Chapt ark

The alley stretches into darkness, the scent of damp earth mingling with the musty aroma of decay. I can feel the cool stone beneath my fingertips, gritty and unyielding. The distant rumble of thunder echoes through the city, a reminder that nature remains untouched by the chaos wrought upon this once-vibrant place. I risk another glance, my heart pounding in my chest, the rhythm mirroring the charm's beat in my hand. It's a small trinket, worn and faded, yet it thrums with an energy that feels both familiar and foreign, as if it knows secrets buried deeper than I could ever imagine.

The man's silhouette is imposing, sharp lines and angles softened only by the shadows that cling to him like a second skin. He steps forward, the light from a flickering street lamp illuminating the edge of his jaw—a harsh, angular feature that somehow feels both dangerous and captivating. My mind races, searching for a way out, but there's something magnetic about his presence, an unspoken challenge that pulls me closer. "What do you want?" I call out, my voice steadier than I feel, a faint echo in the desolation.

His lips curl into a smile that doesn't quite reach his eyes, and for a heartbeat, I feel the thrill of fear mixed with something else—curiosity, perhaps. "You should be asking what I know," he replies, his tone smooth like silk, yet edged with an undeniable sharpness. "The world you cling to is a fragile thing, isn't it? Just like that little charm in your hand."

I clutch the charm tighter, the metal cool against my skin. "It's mine. You can't have it." A foolish statement, yet it's all I can muster. I can't let him know how much it means to me, how it ties me to the remnants of my family, to the home I lost.

"You misunderstand," he says, taking another step forward, and I can see the glimmer of something in his eyes—an intensity that both entices and terrifies. "I don't want it; I want to know how you came by it. It holds more power than you realize."

I swallow hard, adrenaline coursing through my veins, igniting a flicker of defiance. "Why should I tell you anything?" I shift my weight, preparing to dart back into the depths of the alley if I need to, but the curiosity lingers like a persistent itch at the back of my mind.

"Because," he leans closer, the shadows shifting to reveal a flicker of vulnerability beneath the bravado, "your survival depends on understanding the truth. There are those who would stop at nothing to get what you have, and trust me, they won't be as gentle as I am."

His words hang in the air, heavy and charged, electrifying the space between us. My instincts scream for me to run, to escape whatever darkness he is hinting at, but there's a strange thrill in the tension, a dance of danger that tempts me to stay. "What do you know about my family?" I ask, the words escaping my lips before I can think better of it.

His gaze sharpens, interest flickering like a flame. "Your family? They were tangled in things that could unravel this whole city. They knew secrets, and you—" He pauses, taking a step back as if to gather his thoughts. "You're the last piece of a puzzle that could bring the whole thing crashing down. Or perhaps, raise it back up."

A chill runs down my spine, a mix of intrigue and dread coiling tightly in my gut. I've spent so long buried in the ashes of my past, convinced I was simply trying to survive. Now, with him standing before me, the specter of my family looms larger than life, casting shadows I've tried to ignore. "What do you want from me?" The question is almost a whisper, but I can feel its weight.

"I want to help you," he states, the conviction in his voice surprising me. "But first, you need to trust me. There are forces at play that you cannot even begin to comprehend, and they'll stop at nothing to erase your lineage. We need to move—now."

Arcane Rise

Faith Webb

Published by Faith Webb, 2024.

This is a work of fiction. Similarities to real people, places, or events are entirely coincidental.

ARCANE RISE

First edition. November 13, 2024.

Copyright © 2024 Faith Webb.

ISBN: 979-8230587064

Written by Faith Webb.

The urgency in his voice pulls at me, a mix of fear and longing for connection igniting my senses. I'm not sure if I can trust him, but the alternative—remaining in this haunted, desolate place—feels infinitely worse. My pulse quickens as I consider the possibilities. "What's your name?" I ask, though it feels like an irrelevant detail in the grand scheme of things.

"Adrian," he replies, his voice a low murmur, a secret shared between us in the silence of the alley.

"Fine, Adrian," I say, surprising myself with my own boldness. "I'll go with you. But if you try anything—"

He interrupts with a smirk, his eyes dancing with mischief. "You'll do what? Throw your charm at me?"

I can't help but laugh, the sound bubbling up despite the dire situation, and the tension between us shifts, something unspoken passing through the air. "Just know that I'm not the kind of girl who goes down without a fight."

"Good," he replies, his tone lighter now, "I prefer my allies with a little fire."

With one last glance back at the darkness that threatens to swallow me whole, I nod, setting my feet into motion beside him. As we step out of the alley, I can feel the pulse of the charm growing stronger, as if it knows that this moment is merely the beginning of a much larger story waiting to unfold. The streets are empty, the remnants of the past whispering around us, and with each step I take into the unknown, I sense that I am no longer alone in my search for truth. I might be stepping into danger, but for the first time in years, I feel a flicker of hope igniting within.

The city unfurls before us like a forgotten tapestry, threads of what once was tangling with the stark reality of what remains. We step into the open, and the air hangs heavy with the scent of rain-soaked pavement, mingling with the faint tang of rust from the decaying ironwork that lines the streets. Adrian walks with an easy confidence that contrasts sharply with the tension coiling in my stomach. The soft crunch of debris underfoot punctuates the silence, and I can't shake the feeling that we're being watched, as if the shadows themselves are peering out from the remnants of this forsaken world.

"Do you always make a habit of following strangers into the dark?" he teases, casting a sidelong glance my way. His dark hair glints under the streetlights, creating a halo effect that should look ridiculous but somehow enhances his enigmatic charm.

"Only the dangerously handsome ones," I retort, forcing a grin that I don't quite feel. The banter feels like a thin veil over the mounting unease, a distraction from the questions buzzing in my mind like angry hornets. "What's next? You're going to tell me you're a vampire or something?"

"Only on Tuesdays," he quips back, his smile disarming. The warmth in his gaze softens the edges of my anxiety, if only for a moment. I can't afford to let my guard down, though. This man is a mystery wrapped in shadows, and I need to figure out just how deep those shadows go.

We navigate through the remnants of buildings, their facades crumbling like old dreams. I catch glimpses of remnants of lives once lived—faded posters clinging stubbornly to the walls, the shards of glass that catch the light like fallen stars scattered across the ground. There's a sense of intimacy here, as if the city is revealing its heart to me in hushed whispers, and I am both honored and terrified to witness it.

"Why do you keep looking around like that?" Adrian asks, breaking me from my reverie. "You're not afraid of the dark, are you?"

"Not afraid of the dark," I say, my voice steady, "just wary of what might be lurking within it." The truth is, I've been in darker places than this, both inside and out, but I keep that to myself.

"Smart girl." He nods, his expression turning serious. "You should be. The city's not the only thing that's dangerous here. There are people who wouldn't think twice about using you to get what they want."

"Why do I get the feeling you're one of those people?" I shoot back, arching an eyebrow, testing him.

He laughs, a rich sound that echoes off the walls, scattering the gloom. "You're sharp. I like that. But I'm not here to take advantage of you. I want to help you, remember? Just trying to find the right way to do it without sounding like I'm reading from a bad spy novel."

His playful banter does little to assuage my unease, yet it somehow makes him more human. I can't afford to ignore the potential danger of his offer, even if the prospect of understanding my family's legacy is a siren call I can hardly resist.

As we weave through the narrow streets, we eventually arrive at an old bookstore, its windows dusty and cracked but still somehow inviting. The sign above the door hangs precariously, the letters faded but legible enough to read: "Books & Curiosities." A low glow spills from the interior, and I hesitate on the threshold, my instincts battling with the flicker of intrigue in my gut.

"This is where the real stories lie," Adrian says, his voice dropping to a conspiratorial whisper. "And maybe even some answers for you."

I take a deep breath, steeling myself. "Fine. But if I get eaten by a book monster, I'm blaming you."

He chuckles again, stepping aside to allow me to enter first. "I promise you won't be the first to brave the literary horrors."

The moment I cross the threshold, a bell jingles softly above the door, announcing our arrival. The interior is surprisingly warm, filled with the scent of aged paper and wood polish, as if the books themselves are breathing life into the space. Shelves rise from the floor to the ceiling, crammed with volumes that seem to vibrate with stories yearning to be told. The cozy atmosphere belies the air of secrecy that hangs heavy in the corners, and I can't shake the feeling that every book has a tale far more complex than its title suggests.

An elderly woman emerges from behind a counter, her hair a wild tangle of silver curls that halo her head like an ethereal crown. Her eyes, sharp and knowing, scan us with a mixture of curiosity and recognition. "Ah, the seeker returns," she says, her voice gravelly yet rich with warmth. "And you've brought a friend. How delightful."

"Just someone who was curious about the mysteries of the universe," Adrian replies, his tone light, but there's an undercurrent of seriousness that makes my heart race.

The woman nods sagely. "Curiosity is a double-edged sword, dear. It leads to discovery but can also invite danger." She looks at me, her gaze piercing. "And what do you seek?"

I open my mouth to respond, but no words come. The truth of my desire swells within me—the need to understand my family's past, the history that has become a tangled web I can hardly navigate. "I want to know about my family," I finally manage, the confession slipping out as if it has always been waiting for the right moment. "What they did, what they left behind."

The woman's expression shifts, a flicker of surprise crossing her features before she masks it with a knowing smile. "Then you must seek out the tales buried in these shelves." She gestures toward the stacks. "Every book here holds a piece of the puzzle. But be careful. Knowledge can be both a shield and a weapon."

Adrian leans closer, his voice barely above a whisper. "And some stories are best left untold. Are you ready for that?"

I meet his gaze, determination swelling within me. "I've been waiting for too long to back down now."

With a nod, he steps back, leaving me to explore, and I find myself drawn to a section marked with a faded sign that reads "Heritage and Lore." As I scan the spines, a glimmer of silver catches my eye, and I reach for a book adorned with intricate designs, feeling a spark of recognition deep within.

As I pull it from the shelf, the weight of the world shifts ever so slightly, the thrill of discovery igniting my spirit. Little do I know, the truth hidden within these pages may unravel everything I thought I knew about myself—and the dangers lurking in the shadows may be closer than I realize.

As I stand in the warmth of the bookstore, the book in my hands feels alive, its weight both comforting and daunting. I run my fingers over the embossed silver filigree on the cover, tracing patterns that seem to pulse under my touch, as if whispering the stories within. The elderly woman watches me with a knowing smile, her eyes sparkling with a mixture of mischief and wisdom. "That one has a reputation," she says, her voice low and conspiratorial. "It holds truths that many would prefer to keep buried."

"Truths?" I echo, raising an eyebrow. "That sounds ominous."

"Ah, my dear, knowledge often is." She leans closer, her breath a warm gust against my ear. "This book is rumored to contain secrets of the past—your past. Be careful how you proceed."

Adrian moves closer, glancing over my shoulder at the tome, his interest piqued. "What's it called?"

"I'm not sure yet. I just found it," I reply, the words tumbling out as I flip it open. Dust swirls in the air, catching the light like tiny stars as I lose myself in the pages. The text is old, the ink faded but legible, with illustrations that breathe life into the stories—figures in flowing robes, ancient rituals, and symbols that dance across the parchment like echoes from another time.

"Looks like a family tree," Adrian observes, leaning in to study the illustrations. "Are you feeling brave enough to find out where you fit in?"

"Brave or foolish," I mutter, flipping through the pages until a sketch catches my eye—a detailed rendering of a woman with striking features that mirror my own. The resemblance is uncanny, the same sharp cheekbones and dark, penetrating eyes. Beneath the illustration, a name is inscribed: Elara Kleszcz. My heart stutters.

"Do you recognize her?" Adrian's voice breaks through my reverie, his tone tinged with excitement.

"I—I think she might be my great-grandmother," I stammer, my voice thick with disbelief. "But she looks so... familiar." I scan the text, desperately searching for clues.

"Keep reading," he urges, his excitement infectious. "What else does it say?"

My eyes dart across the words, tracing the lineage detailed in a tangle of names and connections that unfurl like the branches of a tree. "It says she was a protector of something... something powerful." My pulse quickens as I continue, a sense of purpose igniting within me. "And she fought against dark forces to keep it safe." I glance up at Adrian, the weight of history suddenly palpable between us. "What if those dark forces are still out there?"

"Then we'd better find out before they do," he replies, a fire igniting in his gaze. "What else does it say?"

I turn the pages, fueled by an adrenaline rush, until I stumble upon a passage that sends a chill through me. "It mentions a ritual... something called the Ember's Binding. It says it can either harness the power of the charm or destroy it completely." The words hang in the air like a threat, and my heart races at the implications.

"Sounds like a choose-your-own-adventure gone wrong," Adrian quips, trying to lighten the mood, but the gravity of what I've uncovered sinks deep into my bones.

"Why would my family have been involved in something like this?" I ask, my voice barely above a whisper. "What power were they protecting?"

"Perhaps they were trying to protect you," he suggests, his expression growing serious. "Maybe they knew this day would come, and that you'd need to be ready."

I close the book, a shiver running down my spine as if the shadows of my ancestors are whispering warnings in the dark. "How am I supposed to be ready for something I don't even understand?"

"By understanding," Adrian replies firmly, placing his hand on the book as if to ground me. "You have to dig deeper. But we can't stay here for long; you know that. If anyone finds out you're looking for answers, they'll come for you."

"What do you mean, 'they'll come for you'?" I frown, unease creeping into my thoughts like an unwelcome visitor.

"Those who want to possess the charm," he explains, his voice low. "They'll stop at nothing to seize its power. And if they know you have it—"

My heart races as I process his words, the threat now looming like a storm cloud overhead. "I can't just leave," I protest. "I need to find out more about Elara and the Ember's Binding. It might be the key to everything."

"Then we find a way to keep you safe while you learn," he says, determination lacing his tone. "But we need to move. Now."

The urgency in his voice sends adrenaline coursing through my veins, but I hesitate, torn between the desire for answers and the instinct to run. "What if it's too dangerous?"

"Dangerous is what makes it worth it," he replies, a spark of mischief returning to his eyes. "Besides, when has caution ever stopped us?"

I can't help but smile at his bravado, even as my stomach knots with apprehension. "Are you always this reckless?"

"Only when it comes to rescuing damsels in distress," he says with a cheeky grin, and I can't help but roll my eyes at his charm.

As we gather ourselves to leave, the air in the bookstore feels charged, the anticipation crackling like static electricity. I glance back at the elderly woman, who watches us with an enigmatic smile that seems to hold a thousand secrets. "Remember," she calls after us, her voice ringing out like a bell, "the past is never truly behind you. It waits in the shadows, eager to reclaim what is rightfully its own."

Adrian pushes the door open, the soft chime of the bell sounding like a warning as we step back into the night. The street is cloaked in darkness, the only illumination coming from the sporadic streetlights that flicker like fireflies in a tempest. I take a deep breath, the air thick with the scent of impending rain, and we start down the street, every instinct on high alert.

As we navigate the alleyways, the weight of the charm feels heavier than ever, the metal pulsing with a strange energy that sends shivers down my spine. The stories of my ancestors weave through my mind, a tapestry of secrets waiting to be unraveled, but before I can formulate a plan, the distant sound of footsteps echoes through the empty streets—a rhythmic pounding that grows louder with each heartbeat.

"Adrian," I whisper, my voice tight with fear. "We're not alone."

He stops suddenly, the playful glint in his eyes replaced with a sharp intensity as he turns to scan the shadows. "Stay close," he warns, and his tone leaves no room for argument.

I take a step back, glancing over my shoulder just as a figure emerges from the darkness—a silhouette that sends a chill racing through my veins. It's tall and cloaked, the edges of its form blurred like smoke. I grasp the charm, its warmth a small comfort against the chill creeping into my bones.

"Run!" Adrian shouts, but before I can react, the figure lunges, a flash of steel glinting in the dim light. My heart pounds in my chest as I turn on my heel, adrenaline surging through my body. I run, the echo of my footsteps mixing with the thundering sound of my heart, as the night swallows us whole.

Chapter 2: Flickers of Resistance

The old diner, with its cracked linoleum and mismatched chairs, buzzed with the low hum of muted conversations and the distant clatter of dishes. A relic of better times, it stood as a sanctuary for the weary and the wary alike, a place where shadows flickered as often as the neon sign that buzzed above the door. I had taken to this place like a moth to a flame, craving its greasy comfort and the familiarity of the regulars. It was a second home, though home had long since become a concept more than a place. My gaze wandered over the assembled group, familiar faces painted with exhaustion and guarded hope. We were all survivors, bonded by unspoken tragedies, clinging to the frayed threads of our lives.

But today, the usual warmth was tinged with something different, a chill that crept through the cracks of the diner's worn exterior. My heartbeat quickened as my attention fixated on him—Reed Mercer. He moved with a predatory grace, his presence carving a path through the bustling crowd as if he were a shadow personified, lurking just outside the edge of light. There was something magnetic about him, an energy that pulled at the edges of my consciousness. Even the hardened patrons seemed to straighten in their seats, eyes darting toward him with a mixture of fear and curiosity.

I had heard the whispers—stories of his exploits that could curdle the blood. They spoke of him with reverence and dread, a bounty hunter whose reputation was woven from nightmares and legend. No one knew where he came from, but the tales of his prowess and ruthlessness echoed long after he left a place. The air thickened with tension as he settled into the booth in the far corner, those dark eyes scanning the room, searching, calculating. And then, unexpectedly, they locked onto mine, pinning me in place as if he had woven an invisible net around my thoughts.

A jolt of heat rushed through me, igniting the charm that hung from my neck, its surface warm and pulsing against my skin, a sensation that had become all too familiar. I had hoped to conceal it, to bury it deep within the layers of my past, but the more I tried to hide, the more it burned—a reminder of the power I was desperate to keep secret. I caught my breath, feeling a mix of dread and defiance. How much longer could I keep the truth at bay, especially from someone like Reed? His gaze was piercing, as if he could see the very core of my being, unraveling my carefully constructed facade.

"Losing your nerve, sweetheart?" The voice broke through my thoughts like glass shattering. It was Jack, the diner's grizzled cook, his arms crossed over his chest, a smirk curling at the corners of his lips. "You're lookin' like you've seen a ghost."

I shot him a glare, grateful for the distraction, even if it was infused with Jack's trademark sarcasm. "I'm fine, Jack. Just... pondering the mysteries of the universe," I replied, the words dripping with irony. "You know, the usual."

"Right." He raised an eyebrow, skepticism etched on his weathered face. "Just don't let that Mercer guy draw you in. He's bad news wrapped in a pretty package."

"Pretty?" I scoffed. "You must be talking about someone else. He looks like he crawled out of a horror flick."

Jack chuckled, the warmth of his laugh chasing away the chill that had settled in my bones. "True, true. Just keep your wits about you. That one's trouble."

With a final nod, he retreated to the kitchen, leaving me alone with my racing thoughts and the heat radiating from my charm. I returned my attention to Reed, who still regarded me with an intensity that made the air feel electric. I was on the brink of standing up, of confronting the undeniable pull he had on me, when a group of newcomers burst through the door, laughter trailing in their wake.

The sudden influx of energy distracted the diner's usual patrons, their conversations bubbling to life, but I remained transfixed by the man in the corner.

It was almost surreal—the way he shifted in his seat, a predator assessing his surroundings, and the way he leaned back, his casual confidence cloaking him like a finely tailored suit. There was a sense of danger about him that both terrified and intrigued me, igniting a spark of rebellion in the pit of my stomach. I shouldn't want to know him; I shouldn't want to rise from my seat and throw caution to the wind. But as I watched him, an almost magnetic pull tugged at my resolve, urging me to uncover the mystery that cloaked him.

With a deep breath, I steeled myself, the charm around my neck now an inferno against my skin. I needed to confront the truth—my truth—and the man who seemed destined to unravel it. As I pushed back my chair, the sound scraping against the linoleum echoed in the sudden hush that followed my movement. Reed's gaze flickered to me, a spark of curiosity igniting the depths of his dark eyes. I moved toward him, each step a declaration, a silent challenge that sent a thrill coursing through my veins.

"Reed Mercer, I presume?" I said, the words tumbling from my lips, infused with bravado I didn't quite feel. His smirk was sly, a predator who had finally cornered his prey.

"Impressive," he replied, his voice low and smooth like the whiskey I imagined he might drink. "You're braver than most, coming over here."

"I'm not brave," I shot back, my heart racing, "I'm desperate for answers."

He leaned forward, the intensity of his gaze sharpening. "Answers can be dangerous, you know. Especially the ones you're seeking."

I couldn't shake the feeling that he knew more than he was letting on, that he was a gatekeeper to a world I had only just begun to glimpse.

The air between us crackled with an electric tension, the kind that could ignite a room or make it implode under the weight of unsaid words. I leaned against the rough wooden table, my heart pounding in tandem with the rhythm of the diner, where the scent of frying bacon mingled with the sweetness of stale coffee. Reed Mercer sat before me, a formidable figure wrapped in layers of mystery, and I felt as if I were standing on the edge of a precipice, staring into a void that promised both peril and revelation.

"Answers can be dangerous, you know. Especially the ones you're seeking," he repeated, his voice smooth, as if carved from stone yet surprisingly warm. The weight of his gaze was both unnerving and exhilarating, sending shivers cascading down my spine. It was as if he could see the very essence of me, the secrets I had woven into the fabric of my being, threads so tightly spun that even I struggled to discern their origins.

I raised an eyebrow, defiance bubbling within me like the coffee pot hissing in the background. "I've survived this long, haven't I? What's a little danger?" I shot back, my bravado a thin veil over the uncertainty gnawing at my insides.

His lips curled into a half-smile, a dangerous invitation that danced at the edges of his mouth. "True, survival has its merits. But there are levels to danger, sweetheart. I don't think you're prepared for what you're about to step into."

His words hung in the air, heavy with implication, as if he were a conductor orchestrating the symphony of tension swirling around us. I felt the charm pulse beneath my fingers, a fiery reminder of the power I desperately wished to keep buried. "And what exactly is it that you think I'm stepping into?" I challenged, emboldened by my own curiosity.

"Why don't we find out?" His reply was casual, but the intensity in his gaze belied the nonchalance. He leaned back, inviting but unyielding, like a lion observing a trespasser in its territory. My heart raced; every instinct screamed at me to back away, to retreat into the safety of the known, yet something deeper urged me forward.

The door swung open again, letting in a rush of cold air, and with it, the cacophony of life outside. A group of rough-looking men entered, laughter echoing off the walls, but the laughter stilled as they caught sight of Reed. An unspoken shift occurred, the atmosphere thickening like fog rolling in off the coast, cloaking the diner in a new layer of tension. They seemed to recognize him, and their playful banter faded into cautious whispers.

"Looks like you have an audience," I remarked, casting a sideways glance at the newcomers. "Are you always this popular?"

Reed's gaze flicked to the men, the ghost of a smirk playing at the corner of his mouth. "Only when I'm in town. Their kind doesn't particularly like me." His eyes flickered back to mine, bright and burning. "But that doesn't matter. What matters is you."

"I'm not a trophy to be claimed, Mercer," I shot back, a hint of irritation lacing my words. "You're not some hunter of hearts here."

"Perhaps not, but I do hunt for truths," he replied, his voice low, dangerously inviting. The sincerity in his eyes caught me off guard, making me question if I had misjudged him.

Just then, the group of men approached, their laughter now replaced by something heavier, almost threatening. The leader, a burly man with tattoos snaking up his arms, planted himself beside our table. "What's this, Mercer? Found yourself a little bird?"

Reed's expression didn't change, a mask of indifference that sent a shiver of admiration through me. "Nothing that concerns you, Turner."

Turner's lips curled into a sneer, his eyes flicking to me, sizing me up as if I were prey rather than a person. "Just thought you should know, trouble follows you like a lost puppy. Best to keep your distance, sweetheart. You don't want to end up burned by the flames he leaves behind."

"Is that supposed to intimidate me?" I shot back, surprised by my own bravado, which seemed to grow stronger in the face of danger. "Because I've dealt with worse than you."

Turner's laughter erupted, braying like a donkey, and it made me cringe. "You think you can stand against the likes of Mercer? He's a storm waiting to swallow you whole."

"Funny, I don't remember asking for your advice," I replied, meeting his gaze with steely resolve. The moment hung suspended in the air, a fragile truce, as the tension thickened around us.

Reed turned slightly, his body language shifting to shield me, his presence suddenly more protective. "You should learn to mind your own business, Turner. Last I checked, you've got enough of your own to worry about."

"Don't let him play you, sweetheart," Turner spat, his voice dripping with condescension. "You have no idea who you're dealing with."

With that, Turner's group turned away, but the lingering threat hung like a storm cloud overhead. I could feel Reed's presence beside me, solid and unwavering, and somehow it emboldened me even more. "What was that about?" I asked, lowering my voice so only he could hear, the adrenaline surging through me.

"Just the usual bluster," he replied, but the shadow in his eyes told a different story. "They've been chasing me for a while now. But you—" He paused, leaning closer, and I caught the scent of something dark and musky, an intoxicating mix of danger and allure. "You've piqued their interest."

"Great, just what I need," I muttered, my mind racing. "I didn't sign up for a sideshow."

"Maybe not, but you're in deeper than you realize," he said softly, almost conspiratorially. "You have something they want, something powerful."

My fingers tightened around the charm as if it were a lifeline. "And what if I don't want to be involved? What if I want to walk away?"

He searched my eyes, a spark of something unreadable flaring between us. "Walking away isn't an option anymore. Not for you. Not for anyone. The world has changed, and you're caught in its currents whether you like it or not."

The weight of his words settled heavily in the air between us, both daunting and thrilling. I had always known I was different, but I never wanted to acknowledge it. But in this moment, standing on the brink of uncertainty, I felt the charm pulsing in rhythm with my heartbeat, urging me to confront the truth that had haunted me for so long. The fight within me flickered to life, ignited by a challenge I couldn't ignore.

"Then what do we do now?" I asked, my voice steadier than I felt.

Reed smiled, a glimmer of mischief flashing across his features. "We make our own rules."

I leaned in closer, the din of the diner fading into a background hum as Reed's presence enveloped me. The air thickened, charged with a mix of curiosity and something deeper, something that fluttered in the pit of my stomach like the wings of a restless bird. "Make our own rules?" I repeated, testing the weight of the words. "You do realize that's a recipe for chaos, right?"

Reed chuckled, the sound low and rumbling, as if it came from the depths of some ancient well. "Chaos is a form of freedom, and freedom is what you need right now." His eyes glinted with a mischief that danced dangerously close to recklessness. "We're not just fighting for survival; we're fighting for control over our own destinies."

I arched an eyebrow, skepticism battling with intrigue. "You make it sound so romantic. But I'm not interested in becoming a pawn in anyone else's game." My voice held more conviction than I felt. After all, the last time I had tried to wrest control over my life, I had only ended up in deeper waters.

"Every game has its players, and you're far from a pawn," Reed replied, his gaze intense. "Trust me, I've seen what happens when you let someone else dictate the terms. You don't want to be a spectator in your own life."

Before I could retort, a loud crash interrupted us, sending the contents of a nearby table sprawling. A glass shattered, the sound sharp and jagged, slicing through the tension like a knife. All eyes turned to the source of the commotion, where Turner and his crew had decided that merely glaring wasn't enough; now they were escalating things. The leader had grabbed a bottle from the counter, the liquor sloshing over the edge as he brandished it like a weapon.

"Looks like your friends are getting restless," I said, my heart racing.

Reed's expression hardened, the playful gleam fading into something more serious. "Stay close," he instructed, rising from his seat with an ease that belied the danger brewing just beyond the edge of the diner's linoleum.

"Are you going to handle this with your usual charm?" I quipped, trying to mask my anxiety with humor.

"I have a few tricks up my sleeve," he replied, a hint of a smile creeping back into his demeanor. "But sometimes, the best trick is to keep the fire contained before it spreads."

With that, he strode toward the group, his posture exuding a confidence that was both intimidating and awe-inspiring. I watched as he approached, my pulse quickening. Every instinct told me to stay back, to hide in the shadows where it was safe, but something tethered me to the spot, a magnetic pull drawing me closer to the storm.

"What's the matter, Turner? Did you run out of manners along with your brains?" Reed's voice rang out, cutting through the murmur of rising tension.

Turner swung around, eyes narrowing at the bounty hunter. "Stay out of this, Mercer. This is between us and her." He gestured toward me, and I felt the blood drain from my face.

Reed's expression was a mask of calm fury. "You're barking up the wrong tree, and you know it. You're just too stupid to back down."

"Stupid? You're the one who thinks you can walk in here and play savior," Turner sneered, his grip tightening on the bottle. "You don't know what you're getting into."

"I'm not the one who's about to make a colossal mistake," Reed shot back, stepping closer, his body radiating a fierce protectiveness that sent a shiver of gratitude through me. "Let her go."

The air was thick with a tension that felt like it could snap at any moment, and I half-expected a fight to break out right then and there. It was absurd; I had come to the diner looking for comfort, not a front-row seat to chaos. My hands trembled slightly as I fidgeted with the charm around my neck, the warmth of it now an insistent pulse against my skin.

"Or what?" Turner taunted, brandishing the bottle as if it were a sword. "You think you can take us all on? You're outnumbered, Mercer."

Reed's expression hardened, a fierce glint in his eyes. "You really want to find out what I'm capable of? That's a dangerous game to play, Turner, and trust me, I always play to win."

Before Turner could respond, the door swung open again, the crisp night air swirling in like a harbinger of change. In strode a figure cloaked in shadows, tall and imposing, the hood of a dark cloak obscuring their features. Instantly, the atmosphere shifted. Whispers cascaded through the diner, a ripple of unease washing over the patrons as they regarded the newcomer with a mix of fear and awe.

Reed's expression darkened as he turned to face the newcomer. "What are you doing here?" he asked, his voice a low growl, barely above a whisper.

The cloaked figure lifted their head, revealing a face partially hidden in the shadows, but their eyes glimmered like shards of ice, cold and piercing. "I'm here for her," they said, their voice smooth and unyielding, sending a wave of apprehension skimming through my skin.

"For me?" I echoed, incredulous. "What do you want with me?"

The figure stepped forward, the cloak flowing like smoke, and I felt the weight of their gaze bore down on me. "You possess something far more powerful than you know. Something that cannot be left unguarded."

Reed stepped protectively in front of me, his frame casting a long shadow, both a barrier and a promise. "You don't know who you're dealing with. You're not taking her anywhere."

"Oh, but I believe you've underestimated the stakes, Mercer," the figure replied, a chilling smile spreading across their lips. "You think you can protect her? There are forces at play far beyond your control."

A ripple of tension surged through the diner as the patrons sensed the danger escalating. It was no longer just a standoff; it was a reckoning. The air felt thick with the weight of secrets, and I could hardly breathe as I glanced between Reed and the stranger, caught in the crossfire of their looming conflict.

"Stay back!" I shouted, an instinctive plea as I clutched the charm tighter, its warmth a fierce contrast to the cold fear gnawing at my insides.

Reed's gaze met mine, fierce and unwavering. "Whatever happens, don't let go of that charm," he said, his voice steady despite the chaos unfolding around us.

The cloaked figure laughed softly, a sound that chilled me to the bone. "You have no idea what you're all up against. But I'll be back, and when I am, you'll wish you had given in."

With that, they turned and slipped out into the night, leaving behind a trail of unease and unanswered questions.

As the door swung shut, silence enveloped the diner, punctuated only by the heavy breaths of the patrons who had held their collective breath. I stood frozen, my heart racing, the charm now burning like a brand against my skin. I could feel the world shifting around me, the ground beneath my feet becoming unsteady, and in that moment, I realized that I had stepped into a game far more dangerous than I had ever imagined.

"Let's get out of here," Reed said, his voice a low murmur, but the urgency in his tone sent adrenaline coursing through my veins.

But just as we turned to leave, the door burst open again, and another figure stepped into the fray, a familiar face emerging from the shadows—someone I had hoped to never see again.

Chapter 3: Sparks of Deception

The bookstore was a relic, its air thick with the scent of aged paper and dust, a sanctuary for forgotten tales. I had often come here to lose myself, but today it felt like a prison. Shelves sagged under the weight of unturned pages, each tome a witness to the secrets of its visitors. I could almost hear their whispers echoing through the aisles as Reed stepped into my carefully curated chaos, shattering the illusion of solitude I'd clung to like a shield. He stood at the end of the narrow aisle, a silhouette of menace draped in a tailored jacket that did little to conceal the intensity radiating from him.

His eyes, a stormy gray, assessed me as if I were a puzzle he was determined to solve. "You don't belong here," he stated, the words low and edged with an authority that made my heart quicken. I feigned nonchalance, a smile barely masking my pulse racing like a caged bird seeking escape. "You don't know me," I shot back, the bravado tasting bitter on my tongue. But even I could hear the tremor that threatened to betray my facade.

"Do I need to? You're the girl whose family charm turned into a shackle." He stepped closer, his presence like a lighthouse cutting through my fog of uncertainty. "Tell me, what did you think you'd find among these pages?" His voice, smooth like honey yet sharp enough to cut, drew me in and pushed me away in equal measure.

I wanted answers, yes, but I also craved the safety of ignorance—something I could hold on to while navigating this fragile dance of deception. "Perhaps I'm here to find the truth," I replied, keeping my gaze steady despite the tumult raging within me. I had rehearsed this moment, imagined every scenario, but reality was unfurling like a story with no author, and Reed was more than just a plot twist; he was a force.

"Truth?" he echoed, almost mockingly. "Or the truth you want to hear?" There was a spark in his eyes, a challenge woven through his words that sent a thrill down my spine. I hated him for it and yet felt an inexplicable pull. "Why don't you enlighten me?" I retorted, taking a step closer, feeling the heat of the moment swirl around us like the dust motes suspended in the sunlit air.

He leaned against the shelf, arms crossed, an unwilling actor playing his part too well. "Your charm, it's not just a bauble, you know. It's a beacon—a siren's call, drawing unwanted attention." The atmosphere thickened, charged with the weight of unspoken words. "Your family's past is like a shadow, and trust me, it's watching."

"Are you implying I'm in danger?" I arched an eyebrow, defiance tinged with a hint of genuine concern. I didn't need another person to tell me my life was tangled in a web of half-truths and darkened corners. But Reed's gaze bored into me, searching for cracks in my facade.

"It's more than danger," he continued, his voice dropping to a conspiratorial whisper. "It's a reckoning." The way he spoke sent shivers along my spine, and my mind raced through the fragmented stories I had heard as a child—warnings shrouded in family lore, cautionary tales disguised as bedtime stories. My childhood had been painted in broad strokes of deceit, and Reed was merely the brush threatening to smear the canvas I'd carefully crafted.

I bit my lip, weighing my next words. "What do you know about my family?" The vulnerability slipped through the cracks I'd fought to seal. I could feel the cracks widening, my carefully constructed walls trembling under the force of his revelations.

"More than you, I suspect," he replied, a hint of a smile tugging at his lips, almost amused by my naivety. "They're not just stories, you know. There are people who want your charm back—people who would go to great lengths to retrieve what was lost."

"Then tell me what you know, Reed. I'm not afraid of the past." The challenge hung between us, a tangible entity that pulsed with potential.

"Fear is just another name for survival," he said, and the weight of his gaze made it hard to breathe. "You're playing a dangerous game, and you don't even have the right cards."

I felt the sharp edges of his words cut through the air, each syllable a reminder of how unprepared I was. "What do you want from me?" I shot back, frustration clawing at my composure. "You have me cornered in this forgotten place, whispering threats like they're gospel. What is it you're trying to achieve?"

Reed hesitated, the flicker of something—regret, perhaps?—crossing his features before it was masked again by the confident veneer he wore like armor. "I want to help you," he finally said, the admission slipping out like a confession. "But help comes at a price."

"Of course it does," I muttered, the cynicism spilling forth. "What's your angle? Are you here to save me, or are you just another player in this twisted game?"

"Why not both?" he shot back, a smirk dancing on his lips. "You see, the lines are blurred when the stakes are this high."

The tension thickened, a palpable entity between us, charged with the electricity of our unresolved conflict. I searched his face for sincerity, for a glimmer of truth amidst the tangled web he wove. There was something in his eyes—a flicker of empathy or perhaps shared pain—that made me reconsider my stance. In this silent bookstore, filled with shadows and secrets, I was teetering on the edge of trust, the promise of revelation luring me closer to the abyss of our intertwined fates.

But the question lingered: Was I willing to take that leap?

The silence stretched, a taut string pulled to the point of snapping, and my heart raced to the rhythm of unspoken truths. Reed leaned in slightly, a predator in a world of prey, and I felt the urge to retreat, to escape the magnetic pull of his presence. Yet, my curiosity anchored me in place. I had waded too far into these murky waters to turn back now.

"Help comes at a price," I repeated, the weight of his words lingering like the musty smell of old paper that enveloped us. "What kind of price are we talking about?" I pushed, determined to peel back the layers of his facade. Reed's brow quirked slightly, amusement flickering across his features as if he were enjoying a private joke that I had yet to grasp.

"Nothing too extravagant," he replied, the lilt of sarcasm evident in his tone. "Just your willingness to play nice and keep an open mind." He straightened, the air between us shifting from confrontational to conspiratorial, his voice dropping to a whisper that beckoned me closer. "And maybe a few secrets of your own."

A laugh escaped me, tinged with incredulity. "You think I'm going to spill my guts to a stranger just because you've put on a show of concern? Spare me the theatrics, Reed." I gestured dismissively, but the challenge simmered beneath my bravado, each word a dance around the truth we both skirted.

"Stranger?" he echoed, cocking his head to the side, amusement evident. "I believe we're well past that point. You know my name, and I can't help but feel you know a little more about me than you let on." His expression turned serious, the playful edge dulled. "Your family's reputation precedes you, even if you've chosen to ignore it. The question is, how much do you actually want to know?"

That struck a nerve, a resonance of uncertainty that sent a shiver down my spine. I had spent years piecing together fragments of my family's history, each story a jigsaw puzzle I couldn't quite complete. The notion that Reed held pieces I was missing ignited a flicker of desperation within me. "I want to know everything," I declared, my voice steadier than I felt. "Everything that's left of the truth."

He took a step back, as if my admission startled him. "Then you're going to have to trust me," he said, the gravity of his tone grounding me in the reality of our precarious situation. "And that's not something you should give lightly."

Trust was a currency I had long abandoned in the economy of my life. I had learned early on that trusting someone could lead to heartbreak or worse, betrayal lurking in the shadows. Yet, I found myself torn, the flicker of vulnerability in his gaze matching the tension coiling in my stomach. "What if I told you I don't trust easily?"

"Then we're in the same boat, love," he replied with a smirk, a hint of mischief dancing in his eyes that momentarily lightened the weight between us. "You see, it's not about trusting blindly. It's about assessing the risk. Right now, I'm offering you the chance to learn what's been kept from you. And in return, all I ask is a bit of honesty."

There was a sincerity in his challenge that tugged at something deep within me, an urge to break down my own defenses. "And what makes you so worthy of my honesty?" I shot back, clinging to my retorts like a lifeline.

"Perhaps because I'm in just as deep as you are," he said, his voice low and laced with sincerity. "I've tangled with your family's shadows long enough to know how they operate. I want to help you untangle them. But first, we need to get past this little dance of ours."

The shift in our dynamic was palpable, a change in the air as if the world outside had paused to eavesdrop on our exchange. "Fine," I relented, my breath catching slightly as I met his gaze. "But know that I'm not some naive damsel waiting to be rescued. I'm not even sure if I want your help."

"Noted," he replied, a flicker of admiration crossing his features. "But if we're going to do this, we need to set some ground rules. First, I need to know everything you've uncovered about your family, and then we can fill in the blanks together."

I nodded slowly, weighing the implications of my next words. "All right, but know this—every story has its monsters, and mine is no different. If we're digging up bones, you might want to brace yourself."

Reed stepped back, his posture shifting from aggressive to contemplative, and he gestured toward a small table tucked in the corner, cluttered with dusty novels and a flickering lamp that illuminated the otherwise dim space. "Why don't we start there? You tell me your story, and I'll share what I know in return."

As we settled into the worn chairs, the ambiance shifted from a confrontation to an alliance of sorts. The flickering lamp cast warm shadows on the walls, wrapping us in a cocoon of secrecy. "So, where to begin?" I asked, feeling the weight of the narrative ahead pressing against my chest.

"Start with the charm," he urged, leaning forward with genuine interest. "What do you remember about it?"

I took a deep breath, the memories flooding back like a tide pulling me under. "It's always been a part of my family, a symbol of protection, or so I was told. My grandmother used to wear it everywhere, claiming it shielded us from harm." My voice wavered as I recalled her warm smile, the way she had always made the world feel safe.

"And what happened to it?" Reed prompted, his gaze unwavering.

"That's where it gets messy," I admitted, my heart racing as I plunged into the shadows of my past. "After she died, everything fell apart. My parents... they started fighting, and soon the charm was just a memory—a symbol of everything that was lost."

"Loss can unravel the strongest of threads," he replied softly, an understanding flickering in his eyes. "But tell me, what do you think it means to you now?"

"Hope, maybe?" I mused, the vulnerability of the moment surfacing as I dared to explore the depths of my feelings. "Or perhaps a curse? It feels like a burden, a weight I've carried for too long."

Reed nodded, his expression softening as if he were a mirror reflecting my unmasked thoughts. "Then let's lighten that load together. Your family's past may be riddled with darkness, but there's always a way to turn the pages toward something brighter."

His confidence was infectious, the flicker of determination igniting a spark within me. I glanced around the bookstore, once a place of refuge, now transformed into a war room of sorts. Here, among the shadows and secrets, we were on the precipice of something far greater than either of us could have anticipated.

In that moment, with the dusty tomes bearing witness to our pact, I realized I was willing to confront whatever ghosts haunted my family's legacy. With Reed by my side, the path ahead might not be as daunting as it had once seemed, and for the first time, the prospect of uncovering the truth felt like an adventure rather than a punishment.

The weight of the moment shifted, my heart beating in sync with the flickering lamp as Reed leaned closer, his curiosity sharpening the air around us. "Tell me about your grandmother's charm," he urged, his voice low and steady, as if trying to draw out a secret long buried.

"It was a silver locket, intricately engraved with a tree—a family tree, I suppose," I began, my fingers instinctively brushing against the hollow space where the charm used to hang. "She said it connected us to our roots, that it would protect us from any evil seeking to disrupt our lives. But it vanished after she died, along with her sense of safety."

"And you believe its loss brought the chaos?" he asked, tilting his head, as if sizing up my belief.

"I don't know what to believe anymore," I admitted, a tremor in my voice betraying my resolve. "Everything changed so quickly. One moment, we were a happy family, and the next, we were just... fragments of what we used to be."

Reed was silent for a moment, his gaze searching mine as if looking for something I hadn't yet revealed. "What if I told you that losing the charm wasn't the end, but the beginning of something new?"

I frowned, skepticism threading through my thoughts. "What new beginnings could possibly arise from a family crumbling apart?"

"Perhaps a chance to reclaim what was lost," he suggested, his eyes flickering with a determination that both intrigued and unnerved me. "If your family has a dark history, then it also holds the key to your present. I've seen it happen before."

"Seen what happen?" I challenged, my fingers tapping on the table in a nervous rhythm. "What are you implying?"

"People with history don't just fade away," he replied, his voice dropping to a conspiratorial whisper. "They rise again, often in the most unexpected ways. It's how legends are born."

I stared at him, a strange cocktail of doubt and curiosity swirling in my chest. "Legends? You make it sound so glamorous. My family's story is one of tragedy, not triumph."

"Maybe it's both," he countered, leaning back, arms crossed, the playfulness in his demeanor replaced by a more serious tone. "You have to confront it to reclaim your narrative. Otherwise, it will keep haunting you."

"Haunting?" I echoed, feeling the familiar chill crawl up my spine. "That's a strong word. Do you have ghosts, Reed?"

"More than you know." He chuckled lightly, the tension easing slightly as he redirected our conversation. "But for now, we can focus on yours. Start with your mother. What did she tell you about the charm?"

"Nothing," I said, the word slipping out harsher than I intended. "She barely spoke of it. It was like a taboo, a wound she refused to acknowledge. All I remember is her tears whenever someone mentioned my grandmother."

"And your father?"

Another hesitation lingered. "He wasn't much better. He left when I was young, and the stories I heard about him were always cloaked in anger and disappointment. I never knew what was true and what was simply gossip."

"That's a heavy load for anyone," Reed observed, nodding in understanding. "But those pieces of your family's past, however tangled, are the foundation of your strength. You need to dig deeper."

"Dig deeper," I repeated, the phrase echoing in my mind like a challenge. "And what if I don't like what I find?"

"Then you deal with it," he replied, his voice steady, unwavering. "You'll find a way to forge a new path, one that isn't dictated by the ghosts of your ancestors."

I wanted to believe him. There was something in his tone, a blend of reassurance and raw truth that cracked open the hardened shell I'd built around my emotions. "I'm tired of living in the shadow of what's lost," I confessed, my voice barely above a whisper. "But how do I even begin?"

"You start by asking the right questions," he urged, his eyes brightening with the thrill of the chase. "And you follow the clues wherever they lead."

Just then, the faint chime of the doorbell startled us, breaking our moment of fragile intimacy. I turned to see a figure entering the bookstore, a tall silhouette that instantly sent a rush of unease coursing through me.

"Speak of the devil," Reed muttered under his breath, his demeanor shifting instantly from ally to something more wary.

I squinted into the dim light, trying to make out the newcomer's features. The stranger's eyes swept over the bookstore with a calculated precision, and as they settled on us, I felt the air grow heavier. There was a familiarity in those eyes that sent a shiver down my spine—a recognition that could be both a blessing and a curse.

"Is this a private conversation, or can anyone join?" the newcomer asked, a sardonic smile playing on their lips.

"Depends on who you are," Reed replied, his voice curt, the friendly banter evaporating.

"Oh, I think you know who I am," the stranger replied, stepping closer, their voice laced with an unsettling confidence. "I'm here for the charm."

I felt my heart stutter, a jolt of adrenaline surging through me. "What charm?" I asked, though the tremor in my voice gave me away.

"The one that belongs to you, my dear," the stranger said, their eyes narrowing with interest. "You're not as lost as you think. Your family's legacy is right in front of you, and I'm here to help you reclaim it."

Reed's body tensed beside me, and I could see the calculation racing through his mind. "You're in the wrong place," he asserted, moving slightly to block my view of the stranger.

But the stranger merely chuckled, unfazed by Reed's attempt at intimidation. "Oh, I assure you, I'm in the right place at the right time. And you, my dear, need to make a choice."

A choice? The weight of that word settled like a stone in my gut. I glanced at Reed, who met my gaze with an intensity that both grounded and terrified me.

"What kind of choice?" I asked, my voice barely more than a whisper, knowing full well that my next words could change everything.

The stranger leaned in closer, their voice dropping to a conspiratorial murmur. "You can either let go of the past or embrace your true inheritance. But be warned—once you step through that door, there's no turning back."

A chill swept through me as the implications hung heavy in the air. I stood at the precipice of a decision, the echoes of my family's history pulling me in one direction, while the allure of the unknown beckoned me forward.

"What will it be?" the stranger pressed, the tension crackling like static electricity, and I knew that whatever choice I made would set the course for the rest of my life, unraveling the tightly knit threads of my existence into something altogether different.

I took a deep breath, feeling the world shift beneath my feet, and as I opened my mouth to respond, the bookstore's door swung shut with a deafening thud, plunging us into a suffocating silence, leaving my heart racing with a choice yet to be made.

Chapter 4: Flames of Confession

The fog curled around my ankles like a ghostly lover, chilling me to the bone as I trudged through the dense underbrush of the city's outskirts. Each step was a battle against the weight of uncertainty that hung in the air, a prelude to something I couldn't quite name but felt in my marrow. I glanced sideways at Reed, whose silhouette loomed just ahead, a figure both infuriating and intriguing, cloaked in shadows and secrets. The soft crunch of leaves beneath his boots punctuated the silence, a reminder that we were no longer in the familiar realm of barbed words and deflected glances; we were now bound by circumstance, our survival entwined.

"I didn't think I'd find myself lost in the woods with you of all people," I quipped, trying to mask the anxious flutter in my chest with humor. "This feels like the start of a very bad romance novel."

Reed cast me a sidelong glance, his lips curling in what might have been a smirk if it didn't also look like a grimace. "Better than being lost alone, I suppose. Unless you think you can charm the fog into revealing a way out."

"I'm not a magician, just a girl with a knack for unlocking secrets," I shot back, my tone light even as the tension coiled between us. "Though if I could conjure a path, I'd have done it before stumbling into your prickly aura."

He chuckled, a low sound that stirred something warm in the cold air. "That prickly aura might just keep you alive longer than your charm. Let's focus on getting out of here before whatever is lurking in the dark decides to make a move."

There it was again—this strange camaraderie that was growing between us, despite the undeniable chasm of distrust. I couldn't deny that I was drawn to Reed's intensity, the way his dark hair fell over his forehead like a shadow of his own. His brows furrowed, and I could see the tension in his shoulders as if he were carrying the weight of something heavier than the fear of the forest. I shifted my gaze ahead, the twisting trees arching over us like sentinels, and let my mind drift to the relic he had mentioned earlier. My heart raced, anticipation mingling with trepidation. It was my family's secret, woven through generations like a tapestry of whispers and half-told tales.

"Tell me about the relic," I urged, forcing the question past the apprehension lodged in my throat. "What exactly does it unlock?"

Reed hesitated, his steps faltering as he paused to study me, the fog swirling like a veil around his features. "It's not just any relic. It's a key to ancient magic, but it's also a curse. Whoever wields it can reshape the world or shatter it entirely."

I raised an eyebrow, my curiosity igniting like a spark in dry brush. "You speak of it like it's a fairytale. What does it mean for us?"

"Us?" He scoffed, a sharp edge to his voice that almost made me flinch. "I don't plan on dragging anyone else into this. You're just... an incidental ally. It's safer that way."

"Safer for whom?" I challenged, stepping closer, needing him to see the resolve in my eyes. "You think I'm just a pawn in your game? I have a stake in this too. My family's past is tied to that relic."

Reed's jaw tightened, his expression hardening into a mask of resolve. "This isn't a game, and your family's past is fraught with peril. The more you know, the more you risk. I'd prefer to keep you out of this. For your own good."

"Since when did you start caring about my well-being?" I shot back, the heat of the moment sparking a fire in my belly. "I'm not some damsel in distress. If there's a way to understand my heritage, I want in, even if it means walking beside you in this fog."

He turned abruptly, and I could see the conflict warring behind his stormy eyes. "I don't want to see you hurt. The forces we're dealing with are not merely threats; they're powerful, unyielding, and hungry. Your charm might unlock the relic, but it could just as easily draw unwanted attention."

"Attention?" I asked, my voice lowering, suddenly feeling the weight of his warning. "You mean like the ambush we just escaped?"

He nodded slowly, the shadows playing tricks on his features. "Exactly like that. If you insist on pursuing this, you need to be prepared for anything."

"Anything?" I echoed, a shiver tracing my spine at the thought of what that might entail. "I thought this journey was about discovery. Now it feels like a descent into madness."

"That's because it is," he replied, his voice low and gravelly, drawing me closer. "And if you're not ready for the truth, it might just consume you whole."

I opened my mouth to retort, but the words caught in my throat as I caught sight of something lurking in the trees. A flicker of movement—quick, almost imperceptible—sent adrenaline coursing through me. "Reed..." I whispered, my voice a tightrope of tension.

He turned, his gaze sharp, and the moment crystallized as the air between us thickened with an electric charge. The forest, once just an ominous backdrop, transformed into a battleground, shadows dancing in the periphery of our vision. I could feel the truth of our situation weighing down on me, a heavy cloak I couldn't shrug off. Whatever lay ahead, the path was fraught with danger, and my fragile trust in Reed was all that anchored me to this reality.

The brush of leaves against my skin sent shivers through me, and I fought to suppress the rising tide of anxiety as Reed scanned the shadows, his every muscle coiled with tension. I stepped closer, drawn to his silent resolve, a flicker of something almost magnetic lingering between us. "You're seriously telling me that ancient magic is just lurking out here? Waiting for me to discover it?" I asked, my voice light but laced with disbelief.

Reed didn't respond immediately, his attention locked on a shadow that flitted just beyond the trees. I could see the gears turning in his mind, the struggle of a man weighed down by burdens he refused to share. "If it were that simple, we wouldn't be in this situation," he finally replied, his voice low and gravelly, tinged with the weight of secrets. "Magic is as much a part of this world as it is a curse. Whoever gets their hands on that relic—"

"Could change everything," I finished, a shiver of realization coursing through me. "But what does that mean for me? What am I supposed to do? Just unlock the mystery and hope for the best?"

He turned to face me, and for a moment, the tension broke, the sharp lines of his face softening as he studied me. "You need to understand, unlocking that relic could put you in danger. There are those who want it for themselves, and they won't stop until they get it."

"Sounds like a fairytale gone wrong," I said, feigning lightheartedness, but the truth was sinking in like a stone in water. The danger was real, and yet, there was an undeniable thrill in the unknown, a whisper of adventure that tickled my insides. "What if I told you I wasn't scared of a little danger?"

Reed raised an eyebrow, his expression caught somewhere between skepticism and amusement. "You've obviously never faced real danger before. It's not romantic, and it certainly isn't charming. It's brutal and messy."

"Sounds like you're projecting," I shot back, a smile tugging at my lips. "I have faced plenty of danger—like when my parents made me go to summer camp. Talk about a life-or-death struggle over who gets the last s'more."

He chuckled, and the sound was warm against the cool air, dissolving some of the barriers between us. "Summer camp? Is that where you learned your survival skills?"

"Absolutely. You wouldn't believe how many knots I can tie," I replied, tapping my fingers against my thighs, trying to maintain the banter even as the shadows loomed closer. "But seriously, Reed, if you're this concerned about my safety, why don't you just let me in on the whole plan? Let me help you."

"Because you don't know what you're asking," he said, the gravity of his words settling around us like the encroaching fog. "This isn't about teamwork; it's about survival. I'm not risking your life because of some misguided loyalty to a family I don't even know."

"And yet, here we are," I pointed out, gesturing around us at the dimly lit forest. "Stuck together, facing whatever lurks in the shadows, and you're not leaving me behind."

Reed sighed, the fight in him wavering just a fraction. "That's because I'm not an idiot. Leaving you behind would only make you a target. It's easier to keep an eye on you if you're right next to me."

"Is that your way of saying you care?" I teased, inching closer, enjoying the way his resolve flickered at my words.

"Care? That's not it," he shot back, though his voice had softened. "It's self-preservation. Keep your enemies closer, right?"

I took a step back, pretending to think it over. "So I'm your enemy, huh? Good to know where I stand in this beautiful mess."

Reed rolled his eyes, a ghost of a smile creeping onto his lips. "You're a headache, but you're my headache."

"Headaches can be manageable," I replied, unable to help myself. "Have you tried an aspirin?"

The sudden rustling of leaves nearby silenced our playful exchange, and I instinctively drew closer to Reed, my heart racing again. "What was that?" I whispered, my bravado evaporating as the tension crackled in the air.

"Stay close," he ordered, his voice low and firm. He scanned the surroundings, and I could see the pulse in his throat, the way his body thrummed with anticipation. "It could be nothing, but it could also be everything."

Just then, a figure emerged from the fog, a dark silhouette that blended into the shadows. I froze, breath hitching in my throat as the shape came into focus—a tall man with piercing eyes, his face obscured by a hood. The air around us thickened, the oppressive weight of his presence wrapping around me like a vice.

"Reed," the man said, his voice smooth and dangerous, like silk threaded with steel. "I see you've brought company. How quaint."

My instincts screamed danger, and Reed's posture shifted, his body tense and coiled like a spring. "What do you want, Dorian?" he asked, the bravado gone from his voice.

"I think you know," Dorian replied, stepping forward into the fading light. "You have something that belongs to me. And I intend to collect."

The tension escalated, crackling in the air as Dorian's eyes flicked to me, a predator sizing up his prey. I stepped back, my heart thundering in my chest as Reed took a protective stance in front of me. "You're not getting anywhere near her," he growled, every bit the guardian.

Dorian chuckled softly, a sound devoid of warmth. "You misunderstand, Reed. It's not about what I want. It's about what you're willing to sacrifice to protect her."

The words hung in the air, heavy and foreboding, as the weight of the moment crashed down upon us. I could feel the truth lurking beneath the surface, a tangled web of choices and consequences that would lead us deeper into a conflict neither of us had anticipated. Reed's fierce protectiveness sent a rush of warmth through me, but the danger was palpable, threatening to unravel everything I had just begun to understand.

Dorian's presence loomed over us, the shadows seeming to twist around him as if the darkness were an extension of his very being. I instinctively edged closer to Reed, a surge of adrenaline flooding my veins. The weight of Dorian's gaze bore down on me, a predatory glint sparking in his eyes. "You've meddled long enough, Reed. This girl is just another pawn in your reckless game," he sneered, his words slicing through the tense air like a dagger.

"Don't you dare speak about her like that," Reed shot back, his voice a low growl that vibrated with barely restrained fury. "She's not part of your twisted plans."

"Ah, but that's where you're wrong," Dorian said, his smile cold and calculating. "She holds the key to a much larger puzzle. And you, my dear Reed, have made a grave mistake in bringing her into this."

I felt the sting of dread curling in my stomach. "What do you want from me?" I demanded, fighting to keep my voice steady. "I'm not a prize to be claimed."

Dorian stepped forward, his presence overwhelming, a shadow that swallowed the light around us. "Oh, but you are," he said, his tone almost reverent. "You carry a legacy that has the power to shift the balance of this world. That charm of yours—it's the doorway to unimaginable power."

Reed's body shifted, positioning himself protectively in front of me as he stared down Dorian with fierce determination. "She won't be your weapon, Dorian. Not now, not ever."

The tension thickened like the fog around us, and for a moment, the world narrowed to just the three of us—the predator, the protector, and the prize. Dorian laughed softly, a sound laced with disdain. "You think you can shield her from this? You're playing a dangerous game, Reed. And I don't intend to lose."

With a sudden movement, Dorian flicked his wrist, and the air crackled with a sinister energy. I stumbled backward, my heart racing as an invisible force slammed against my chest, pinning me against a tree. The world blurred, the edges of my vision dimming as fear clawed at my throat.

"Let her go!" Reed roared, launching forward, but Dorian simply waved a hand, the magic coiling around me like a serpent, tightening its grip. I gasped, struggling to breathe, the panic threatening to pull me under.

"I suggest you reconsider your position," Dorian said, his voice smooth and unyielding. "There are worse fates than losing your life. Imagine what it would be like to lose everything you hold dear. Your family, your friends—all gone in an instant. Just to keep this girl safe."

Reed's eyes blazed with fury, the kind of rage that could ignite the very air around us. "You're a monster," he spat, every word heavy with contempt. "I'll never let you have her."

"And yet, here we are," Dorian replied, his expression almost triumphant. "You may be strong, Reed, but strength alone can't win this battle. You're outnumbered, outmatched, and out of time."

I felt the air shift, a slight tremor coursing through the ground beneath me as Dorian's grip on my energy began to fracture. In that moment of desperation, a flicker of light ignited in my mind, a memory of my charm—the source of my family's secrets and the key to ancient magic. I focused all my strength on it, willing it to respond, to break free from Dorian's hold.

"Stop!" I shouted, my voice echoing in the stillness as I summoned the energy of the charm, feeling it pulse with life in the depths of my being. "I won't let you take anything from me!"

The moment I spoke, the charm flared to life, a radiant glow cutting through the darkness, illuminating the fear on Dorian's face. The magic surged around me, shattering the oppressive force pinning me to the tree. I gasped for air, my body released from the invisible bindings that had constricted my breath.

Reed's eyes widened in surprise, and for the first time, I saw a flicker of hope. "That's it! Use it, unleash your power!" he urged, his voice fierce and filled with determination.

Dorian stumbled back, his confidence wavering as the light intensified, casting away the shadows that had wrapped around us.

"No! You don't know what you're doing!" he shouted, panic threading through his tone.

"Neither do you," I shot back, my voice steadying as I stepped forward, channeling the energy of my charm. I could feel its warmth radiating through my veins, fueling my resolve. "I may not know what lies ahead, but I refuse to be anyone's pawn!"

As I unleashed the power within me, a surge of energy exploded outward, pushing against Dorian, who staggered under the force. The fog parted like a curtain, revealing a path that had been obscured by darkness. For a heartbeat, the air was alive with electric potential, and I could sense the shifting tides of fate.

Dorian's expression transformed from confidence to desperation as he fought against the magic I wielded. "You're making a mistake, girl! You don't understand the consequences of your actions!"

"Maybe not," I retorted, feeling the tide of the battle shifting in my favor. "But I refuse to stand by and let you dictate my life!"

In that moment, the fog began to swirl violently, as if responding to our confrontation. Reed stepped closer, ready to support me, but the ground beneath us trembled, a warning of the forces at play.

Dorian recovered, his eyes narrowing, fury igniting his features. "You think you can control this? You're only scratching the surface!"

Before I could react, he extended his hand, and the ground erupted beneath us. A fissure opened, a dark chasm threatening to swallow everything whole. I barely had time to scream as I felt the world tilt, the earth crumbling away, and just as I reached for Reed, the ground buckled, separating us in a violent surge.

"Reed!" I cried, panic rising as the space between us widened, the darkness clawing at the edges of my vision. "No!"

His face was etched with determination, but I could see the frustration in his eyes as he reached for me. "Stay focused! Don't lose the charm's power!"

The last thing I saw before the chasm closed was Dorian's triumphant smile, a promise of chaos and despair lingering in the air. My heart raced as the ground settled, the fog swirling around us once more, but I could still feel the connection, the magic thrumming within me, a fire waiting to be unleashed.

And then there was silence—an oppressive quiet that hung heavily in the aftermath of the chaos, leaving me breathless and alone, with uncertainty spiraling around me like the mist.

Chapter 5: Inferno of Trust

The library, a crumbling monument to lost knowledge, loomed before us like an ancient sentinel, its stone facade covered in twisting vines that clawed at the weathered bricks. Each step I took into its shadowy depths stirred the musty scent of parchment and dust, a perfume of ages past that whispered secrets in a language I was only beginning to decipher. The moon hung low in the sky, its silvery light cascading through shattered windows, illuminating the remnants of a world once vibrant with stories and wisdom.

Reed stood beside me, his silhouette sharp against the dim glow, arms crossed and expression unreadable. There was something almost fierce in the way he surveyed the room, as if he were a guardian of its mysteries, yet I could sense the tension beneath his calm exterior. I felt the urge to bridge that distance, to pull him closer to the warmth of camaraderie that flickered between us like a candle's flame. "So, where do we start?" I asked, trying to sound confident despite the fluttering uncertainty in my chest.

He snorted, a sound that was equal parts amusement and disdain. "You think this is a classroom? It's a graveyard of knowledge." His voice was low, laced with an edge that made my spine tingle. "What do you even know about magic, anyway?"

"More than you might think," I retorted, matching his tone. "You're not the only one who's been digging through dusty old tomes, Reed." I gestured towards the towering shelves, their spines cracked and faded. "There's power here. We just have to find it."

With a reluctant grunt, he stepped closer to a nearby shelf, his fingers trailing over the bindings, each one a portal to a different reality. "Fine," he said, his voice softer now, as if he were letting down a shield. "But it's not as simple as flipping pages. Magic comes with a price, and not all of it is worth paying."

The weight of his words settled around us like a shroud. I watched him, intrigued and slightly unnerved. This was the same Reed who could effortlessly wield power, yet here he was, revealing a glimpse of vulnerability. There was more to him than the hardened exterior he displayed to the world, and for the first time, I felt a flicker of connection, a bond forged in our shared quest for understanding.

"Let's start with something basic, then," I suggested, my heart racing at the thought of delving into the unknown. "What about spells? We have to have a few tricks up our sleeves if we're going to face what's coming."

He shot me a sidelong glance, a mixture of surprise and begrudging respect flashing across his features. "You really want to learn?"

"I do." My voice was firm, a declaration. "Teach me."

The dawn began to break, casting an ethereal light through the shattered windows. Reed's demeanor shifted slightly, as if the soft glow revealed a version of him I had yet to meet—a reluctant mentor, perhaps, or a weary traveler looking for purpose. "Alright. But you need to listen closely. This isn't a game."

We settled down in a small clearing among the ruins, a space littered with scrolls and broken relics, remnants of the past that seemed to breathe with a life of their own. He reached for a tattered book, its cover embossed with intricate symbols that seemed to shift in the light, teasing at secrets within. "This is a basic spellbook," he said, flipping it open to reveal pages filled with elegant script and illustrations that danced before my eyes. "We'll start with something simple."

As he began to explain the intricacies of the first spell, a warm energy crackled in the air between us, an unspoken understanding blooming like the dawn outside. "You'll need to focus your thoughts, channel your emotions," he instructed, his voice steady yet layered with intensity. "Magic isn't just about words; it's about intention."

I nodded, trying to absorb his every word. "So, it's like... like a dance? You have to move in sync with it?"

"Exactly," he replied, a hint of a smile creeping onto his lips. "But be careful; even the most graceful dancers can trip and fall."

"Don't worry," I said, flashing him a grin. "I've tripped plenty of times in my life. I'm practically an expert."

He chuckled, a rich sound that sent a thrill through me. It was a surprising shift, this lightness between us, and I could feel the walls he had built beginning to crack. As we practiced, my initial clumsiness faded, replaced by an exhilarating sense of empowerment. With each attempted incantation, the connection between us deepened, threading through our shared laughter and shared failures.

But just as the first rays of sunlight poured into the library, illuminating the dust motes dancing in the air, an unease settled in the pit of my stomach. Reed's demeanor shifted once again, his brows furrowing as he caught the shift in the atmosphere. "We need to be cautious," he murmured, eyes narrowing as if sensing an unseen threat. "This place has been untouched for years, but something is stirring. I can feel it."

My heart raced, the earlier exhilaration now mingling with a sense of dread. "What do you mean?"

He stood, scanning the room with a predatory grace, every muscle in his body taut. "It means we're not alone. And whatever lurks in the shadows may not welcome our presence."

As the words hung in the air, the warmth of our newfound bond felt fragile, like a thread stretched too tight. I took a step closer, driven by instinct. "Then we'll face it together," I declared, determined not to let fear fracture the trust we had begun to build.

Reed's gaze met mine, and in that moment, the world beyond the library faded, leaving only us and the echo of our shared resolve.

The dawn light poured through the remnants of the ancient structure, wrapping us in a golden embrace, and for the first time, I believed that perhaps we could unravel the mysteries that bound us both. Together.

The warmth of the sun spilled into the library, transforming the dust motes into glittering diamonds that danced in the golden light. Reed stood across from me, a stoic figure framed by the remnants of a forgotten era, his jaw set and eyes scanning the room like a hawk assessing its territory. I could feel the electric hum of magic lingering in the air, thick and intoxicating, as if the very walls held their breath, waiting for our next move.

"Alright, let's try this again," he said, the edge in his voice hinting at impatience, but his eyes sparkled with a challenge. "Focus on your emotions. Channel them into the words."

I squared my shoulders, determined not to let his intensity intimidate me. "So, all I need to do is harness my inner whirlwind of feelings, then?" I shot back, feigning nonchalance, though the flutter in my stomach suggested otherwise. "Easy peasy."

He raised an eyebrow, a smirk tugging at the corners of his mouth. "Just remember, last time your 'inner whirlwind' nearly blew up the shelf of relics."

"Hey! That wasn't my fault; that spell clearly had a wicked sense of humor." I crossed my arms, pretending to pout. "Besides, you didn't exactly warn me about the explosive part."

"Explosive, indeed," he chuckled, shaking his head. "You have a gift for attracting chaos."

"Chaos? I prefer to think of it as...enthusiasm." I leaned in closer, the shared laughter lightening the air between us, binding us in a moment of camaraderie. The warmth of our connection swirled like the golden light filtering through the shattered windows, but beneath it, the undercurrents of uncertainty remained.

"Let's see that enthusiasm in action, then," he challenged, stepping back to give me space. "This time, focus on a small object—something simple. How about that?" He pointed at an unremarkable pebble resting among the debris.

With a mock sigh, I bent down to pick it up, feeling the coolness of the stone against my palm. "You really aim low, don't you? A rock? Is this a magical initiation or a scavenger hunt?"

"Don't underestimate the power of the mundane," he replied, his voice steady. "It's not the object that matters but the intention behind it. Concentrate."

I nodded, feeling the weight of the pebble settle into my hand as I closed my eyes, breathing in the scent of aged parchment and the earthy aroma of the stone. I tried to visualize the energy swirling around me, tapping into that inexplicable connection I felt with the magic of this place. Words tumbled in my mind like leaves caught in a gust of wind.

As I opened my eyes, I uttered the incantation, pouring every ounce of focus into the pebble. At first, nothing happened, and I felt the creeping tendrils of doubt slither into my thoughts. But then, a soft glow began to emanate from the stone, pulsing like a heartbeat, and I gasped as it lifted slightly from my palm. The thrill of success surged through me, electric and exhilarating.

"Not bad," Reed admitted, a hint of admiration breaking through his guarded demeanor. "But don't let it go to your head. It's a pebble."

"Hey, it's a magically levitating pebble," I corrected, unable to suppress a grin. "That's like, an upgrade from regular rocks. Watch out, I might start my own collection."

"Just remember to keep your enthusiasm contained. Not everything needs to be levitating." His tone was teasing, but the underlying tension in his expression reminded me that the stakes were higher than mere tricks.

I dropped the pebble, letting it fall back to its rightful place, and turned to Reed, feeling emboldened. "So, what's next? More levitating rocks, or are we going to tackle something with a bit more...pizzazz?"

He crossed his arms, regarding me with a mixture of caution and intrigue. "Pizzazz, huh? Alright, let's step it up. How do you feel about conjuring something more complex? Like an elemental spirit?"

"Elemental spirit?" I echoed, my heart racing at the prospect. "You mean, like, a mini tornado or a friendly little fireball?"

"Less tornado, more...subtlety. Think of it as manifesting a companion—one that's more helpful than destructive." He moved towards the far wall, brushing away cobwebs to reveal an intricate mural depicting swirling clouds and flames entwined with graceful, ethereal beings. "But it requires more energy and focus than what you've just done."

"Great," I said, eyeing the mural with trepidation. "I'm basically summoning a roommate. I hope they come with their own snacks."

"Just keep your sense of humor in check; it won't be helpful when things go sideways." Reed took a deep breath, the shadows playing across his features. "Remember, the key is to connect with the element you're summoning. Feel its essence, and let it guide you."

I took a moment, allowing the vibrant energy of the library to seep into my bones. The connection with magic felt almost palpable, a living entity pulsing through the air. "Alright, let's do this," I said, steeling myself. "But if I end up with a fireball that's more 'hothead' than 'helpful,' I'm blaming you."

With that, I closed my eyes once more, channeling every ounce of intention into the air around me. I visualized the essence of fire—its warmth, its flickering light, its potential for both destruction and creation. Words of the incantation flowed from my lips, each syllable tinged with a nervous excitement. I could feel the energy swirling around me, responding to my call, beckoning to be shaped.

The temperature in the room began to rise, and a flickering light danced behind my closed eyelids. As I opened my eyes, there, hovering before me, was a small flame, bright and vibrant, swirling like a playful dancer in the air. It flickered and flared, a tiny beacon of heat and light.

"Impressive," Reed breathed, his eyes wide with a mix of surprise and approval. "But be careful; it's lively."

"Lively? It's practically a party," I exclaimed, grinning at the small fire spirit as it twisted and curled, delighting in its own existence. But even as I reveled in the moment, the shadows of the library seemed to shift, darkening the corners and deepening the creases in Reed's brow.

"Focus on control," he warned, stepping closer. "Lively spirits can turn unpredictable if they sense fear."

"Great. Just what I needed to hear." I drew a breath, centering myself, feeling the warmth of the flame on my skin. "Okay, little guy. Let's dance, but stay close to me."

As the fire spirit twirled around, a sudden gust of wind swept through the library, swirling the dust into a frenzy and snuffing out the warmth of my flame in an instant. My heart raced as the air grew heavy with an unseen presence, the very atmosphere shifting with tension.

"What was that?" I gasped, scanning the shadows, my earlier confidence evaporating. Reed's expression darkened, and the light in the room seemed to dim.

"I told you we're not alone," he murmured, eyes narrowing as he stepped protectively in front of me. The walls of the library felt alive, pulsating with a magic that was both inviting and foreboding. I could sense it then, a looming darkness that encroached upon our fragile bubble of trust, threatening to tear apart everything we had just begun to build.

The air thickened around us, a palpable tension coiling like a serpent poised to strike. I shifted my weight, heart pounding as the shadows deepened, morphing into ominous shapes that seemed to crawl along the walls of the library. Reed's posture changed; he was no longer the reluctant mentor, but a sentry, alert and watchful.

"Stay close," he said, his voice low and urgent. "We need to be prepared for whatever that was."

"What exactly is 'that'?" I whispered, my voice barely above a breath. My eyes darted around, searching the dim corners for any sign of movement. "You know, besides the fact that I just summoned a rogue wind."

"I don't know yet, but I can feel it," he replied, scanning the room with a focus that sent chills down my spine. "There's a darkness here, something that's been disturbed. We've awoken it."

"Fantastic," I muttered, feeling the weight of dread settle like a heavy cloak on my shoulders. "First levitating rocks, now dark forces. I should've brought a sage bundle or something."

"Humor won't help us now." His tone was sharp, but there was a flicker of something softer beneath it, an unspoken understanding that we were in this together, even as danger loomed.

I took a deep breath, squaring my shoulders. "Okay, so what's the plan? Fight or flight?"

"Neither. We observe," he replied, his eyes narrowing as he focused on the far side of the library, where the shadows pooled thicker. "We need to find out what we're dealing with before we make any moves."

I nodded, though my instincts screamed for action. There was something unsettling about the way the shadows curled and shifted, almost as if they had a mind of their own. "And how exactly do we do that?" I asked, my voice steadier than I felt.

"By listening. Sometimes, the most dangerous things reveal themselves if you're patient enough."

I glanced at him, realizing how much his demeanor had shifted. This was a side of Reed I hadn't seen before, the tactical thinker who was accustomed to navigating perilous waters. But as we stood there, the silence around us stretched, thick and foreboding, my patience began to wear thin.

"Are we going to just stand here, or—"

A sudden gust rushed through the library, and a voice, low and melodic yet laced with menace, echoed off the walls. "Why do you disturb my sanctuary?"

I jumped, the voice wrapping around me like icy tendrils. Reed instinctively stepped in front of me, a protective barrier against the unseen threat. "Show yourself!" he called, his voice firm but laced with an undertone of tension.

The shadows flickered, momentarily coalescing into a figure that shimmered like heat waves rising off asphalt. It was a woman, or what once might have been a woman, her form undulating like smoke. Her features were indistinct, her eyes two dark voids that seemed to suck in the light around her. "You tread where you do not belong," she intoned, each word dripping with ancient authority.

I could feel Reed's muscles tense beside me. "We seek knowledge, nothing more," he said, voice steady but laced with an underlying urgency. "We didn't mean to intrude."

"Knowledge is power, and power demands a price," she hissed, the shadows swirling around her like a storm ready to break. "What will you offer in exchange for what you seek?"

I exchanged a glance with Reed, uncertainty swirling in my gut. "What kind of price?" I ventured, my heart racing. "We didn't come here to barter our souls or anything."

The figure laughed, a sound that sent shivers skittering down my spine. "Not souls, child, but perhaps something of value. Something personal." Her eyes glinted with a predatory delight, as if she savored the moment of our fear.

"What do you mean?" Reed asked, his tone sharper now. "We have nothing you would want."

"Oh, I beg to differ," she purred, her gaze fixed on me with unnerving intensity. "You hold more than you realize, dear girl. You are a vessel of untapped potential, a beacon in the dark. I can sense the magic thrumming beneath your skin, but it is not yet fully yours."

I swallowed hard, the weight of her words sinking in. "So you want... me?" I asked, incredulous. "You want to take my magic?"

"Not take, merely guide," she replied, her smile sharp as glass. "I could teach you to harness it fully, to wield it with the finesse you currently lack. In exchange, I only ask for a small token—your trust, your commitment to this path."

"Why do I feel like you're trying to sell me a used car?" I shot back, unable to contain my skepticism. "What's the catch?"

"Clever girl," she said, her voice dripping with approval. "The catch is simple. Once you accept my offer, you can never turn back. You will be bound to me, to this library, to the magic that flows through you."

Reed shifted beside me, concern etched in his features. "Don't listen to her. This is a trap."

"But what if it isn't?" I countered, torn between fear and an insatiable curiosity. "What if this is the opportunity we need?"

"The opportunity to lose yourself?" Reed snapped, frustration creeping into his voice. "Don't let her weave her lies into your heart."

I hesitated, the weight of their words pulling me in two directions. The shadows around the woman flickered, her form almost playful, as if she could sense my uncertainty. "Think carefully, child," she urged, her voice a sultry whisper that sent shivers through me. "I can show you wonders beyond your imagination, but you must be willing to take the leap."

The library felt alive, the air crackling with tension as I wrestled with the choice before me. Reed's presence was a steadfast anchor, a reminder of the danger lurking just beyond the shadows. Yet the allure of power, of true understanding of the magic within me, tugged at my core.

"Choose wisely," the woman said, her tone turning sinister, a warning woven into her honeyed words. "Time is not on your side, and I do not wait for the indecisive."

In that moment, the ground beneath us trembled, sending vibrations up through my legs, jolting me from my thoughts. Reed's hand found mine, his grip firm and reassuring, yet the shadows seemed to deepen, ready to swallow us whole.

"I—" I began, my voice wavering as the weight of my decision bore down on me. But before I could finish, the walls of the library shuddered, and the figure burst into a flurry of shadows, swirling violently as an unseen force rattled the very foundations of our sanctuary.

"Choose!" she roared, her voice echoing in the chaos, reverberating through the ancient stones. And in that moment of turmoil, I felt the power within me flare, a bright spark against the encroaching darkness.

Before I could grasp what it all meant, the world tilted, and I was left dangling in uncertainty, teetering on the edge of a decision that could change everything. Would I embrace the unknown or retreat into the safety of ignorance?

The ground quaked again, and as the shadows closed in, I took a step forward, my heart racing. But would it be towards enlightenment or into the abyss? The answer slipped through my fingers like sand, leaving only the lingering echo of her demand: "Choose."

Chapter 6: Blazing Betrayal

The air crackled with the heat of the sun bearing down on us, turning the forest path into a shimmering ribbon of gold and shadow. Reed walked ahead, his silhouette cutting an imposing figure against the verdant backdrop, the light glinting off the sharp angles of his jaw and the muscles that shifted beneath his shirt. Every step felt deliberate, as if he were attuned to the very heartbeat of the earth beneath him, the soft crunch of twigs echoing like a whispered promise that adventure awaited us just beyond the bend.

I followed, my heart a tumult of excitement and uncertainty. The thrill of our partnership had sparked something within me, a fire kindling in the pit of my stomach that threatened to spill over into reckless abandon. Every moment with him felt charged, like we were striding through a realm where danger and possibility danced a tantalizing waltz. Yet, the deeper we wandered into the woods, the more the shadows stretched around us, and a shiver traced down my spine—a premonition that something was amiss.

Reed paused, his senses sharpening as he scanned the thick foliage ahead. I could see the tension ripple through him, the way his shoulders drew back, muscles coiling like a snake preparing to strike. It was then that I felt it—a prickling sensation crawling up my neck, warning me that we were not alone. I opened my mouth to voice my concern, but the words caught in my throat as a chorus of snarls erupted from the underbrush.

A group of men emerged, their eyes cold and devoid of compassion, like wolves hungry for a long-overdue meal. They advanced with predatory grace, faces obscured by masks that seemed to blend with the shadows of the trees. My pulse quickened, and I instinctively stepped closer to Reed, my heart pounding an erratic rhythm.

"Stay behind me," he commanded, voice low and steady, as he unsheathed a knife that glinted menacingly in the light. I nodded, though dread clawed at my insides. I had trusted him, let down my guard, and now it felt like the ground beneath my feet was crumbling away.

"Reed!" one of the men spat, the sound laced with contempt. "You think you can just walk away from us? From everything we've built?"

Their leader, a burly figure with a scar running across his brow, stepped forward. Recognition flickered in Reed's eyes, and in that moment, I understood. The warmth that had radiated from our shared experiences began to cool, replaced by a frigid tension as the reality of Reed's past crashed over me like a wave.

"You led us," I whispered, disbelief lacing my words. "You were one of them."

Before Reed could answer, the men charged. The world exploded into chaos. Reed moved like a whirlwind, his body a blur as he engaged the hunters with a grace that was both mesmerizing and terrifying. I clung to the edge of the chaos, my heart racing, adrenaline coursing through me like wildfire. I had never witnessed such ferocity.

He was a force of nature, and yet each swing of his knife felt like a dance with demons, shadows of his past lashing out with every strike. The air was thick with the metallic scent of blood and the raw, earthy smell of sweat and desperation. I wanted to help, to join him in this battle, but fear anchored my feet to the ground. Instead, I could only watch as he fought to protect not just himself, but the secret we'd shared—the charm, our bond, everything that had begun to bloom between us.

The fight escalated, the men circling us like vultures, and I felt a panic rise within me. Just when I thought Reed had gained the upper hand, one of the hunters lunged, a wicked glint in his eyes. Time slowed as Reed dodged, his movements fluid and instinctual, but not fast enough. The hunter struck, a dagger slicing through the air, and I gasped as I saw the flash of pain etch across Reed's face.

"Reed!" I screamed, the sound raw and desperate. I pushed forward, my instincts overtaking my hesitation, and in that moment, I realized I would do anything to protect him.

He turned, eyes blazing, and I saw the flicker of surprise in his expression—an unexpected warmth that nearly shattered the icy tension between us. "Get back!" he shouted, but I refused to retreat.

With a surge of courage, I grabbed a fallen branch and swung it at the nearest hunter, the impact sending shockwaves through my arm. The man staggered back, surprised by my sudden defiance. Reed seized the opportunity, launching himself into the fray with renewed ferocity, his movements sharp and decisive.

As we fought side by side, an unspoken understanding passed between us—this wasn't just about survival anymore; it was about confronting the ghosts of Reed's past and the truth that had woven its way into our lives like a dark thread in a tapestry of light.

When the last of the hunters fell, panting and defeated, the forest fell silent, the echoes of battle fading into a tense stillness. Reed stood before me, chest heaving, the blade still clutched tightly in his hand. The remnants of the fight clung to him—sweat glistened on his brow, and the scarlet stains on his shirt told tales of violence and survival.

The weight of betrayal hung between us, heavier than the aftermath of battle. "I didn't choose them," he finally said, voice thick with a mixture of anger and regret. "I was trying to escape—"

"Escape what?" I cut in, frustration boiling over. "You led them! You were one of them!"

His eyes softened, and I could see the battle within him, the flicker of remorse that contrasted sharply with the man who had fought to protect me. "I left them for a reason," he said quietly, the intensity of his gaze boring into me. "I thought I could make something better. But I should have known they'd come for me. For you."

My heart twisted painfully as the truth settled into the crevices of my mind, the realization that our connection was forged in the flames of betrayal. "You were tracking me," I breathed, the betrayal hitting harder than any blow. "This was all a part of your plan."

The silence that followed was deafening, a chasm opening between us that seemed insurmountable. Reed's shoulders slumped, his bravado crumbling under the weight of his own confession.

The silence stretched between us, thick and suffocating, as the reality of Reed's betrayal hung in the air like a storm cloud, heavy and ominous. The forest, once a sanctuary filled with the rustling of leaves and the gentle whisper of the breeze, now felt like a cage, trapping me with the truth that threatened to unravel everything I thought I knew. I took a step back, the world around me blurring as I grappled with the weight of his words.

"I didn't come here to hurt you," Reed said, his voice low and steady, but I could see the tension coiling within him. His fists clenched, his gaze searching mine for some flicker of understanding, but all I could feel was betrayal, a cold, jagged edge that cut deeper than any knife could.

"But you did," I replied, my voice trembling with the force of my emotions. "You used me. You waited for the moment I'd lead you to the charm, and for what? Power?" The word tasted bitter on my tongue. The very idea that our connection had been tainted by manipulation twisted my insides, made my heart race with anger and confusion.

"I thought—" he started, but I held up a hand to stop him. I didn't want to hear his rationalizations, his excuses. Not now. Not when I felt like I had been living a lie.

"Thought what? That it was okay to track me like some kind of game? That you could just walk away from your past and start fresh with me without telling me the truth?" My heart raced, each syllable laced with a frustration I could no longer contain.

"I thought I could protect you," he said, his expression shifting as if he were wrestling with his own demons. "I didn't want to drag you into this. I didn't want to expose you to what I've left behind."

The sincerity in his eyes was like a beacon cutting through the fog of my anger, but I didn't want to follow it. Not yet. "Protect me?" I scoffed, crossing my arms tightly over my chest. "Is this your idea of protection? Putting me in the crosshairs of your past?"

He stepped closer, the space between us crackling with tension, and I felt an unwelcome rush of longing mixed with fury. "You have to believe me when I say I didn't think they'd find us. Not like this."

"Maybe I should have kept running," I snapped, but the truth was, I didn't want to run anymore. Not from him. Not from the adventure that had ignited something inside me. But the betrayal felt like a dark stain on everything, and I wasn't sure how to wash it away.

Before he could respond, the distant rustle of leaves drew my attention. I turned sharply, instincts kicking in, but when I looked back at Reed, I found him watching me with an intensity that set my heart racing. There was so much unsaid between us—so many layers of hurt and trust that needed peeling back.

"Let's move," he said, urgency creeping into his tone. "We can't stay here."

I nodded, my mind still spinning, and together we retraced our steps along the path, the air heavy with unspoken words. As we navigated through the trees, I caught sight of the remnants of the fight—discarded weapons, the faint scent of blood mingling with the earthy aroma of the forest floor. It was a stark reminder of the danger lurking in the shadows, not just from the hunters, but from the secrets that now lay bare between us.

The forest was thick with anticipation, the kind that sent shivers racing down my spine. I stole glances at Reed, his jaw set in determination, his expression taut. I wanted to reach out, to bridge the gap that had opened up between us, but I couldn't shake the feeling that every step forward was a step deeper into unknown territory.

As we moved further from the scene of the ambush, the underbrush began to thin out, revealing a small clearing bathed in the golden light of the late afternoon sun. It felt almost surreal, like stepping into a dream where the colors were too vibrant and the shadows too deep. I could hear the faint trickle of a stream nearby, a sound that promised clarity but felt miles away from the chaos of our reality.

"We should rest," Reed said, finally breaking the silence that had enveloped us. He dropped to a log at the edge of the clearing, and I followed suit, the weight of my emotions making the ground feel like a welcome respite.

"Why didn't you just tell me the truth?" I asked, the question tumbling out before I could hold it back. "You could have trusted me."

He ran a hand through his hair, a gesture that spoke of frustration and regret. "I didn't want to drag you into this mess. I wanted to keep you safe. When I first found you, I was drawn to your light, your spirit. I thought I could—"

"Thought you could what?" I challenged, leaning forward. "Save me? From what? Your past? Your mistakes?"

"No," he said, his voice a fierce whisper. "From the consequences of my choices. I thought if I stayed close enough, I could protect you from everything. I didn't realize how deep the shadows ran until it was too late."

My heart softened for a moment, but the sharp edges of betrayal remained. "And what about the charm? Is that all this was to you—a means to an end?"

"It was never just about the charm," he replied, eyes locked onto mine with an intensity that nearly stole my breath. "That charm is powerful, yes, but it's also a part of something larger—a history that I've been trying to escape. When I met you, everything changed. I thought I could find a way to reconcile my past without losing you in the process."

The air between us felt charged, electric. My pulse quickened as I weighed his words, a delicate dance of emotions swirling within me. "And what happens now?" I asked, the question lingering in the air like a dare.

Reed's gaze darkened, determination flickering in his eyes. "Now, we find a way forward. Together. I won't let them take you from me. Not now. Not ever."

The weight of his promise settled over me, a blanket of warmth amidst the cold uncertainty. In that moment, I realized that despite the betrayal, despite the lies, there was still a flicker of something undeniable between us—a connection forged in fire, a bond that could either break us apart or bring us closer than we'd ever imagined.

As the sun dipped below the horizon, painting the sky in hues of purple and gold, I took a deep breath, letting the crisp air fill my lungs. The forest around us was alive with the sounds of twilight, the chorus of crickets and rustling leaves providing a rhythm to the tumultuous emotions that swirled within. Whatever lay ahead, I knew I had to face it—together.

The air hung heavy with tension as the last remnants of daylight faded into the embrace of dusk, shadows stretching and intertwining like the tangled web of emotions that now separated Reed and me. The clearing was silent, save for the occasional rustle of leaves in the gentle evening breeze, but the quiet felt deceptive, charged with the possibility of danger lurking just beyond the trees. I could almost taste the adrenaline still buzzing in my veins, a visceral reminder of our earlier confrontation.

"Together," Reed had said, a promise wrapped in sincerity, but I found myself grappling with the weight of his past. How could I trust him again when every inch of my being screamed that his intentions were shrouded in darkness? I took a breath, letting the cool air fill my lungs, trying to dispel the remnants of my anxiety. But the doubt clung to me like a shadow.

"Is this how you intend to protect me?" I asked, my voice barely above a whisper. I gestured around us, taking in the remnants of our recent battle—the broken branches, the scattered leaves, the faint traces of blood that seemed to seep into the earth like spilled secrets. "By lying? By keeping me in the dark about who you are?"

He ran a hand through his hair, a gesture of exasperation. "I thought I could keep you out of it. I thought if I could just find the charm, we could be free. Start fresh. I was wrong."

"Wrong? That's an understatement," I shot back, feeling the heat of anger flush my cheeks. "You put me in danger, and for what? A chance at redemption? A few moments of adventure?"

Reed's expression hardened, the intensity of his gaze piercing through the softening twilight. "This is not a game to me. I thought you understood that."

"Oh, I understand plenty," I replied, my voice rising. "I understand that trust is a fragile thing, and you shattered it. You thought you could control this? Control me? You might have been tracking me, but you didn't realize I'm not some pawn on your chessboard."

A flicker of pain crossed his features, and for a moment, the anger between us felt like a living thing, pulsing and vibrant. "I know that now," he said, his tone low and heavy with regret. "I've spent so long running from my past, I didn't think about how it would affect you. I wanted to protect you from all of this." He waved his hand, encompassing the tangled web of trees and shadows surrounding us, as if they were somehow responsible for the chaos between us.

"By keeping me ignorant?" I countered, folding my arms defiantly. "How does that protect me?"

Reed sighed, the sound heavy with the weight of unspoken words. "You're right. It doesn't. But I thought if I could get the charm, I could finally sever the ties to my past. I could make it all go away."

"And what about us?" I pressed, the question lingering in the air like a promise unfulfilled. "What happens when your past catches up with you again? Because it will."

"I'll deal with it," he replied, the certainty in his voice both comforting and unsettling. "And I'll protect you while I do. You mean more to me than this—" he gestured again, frustration clear in his eyes, "than this entire mess."

Something in his gaze shifted, an urgency that snapped my attention back to the shadows creeping at the edges of the clearing. Just as the last slivers of sunlight slipped beneath the horizon, a low growl broke the silence, reverberating through the air like an ominous warning. Reed's body tensed, and I felt the hairs on the back of my neck stand on end.

"Get behind me," he ordered, instinctively positioning himself between me and the encroaching darkness. My heart raced as I peered into the depths of the forest, shadows twisting and shifting with a life of their own.

"What is it?" I whispered, dread curling around my insides.

"Hunters," he replied grimly, his voice barely audible. "They won't give up easily."

Panic surged through me, propelling my heart into a frantic rhythm. "We can't just stand here. We need to run!"

"We can't let them know we're afraid," he said, scanning the treeline for any sign of movement. "They'll use it against us."

Before I could argue, the shadows coalesced into shapes—figures moving stealthily, their intent as clear as the glint of steel reflecting in the faint moonlight. Reed's grip tightened on his knife, and I felt an exhilarating rush of fear and adrenaline flood through me.

"Stay close," he said, his eyes flicking to mine, the resolve in his gaze igniting something fierce within me. "We can fight them."

"Fight them?" I echoed incredulously. "There are too many!"

He shot me a quick look, his determination radiating like heat from a fire. "We'll find a way."

The growls grew louder, and the hunters emerged from the underbrush, their faces obscured by masks that made them appear more like phantoms than men. Their eyes gleamed with a predatory hunger, and as they advanced, a mixture of terror and fierce loyalty surged through me, binding me to Reed.

"I won't let them take you," he promised, and there was a fierce conviction in his voice that made my heart flutter, despite the fear clawing at my insides. "Whatever happens, we stand together."

"Together," I echoed, the word feeling foreign yet strangely right. It was a promise forged in the heat of chaos, in the shadow of betrayal.

With a roar, one of the hunters lunged, and Reed was immediately engaged, the two of them colliding in a flurry of motion. I felt a surge of instinct—my body moving without thought as I grabbed a fallen branch, rushing into the fray. Adrenaline coursed through my veins as I swung it, striking the nearest hunter with a satisfying crack.

"You're not so fragile after all!" Reed shouted, a grin breaking through the tension as he dispatched another foe.

"I'm full of surprises!" I quipped back, the thrill of battle igniting a fierce determination within me.

But the hunters were relentless, a dark tide threatening to engulf us. I could see Reed working to keep them at bay, his movements fluid and practiced, yet with each passing moment, the numbers grew, and my heart sank with the realization that we might not escape this.

A sudden shout echoed from behind me, and before I could turn, a figure burst into the clearing—someone familiar, someone I hadn't expected to see. The chaos around me faded as recognition pierced through the adrenaline.

"Get down!" the voice called, a sharp command that cut through the noise.

I turned, just as another hunter lunged toward me, and the world seemed to slow. I dropped to the ground instinctively, the branch slipping from my grasp as I caught a glimpse of a weapon glinting dangerously close.

But before I could fully process the scene, a figure moved swiftly, stepping in front of me. The unmistakable outline of a woman appeared, her hair catching the moonlight like a silver halo. "I told you to stay away!" she shouted at Reed, eyes blazing with a mix of anger and worry.

"Lila?" Reed breathed, shock mingling with disbelief as he parried a blow from the hunter, the clash of metal ringing sharply in the night.

"You don't get to decide when I come and go!" she retorted, swinging a dagger with lethal precision, forcing the hunters back.

I scrambled to my feet, heart racing, confusion swirling in my mind as I watched the chaos unfold. The once familiar world of trust and betrayal had spiraled into a battlefield of conflicting loyalties, and I was caught in the middle, unsure of where my allegiances lay.

"Lila, we need to leave!" Reed shouted, his voice cutting through the clamor.

"Not without the charm!" she shot back, her eyes locked onto mine with an intensity that sent a shiver down my spine. "Where is it?"

The question hung in the air, thick with implication, and suddenly the gravity of our situation crashed down upon me. The charm—the very object that had drawn us together and now threatened to tear us apart—was the focal point of this chaos.

Just as the realization dawned, a sharp pain lanced through my side, and I gasped, stumbling back as a hunter had found his way past Reed and Lila. I could feel the heat of blood against my skin, and the world around me dimmed as I fell to my knees, the reality of our fight pressing down on me like a weight I could no longer bear.

"NO!" Reed shouted, a primal scream that echoed through the clearing, and in that moment, I knew that everything had changed. The battle was far from over, and the truth of what lay ahead would redefine us all, pulling us into an abyss from which we might never return.

Chapter 7: Ashes of Redemption

The sun had dipped below the horizon, leaving behind a smattering of twilight hues that painted the sky in soft purples and golds. The chill of the evening air slipped into the clearing like a whisper, urging us to build a fire. Reed knelt on the damp earth, his broad shoulders tense as he scraped together twigs and dry leaves, an errant flame flickering to life under his careful hands. I watched him, my heart a conundrum of distrust and intrigue, the warmth of the fire contrasting sharply with the icy grip of betrayal still lingering in my chest.

"Are you going to just stare at me all night?" he asked, glancing over his shoulder with a sardonic lift of his brow. "Or do you plan to actually help?"

I huffed, arms crossed, a defensive stance I had perfected. "What's the point? You'll probably set us on fire, and I'm not in the mood for an impromptu barbecue."

He chuckled, the sound a low rumble that sent a shiver of unexpected warmth through me. "You know, for someone who's supposed to be angry at me, you sure are witty."

"Witty?" I retorted, stepping closer, my fingers brushing against a few stray twigs. "I prefer 'survivor.' It's more fitting given the circumstances."

He raised an eyebrow, the flickering light illuminating the shadows that danced across his face. "Survivor, huh? That's a fancy title for someone who nearly got captured by those hunters."

"Funny, I thought that was your job. Not mine." The bite in my tone surprised even me.

His gaze softened for a moment, and I caught a glimpse of the vulnerability that had been hidden beneath layers of bravado. "I didn't mean for any of this to happen," he said quietly, returning to the fire as it roared to life, casting flickering shadows on his face. "I was trying to protect you."

"Protect me?" I scoffed, the word tasting bitter on my tongue. "By throwing me to the wolves?"

The fire crackled, breaking the tension, and for a heartbeat, we both fell silent, the truth of our circumstances hanging between us like a heavy shroud. Reed stared into the flames, his expression a mix of regret and something deeper, a darkness I couldn't quite decipher.

"My sister..." he began, the words slow and weighed down by grief. "She was taken by the same hunters. I should have done more to save her."

There it was—the first thread of his story, the piece I hadn't known existed. I leaned in, curiosity pulling me closer. "What happened?"

His jaw tightened as if the memories were physical pain. "We were supposed to leave together. But I was reckless, focused on my own plans. By the time I realized she was in danger..." He trailed off, eyes darkening, a storm of regret swirling behind them.

In that moment, I saw him—really saw him. The bravado, the bravado, the reckless swagger, all stripped away to reveal a man weighed down by grief and guilt. I shifted, the warmth of the fire mingling with an uncomfortable empathy. "You're not a monster," I said softly. "You're just a man who made a mistake."

He glanced at me, surprise flickering in his expression. "And what do you know about mistakes?"

"More than I care to admit." I drew a breath, the cool air filling my lungs with a sharp clarity. "We're all just trying to survive. Just trying to do what's right."

Reed shifted, the weight of his own burden evident in the way he held himself. "And what does that look like for you?"

"Right now? It looks like staying alive long enough to figure out how to get away from these hunters." I met his gaze, a fire of determination igniting within me. "But after that? I don't know. Maybe it means finding my own way back."

"Back to where?"

"To myself, I suppose. Before all this." I gestured vaguely, encompassing the shadows that loomed around us. "Before I lost my way in all this chaos."

He studied me, his eyes piercing yet oddly soft, as if he were peeling back the layers of my soul. "You've got more fight in you than I gave you credit for," he said finally, a hint of admiration lacing his voice.

"Maybe I'm just tired of being hunted." The confession slipped out, raw and unguarded, the admission lingering in the air between us.

The fire crackled, its warmth wrapping around us like a cocoon. Reed drew closer, the heat of his body mixing with the firelight, creating an intimate space amidst the chaos. "Then let's make a promise," he said, his voice low, almost conspiratorial. "You keep fighting, and I'll protect you. No more betrayals. I swear it."

"Promises are easy to make," I countered, heart racing at the proximity, "but keeping them? That's where things get complicated."

"Then let's simplify it." He leaned in, sincerity etched on his face. "If we survive this, we can figure out what comes next."

Something in me wanted to believe him, to trust him despite the betrayals that lay between us. I swallowed hard, the tension thick and tangible. "Fine. But don't expect me to go easy on you if you screw up again."

"Wouldn't dream of it," he replied, a teasing grin breaking through his somber mask.

The atmosphere shifted, our shared resolve lighting a flicker of hope in the darkness. As we sat together, the fire crackling like the embers of our newfound alliance, I felt the first stirrings of something deeper—an understanding that maybe, just maybe, this journey could lead us both to a redemption we had not anticipated.

The fire crackled with life, illuminating the forest clearing and casting playful shadows that danced along the trees. The air was thick with the scent of burning wood, a comforting aroma that mixed with the earthy undertones of damp leaves and moss. I watched as Reed added a few larger logs to the fire, the flames licking greedily at the fresh fuel, creating a warmth that seeped into my skin and eased some of the tension coiling in my stomach.

"Can't believe you almost let me walk off that cliff yesterday," I teased, trying to lighten the weight that hung between us. "What were you hoping for? A dramatic exit? 'And she fell to her doom, never to be seen again'?"

Reed chuckled, the sound rumbling low in his throat. "I was trying to save your life, not orchestrate a tragic romance. But if I'd known you'd take it so personally, I would have tried a little harder to catch you."

I rolled my eyes, feigning exasperation. "Oh, please. You were just waiting for the right moment to swoop in and play the gallant hero, weren't you? How very cliché."

"Cliché is better than dead," he shot back, a grin breaking through the remnants of his earlier melancholy. "But if I'm going to be a hero, I need to work on my timing. No one wants to see a hero arrive fashionably late to the disaster."

"Maybe you should start by paying more attention to your sidekick," I replied, smirking at him. "I could have used a little more foresight yesterday."

The playful banter rolled between us like the fire's crackling flames, chasing away the shadows that loomed over our past. But underneath the teasing, the weight of our circumstances simmered, unresolved and precarious. I watched Reed as he focused on the fire, the flickering light reflecting in his eyes, revealing a depth of emotion that stirred my curiosity.

"What do you miss most about her?" I asked, my voice softening, the question hanging heavy in the air.

He was silent for a moment, the fire popping as if it shared in his contemplation. "Her laughter," he finally said, his tone more serious. "It was contagious, you know? She could make even the darkest days seem bearable. It's hard to explain, but when you lose someone like that... it's like carrying a shadow with you."

I nodded, understanding the kind of loss that etched itself into a person's soul. "Sometimes, I think those shadows are what make us human," I replied. "They remind us of what we've loved, even as they weigh us down."

Reed looked at me then, his expression a blend of surprise and admiration, and I felt a flicker of warmth spread through me. "You're wiser than you look," he said, a teasing lilt returning to his voice. "What else do you miss?"

"Home," I confessed, my thoughts drifting to the small, unremarkable house I had once known, filled with the warmth of shared meals and laughter that now felt like a distant dream. "The smell of fresh bread baking, the sound of my mother's voice calling me for dinner... everything felt so simple back then."

"Sounds like a dream," he replied, his gaze steady. "I wouldn't know. My home was never anything special—just a collection of rooms with no love in them."

"Maybe that's why we're here," I said, leaning forward, the firelight casting our faces in warm hues. "To find something real, something worth fighting for."

He met my gaze, and in that moment, it was as if the world outside our little sanctuary fell away. It was just the two of us, two lost souls in a wilderness of uncertainty.

"Together?" he asked, his voice a low whisper, vulnerable and raw.

"Together," I confirmed, my heart racing at the weight of the promise that lingered in the air.

As if on cue, a rustle in the underbrush interrupted our moment, the quiet shattering with the unmistakable crunch of leaves. My heart lurched, a primal instinct kicking in. "What was that?" I whispered, my earlier bravado evaporating like mist in the morning sun.

"Stay close," Reed ordered, his tone shifting from playful to serious in an instant. He positioned himself protectively in front of me, eyes scanning the darkened tree line, alert and vigilant.

The rustling grew louder, and my breath caught in my throat as a figure emerged from the shadows. My muscles tensed, ready to flee, but then the silhouette stepped into the firelight, revealing a wild-haired woman with piercing blue eyes that glinted with defiance.

"Fancy meeting you here, Reed," she said, a smirk playing on her lips.

"Zara," he breathed, surprise flashing across his face. "What are you doing here?"

"I came to find you, obviously," she replied, crossing her arms over her leather-clad chest. "I heard you were making waves again, and I couldn't resist the chaos. But it looks like you've already got company."

"Yeah, well, this is... complicated," Reed muttered, shifting slightly as if to shield me from her scrutiny.

Zara's gaze flicked to me, sizing me up with an intensity that made my skin prickle. "Another one of your charity cases?"

"She's not a charity case," Reed snapped, his voice firm, and I could see the protective edge surfacing again. "She's with me."

"Interesting," Zara mused, her smirk deepening. "But tell me, does she know what she's getting into?"

I stepped forward, defiance flaring within me. "I'm not some delicate flower, ready to wilt at the first sign of trouble. I can handle myself."

"Oh, I believe you can," Zara said, her tone almost playful. "But handling trouble is one thing. Surviving it is another."

"And I suppose you're here to give us survival tips?" I shot back, my heart racing with adrenaline.

"Actually, I'm here to help." Her smile faded, replaced with an earnestness that took me off guard. "There's a storm coming, and it's not just the hunters. You two are in over your heads, and I might just be the ally you need."

Reed's expression darkened, the tension in the air shifting as he weighed her words. "Why should we trust you?"

"Because," she replied, stepping closer, her voice low and steady, "I've been where you are, and I know what it takes to survive. The hunters aren't just hunting for sport—they want something from you, Reed. Something big."

I glanced at Reed, the implications of her words hanging heavily between us. "What does she mean?" I asked, dread pooling in my stomach.

Reed met my gaze, his expression inscrutable. "I'll explain later."

Zara's smile returned, sharp and predatory. "No time for later, darling. The hunters won't wait, and neither should we."

The fire crackled ominously as I felt the weight of our precarious situation settle in, the reality of our journey morphing into something darker. With Zara's arrival, everything had shifted, the path ahead now fraught with uncertainty, and the stakes were higher than I could have ever anticipated.

The atmosphere shifted with Zara's arrival, charged with an energy that crackled in the air like static before a storm. Reed's eyes narrowed, suspicion coloring his features as he stood protectively beside me. I felt the tension coiling between us, the firelight flickering shadows across our faces, revealing unspoken fears and uncharted alliances.

"What do you mean, they want something from you?" I pressed, my voice barely above a whisper, as if the very act of speaking could summon the hunters lurking just beyond the tree line.

Zara's gaze was steady, unwavering. "They know about your sister, Reed. They think you have information—something that could turn the tide in their favor. That's why they've been hunting you both."

Reed stiffened, his expression a mixture of confusion and dread. "I don't have anything they want. I've buried that past."

"Maybe not deep enough." Zara leaned in, her intensity palpable. "If they're after you, it's only a matter of time before they find a way to squeeze the truth out of you."

I shot Reed a look, my stomach tightening at the implication. "What does that mean for us? Are we in danger?"

"Danger? That's an understatement," Zara replied with a wry smile that didn't reach her eyes. "You're both in the crosshairs, and I doubt they'll let you go without a fight. But I can help. We can come up with a plan."

Reed shifted, his protective stance faltering. "And why should we trust you? You have a reputation, Zara. You don't just help people without expecting something in return."

Zara raised an eyebrow, her confidence unwavering. "You're not wrong. But right now, my interests align with yours. I want to take down those hunters, too. I've had my share of run-ins with them, and they're not just after you for sport. They're building something—an army, a movement. And I won't let them turn this world into their playground."

The weight of her words pressed heavily on me. "An army?"

"Not just any army. They're gathering followers—people desperate for a sense of belonging. They prey on the lost and vulnerable, twisting them into something they're not. They're using fear to manipulate, and it's only going to get worse if we don't act."

The implications of her statement hung in the air, thick and suffocating. My mind raced with possibilities, and I glanced at Reed, searching for a flicker of reassurance. He met my gaze, uncertainty lingering in his eyes.

"Zara, we can't just jump into a fight without a plan," he said, a hint of hesitation creeping into his tone. "We need to gather information first."

"Oh, we'll gather information," Zara replied, a fierce glint in her eyes. "But we also need to act. Sitting idle is the same as giving up. Trust me, I've been through this before. Waiting for the right moment often leads to the wrong consequences."

"I'm not in the mood for more casualties," Reed shot back, his voice a low growl. "I've lost enough already."

Zara's expression softened slightly, a flicker of understanding passing between them. "I get it. We've all lost someone, but it's time to channel that loss into something productive. Together, we can become the storm rather than just weather it."

I looked between them, feeling a strange sense of camaraderie forming in the space between our fears and hopes. "So, what's the plan?" I asked, my heart racing with a mixture of anticipation and dread.

Zara crossed her arms, her posture confident. "We move at dawn. We scout their camp and see how many they have. From there, we can strategize. If they're expecting a show of force, we can use that to our advantage."

"And what if they're already aware of us?" Reed interjected, his brow furrowing. "What if they've been tracking us all along?"

"Then we'll need to be smart," Zara said, her voice steady. "Every hunter has a weakness. We just need to find theirs."

A plan began to form in my mind, though it felt fragile, like the flames dancing before us. "And what about the people they've already captured? What if they're using them as bait?"

Zara nodded, her expression grave. "Exactly. We can't afford to leave anyone behind. We'll go in, gather intel, and extract anyone still alive. But it'll be risky."

"Risky is our middle name," I quipped, trying to inject some humor into the situation, though my heart was pounding with fear.

Reed shot me a lopsided smile, the kind that made my insides flutter, but then he turned serious again. "We'll have to be careful. Once we engage, there's no turning back."

"Agreed," Zara added, her eyes gleaming with a mix of excitement and apprehension. "But I promise you this: if we do it right, we'll walk away with more than just our lives. We'll have a chance to put a stop to their plans before it's too late."

As the fire flickered and the shadows deepened, we forged a silent pact. We were no longer just three people caught in a web of uncertainty; we were allies now, bound by a common purpose. The weight of our mission settled on my shoulders like a cloak, heavy yet oddly comforting.

We spent the rest of the night discussing tactics, the fire casting a warm glow on our determined faces. I couldn't shake the feeling that we were standing on the edge of a precipice, poised to leap into the unknown.

Just as dawn began to break, casting a pale light over the clearing, the atmosphere shifted once more. An eerie silence fell, the kind that made my skin crawl. I peered into the trees, heart pounding, instinctively knowing something was wrong.

"Do you hear that?" I whispered, straining my ears to catch any hint of movement.

"Nothing's ever quiet in these woods," Zara muttered, her eyes narrowing.

A sudden rustle erupted from the thicket, a flurry of movement that sent adrenaline surging through my veins. My breath caught as figures emerged from the underbrush—hunters, armed and glaring with predatory intent.

"Time's up," one of them snarled, stepping forward, a cruel smile twisting his lips. "We've come for what's ours."

The air thickened with tension as I glanced at Reed and Zara, their faces mirroring the shock I felt. We had ventured too far into their territory, and now we were cornered, the shadows closing in.

"We need to move—now!" Reed shouted, adrenaline coursing through him as he positioned himself between me and the encroaching threat.

But before we could react, a sudden crack echoed through the trees, sharp and final. My heart dropped as the world around me spiraled into chaos, the realization settling in that we were no longer the hunters; we were the hunted.

Chapter 8: A Dance of Flames

The moment we stepped into Ashford, a shiver rippled down my spine, a blend of excitement and apprehension that danced in time with the flickering shadows cast by the streetlamps. The town sprawled before us, its quaint charm marred by the whisper of neglect that hung thick in the air. The cobblestones glistened with the remnants of a recent rain, slick and treacherous, glinting under the amber glow as though beckoning us deeper into its embrace. Reed walked beside me, his presence a reassuring weight against the uncertainty that surrounded us.

There was something almost magnetic about Ashford, a hidden energy that pulsed beneath the surface of everyday life. The buildings, with their faded paint and sagging roofs, seemed to lean in closer as if straining to overhear the secrets we carried. Shop windows displayed dusty trinkets that spoke of forgotten tales and dreams unfulfilled, while the occasional burst of laughter or raised voice hinted at the lives weaving through the fabric of this town. I found myself drawn to the hum of it all, the way the past clung to the present like a stubborn stain.

"Do you think anyone here remembers my family?" I asked, half to myself, half to Reed, as we wandered past a bakery where the scent of freshly baked bread wafted through the door. It wrapped around me like a warm embrace, pulling me closer to the threshold.

Reed glanced over, his brow furrowing in thought. "If they do, I doubt they'll be eager to share. Secrets here are as guarded as the bread in that bakery." His voice had a roughness to it that belied the sincerity behind his words.

I chuckled, a light sound that surprised even me. "You think they'll throw bread at us if we ask too many questions?"

"Only if we're lucky," he shot back, a hint of a smile teasing at the corners of his mouth. It was the first time I'd seen him crack even the slightest grin since we'd arrived.

As we walked, I felt the spark of something elusive hover between us, a tension that thickened the air. Each shared glance lingered longer, our shoulders brushing occasionally in a way that made my heart race. It was absurd to feel this way about someone I had set out to distrust, yet here we were, caught in a dance of uncertainty and attraction that seemed as old as the cobblestones beneath our feet.

The sun dipped lower, spilling hues of orange and pink across the sky, transforming Ashford into a canvas of warm colors. The townsfolk began to gather for the evening's festival, their faces illuminated by the glow of lanterns strung overhead. Laughter erupted from the crowd, a stark contrast to the wary glances exchanged earlier. It was a simple celebration, yet it felt monumental, a fleeting moment of joy amid the whispers of the past.

"Should we join them?" Reed asked, his voice tinged with a mix of curiosity and wariness.

"Why not? It's not every day we stumble upon a festival in a town like this." I gestured toward a gathering of people dancing in a circle, their movements fluid and carefree.

As we approached, the atmosphere enveloped us, the music vibrant and alive, a sweet melody that wrapped around the tension between us. I couldn't help but let out a small laugh at the absurdity of it all—two strangers drawn together by an unknown quest, now standing amidst a celebration.

"Let's dance," I said, my words surprising both Reed and myself.

"Dance?" he echoed, the incredulity clear in his voice.

"Yes, dance. You know, that thing people do when they want to have fun?" I smirked, daring him to say no.

With a resigned shake of his head, he stepped forward, taking my hand in his, and suddenly the world narrowed to the space between us. The music swelled, and I was pulled into the rhythm of the dance, twirling and laughing with reckless abandon. Reed's hand at my waist was firm and guiding, his presence grounding me as I swayed and spun.

"What are you doing?" he asked, laughter bubbling in his chest, the sound warming me more than the lantern light.

"Having fun, remember? That thing people do?" I shot back, relishing the way his eyes sparkled with an unexpected delight.

The dance became a whirlwind of laughter and light, the worries of our quest momentarily forgotten. As the evening deepened, the laughter and music mingled with the scent of roasted chestnuts and spiced cider, wrapping around us like a cozy blanket. Yet, beneath the joy, an undercurrent of tension surged; the charm I sought and the truth about my family loomed ever closer, reminding me that our lighthearted distraction couldn't last forever.

But for that moment, I allowed myself to be swept away. The world spun around us, a blur of colors and sounds, and with every beat of the drum, every note of the melody, I felt the weight of Reed's gaze on me, intense and penetrating. It ignited something deep within me, something that felt forbidden yet exhilarating.

"Is this all you've got?" he challenged playfully, a teasing glint in his eyes as he twirled me once more, my laughter bubbling up uncontrollably.

"Oh, just you wait," I said, the thrill of the moment pushing me to tease him back. "I have moves you've never seen."

His laughter mingled with mine, a perfect symphony of joy in the midst of uncertainty. It was a brief reprieve, a chance to forget the stakes of our journey, even if just for a heartbeat. And as the dance unfolded, I couldn't shake the feeling that something was shifting between us, a spark that had ignited in the shadows of this enigmatic town, a dance of flames flickering to life in the dark.

As the music swirled around us, I became acutely aware of the people around us, their laughter echoing like the chime of distant bells. The festival pulsed with life, drawing in townsfolk and visitors alike, a tapestry of stories woven into the fabric of Ashford. Reed's grip on my waist tightened as we moved together, the heat from our bodies blending in a dance that felt both electric and unnerving. The world melted away, leaving just the two of us swaying beneath the glowing lanterns, our surroundings blurring into a backdrop of color and sound.

"Careful," Reed teased, leaning in close enough that I could catch the hint of citrus on his breath. "If you keep dancing like that, I might think you enjoy my company."

"Let's not get ahead of ourselves," I shot back, matching his playful tone with a smirk. "I'm merely trying to survive your clumsy footwork."

His laughter was a low rumble, a sound that danced around my heart like a flickering flame, both comforting and alarming. "Clumsy? I'll have you know, I'm an excellent dancer—at least in my imagination."

"Imaginary dancing? Now that's a skill I would like to see," I countered, spinning away from him, feeling the air rush past as I let the moment carry me away. The thrill of the festival swept through me, and I couldn't remember the last time I'd felt this carefree. But just as I was about to lose myself completely, a sudden gust of wind swept through the square, causing the lanterns to flicker wildly, casting eerie shadows that danced along the cobblestones.

The laughter faded into a whisper, and I could sense the shift in the crowd's energy, the way they turned their heads toward the shadows as if expecting something to emerge. Reed's hand found mine again, firm and grounding, as we both instinctively stepped closer. "What was that?" he murmured, his playful demeanor evaporating like morning mist under the sun.

"Just the wind," I said, though a sliver of unease twisted in my gut. Yet, the way the townsfolk were now glancing around, their faces taut with concern, suggested that perhaps there was more to fear than a mere gust.

"I don't think they like the wind much," Reed observed, scanning the crowd. "Or maybe it's what comes with it."

Before I could respond, a figure emerged from the shadows—a tall woman clad in a flowing cloak, her face partially obscured by a hood. She moved with an ethereal grace, her presence commanding attention even from the most engrossed revelers. The music dimmed as she approached, the air thickening with a tension that felt palpable.

"Who is she?" I whispered, my heart quickening as the crowd parted to let her through.

"I'm not sure," Reed replied, his tone serious. "But it looks like she has something to say."

The woman halted in the center of the square, and as the last notes of the song faded, a hush fell over the crowd. Her voice, when she spoke, was rich and melodic, a whisper that carried like a gentle breeze. "People of Ashford," she began, her gaze sweeping across the gathered faces, "the time has come to face the truth that dwells in the shadows."

Unease rippled through the crowd, and I could feel Reed's grip tighten around my hand. "What truth?" I murmured, glancing up at him.

"The kind that makes people uneasy," he replied, his voice low, almost thoughtful.

The woman continued, her presence commanding as she wove tales of the town's history—stories of lost magic and hidden secrets, of a charm that had once thrived among them, now reduced to a mere whisper of its former glory. "There are those who seek the charm," she declared, her voice rising above the murmurs. "They wish to control its power for their own ends, and we must protect it."

I exchanged a look with Reed, my mind racing. "Is she talking about the charm I'm looking for?"

"I think so," he replied, his eyes narrowing as he listened intently. "But it sounds like there's more to it than just your family's connection."

The woman paused, her eyes fixing on me as if sensing my presence amidst the crowd. "Those who seek the truth must tread carefully. There are dangers that lurk in the corners of this town, shadows that watch and wait."

A chill raced up my spine, a reminder that the comfort of the festival was an illusion, quickly shattered by her words. I felt Reed's hand tighten around mine, our fingers interlacing as though we were clinging to each other against the encroaching darkness.

"Dangers?" I echoed, my voice barely above a whisper. "What kind of dangers?"

But before the woman could answer, a commotion erupted from the edge of the crowd. A group of men, their faces twisted in anger, pushed their way toward the center, shouting over one another. "Enough of this nonsense!" one of them bellowed, his eyes blazing with fury. "We don't need more tales of danger! We need action!"

"Action?" the woman retorted, her voice steady and unwavering. "You want action without understanding? That is a path to ruin."

Reed and I exchanged worried glances, the tension in the air palpable as the crowd began to shift uneasily. My heart raced as the confrontation escalated, the laughter and music replaced by a heavy silence fraught with uncertainty. The festival had morphed into something altogether different—a brewing storm, the calm before the chaos.

I could feel the magic in the air, crackling like static electricity, and it made me acutely aware of the stakes. "We should leave," I said, my voice tinged with urgency.

Reed nodded, but before we could turn away, the leader of the angry men stepped forward, his gaze locking onto mine. "And what about you, girl? You think you can come here, dig into our past, and leave without consequences?"

His words struck like a physical blow, and I felt a surge of defiance rise within me. "I'm not here to hurt anyone," I shot back, surprising myself with the strength in my voice. "I'm trying to uncover the truth about my family. If you have a problem with that, then perhaps it's you who should be concerned."

The crowd gasped, and for a moment, all eyes were on me, the weight of their scrutiny heavy and suffocating. Reed stepped closer, his presence a solid wall beside me, lending me strength I didn't know I had. "Let's go," he urged, but I stood firm, determined to hold my ground.

"Do you even know what you're getting into?" the man spat, his disdain palpable. "You don't belong here."

A thrill of fear danced along my spine, but I couldn't back down now. "Maybe you should consider that Ashford belongs to everyone who seeks its truth, not just those who are afraid of it."

The tension in the air thickened, and I felt Reed's hand squeeze mine tighter as the crowd shifted restlessly. But just as the confrontation threatened to boil over, the woman raised her hand, her voice slicing through the chaos like a blade. "Enough!" she commanded, her eyes fierce and unwavering. "This town is more than your anger. It is time to choose—embrace the truth, or let it consume you."

With that, the festival's vibrancy dimmed further, the flickering lanterns now casting long shadows that whispered of uncertainty. As the crowd began to disperse, Reed pulled me close, his breath warm against my ear. "We need to find answers. Now."

I nodded, the gravity of our situation sinking in. The night was still young, but the dance of flames we had stepped into was far from over.

The moment we left the festival, a blanket of darkness enveloped us, the cheerful lanterns and lively music fading into a haunting silence. Reed and I maneuvered through the winding streets of Ashford, the cobblestones slick beneath our feet, reflecting the slivers of moonlight that pierced the clouds above. The tension from the confrontation lingered in the air, thickening our breaths and urging us forward as if we were fleeing from the weight of our own decisions.

"I can't believe you stood up to him like that," Reed said, his voice a low murmur that broke the silence as we turned a corner. His tone was both incredulous and admiring, and I felt a flush creeping up my neck at his words. "Most people would have just backed down."

"Well, I didn't come all this way to be intimidated," I replied, a hint of bravado in my voice, though inside, I felt a flicker of doubt. "I need to find the truth about my family, and I won't let some angry townsfolk stop me."

"Determined, aren't you?" he said, a teasing lilt in his tone. "I suppose you think that will charm everyone into submission?"

"Not charm," I shot back, grinning despite the seriousness of our situation. "More like a firm reminder that I'm not here to play games."

He chuckled softly, a sound that sent a flutter through me, as we reached a fork in the path. To the left, the street faded into a deeper shadow, lined with crumbling buildings that looked as though they might whisper secrets if only we dared to listen. To the right, a flickering light beckoned us forward—a small tavern with a sign creaking in the night breeze, promising warmth and perhaps a measure of solace.

"I vote we investigate the tavern," Reed suggested, nodding toward the light. "It might be filled with folks more inclined to share their secrets over a drink than in a heated square."

"Only if they have something warm," I replied, my stomach rumbling in agreement. "I could use a distraction from the ghosts lurking around here."

We made our way to the tavern, its wooden door swinging open to reveal a cozy interior filled with the soft glow of candles and the inviting aroma of spiced cider. The patrons, a mix of locals and travelers, looked up as we entered, their expressions a mix of curiosity and wariness. I could feel the weight of their gazes, each pair scrutinizing us as we stepped inside, as if judging our worthiness to intrude upon their world.

Reed guided me to a small table in the corner, far enough from the bar that we wouldn't be overheard but close enough to catch snippets of conversation. A fire crackled in the hearth, casting a warm light that flickered across the walls, chasing away the chill of the night. As we settled into our seats, I took a deep breath, allowing the warmth to seep into my bones.

"What'll it be?" he asked, glancing over the menu, though I could sense he was as unsure as I was.

"I'll take whatever has the most alcohol," I declared, half-joking. "At this rate, I need something to dull my senses after all that drama."

He raised an eyebrow, a smile teasing the corners of his lips. "Not one for a calming chamomile tea, then?"

"Please, I need something stronger to cope with the fact that we just barged into a town on the brink of chaos."

Reed called over the server, a wiry man with a friendly grin, and placed our orders. As he left, I leaned in closer to Reed, the firelight illuminating his features, accentuating the sharp angles of his jaw.

"So, what do you think? Will anyone here actually tell us what's going on?"

"Doubtful," he replied, his tone sober. "But we can at least try to pick up some loose threads. Maybe someone knows more about the charm or what that woman was talking about."

I nodded, the thought gnawing at me. The charm held the key to my family's past, and as we sat in the tavern's warmth, I felt the weight of that knowledge pressing down. "And if they don't?"

"Then we regroup and think of another plan," he said, though the hint of frustration in his voice betrayed the urgency behind our quest.

The server returned with our drinks, the warm cider steaming in front of us. I took a tentative sip, the flavors bursting across my palate—a perfect blend of sweetness and spice, and I couldn't help but smile. "This is good," I said, savoring the warmth as it spread through me.

"Glad you approve," Reed said, taking a sip of his own drink. "Now, let's see if we can blend in enough to eavesdrop on some gossip."

The tavern's atmosphere shifted slightly as I observed the conversations around us. Locals huddled in tight-knit groups, their laughter tinged with a hint of desperation, while others whispered in hushed tones, their eyes darting toward us as though we were intruders in their circle. I caught snippets of conversation—references to the charm, stories of disappearances, and warnings about the dangers lurking in the shadows.

"Did you hear that?" I leaned closer to Reed, excitement bubbling within me. "They're talking about the charm! We might be onto something."

"Let's see if we can get a little closer," he murmured, his eyes scanning the room.

We edged our way toward the bar, where a group of older men sat, their voices rising above the rest, animated yet cautious. I caught phrases like "darkness," "the watchers," and "the charm's true power." My heart raced as we settled onto the stools beside them, our presence casual yet intentional.

"Seems like you've got something on your minds," one of the men said, his eyes narrowing with suspicion.

"Just curious about the town's legends," Reed replied smoothly, leaning in with an air of feigned nonchalance. "Heard some interesting stories tonight."

The men exchanged wary glances, but one of them, his beard streaked with gray, snorted. "Legends? They're more like warnings at this point. You best not go digging where you don't belong."

I couldn't resist the urge to interject. "But what if someone needs to know the truth? Isn't that worth the risk?"

"Truth is a dangerous thing here," another man warned, his voice low and gravelly. "And the charm? Best left undisturbed. You're new, and new folks tend to attract trouble."

"Trouble finds us no matter where we go," Reed said, his tone light yet firm. "We're just looking for answers, that's all."

"Answers," the gray-bearded man echoed, his expression shifting from suspicion to something more contemplative. "Sometimes, the answers are better left buried."

Just as I opened my mouth to respond, a loud crash echoed from the back of the tavern, drawing everyone's attention. Glass shattered, and a figure stumbled into view, wild-eyed and panting, the remnants of a shattered lantern at their feet. The atmosphere shifted instantly, tension crackling like static as the crowd fell silent, all eyes turning toward the newcomer.

"They're coming!" the figure gasped, their voice a frantic whisper that hung in the air. "We have to warn them! The watchers are here!"

My heart plummeted as panic rippled through the tavern, the realization settling in like a stone in my gut. The dance of flames we had stumbled into was about to ignite into something far more dangerous, and with Reed beside me, I knew we would have to face whatever shadows emerged from the dark.

But just as the fear took root, I noticed the glint of something sharp in the newcomer's hand—something that sparkled ominously in the firelight, drawing my gaze like a moth to a flame.

Chapter 9: The Flicker Before the Blaze

The old chapel loomed before us, a relic of a time when faith was written in the stone and whispered through the wind. Its weathered façade was cloaked in ivy, the tendrils wrapping around the crumbling bricks like secrets held too tightly for too long. Reed stood beside me, his silhouette framed by the evening light, casting long shadows that danced with the rustling leaves. There was a charge in the air, an electric promise that crackled between us, drawing us closer, even as uncertainty loomed like the gathering storm clouds above.

"Are you sure you want to do this?" Reed's voice was low, a velvet murmur that sent shivers racing down my spine. It felt both comforting and ominous, a soothing balm against the jagged edges of my fear. I turned to him, my heart hammering against my ribs, a wild creature desperate to escape.

"Do we have a choice?" I replied, my tone sharp yet playful, the remnants of a smirk tugging at my lips. I wanted to sound brave, to mask the tremor in my voice, but the truth hung between us, heavy and undeniable. Trust was a fragile thing, especially in a world where deception thrived like weeds in the cracks of a forgotten sidewalk.

With a resigned sigh, I stepped through the creaking door of the chapel, the scent of aged wood and musty parchment enveloping me like a shroud. The interior was dim, shadows pooling in the corners where flickering candles fought against the encroaching dark. I could feel the weight of the past pressing down on me, the whispers of those who had sought solace within these walls mingling with the secrets I carried.

"We need to find the altar," Reed said, his voice breaking the silence like a pebble skipping across still water. As he moved deeper into the chapel, I trailed behind, captivated by the way he navigated the gloom, confidence radiating from him in waves. He pushed aside a tattered curtain, revealing an ancient stone altar, its surface etched with symbols I couldn't decipher.

As I approached, something caught my eye—a glint of metal peeking out from beneath a loose stone. I knelt, my fingers brushing against the cool surface, and with a gentle tug, I freed the object from its resting place. It was a map, its parchment yellowed with age, the ink faded but still legible. My breath caught in my throat as I unfolded it, the lines twisting and turning like a labyrinth of secrets waiting to be unraveled.

"Look at this," I breathed, the map trembling in my hands as I traced the lines with my fingertip. Reed leaned closer, his shoulder brushing against mine, igniting a spark that ignited both curiosity and apprehension.

"What does it say?" he asked, his breath warm against my ear, sending a thrill through me that I couldn't quite shake off. I could feel the anticipation rising between us, a shared sense of purpose igniting a fire within the shadowy confines of the chapel.

"It's a valley," I murmured, piecing together the faded markings. "It's supposed to be where the charm's power can be unlocked. But..." I hesitated, my heart stuttering as I read the words that followed. "There's a ritual, and it requires trust. Immense trust and sacrifice."

Reed's expression shifted, his brows furrowing as he processed the implications. "Sacrifice? What kind of sacrifice?"

I shrugged, uncertainty gnawing at my insides. "I don't know. But it can't be good."

"Nothing ever is, is it?" He ran a hand through his hair, the disheveled strands falling over his forehead in a way that was both endearing and infuriating. I wanted to tell him he was overthinking, that we could figure this out, but the truth was I felt the same gnawing fear, a pit of dread unfurling in my stomach.

"You're thinking too much," I said lightly, trying to lighten the mood, but I could see the flicker of doubt in his eyes. "It's just a map, right? We can—"

"Maps lead to places," he interrupted, his gaze intense, a storm brewing behind his eyes. "Sometimes they lead to treasure, sometimes to traps. We have to be careful."

I nodded, swallowing hard. "Yeah, careful." But the thrill of adventure coursed through my veins like wildfire, and it was difficult to suppress the excitement bubbling beneath my anxiety. What lay in that valley? What secrets were waiting to be uncovered?

He studied me for a moment, the silence between us heavy with unspoken questions. "And what about us?" His voice was barely above a whisper, laced with an edge of vulnerability that tugged at my heart. "Can we trust each other?"

I took a breath, the weight of his question settling over us like a fog. Could we? Our history was a tapestry woven with threads of both truth and deceit, and yet, in that moment, I felt a flicker of hope igniting.

"Maybe we have to," I said, my voice steadying as I met his gaze. "If we're going to do this, we need to believe in something—each other, this map, whatever's waiting for us."

He stepped closer, and in that fleeting moment, the world outside faded away. My heart raced as his hand brushed against mine, a spark igniting in the air between us, swirling with the tension of unspoken words. I could feel the heat rising, a dangerous flame licking at the edges of our resolve.

"Okay," he said, a small smile breaking through the gravity of the moment. "Then let's find this valley. Together."

Together. The word hung in the air, a promise laced with uncertainty, and yet, as I met Reed's unwavering gaze, I felt a sense of resolve washing over me. Whatever awaited us in that valley, we would face it side by side, trusting each other in a world where trust felt like a rare commodity.

With renewed purpose, we set forth into the night, leaving the shadows of the chapel behind, our hearts entwined in a dance of hope and trepidation. The flicker of what could be ignited within us, a blaze waiting to be unleashed as we stepped into the unknown.

The moon hung low in the sky, a silver sentinel watching over us as we made our way through the underbrush, the map clutched tightly in my hands. Each step felt heavy with the weight of what we were about to undertake. Reed walked beside me, his presence a steadying force, though the tension in the air was palpable, a taut string vibrating with possibilities.

"Do you think we'll actually find it?" I asked, my curiosity mingling with apprehension. The shadows cast by the trees danced like ghosts around us, whispering secrets that only the night could hold.

Reed shrugged, a grin tugging at the corners of his mouth. "Well, if we do find it, let's hope it's not guarded by a dragon or a bunch of angry villagers with pitchforks."

"Right, because that would make our day even worse," I replied, laughing lightly, but the truth was, the map seemed to promise adventure and peril in equal measure. "I'm not exactly dressed for a dragon encounter."

He glanced down at my outfit—a pair of worn jeans and a cozy oversized sweater that I'd chosen more for comfort than practicality—and chuckled. "Trust me, I don't think anyone is ever 'dressed' for a dragon encounter. We might just have to settle for a little old-fashioned treasure hunting."

As we ventured deeper into the woods, the air turned crisp, and the scent of pine filled my lungs, grounding me in the moment. The forest was alive with sounds—the rustle of leaves, the occasional call of a night bird, and the distant babbling of a brook. It was a beautiful tapestry of nature, and in that stillness, I felt the pulse of something ancient, something that stirred deep within me, weaving together the threads of destiny that had led us here.

"Do you ever think about how we ended up together on this crazy adventure?" I asked, breaking the comfortable silence that had enveloped us.

"Only when you remind me," he shot back playfully, his eyes glinting with mischief. "I'm still trying to figure out if this is your idea of a romantic getaway or a twisted survival challenge."

"Both, clearly. Nothing says romance like dodging mythical beasts and potentially saving the world." I nudged him playfully, my heart lighter, buoyed by the banter.

Our laughter echoed through the trees, a bright note against the dark backdrop of uncertainty. But as quickly as the lightness came, it dissipated, replaced by the gravity of our quest. My thoughts drifted to the ritual the map spoke of, the trust it demanded. Could we truly trust each other enough to unlock whatever lay at the end of our journey?

A sudden rustle in the underbrush drew my attention, and I froze, my instincts kicking in. "Did you hear that?"

Reed halted beside me, his expression shifting to one of alertness. "Yeah, I did."

My heart raced as the sound grew closer, and for a split second, the thought of facing a feral creature made my stomach churn. But then, out of the shadows, emerged a figure—a girl, maybe a year or two younger than me, with wild hair and an expression that was equal parts fierce and frightened.

"What are you doing here?" she demanded, her voice sharp, as if we had trespassed on sacred ground.

"Uh, looking for a treasure?" I replied, bewildered but trying to match her intensity.

"Right. Because every adventurous duo wanders into the woods at night for a little light treasure hunting." Her eyes darted between Reed and me, skepticism written all over her face.

Reed stepped forward, his demeanor calming yet assertive. "We found a map that leads to a valley, and we think it might lead us to something significant. Do you know anything about it?"

The girl's expression shifted, her wariness giving way to curiosity. "Significant, huh? What's so significant about it?"

I exchanged glances with Reed, and without a word, we decided to share the truth, knowing that trust was our only currency in this moment. "There's a charm," I said, my voice steadying. "It's supposed to have power, but it can only be unlocked through a ritual. We need to gather whatever we can to prepare."

She considered us, a calculating look in her eyes. "You really don't know what you're getting into, do you?"

"Enlighten us," Reed replied, crossing his arms, a faint smile playing on his lips.

"Fine," she said, a reluctant smile creeping onto her face. "But you're going to owe me a favor. The valley isn't just any valley—it's a place where the boundaries between our world and… other things blur. There are forces at play there, and if you're not careful, you could end up as part of the scenery."

"Scenery?" I echoed, trying to mask my rising anxiety with humor. "What, like a tree? I don't think I'm ready to become a shrub."

"No, not a shrub," she replied, rolling her eyes, though the corner of her mouth twitched. "You'd make a terrible shrub. More like a cautionary tale. But let's be real here; we've got to go fast if you're serious about this."

"Wait, what's your name?" I asked, eager to know more about this unexpected ally.

"Juno," she said, crossing her arms defiantly, as if daring us to question her. "And I might just know the way to this valley, but you'll need to stick close to me."

As we set off behind Juno, I couldn't shake the feeling that our encounter had shifted the dynamics of our mission. The air was charged with new energy, and a spark of hope ignited within me. Whatever trials lay ahead, we wouldn't face them alone. The flicker of camaraderie began to burn brighter, and with every step, I felt the tendrils of fate weaving a tapestry that held promise—of discovery, of danger, and perhaps of something that had nothing to do with treasure at all.

"Just so we're clear," I said, glancing at Reed, who matched my intensity with a determined look. "If we end up as cautionary tales, I'm blaming you."

Reed chuckled, shaking his head. "And if we find a dragon, you'll be the one to negotiate our way out. Deal?"

"Deal," I replied, and for the first time in what felt like ages, I felt the weight of uncertainty lift, replaced by the thrill of adventure and the unexpected company of newfound friends. We plunged deeper into the woods, ready to face whatever awaited us in the dark embrace of the unknown.

As we followed Juno deeper into the heart of the woods, the shadows stretched long, shifting with every flicker of the moonlight filtering through the thick canopy overhead. The air was cool and fresh, filled with the scent of damp earth and pine. With each step, I could feel the weight of our journey pressing down, the tension coiling like a spring ready to release.

"What kind of forces are we talking about?" I asked, trying to mask my apprehension with a light tone. "Ghosts? Vengeful spirits? Or maybe just angry squirrels?"

Juno shot me a sideways glance, her expression both amused and exasperated. "If only it were just squirrels. There's something much darker at play. This valley has a history, and not all of it is friendly. If you're going to unlock that charm, you need to be ready for anything."

"Anything? That sounds... vague." Reed chimed in, his brow furrowing as we picked our way over a gnarled root that jutted from the earth like a warning finger.

Juno halted abruptly, spinning to face us, her green eyes gleaming like emeralds in the low light. "Vague is the best I can do without getting into the details. The valley reacts to those who enter. It's like it knows your fears and weaknesses. You might face illusions, shadows of your past, or even... manifestations of your worst traits."

"Great. I always wanted to battle my inner demons while trying to find a treasure," I quipped, attempting to maintain the lightness in my voice even as my heart thudded in my chest.

"Welcome to the club," Juno replied with a wry smile. "But don't worry; you won't be alone in your battle. If it helps, I've faced it all before."

The woods thickened around us, the path narrowing as we wound deeper into the wilderness. It felt as if the trees themselves were closing in, creating an intimate tunnel where secrets whispered between branches. I found myself stealing glances at Reed, whose quiet confidence lent me strength, a steadiness I clung to as the gravity of our task settled upon us like a heavy cloak.

"Just remember," Juno said, breaking the silence that had settled between us. "If things get too intense, don't stray from the path. The valley is a tricky place, and losing your way can lead to... well, let's not think about that."

"Good advice," I said, the humor in my voice forced, "but what if the path isn't as clear as it seems?"

"Trust me," Juno replied, her tone becoming more serious. "You'll know when you're getting close. Just listen to your instincts."

As we trudged forward, the canopy above thinned slightly, revealing a patch of starlit sky that glimmered like scattered diamonds against the deep blue expanse. I paused, captivated by the sight, the momentary beauty contrasting sharply with the mission at hand. It felt almost surreal, standing in this hidden world where magic and danger coexisted, urging me to step further into the unknown.

"Why do you even care about this charm?" Juno's question cut through my reverie, drawing my attention back to her. "What's your stake in all of this?"

Reed answered before I could. "We're looking for answers. My past is tangled in this mess, and I can't just walk away. Plus, I think the charm could help people."

"Help people?" Juno repeated, skepticism coloring her tone. "Or help yourself?"

"Both," I interjected quickly, wanting to clear the air. "We have our reasons, and they aren't selfish. Trust me."

"Trust is a slippery concept," Juno replied, a challenging glint in her eyes. "Just make sure you remember that when you're faced with whatever awaits in the valley."

We trudged on, the underbrush thickening again, and I could feel the tension rising. I thought about Juno's warning, the shadows that might take form, and my heart raced with the uncertainty of what we might encounter. Would I face my own fears? Would the charm truly be worth it?

As we rounded a bend, the trees parted dramatically to reveal a breathtaking sight: a wide clearing bathed in silver moonlight, with the valley sprawled out before us like an ancient secret waiting to be unearthed. The ground sloped gently downward, carpeted in soft moss that glowed with a faint luminescence, casting an ethereal light across the scene.

"Here we are," Juno announced, her voice barely above a whisper, reverence and trepidation mingling in the air. "Welcome to the Valley of Echoes."

I stepped forward, taking in the mesmerizing beauty of the landscape. The air felt thick with magic, a shimmering energy that raised the hairs on my arms. In the distance, I could see the outline of stone structures, ancient and worn, their surfaces covered in intricate carvings that seemed to pulse with life.

Reed moved closer to me, his presence grounding amidst the overwhelming beauty. "This is it," he said, his voice a mixture of awe and determination. "We're really here."

Juno led us toward the nearest stone structure, a towering monolith draped in vines. The markings on its surface glowed softly, pulsing like a heartbeat. "This is where the ritual will begin," she said, her tone now more serious. "But before we proceed, we need to understand what we're up against. The valley won't just let us take the charm. We must be prepared to confront our pasts."

"What if our pasts aren't ready to be confronted?" I asked, my voice shaky as the reality of her words sank in.

"Then we'll face them together," Reed replied, gripping my hand.

"Together," I echoed, though doubt clawed at my insides.

Juno stepped forward, examining the glowing symbols etched into the stone. "The key is in the connection. If we can channel our trust into this, it might just work."

"Great, let's just add a little more pressure," I muttered, the nerves gnawing at my resolve. "No big deal."

With a deep breath, Juno began to trace the symbols with her fingers, her voice low and incantatory as she chanted softly, the words weaving through the air like a melody. I felt the energy shift around us, the atmosphere thickening as if the valley itself was listening.

"Are you ready?" Reed asked, his eyes searching mine, the warmth of his hand steadying me amidst the uncertainty.

I nodded, my heart racing as the air crackled with anticipation. "As ready as I'll ever be."

Just as Juno's chant reached a crescendo, the ground beneath us trembled, a low rumble resonating through the air. I stumbled, fear coursing through me as the stone structure began to glow brighter, a pulsating light that seemed to awaken something deep within the valley.

"What's happening?" I cried out, my voice rising above the chaos.

Juno's eyes widened, panic flickering across her features. "It's reacting to us! We need to hold on!"

Suddenly, a blinding flash of light erupted from the stone, enveloping us in an otherworldly glow. I felt a jolt, as if something ancient was awakening, the very fabric of reality bending around us.

"Stay close!" Reed shouted, his grip tightening as the energy surged.

The light enveloped us, a brilliant torrent of colors and sensations, and for a moment, everything felt suspended in time. The valley roared to life, a cacophony of voices swirling around us, echoing with fragments of our pasts, our fears, and our desires.

And just as quickly as it began, the light exploded outward, a shockwave that sent us tumbling backward. I hit the ground hard, the world spinning around me, and in that moment of chaos, everything went dark.

The last thing I heard was the distant echo of Juno's voice calling my name, fading into silence as the shadows closed in, leaving me teetering on the edge of consciousness and the unknown.

Chapter 10: Veil of Illusions

The valley looms before us, steeped in fog so thick it almost feels alive. Each breath is an effort, the damp air clinging to my skin like a shroud. As I step forward, the gnarled roots of ancient trees reach out like twisted fingers, their bark engraved with strange symbols that seem to murmur secrets of the past. Reed walks beside me, close enough that I can feel the warmth radiating from him, yet not so close that I dare reach out. The distance between us is a palpable tension, an unspoken understanding that simmers beneath the surface, and I'm caught between wanting to close that gap and fearing what it might bring.

The shadows dance in the underbrush as we move deeper into the valley, flickering like phantoms in the twilight. My heart races, not just from the chill that seeps through my clothes, but from the weight of memories that claw at my mind, rising with every step. There's something unsettling about this place, a feeling that the very earth is watching, waiting for us to unveil our intentions. Reed's presence beside me is a tether, yet I can't shake the feeling that he might be the very storm I'm trying to outrun.

"Do you think we'll find anything here?" he asks, breaking the silence with a voice low and smooth, as if he's afraid the fog might snatch his words away. There's a hint of something in his tone—curiosity, maybe, or perhaps a longing that mirrors my own.

"Depends on what you mean by 'anything,'" I reply, my lips curving into a half-smile that feels foreign on my face. "If you mean treasure, I think we're more likely to find a haunted tree than a chest of gold."

Reed chuckles, and the sound is a brief reprieve from the oppressive atmosphere around us. "A haunted tree would certainly add some flair to our adventure. Just think of the stories we'd tell afterward."

"Aren't you the one who's always trying to keep things serious?" I challenge, nudging him playfully with my elbow. It's a small gesture, yet it feels monumental, a fragile bridge across the chasm of our uncertain relationship. But just as quickly as it appears, my humor fades, swallowed by the shadows that loom ahead.

The fog shifts, curling around us like a living thing, and for a moment, I'm lost in the swirling haze. The world blurs, and I find myself standing in a memory I'd thought long buried—an echo of laughter and sunlight filtered through leaves. It feels so real that I almost reach out, but then it shatters, the laughter morphing into whispers, voices I once knew but can't bear to hear. "You shouldn't have trusted him," they murmur, the words weaving through the mist, taunting me.

I shake my head, willing the phantoms away. "We need to keep moving. This place... it plays tricks on you."

Reed's gaze sharpens, and I catch the concern flickering in his eyes. "What did you see?"

I hesitate, torn between honesty and the urge to protect him from the jagged pieces of my past. "Just... ghosts of my mistakes."

"Everyone has ghosts," he says, his voice a soothing balm against the tumult in my mind. "The trick is learning how to face them."

The path before us narrows, and I feel the weight of his words settling on my shoulders. "Easier said than done," I murmur, my mind racing with half-formed thoughts and tangled emotions. Yet somehow, I manage a smile that doesn't quite reach my eyes. "What if my ghosts are more of a... horror show?"

"I've seen horror movies," Reed replies with a teasing lilt. "Trust me, I can handle it. Besides, I've got my trusty flashlight." He brandishes the small beam of light he carries, illuminating the ground ahead. "Just stick close, and I'll guide us through."

I snort at his bravado, but it's a welcome distraction from the dread creeping in. "You'd better hope it's enough to ward off any vengeful spirits."

The terrain shifts beneath our feet, the once-tame ground becoming rocky and uneven. I stumble, catching myself against a tree, its bark rough and warm. The air grows heavier, thick with the scent of damp earth and something metallic, as if the valley itself were bleeding. I glance up at Reed, and in the fleeting light, I see a flicker of something in his expression—an uncertainty, perhaps, or a flickering doubt that he's just as haunted as I am.

"This place feels like it's holding its breath," he says, voice low as we navigate through the thickening fog. "Like it's waiting for us to unravel its mysteries."

"Or for us to become part of its stories," I counter, an involuntary shiver racing down my spine. The thought of being lost in these woods, of becoming yet another ghost wandering through its depths, tightens the ache in my chest.

But Reed steps closer, his shoulder brushing against mine, and suddenly, I'm reminded that I'm not alone in this. "Whatever happens, we face it together," he promises, a vow that wraps around me like a cloak of warmth. It's a fragile reassurance, yet in that moment, it's enough to kindle a spark of hope in my heart, flickering defiantly against the dark.

Just then, the fog shifts again, and out of the corner of my eye, I catch a movement—a shadow darting between the trees. My pulse quickens, and I grip Reed's arm tighter, the grip of a lifeline. "Did you see that?"

Reed pauses, his eyes narrowing as he scans the tree line. "I did. We should—"

A rustle, then a low growl reverberates through the air, cutting him off. The sound coils around us, heavy with menace, and instinct kicks in. My breath catches as fear slithers into my veins, and I step back, feeling Reed's presence solid beside me.

"Let's not stick around to find out what's lurking," he whispers, urgency seeping into his tone. We turn to run, hearts pounding in unison, the mist swirling around us like the arms of a spectral dancer eager to reclaim what we dared to disturb. Each step feels like a race against the darkness that seeks to engulf us, but even in the chaos, I feel Reed's hand find mine, grounding me as we flee into the unknown.

The ground beneath us shifts from solid earth to a carpet of moss, its vibrant green a stark contrast to the encroaching darkness. Each step squelches softly, a reminder that we are intruders in this damp realm, where secrets cling to the air like the lingering scent of rain. The path is narrow, flanked by towering trees that loom above us like ancient sentinels. Their twisted branches reach out, casting shadows that dance across the fog, playing tricks on our eyes as if they were eager to share their forgotten tales.

"Do you think it's too late to turn back?" I ask, trying to inject some levity into the oppressive atmosphere. Reed glances at me, a smirk tugging at the corners of his mouth, his eyes bright against the gray backdrop.

"Only if you're afraid of a few ghost stories," he replies, his voice teasing. "Come on, you can't be serious. Think of the adventure! It's practically a rite of passage at this point."

I shake my head, half-amused and half-serious. "You're right, because nothing says 'fun' like wandering through a haunted forest in the dead of night."

We laugh, the sound a small beacon of light in the enveloping gloom. But the laughter fades as the air thickens with an unsettling energy. A sudden rustle nearby sends us both jumping, and I can feel the heat rising in my cheeks, a mix of embarrassment and adrenaline.

"Did you hear that?" I whisper, trying to keep my voice steady as the fog rolls in thicker, wrapping around us like a cloak.

"Yeah," Reed admits, his gaze narrowing as he scans the darkened trees. "It's probably just a rabbit or something. They can be surprisingly loud in the quiet."

"Right, because we're just two unsuspecting travelers out for a moonlit stroll," I murmur, eyeing the shadows with suspicion. "I'd feel a lot better if I had a sword or at least a really sharp stick."

Reed chuckles, his bravado slightly reassuring, yet I can see the tension flickering in his eyes. "You know, I always thought I'd die an epic hero's death, not chased down by a rabid rabbit."

I can't help but smile at his absurdity, even as my heart races. "At least you'd get a good story out of it."

As we move further along the path, the statues rise up like guardians of forgotten lore, their features worn smooth by the passage of time, yet their eyes—if they had eyes—seem to follow us, watching with an intensity that makes the hairs on the back of my neck stand on end. Each statue tells its own story, but I can't help but feel that they harbor secrets darker than mere stone.

"Do you think these statues are real?" I ask, my curiosity piqued. "I mean, like... real people turned to stone?"

"Like Medusa?" Reed raises an eyebrow, his playful tone returning. "I'd say if they were, we should really tread carefully. I'm not ready for a stare-down with anyone who can turn me to stone."

"Charming. But let's hope it's not that dramatic." I glance at him, noting the way his shoulders relax a bit in the shifting light. "What if they're here to protect something? Like treasure or a portal to another world?"

"Or just a really bad Yelp review waiting to happen," he quips. "I mean, this place is not exactly five stars."

Our laughter echoes, a fragile defiance against the heavy silence that envelops us. But it fades quickly as we push onward, the air growing thicker, almost electric, as we tread deeper into the heart of the valley. The mist swirls with an uncanny intelligence, wrapping around my legs like tendrils, beckoning me to step forward into its depths. My heart pounds in my chest, a primal rhythm that quickens with every cautious movement.

Suddenly, a figure looms ahead, half-hidden in the fog—a silhouette that sends my heart skittering into a frantic race. "Reed?" I hiss, gripping his arm tightly. "What is that?"

He squints into the haze, his confidence faltering. "I... I don't know. Just stay close."

As we approach, the figure sharpens into focus, revealing a woman cloaked in shadows, her features obscured but her presence undeniable. She stands still as a statue, yet there's a strange vitality about her, an energy that crackles in the air between us. I can't tell if she's a guardian or a warning.

"Travelers," she says, her voice a soft melody that echoes through the trees, unsettling in its calmness. "You tread on sacred ground."

Reed's grip tightens around my hand, and I can feel the tension radiating from him like heat. "We mean no harm," he replies, his voice steady despite the uncertainty coiling in my stomach. "We're just exploring."

"Exploring?" The woman laughs, a sound that ripples through the fog like a whisper of wind. "Many have come seeking knowledge, yet few have returned unscathed. The valley has a mind of its own, and it will reveal what you fear most."

"What do you mean?" I step forward, curiosity driving me despite the warning bells ringing in my head. "What do you fear?"

"Not what I fear," she replies cryptically, her gaze piercing into me like a beam of light cutting through the fog. "What do you fear?"

The question hangs in the air, heavy with implications. A flicker of vulnerability crosses my mind, but I shake it off, unwilling to delve into the abyss of my fears in front of this enigmatic figure. "We're here for answers, not... whatever this is," I say, my voice firmer than I feel.

She smiles then, a mysterious curve of her lips that could mean anything—or nothing at all. "Answers come with a price. Are you willing to pay?"

"What kind of price?" Reed interjects, his voice low but laced with determination. "We're not here to barter with shadows."

The woman tilts her head, studying us with an intensity that feels almost invasive. "Every truth has its cost, and sometimes, it's more than you're willing to give."

"Great, just great," I mutter under my breath, feeling the panic rise within me. "Another cryptic riddle. I didn't sign up for this."

Reed squeezes my hand, a silent reassurance, as if he's willing to face whatever challenge this valley throws our way. "We'll find a way through," he promises, glancing back at the woman. "We're not afraid of the truth."

"Fear is not the enemy," she counters, her voice suddenly grave. "The shadows within you are. Only by confronting them can you hope to escape this valley's grasp."

With that, the woman steps back, dissolving into the fog as quickly as she appeared, leaving behind only the echo of her words. I stand frozen, the weight of her warning settling over me like a heavy shroud. Reed looks at me, a mixture of concern and determination in his gaze, and I know we're faced with choices that will stretch far beyond the confines of this valley.

"Are we ready for this?" I ask, uncertainty creeping back in.

"Ready or not, we've come too far to turn back now," he replies, the spark of courage igniting in his eyes. "Together, we'll face whatever comes next."

And with that, we press onward, hand in hand, into the heart of the fog, the looming shadows of our past trailing close behind, whispering secrets that threaten to unravel everything we thought we knew.

The path ahead twists like a serpent, winding deeper into the heart of the valley where the fog thickens into a shroud. Each step feels heavier, as if the ground itself is reluctant to let us pass. The air vibrates with an energy that is both unsettling and intoxicating, filling my lungs with a damp heaviness that is all too familiar. The statues loom larger now, their expressions carved with such emotion that I feel they might come alive at any moment. I steal a glance at Reed, whose brow is furrowed, his mouth set in a thin line of concentration. The weight of the unknown hangs between us, and I can't shake the feeling that we are on the brink of uncovering something monumental—something that could change everything.

"You ever think about what happens if we find something?" I ask, trying to break the tension that clings to us like the fog. "Like, what if we discover a secret so big it makes us rethink everything we've believed?"

Reed pauses, his gaze flicking to the dim outlines of the statues around us. "I don't know. But I'd rather find out than just turn back, wouldn't you? Besides, I'm not a fan of living my life in ignorance."

I laugh softly, though my heart races at the implications of his words. "Ignorance is bliss, my friend. Or at least less terrifying."

"True," he admits, the corners of his mouth quirking up. "But think about it: you can't unlearn something once you've seen it. It's like going to a magic show and discovering all the tricks. Kind of ruins the fun."

"Or makes it infinitely more interesting," I counter, a spark of mischief igniting within me. "So you're saying we should embrace the chaos?"

"Exactly," he replies, his tone suddenly earnest. "If we're going to confront our fears, we might as well have a good time doing it."

With a renewed sense of purpose, we continue along the winding path, our feet crunching over fallen leaves that scatter like whispers beneath us. The statues seem to whisper their own tales as we pass, their stone lips sealed but their expressions telling stories of regret, sorrow, and perhaps a hint of hope. My skin prickles with the sensation of being watched, and I can't shake the feeling that the valley is holding its breath, waiting for us to unlock its secrets.

Just ahead, the path opens up into a small clearing. The fog parts like a curtain, revealing a stone altar at its center, draped with vines and moss that have grown thick over the years. The altar is surrounded by a circle of stones, each one larger than the last, standing like guardians watching over the secrets hidden within. My breath catches in my throat as I take in the sight, an undeniable aura of power radiating from the altar.

"Whoa," Reed breathes, stepping forward cautiously. "This is... something else."

"It looks ancient," I murmur, drawn closer. "Like it's been waiting for us."

"Or for someone else," Reed adds, his voice a low rumble filled with concern. "Do you think it's safe?"

"Safe?" I repeat incredulously, my eyes darting around the clearing. "We're deep in a haunted valley, Reed. I don't think safe is really part of the deal."

"True." He takes another step closer, peering at the altar. "But look at those markings. They're similar to what we saw on the trees. What if they mean something?"

I step beside him, my pulse quickening as I lean closer to examine the engravings. They swirl around the surface of the altar, intricate designs interwoven with symbols I can't decipher. "What do you think they are?"

"Looks like a language," he muses, tracing one of the symbols with his finger. "Maybe an old one. Something lost to time."

As his finger glides over the stone, the air around us crackles with a sudden energy, and I feel a shift, a pulse that reverberates through my bones. The ground trembles beneath our feet, and the fog swirls violently, swirling like a tempest ready to unleash its fury. I gasp, pulling back as a rush of wind bursts from the altar, catching us off guard.

"Reed!" I shout, scrambling to regain my balance as the stones around us seem to hum with life. The fog thickens, enveloping us in a swirling vortex, and I can barely see his face through the chaos. "What did you do?"

"I didn't do anything!" he yells back, his voice barely audible over the roar of the wind. "It must be reacting to the markings!"

"Reed, we have to get out of here!" I scream, feeling the weight of fear settle over me like a heavy cloak. The wind howls, and for a moment, I'm paralyzed, trapped in a whirlwind of confusion and panic.

Then, without warning, a blinding light erupts from the altar, cutting through the fog with a sharp brilliance. It envelops us, and I feel my heart race, adrenaline coursing through my veins. Everything shifts—the ground beneath me, the air around me—and for an instant, I'm weightless, suspended between this world and something far beyond it.

"Hold on!" Reed shouts, his hand gripping mine tightly, anchoring me as the light expands, wrapping us in its embrace. My mind spins, and I can feel the pull of the valley's energy, dragging me toward an unknown fate.

As the light envelops us completely, the fog recedes, and I find myself standing in a new place, the landscape transformed. The valley is gone, replaced by a vibrant field under a brilliant sky, the colors more vivid than anything I've ever seen. Wildflowers sway in a gentle breeze, their petals shimmering like jewels in the sunlight.

"What just happened?" I breathe, looking around in disbelief. "Where are we?"

Reed's grip on my hand tightens as he surveys our surroundings, his brow furrowed in confusion. "I don't know, but this doesn't feel like home anymore. It feels... too perfect."

Just as I start to process the beauty of our new surroundings, a figure emerges from the field, radiant and ethereal, as if she's woven from the very light that surrounds us. She glides toward us, her presence commanding yet serene, and I feel an instinctual urge to kneel before her.

"Welcome," she says, her voice resonating like a soft chime. "You have awakened the valley's secrets."

"Awakened?" I echo, my heart pounding. "What do you mean?"

"The choice you made brought you here," she replies, her gaze piercing through me. "But every choice has its consequences. You must decide—will you face the truths that await you, or return to the safety of your ignorance?"

Before I can respond, the ground beneath us shifts again, and I glance back at Reed, who looks as bewildered as I feel. "What do we do?" he whispers, his voice barely containing the tremor of uncertainty.

The radiant figure tilts her head, a knowing smile playing on her lips. "The path is yours to choose, but be warned: once you take the first step, there may be no going back."

My mind races with possibilities, a thousand questions bubbling to the surface, but as I take a step toward her, the ground trembles again. "Reed—"

And just like that, the radiant light begins to fade, swallowed by a darkness that churns with a life of its own, creeping back toward us with a hunger that feels all too familiar. The valley isn't finished with us yet.

Chapter 11: Echoes of Betrayal

The clearing was bathed in a golden light that filtered through the dense canopy above, casting intricate shadows on the forest floor. I could feel the soft crunch of fallen leaves beneath my feet, each step resonating with the pulse of the earth, urging me forward. Reed walked beside me, his presence a comforting weight in the midst of the encroaching uncertainty. My heart raced as we drew nearer to the stone altar, its surface adorned with symbols that danced and shimmered under the sun's embrace. They whispered secrets, tales of ancient power that pulsed through my veins, mingling with the thrum of my anxious thoughts.

"Can you believe it?" I murmured, tracing the cool stone with my fingertips. "It's beautiful. These symbols... they're just like the ones on my charm." The weight of the charm rested heavy against my chest, a constant reminder of my lineage and the legacy I was destined to explore. I felt a sense of connection to the past, a link to my ancestors who had once stood in this very place, weaving their destinies with the threads of magic and intention.

Reed's gaze flickered between the altar and me, his brow furrowing in concentration. "This could change everything, you know," he said, his voice low but steady. I looked at him, really looked, searching for a glimpse of the man I had once known, the one who had shared laughter and fleeting moments of vulnerability. Yet, there was a storm brewing in his eyes, a conflict that left me uneasy.

"Are you ready?" I asked, my voice barely above a whisper, as if saying it out loud might shatter the fragile atmosphere that enveloped us. He hesitated, the moment stretching like a taut string between us. I felt the tension crackle in the air, an electric pulse that threatened to snap at any moment.

Before he could respond, a rustle from the treeline shattered the stillness, and my heart dropped into my stomach. Figures emerged, their silhouettes dark against the sunlight—a gang I had hoped never to see again, Reed's old crew, their intentions as murky as the shadows they cast. I could see Carrick at the forefront, his presence commanding, a wolf among sheep. The flicker of recognition in Reed's eyes told me everything I needed to know. This was more than just an encounter; it was a reckoning.

"Reed!" I called, my voice shaking with an urgency I couldn't contain. But he remained rooted in place, a statue carved from indecision. The air thickened around us, and I could sense the shift in the dynamic, the impending clash of loyalties and shadows that would soon unfold. My breath quickened as Carrick stepped forward, a predatory smile stretching across his face, the kind that sent chills skittering down my spine.

"Well, well, well, if it isn't our dear Reed," Carrick taunted, his voice smooth like honey but dripping with malice. "And you've brought a little trinket with you, I see. How charming." He gestured toward the altar, his eyes gleaming with a hunger that made my skin crawl. "We've come for what's ours, and I do believe you're holding onto it quite tightly."

I clutched the charm, its surface warm against my palm, as if urging me to draw strength from its power. "You won't get away with this," I said defiantly, even as doubt crept into my mind like a slow poison. Carrick's laughter rang out, echoing through the clearing, and I felt a sickening twist in my gut.

"Is that so?" he said, advancing with a predatory grace. "We have everything we need to unearth a power that could bring this world to its knees. And you, my dear, will witness it all."

"Reed, do something!" I turned to him, my voice a mixture of desperation and disbelief. The man I had trusted now seemed a stranger, caught in a web of his past choices. He looked at me, a storm of emotions brewing in his eyes, and for a fleeting moment, I saw the spark of defiance there. But it flickered and died as quickly as it had appeared.

The moment hung heavy, and I felt time stretch into eternity. Reed's silence cut deeper than any blade, severing the fragile tether of trust that had bound us together. "I didn't want this," he finally said, his voice barely a whisper, lost in the cacophony of Carrick's approaching footsteps. "I thought I could keep you safe."

"Safe?" I spat, the anger flaring like a wildfire in my chest. "By doing nothing? By standing here while they take everything from us?"

Carrick's crew surged forward, their movements a coordinated dance of malice. I could see the glint of metal, the promise of violence wrapped in their eagerness. Reed stepped back, his face pale, and I felt the ground beneath me shift. The realization dawned like a heavy fog—this had been his plan all along, hadn't it? To let them come, to let them take the charm. My heart shattered, the pieces sharp and jagged as they tumbled down into the abyss of betrayal.

"You should have trusted me," Reed murmured, his voice breaking against the weight of his regret. "I thought I could protect you, but I was wrong."

In that moment, the air thickened with tension, and I felt a swell of determination rising within me. Betrayal was a bitter poison, but I refused to let it define me. I would fight. For my ancestors, for the power that coursed through my veins, and for the chance to reclaim what was rightfully mine. I squared my shoulders, steeling my resolve as I faced Carrick and his crew.

"No," I said firmly, as the echoes of betrayal reverberated around us. "You will not take anything from me."

The clearing buzzed with tension, and the sunlight suddenly felt like a spotlight on our impending doom. As Carrick stepped closer, his imposing figure eclipsed the warmth of the sun, making me shiver as if a winter chill had swept through the air. His crew flanked him, a rough-and-tumble band of faces I didn't recognize, but their predatory grins and hardened gazes told me all I needed to know. They were here to claim not just the charm, but to assert their dominance in a game I had unwittingly become a part of.

"Don't underestimate the power we'll unleash," Carrick sneered, brushing his fingers against the altar as though he had a claim to it. "You're in way over your head, girl." His gaze darted back to Reed, and a flicker of something passed between them—an acknowledgment, a shared history steeped in darker dealings. I felt the familiar pang of betrayal swell inside me, sharper than the afternoon sun glaring down on us.

Reed took a step back, a fragile thing caught in a tempest. "I'm not with them," he said, but the words sounded hollow, a feeble whisper against the backdrop of Carrick's booming laughter.

"Oh, but you are," Carrick countered, his voice low and mocking. "You think just because you're holding hands with this little treasure, you can turn your back on us? It doesn't work that way, Reed. You can't just walk away from family." He emphasized the last word, twisting it like a knife, and I could see the flicker of doubt in Reed's eyes.

"Family?" I scoffed, finding my voice amid the chaos. "Is that what you call betrayal? Because that's what this feels like." My heart raced, adrenaline surging through my veins as I clenched the charm tighter, its surface warm against my palm, a lifeline in the storm.

Carrick's grin widened, and he took a step toward me, closing the distance. "You have no idea what you're holding, do you? That little trinket of yours is a key, and not just to some dusty old legends. It has power, power that could rewrite the rules of our world." He leaned in, his breath hot and sour, and I resisted the urge to recoil. "But it will come at a price."

I couldn't let fear root me to the spot. "What kind of price?" I shot back, refusing to give him the satisfaction of seeing me flinch. "The kind that sacrifices innocent lives for your twisted ambitions?"

"Such a fierce little thing," Carrick said, stepping back with a chuckle, clearly enjoying the exchange. "You really think you can protect the world from what lies ahead? You'll learn quickly that there's no stopping the darkness once it has its claws in you."

Behind me, I could sense Reed's turmoil, an inner battle that left the air thick with unresolved tension. "This doesn't have to happen," he said, almost pleadingly, yet there was a distance in his voice that suggested he was still weighing his loyalties. "We can work together."

Carrick's eyes glinted with mock sympathy. "Oh, Reed, you've grown soft. You forget, we don't need you anymore. And now, neither does she." With that, he signaled his crew to move, and in an instant, chaos erupted. They surged forward, a tidal wave of greed and ambition, and I instinctively stepped back, the altar pressing into my back like a protective barrier.

"Reed!" I shouted, panic rising as the gang closed in. It felt like time stretched and warped; every heartbeat echoed like thunder in my ears. With a burst of instinct, I reached for the charm, holding it aloft. "You'll never take this!"

A murmur rippled through the crew, their confidence faltering momentarily as they regarded the charm with a mix of fear and greed. "What's she doing?" one of them hissed, but Carrick merely chuckled, his bravado unyielding.

"Show me what you've got, then!" he shouted, urging me on. "You think that little glow will stop us? We've faced worse than you, girl."

I drew a deep breath, drawing on the energy I felt emanating from the charm. The symbols seemed to pulse in response, a rhythm echoing the chaos around us. I closed my eyes for a heartbeat, focusing on the legacy of my ancestors, the stories woven into my blood. The power surged within me, and as I opened my eyes, I felt a sudden clarity—this was not just a fight for survival; it was a stand for everything I believed in.

With a sudden thrust of will, I directed the charm towards Carrick and his crew, feeling the warmth radiate from my fingertips. Light exploded from the charm, a brilliant burst that illuminated the clearing and sent the shadows recoiling. Gasps erupted from the crew as the glow enveloped them, a shimmering barrier that stopped them in their tracks.

Carrick staggered back, his bravado faltering as confusion flickered across his features. "What is this?!" he roared, the bravado dissipating like mist in the sun.

"Just a taste of what you'll never control," I replied, my voice steady despite the whirlwind of fear and anger churning inside me. I stepped forward, emboldened by the power that surged within, but I felt Reed's hand grip my arm, his touch grounding me amidst the chaos.

"Wait!" he shouted, and I turned to meet his gaze. There was a mix of desperation and something softer there, and it pulled at my heart. "We can't let them have it. They'll use it to hurt people."

"I know," I said, my voice low but firm. "But if we let them go now, it'll be worse. We have to stand our ground." The tension in the air thickened, a taut string ready to snap, as Carrick regained his composure and edged closer, the determination in his eyes morphing into something darker.

"You think this little light show intimidates me?" Carrick snarled, a flash of menace crossing his face. "You're just a girl playing with magic she doesn't understand. This charm belongs to me, and I will take it, one way or another."

"No," I countered, my voice ringing with resolve. "This charm belongs to my ancestors, and I won't let you twist it to serve your dark ambitions. Not today, Carrick."

As the tension hung heavy between us, I could feel the line drawn, the clash of wills and destinies colliding like storms. The outcome was uncertain, but one thing was clear: I wasn't backing down without a fight. In this game of shadows and betrayals, I was no longer a mere pawn. I would be the one to rewrite the rules, and I could only hope Reed would stand beside me when the storm broke.

The light from the charm pulsed around us, casting intricate patterns on the ground, but it didn't seem to deter Carrick and his crew. They exchanged wary glances, but the allure of power hung thick in the air like a heady perfume, intoxicating and dangerous. Carrick, his confidence rekindled, stepped forward again, eyes glinting with the promise of chaos.

"Do you really think you can hold us off?" he sneered, sweeping his arm in a grand gesture as if to encompass his crew, the shadows gathering at their feet. "You're just delaying the inevitable. Power doesn't bow to little girls with pretty trinkets. It demands loyalty—and that's something you'll never understand."

I felt the heat of anger flush through me, fueling the magic that crackled at my fingertips. "I understand plenty, Carrick. Like how you're too blinded by your own greed to see that true power lies in unity, not fear."

His laughter echoed, dark and cruel, as if my words were a joke to him. "Unity? Oh, darling, I'd love to see you try and unite with the very shadows you seek to control. It's amusing, really." He glanced at Reed, a knowing look passing between them that made my stomach churn. "You should be careful, Reed. A pretty face can mask a treacherous heart."

"Enough!" I shouted, my voice cutting through the tension like a blade. "You don't get to threaten us anymore. This ends now." With a surge of determination, I pushed the charm out further, the light intensifying, and for a moment, I could see the crew hesitate, fear flickering across their faces.

"Get her!" Carrick bellowed, breaking their trance, and the chaos that followed erupted like a wildfire, each member of the crew lunging forward, their hands outstretched as they tried to snatch the charm from me.

I moved instinctively, weaving between them, the pulse of the charm guiding my every step. "Reed, help!" I called, dodging a hefty arm that swung too close. In the whirlwind, I could see him, rooted in indecision, his brows knitted together as if caught in the throes of a storm. I couldn't let his hesitation become my downfall.

"Stop standing there!" I shouted, and in that instant, I saw a flicker of resolve spark in his eyes. He stepped forward, and as if a dam had burst, he charged into the fray beside me.

"Get back!" he yelled, pushing through the crowd, and with each shove, I felt the momentum shift slightly in our favor. But just as hope began to bloom, Carrick roared, his voice a low rumble that seemed to shake the very ground beneath us.

"Fools! You don't understand what you're playing with!"

In that moment, the charm flared again, and a blinding light erupted from it, forcing Carrick and his crew to shield their eyes. I felt the power surge through me, invigorating and fierce, but it came at a cost. The energy was draining fast, and I could already feel my fingers starting to tremble.

"Hold them off! I just need a moment!" I cried, feeling the last vestiges of strength gathering in my core. I couldn't let this chance slip away. This was my moment to not only reclaim the charm but to forge my own destiny.

With a defiant shout, Carrick thrust his hand into the air, summoning his crew to rally against us, their faces set with grim determination. "You think you can protect her?" he bellowed at Reed. "You're nothing but a traitor to your own blood. You will regret this!"

"Not as much as you will," Reed shot back, determination carving lines into his expression. "I won't let you take her or the charm."

The atmosphere crackled as I felt the power of the charm reaching its zenith. "We can do this together, Reed!" I urged, my heart pounding. "We just have to believe we can beat them!"

Carrick lunged, a wild look in his eyes, and I braced myself, adrenaline coursing through my veins like wildfire. Just as he reached for the charm, I focused every ounce of energy within me and hurled the light forward. The brilliance enveloped us, a protective barrier that surged toward Carrick and his crew, pushing them back, forcing them to stumble in shock.

But then, amid the confusion, I saw something glint at the edge of my vision—a figure hidden in the treeline. My stomach dropped as I recognized the silhouette of a woman, her long hair flowing in the wind like a banner of chaos. She stepped into the clearing, and with a flick of her wrist, she unleashed a dark energy that swirled like a storm.

"Carrick, darling, you've been so naughty!" she chimed, her voice smooth as silk, yet filled with a biting edge. "Let me show you how it's done."

In an instant, the atmosphere shifted, the air thick with a palpable dread that seeped into my bones. Carrick's confidence faltered as he turned to the newcomer, confusion mingling with fear. "Who are you?" he demanded, but his voice was no longer the commanding roar it once was.

The woman smiled, her gaze flitting between Carrick and me, a knowing spark igniting her dark eyes. "You've messed with forces beyond your comprehension, my dear. I'm here to collect what's owed."

Before I could process her words, she waved her hand, and a blast of energy surged through the clearing, throwing me back against the altar. Pain jolted through me, and I gasped for breath, the charm slipping from my fingers as darkness enveloped my vision.

"No!" Reed's voice cut through the haze, filled with desperation and fury. I reached out, but the world around me began to fade, the brightness of the charm dimming as I fought to keep my consciousness. The last thing I saw was Reed, desperately trying to reach me, his silhouette swallowed by the shadows.

And then, everything went black.

Chapter 12: Shards of Trust

The dim light of dawn filtered through the frayed edges of the tarp that hung above us like a guilty secret, casting flickering shadows on the ground littered with remnants of the previous night's revelry. The air was heavy with the scent of damp earth and the lingering acrid smoke of last night's fire, remnants of Carrick's crew celebrating their temporary victory over us. I lay on the ground, the roughness of the earth jarring against my skin, each grain of sand a reminder of my vulnerability. My heart raced as I replayed the events that had led us here, trapped in this makeshift camp with danger lurking at every corner.

The memory of Reed's betrayal stung deeper than the chill in the air. I could still feel the weight of his gaze, a mixture of longing and regret, pressing down on me like a stone. The connection we had felt so profound, so real, but now it seemed to dissolve like mist in the morning sun. How could I trust him again? The glimmer of hope he had ignited within me flickered weakly, overshadowed by the betrayal that had thrust me into this nightmare. The very thought of escape tugged at my heart, a siren song whispering promises of freedom, yet tethered by uncertainty and fear.

I shifted my position, trying to find some semblance of comfort amidst the chaos. The ropes binding my wrists were rough, biting into my skin, a physical reminder of my captivity. I could hear Carrick's laughter echoing through the camp, a sound that twisted in my gut, each peal ringing out like a bell tolling for the end of our hopes. The man thrived in chaos, feeding off the fear that hung in the air like a thick fog. The power he sought was not just magical; it was deeply human, rooted in the very essence of trust and betrayal.

As I sat there, a soft rustle of leaves announced Reed's arrival. My breath hitched as I turned, his figure emerging from the shadows, his presence both a comfort and a torment. He knelt beside me, close enough that I could see the lines of worry etched on his brow, but far enough to maintain a barrier I wasn't sure I was ready to breach. "I won't let them keep you," he whispered, his voice rough, raw from the strain of the night.

I narrowed my eyes, searching for the sincerity that once danced in his gaze. "And why should I believe you? You've already shown me what you're capable of."

Reed's expression shifted, anguish twisting his features. "What you saw wasn't the whole truth. Carrick—he manipulates everything. I was trying to protect you, but I made the wrong choice. I thought I could—"

"Protect me?" I scoffed, incredulous. "By aligning yourself with him? You've put me in more danger than I could ever imagine."

The vulnerability in his eyes pierced through my anger, and I could see the truth of his words battling within him. "I know I messed up. But if you let me, I can fix this. We can escape. Together."

Together. The word lingered between us, heavy with unspoken promises and fraught with the weight of betrayal. I wanted to believe him, wanted to grasp onto the hope he offered like a lifeline in stormy seas. But doubt coiled tightly around my heart, whispering insidious thoughts that spoke of pain and disappointment. I had trusted him once, and now I found myself standing at the precipice of another choice: embrace the familiar warmth of his promise or venture alone into the dark unknown.

My resolve wavered, the chill of the morning air seeping into my bones. "How do I know this isn't another trick?" I asked, my voice barely more than a whisper, the words tasting like ash on my tongue.

He leaned closer, his voice earnest and low, "Because I'm here. I could have left you with Carrick, let him do what he wanted. But I came back. I'll always come back."

In that moment, the sincerity of his promise ignited a flicker of warmth within me, a defiance against the cold logic that warned me to run. I searched his face for any trace of deceit, but all I found was the raw honesty that had first drawn me to him. "What's your plan?" I asked, curiosity threading through my fear.

"I overheard Carrick last night. He's distracted, celebrating his success. It's the perfect time to make our move."

Hope began to weave through my veins, curling around the fear that had taken root in my heart. The thought of escaping this place, of leaving behind the shackles of doubt and fear, was intoxicating. But the journey ahead was fraught with uncertainty, the shadows of Carrick's crew lurking in every corner. "What if we get caught?"

Reed's gaze hardened, determination radiating from him like a beacon. "Then we fight. I won't let you go back to Carrick. I promise."

The way he said it, with such conviction, stirred something deep within me—a fragile hope tempered by the embers of my earlier anger. "Okay. But if we're doing this, we do it my way."

A flicker of surprise danced across his features, quickly replaced by a grin that seemed to banish the shadows lingering in the corners of my mind. "Your way? I'm all in, as long as it means getting you out of here."

And just like that, the tension that had coiled around us began to unravel, replaced by a shared purpose. The world outside remained bleak, the danger still palpable, but together, we could challenge the chaos that surrounded us. The path ahead would be treacherous, but I refused to back down. Reed's presence felt like an anchor amidst the storm, reminding me that trust could still exist even in the darkest of times. And so, with a plan forming in our minds, we set our sights on the horizon, ready to reclaim our freedom.

The camp was stirring with the sounds of awakening—a chorus of gruff voices, clattering metal, and the low crackle of the dying fire, which had kept the night's chill at bay. I could barely remember how long we had been held captive; time had lost its meaning amid the tension and uncertainty. The weight of impending decisions settled on my shoulders like a heavy cloak. The vibrant hues of dawn spilled across the sky, illuminating the jagged outlines of our captors' tents. I felt a mixture of dread and determination swirling in my gut, as if I were about to dive headfirst into the unknown.

Reed was no longer just the man who had betrayed me; he was the only ally I had in this twisted game. I watched him from the corner of my eye, his brow furrowed in concentration as he scanned the camp. The way his muscles tensed under his shirt, the firelight flickering off his features—it reminded me that beneath the façade of confidence, he was just as vulnerable as I was. He glanced my way, our eyes locking for a brief moment, and a jolt of something—fear, hope, or perhaps a reckless mix of both—passed between us.

"Ready to enact your brilliant escape plan?" I murmured, sarcasm threading through my voice like a lifeline.

"Brilliant? I thought I'd just wing it." He grinned, that crooked smile tugging at my heartstrings, even in this chaos. "But I suppose that won't work for the grand design of our heroic rescue."

"Winging it tends to end in disaster, you know," I replied, rolling my eyes but unable to suppress the flicker of amusement at his bravado.

As we exchanged jabs, a part of me clung to that banter like a safety net, grounding me in the face of the imminent threat that loomed just beyond the boundaries of our camp. It was as if our words wrapped around us like a shield, momentarily warding off the fear that threatened to creep back in.

Before I could delve further into my musings, Carrick sauntered into view, his silhouette casting a long shadow over our makeshift refuge. His presence demanded attention, and the air grew thick with tension. "What's this? A moment of bonding before the show begins?" he taunted, his voice laced with mockery.

Reed stiffened beside me, a predator ready to defend its territory. "Nothing you'd understand," he shot back, his tone defiant.

Carrick chuckled, the sound low and menacing, sending shivers down my spine. "Ah, the defiance of youth. It's quite entertaining. You two think you have a way out of this? I admire your optimism." His gaze narrowed, scrutinizing us as if we were mere pawns in a game he had already won. "But let's not forget who holds the real power here."

I exchanged a glance with Reed, the weight of Carrick's words sinking in. We were outmatched, surrounded by those who reveled in cruelty and had no qualms about using the charm's power for their own gain. The realization that our escape relied on a flicker of trust in Reed's plan sent a shiver down my spine.

"Let me guess, you're going to showcase your magnificent abilities today?" Reed challenged, defiance dripping from his words.

"Something like that," Carrick replied, amusement dancing in his eyes. "You see, this little charm of yours? It's not just a trinket. It's a beacon of power, and soon, it will be mine to wield."

With that, he turned away, leaving a heavy silence in his wake. I felt my stomach twist. The charm—its very essence was tied to us, to me. I had thought it could be our salvation, a key to unlocking the mysteries that had ensnared us, but now it felt like a noose tightening around our necks.

"Look, we need to move before he decides to demonstrate his power on us instead," I whispered urgently to Reed.

He nodded, determination flashing in his eyes. "Follow my lead. There's a gap between the sentries just past the trees. We'll have to be quick."

With every step we took toward the edge of the camp, I felt the atmosphere thrum with impending danger, every heartbeat echoing in my ears like a countdown to our freedom or our downfall. Reed led me through the shadows, our movements careful and deliberate.

The thrum of life around us intensified as we approached the perimeter, the clamor of Carrick's men rising as they prepared for whatever dark magic he planned to unleash.

Suddenly, a shout rang out, slicing through the air like a knife. My heart raced as I whipped around to see a hulking figure—a guard—barrelling towards us, eyes wild with recognition.

"Stop! You're not going anywhere!" he bellowed, lunging for us.

"Run!" Reed shouted, shoving me ahead as he positioned himself between me and the guard.

Panic surged through me as I dashed into the thicket of trees, the underbrush scratching against my legs. Branches snagged at my clothes, but I didn't dare look back. The thudding of footsteps grew louder, and I could almost feel the guard's breath on my neck. My heart raced, an adrenaline-fueled rhythm propelling me forward.

"Over here!" Reed called, his voice cutting through the chaos as he ducked behind a large tree. I followed instinctively, my lungs burning as I pressed against the rough bark, trying to catch my breath.

"What now?" I gasped, my mind racing.

Reed's eyes darted around, searching for an escape route. "We need to create a diversion. If we can draw them away, we can slip out."

"Right, and how do you propose we do that? Wave a magic wand?" I quipped, though the edge of fear laced my voice.

He smirked, a glimmer of that wry humor shining through the tension. "No, but we can make some noise. Follow my lead."

With that, he leaned back against the tree, cupping his hands around his mouth. "Hey! Over here, you thugs!" His voice rang out, loud and mocking, echoing through the woods.

It worked like a charm—or perhaps it was the madness of desperation. The guard paused, confusion flickering across his face before he took off toward Reed's voice.

I watched, my heart racing, as Reed glanced back at me, his expression a mix of urgency and exhilaration. "Now!" he urged, and together, we sprinted deeper into the forest, leaving the chaos behind us.

With each step, the freedom I craved felt closer, the shadows of our captors fading behind us. But the journey was just beginning, and the reality of our situation weighed heavily on my heart. Trust was a fragile thing, easily shattered, and yet in that moment, it was the only thing tethering us to hope.

The forest enveloped us in a cocoon of shadows and rustling leaves, the scent of damp earth mingling with the sweetness of pine. Each step felt heavy with the weight of uncertainty, the thrill of potential freedom battling against the lingering fear of capture. Reed was a few paces ahead, his body a taut line of focus and urgency. I followed closely, my heart racing in sync with the muffled sounds of the camp fading into the distance.

"Do you think they've noticed yet?" I asked, forcing a nonchalance into my tone that didn't quite match the fluttering in my chest.

Reed glanced over his shoulder, his eyes sparkling with mischief. "They'll figure it out soon enough. Let's just hope they're more concerned with catching us than with what they're leaving behind."

"Leaving behind? Like their dignity?" I shot back, the tension easing slightly between us.

"Right, because nothing says 'intimidating pirate crew' like being outsmarted by a couple of scared kids." His grin was infectious, and despite the perilous situation, I felt a warmth growing in my chest.

But that warmth was soon overshadowed by a harsh reality. The further we moved, the more the forest transformed into a labyrinth of confusion, branches clawing at us like the hands of a thousand hidden threats. Just as I thought we might find a path away from danger, a cacophony of shouting erupted behind us, echoing through the trees like a haunting warning.

"Reed!" I cried out, panic rising in my throat. "They're coming!"

"Keep moving! We can't stop now!" he urged, pulling me along as adrenaline surged through my veins.

We darted deeper into the thicket, the underbrush snapping beneath our feet. I could hear the men's voices growing louder, their laughter menacing. They were relishing the hunt, their confidence a chilling reminder of how precarious our situation was. "If we can just make it to the river," Reed muttered, almost to himself, "we can lose them in the current."

"Great plan if we don't get caught first!" I shot back, trying to keep up with his long strides.

A sudden noise to our right—a rustling that grew louder—had my heart leaping into my throat. I turned to see a dark figure emerging from the foliage, and for a moment, my mind went blank with fear. My instincts screamed to run, to flee from whatever creature lurked in the shadows.

But it was just another guard, a burly man with a wild look in his eyes and a weapon drawn, blocking our escape route. "There you are!" he bellowed, a crazed smile spreading across his face. "Thought you could get away so easily?"

"Not on my watch!" Reed exclaimed, shoving me back as he confronted the guard. The desperation in his voice ignited a spark of courage within me, and without thinking, I lunged forward, grabbing a fallen branch from the ground. It was a flimsy weapon, but it would have to do.

The guard took a step closer, clearly underestimating the two of us. "You think you can fight me? I'll enjoy taking you back to Carrick myself," he sneered.

"Or maybe you'll enjoy this!" I shouted, swinging the branch with all my might. It connected with a dull thud against his shoulder, and for a split second, he faltered, surprise flickering across his face. Reed took advantage of the moment, tackling him to the ground.

The two of them wrestled in a tangle of limbs, but the guard was bigger, stronger, and his rage fueled him like a raging fire. Reed grunted as the man managed to throw him off, scrambling to regain his footing. My heart raced as I watched, torn between helping Reed and running for our lives.

"Get the charm!" Reed shouted, desperation spilling from his lips. "I can hold him!"

The mention of the charm sent a jolt of clarity through me. It was our only hope, our tether to freedom, and I wasn't about to let Carrick take that from us. With a quick glance back, I made a split-second decision, sprinting toward the direction we had come from, where our packs had been discarded in the chaos. I could still hear Reed's grunts of exertion as he battled the guard behind me, the sound a harsh reminder of how quickly our luck could change.

Racing through the trees, I pushed aside the panic threatening to overwhelm me. My fingers brushed the cool fabric of our packs, and I felt around frantically, my breath quickening. Where was it? Where was the charm? I could almost hear Carrick's laughter, a dark echo that promised suffering if I failed.

Finally, my fingers closed around the small pouch, the charm nestled inside like a heartbeat waiting to be awakened. Relief surged through me, and I turned to head back to Reed, but a sharp crack of a branch broke my focus. I froze, the air thick with tension. The guard had escaped Reed's grasp, and now he was looming just a few yards away, a menacing smile plastered on his face.

"Look what we have here," he taunted, taking a step toward me. "You're all alone now."

I tightened my grip on the charm, my heart pounding wildly. "Get away from me!" I shouted, feeling the fight surge through me once again.

"Or what?" he sneered, raising his weapon menacingly. "You think that little trinket can save you?"

The charm pulsed in my hand, its energy thrumming with potential, urging me to unleash its power. I took a step back, weighing my options, feeling cornered and desperate. Reed's voice echoed in my mind, urging me to be brave, to harness what we had discovered together. With my heart pounding, I drew on the energy of the charm, summoning every ounce of will I had.

"Stay back!" I warned, channeling my fear into defiance.

But just as I prepared to unleash its power, a figure dashed through the trees behind the guard—Reed, breathless and fierce, tackling the man from behind. They both stumbled, and the guard's weapon flew from his hand, landing with a soft thud at my feet.

"Now!" Reed shouted, urgency woven into his voice.

In that heartbeat, I had a choice to make—pick up the weapon and fight alongside Reed or use the charm to create a distraction that could give us the upper hand. The decision hung in the air, and I could almost hear the chorus of doubt swirling around me, urging me to act.

Before I could decide, the guard swung around, his eyes wild with fury as he reached for Reed. In that moment of chaos, everything slowed, and I felt the world narrow down to a single choice.

"Let's see who has the real power," I breathed, grasping the charm tight and preparing to unleash its potential, unaware of the consequences that would follow. As the energy surged, the ground beneath us trembled, and I realized too late that some powers came with a price, one we might not be ready to pay.

The last thing I saw was the guard's eyes widening in shock, and then—darkness engulfed us all.

Chapter 13: Fire and Flight

Firelight danced around us, its flickering glow illuminating the chaos that had unfurled in Carrick's camp. Shadows stretched and twisted, mirroring the turmoil that churned within me. Reed moved with a fluidity that spoke of desperation and determination, his blade slicing through the air like a whisper of vengeance. As the flames licked hungrily at the tents, consuming the remnants of our captors' world, I felt a surge of exhilaration mixed with an unmistakable thread of fear. We were no longer pawns; we were wild cards in a game we barely understood.

The acrid scent of smoke filled my lungs, sharp and bitter, blending with the earthy aroma of the forest surrounding us. The night had turned into a cacophony of crackling firewood and the distant echo of our footsteps, now unshackled from the oppressive weight of Carrick's authority. Each stride I took was a release, a defiance against the chains of my past that had kept me bound for too long. But even in our escape, doubt clung to me like a second skin. Reed was a man of secrets, and though he fought fiercely at my side, the shadows in his eyes spoke of battles I could not yet fathom.

We stumbled through the underbrush, the moonlight filtering through the canopy above, casting a silver hue on the world that felt both foreign and familiar. Each branch we brushed against felt like a caress of fate, guiding us toward an uncertain freedom. Reed glanced back, his expression a mix of relief and apprehension. "We're not safe yet," he said, his voice low and steady, betraying none of the turmoil I felt surging within.

"Then we keep moving." I replied, the determination in my voice surprising even myself. I had learned to navigate the darkness within me, and tonight, I would not falter.

We reached a small clearing, the moon illuminating the world with an ethereal glow. The silence here was a stark contrast to the chaos we'd just escaped, and for a moment, we simply breathed, catching our bearings as the night wrapped around us like a soft blanket. The weight of the charm rested heavy in Reed's pocket, a talisman of both hope and horror, and I could see the conflict writ large across his features.

"What was your sister like?" I asked, hoping to peel back the layers of his guarded soul.

Reed hesitated, and I watched as memories flickered in his eyes like the dying embers of our fire. "She was... stubborn, brave. Always charging into danger without a second thought." He chuckled softly, a sound that felt fragile, like glass on the verge of shattering. "Thought she could save the world, you know? I admired that about her, even when it drove me mad."

"And now?" I pressed, my heart racing. "What do you want?"

His gaze turned toward the stars, as if searching for answers hidden in their ancient light. "I want to honor her memory," he said finally, his voice thick with emotion. "To stop Carrick from using the charm. To keep it from falling into the wrong hands." He paused, a dark shadow crossing his face. "But I can't do it alone."

The admission hung between us, thick with unspoken fears and unyielding hopes. I wanted to reach out, to comfort him, but something held me back. Perhaps it was the fear that my own heart was not yet ready to be laid bare. "And if I say no?" I challenged, testing the boundaries of our new alliance.

He met my gaze, his eyes fierce, unyielding. "Then we'll both lose. This charm is not just a key; it's a curse. We don't understand its true power yet, but it binds us, and I can't let Carrick exploit it."

His sincerity struck a chord within me. I had felt the charm's pull, its seductive promise of power and control, and I could not deny the thrill that coursed through me when I held it. But I also sensed the dark tendrils of its influence wrapping around my soul, threatening to ensnare me in its web of manipulation.

I took a deep breath, letting the forest's cool air fill my lungs, cleansing the remnants of fear and uncertainty. "Then let's make a plan," I said, my voice steady. "We need to understand what we're dealing with if we're going to confront Carrick."

Reed nodded, a flicker of hope igniting in his gaze. "We start with the charm itself. There must be something in the legends or texts that can help us."

As we spoke, the shadows of the trees seemed to lean in, listening to our whispered secrets, guarding our newfound purpose. But even in this moment of clarity, the weight of betrayal lingered. I couldn't shake the feeling that Carrick would not take our escape lightly. The air felt charged with a tension that promised more than mere confrontation; it whispered of consequences yet to come.

The fire had become a distant glow behind us, but its heat remained, a reminder of what we'd left behind. I felt the remnants of Carrick's camp still clinging to me—the fear, the darkness—but I also felt the rising pulse of determination thrumming in my veins. We would not be defined by our pasts; we would carve our own futures, step by tentative step, toward whatever lay ahead.

With each word exchanged, I sensed the boundaries of our alliance shifting, solidifying into something more than mere survival. There was a connection forming between us, one forged in shared purpose and the promise of freedom. We were no longer just a fugitive and a warrior; we were allies in a battle that was only beginning.

The forest wrapped around us like a thick shroud, each tree a sentinel standing guard over our fraught escape. As we leaned against the gnarled trunk of an ancient oak, I tried to catch my breath, the adrenaline of our flight still coursing through my veins. Reed's presence beside me was both a comfort and a source of lingering unease; he was the enigma I had started to understand, yet I couldn't shake the remnants of doubt swirling in my mind.

"Where do we go from here?" I asked, my voice low as I scanned the shadowy woods, half-expecting Carrick's men to burst forth from the trees. The remnants of his camp still smoldered behind us, a haunting reminder of the chaos we had unleashed.

Reed pushed a hand through his tousled hair, his eyes narrowed in thought. "There's an old safe house, a relic from my sister's days with the Resistance. It's not far from here, but I doubt it's been untouched."

"Of course it hasn't. Why would it be?" I shot back, a mix of sarcasm and fear escaping my lips. It was easier to mask my anxiety with wit, to cloak the uncertainty in humor, even as dread gnawed at my insides. "We've only been chased through a burning camp; it's not like we're high on the list of priorities."

His lips quirked into a small smile, a fleeting moment of levity in the heavy atmosphere. "You're right. We should've sent out invitations."

"Fancy that. 'Join us for an evening of chaos and potential death!'" I laughed, a sound tinged with the sharp edge of reality. It felt good to share a joke, even if only briefly.

"Maybe a little too optimistic for our current situation," Reed said, his tone shifting as he gestured toward the dense thicket ahead. "But we need to keep moving. I'll lead; you stay close."

As we trudged deeper into the woods, the air grew thick with the scent of damp earth and the pungent aroma of crushed pine needles. Each step felt like a step away from the life I had known, and the weight of the charm in Reed's pocket felt heavier than before. I could almost feel its pulse, a wicked heartbeat that echoed the chaos in my mind.

"Tell me more about this charm," I prompted, wanting to draw out the story, to keep my mind occupied. "What exactly does it do? Why is it so dangerous?"

Reed hesitated, his face shadowed by the moonlight as he glanced back at me. "Legends say it can grant immense power—enough to reshape reality itself. But it comes at a cost, one that tends to destroy whoever wields it."

"Sounds delightful," I said dryly, my heart racing as I envisioned the power it could unleash. "So, just a casual trinket, then?"

He chuckled softly, the sound surprising me with its warmth. "I wish it were that simple. The charm feeds off darkness. It amplifies desires, yes, but it also knows your fears, your insecurities. It twists everything until it devours you whole."

I shivered at the thought. "So basically, Carrick's been playing with fire and hasn't noticed he's already singed his eyebrows off."

"Pretty much," he agreed, a flicker of admiration in his eyes. "But it's not just Carrick we have to worry about. Others want the charm too, and they won't hesitate to eliminate anyone in their way."

The reality of our situation sank in like a stone in a pond, the ripples of danger spreading wide. As we navigated the dense underbrush, I could feel the tension building, thick and palpable, an unspoken acknowledgment of the stakes we faced. Each rustle of leaves sent a jolt of adrenaline through me, and my instincts screamed at me to stay alert.

We rounded a bend, and Reed suddenly stopped, raising a hand. "Listen."

I strained to hear, heart pounding as the distant sound of footsteps approached, heavy and deliberate. My pulse quickened, and the hairs on the back of my neck prickled. "How close are we to this safe house?" I whispered, anxiety creeping into my voice.

"Not far, but we need to move fast," Reed said, his tone clipped. "Follow me, stay low, and don't make a sound."

We slipped through the undergrowth like shadows, every crack of a twig beneath our feet felt like a shout in the stillness. The footsteps grew louder, echoing the threat looming behind us. I could sense the presence of others, a force lurking just out of sight, and the urge to flee gripped me fiercely.

"Do you think they know we escaped?" I muttered, the question barely escaping my lips.

"They will soon enough. Carrick won't let this go lightly." His expression hardened, the playful banter replaced by grim determination.

We pressed on, the darkness enveloping us, but I felt a surge of hope igniting within me. Reed's resolve pushed me forward, urging me to believe that there was a way out of this nightmare. As we reached the edge of a clearing, the silhouette of an old cabin appeared, weathered and worn but standing defiantly against the night.

"There it is," Reed said, a glimmer of relief in his voice. "Quickly now."

We sprinted toward the cabin, our footsteps muffled by the underbrush, hearts pounding in unison. As we reached the door, Reed pulled it open with a creak that echoed like thunder in the stillness, and we slipped inside, hearts racing.

The interior was dim, dust motes dancing in the shafts of moonlight that filtered through the cracked windows. Old furniture lay scattered, a testament to the lives once lived here. I could feel the weight of history pressing down on me as I surveyed the space, the air thick with the scent of aged wood and a hint of forgotten secrets.

"Stay close," Reed said, moving deeper into the shadows as he began to search through the remnants of the cabin. "We need to find anything that could help us."

I nodded, the flickering shadows creating a tapestry of uncertainty on the walls. As I sifted through a stack of tattered books and brittle papers, a sudden noise shattered the silence, and my heart leaped into my throat.

"Did you hear that?" I whispered, my voice barely above a breath.

Reed froze, his gaze locked on the door. "We're not alone."

A surge of fear washed over me, but alongside it was a fierce determination. Whatever was coming, I wouldn't let it steal my newfound resolve. Together, we could face whatever lay beyond those walls, but only if we held tight to the spark that had ignited between us—a fragile connection born of fire, flight, and the unwavering belief that we could change our destinies.

The air crackled with tension as we stood in the dim light of the cabin, the weight of uncertainty heavy between us. Reed's expression was set, eyes narrowed in focus as he listened intently for the faint sounds echoing outside. My heart raced, pounding like a war drum against my ribcage, urging me to move, to act, while my mind screamed for caution.

"Can you hear anything?" I whispered, straining to listen, my pulse thrumming in my ears.

"Not yet," he replied, scanning the corners of the room, searching for anything that could serve as a weapon or a means of escape. "But they're close. I can feel it."

The last light of dusk slipped away, plunging the cabin into a deeper darkness that felt almost suffocating. I stepped further inside, stepping over a cracked floorboard that creaked beneath my weight, the sound echoing in the stillness. The cabin was a relic of a different time, filled with remnants of lives long forgotten—dust-covered furniture draped in sheets like ghosts waiting to be remembered.

"Are you sure this place is safe?" I asked, glancing at the door as if it could somehow sprout legs and run away from the impending danger. "Or is this just a really elaborate trap?"

Reed turned to me, a smirk tugging at the corner of his lips despite the situation. "Welcome to the world of adventure. A bit of danger keeps things interesting, don't you think?"

"Interesting isn't the word I'd use." I shot back, crossing my arms defiantly, though I couldn't help but admire his easy bravado. It was infuriatingly charming.

He chuckled, a sound rich with warmth that momentarily eased the knot in my stomach. "You're going to have to learn to embrace the chaos. Besides, there's a certain thrill in living on the edge, don't you agree?"

"Only if we survive to tell the tale," I replied, an eyebrow raised. "I'd rather not become a cautionary legend."

Reed's smirk faded slightly as he leaned closer to me, his voice dropping to a whisper. "If they find us here, it won't just be a legend. We need to figure out our next move."

As if on cue, a loud bang reverberated outside, causing the walls to tremble as if they too were frightened. I instinctively recoiled, pressing my back against the cool wood of the cabin. "What was that?"

"Sounds like our friends have arrived," Reed said grimly, moving to the window. "We need to keep quiet and—"

The door splintered, crashing inward with a force that sent shards of wood flying. I gasped as men dressed in dark cloaks surged into the cabin, their eyes scanning the room with a predatory gleam. Reed lunged forward, pushing me behind him as he brandished his blade, the silver catching the faint light like a beacon of defiance.

"Get out!" he shouted, his voice rising above the chaos. "Now!"

I didn't need telling twice. Heart pounding, I bolted for the back of the cabin, my instincts kicking in. The sharp edges of the room blurred as I weaved around broken furniture, my breath quickening. I heard Reed's blade clash against metal, a sound so visceral it sent chills racing down my spine.

In the shadowy corner, I spotted a door leading to the back. With trembling hands, I yanked it open, revealing a darkened hallway that felt like a tunnel into oblivion. "Reed!" I called out, desperation clawing at my throat as I turned to face the chaos behind me.

"Go!" he yelled again, his voice a fierce command. "I'll hold them off!"

"No!" I protested, horrified at the thought of leaving him behind. "I'm not leaving you!"

"Do you want to live?" he shot back, determination etched into his features. "Because if you stay here, you won't have that option! Now, move!"

His words hung in the air, heavy and urgent. I hesitated, torn between loyalty and survival, but the rapid footfalls and shouts from outside left me no choice. "Fine," I hissed, biting back tears. "But you better follow me!"

I sprinted down the hallway, adrenaline fueling my every step. The air was cooler here, the faint scent of mildew and decay a stark contrast to the raging chaos outside. The hallway twisted, leading me to a small back door that opened into a moonlit grove.

Bursting through, I paused to catch my breath, the cool night air refreshing yet tainted with the lingering fear of what lay behind me. I glanced back at the cabin, its silhouette framed against the night sky, and the sounds of struggle resonated like a heartbeat. Reed was still inside, fighting against the odds, and the thought filled me with dread.

Suddenly, a voice pierced the darkness, slicing through my thoughts like a knife. "There you are!"

I turned, my heart dropping as I faced a figure emerging from the shadows. It was a woman, her presence commanding and fierce, with eyes that shimmered like starlight, filled with a dark intensity that sent a shiver down my spine. "You shouldn't have run. It makes this so much more difficult."

"Who are you?" I demanded, trying to summon courage as fear threatened to claw its way back in.

"Someone who has been waiting for you," she said, her lips curling into a sly smile that revealed nothing of her intentions. "You've unwittingly entered a game far bigger than yourself. And now, it's time for you to play your part."

Before I could respond, a loud crash resonated from the cabin, followed by Reed's voice, strained yet defiant. "Get away from her!"

The woman's smile widened, a glint of amusement dancing in her gaze. "Ah, your brave knight returns. But I'm afraid the game has already begun."

And with that, the world spun on its axis, my heart plunging as I realized we were trapped in a web of power and deception far more intricate than I had ever imagined.

Chapter 14: Embered Hearts

The rain pounds the earth with a relentless rhythm, each drop splattering against the windshield as if the sky itself were trying to drown out the memories swirling in my mind. Reed walks beside me, his expression a storm of its own, dark and brooding. The air is thick with the scent of wet earth and pine, a heady combination that feels both familiar and foreign, reminding me of summer evenings spent chasing fireflies. Yet now, as we traverse the rugged trail leading to the heart of the mountain, the landscape seems to echo our unease. Shadows stretch long and distorted under the encroaching night, making the world around us feel more alive than ever, and somehow more treacherous.

"Do you think it'll ever stop?" I ask, my voice barely audible over the roar of the rain.

Reed glances at me, his brow furrowed, then looks back to the path ahead. "Not tonight," he replies, his tone low and gravelly, like stones tumbling through a brook. There's a finality to his words that sends a shiver down my spine. I can't help but wonder if he's not just talking about the weather. A tension hangs between us, thick and unyielding, the remnants of our fractured past bleeding into the present.

As we round a bend in the path, a small cabin emerges through the trees, its rustic charm softened by the heavy veil of rain. Smoke curls from the chimney, promising warmth and refuge. My heart quickens. It's a place that feels suspended in time, a haven far removed from the chaos that has chased us up this mountain.

"Let's go," I say, my voice laced with urgency. Reed nods, and we pick up the pace, splashing through puddles that form along the uneven ground, our footsteps a chorus of determination.

Inside, the cabin is cozy, illuminated by the flickering light of a fireplace that crackles cheerfully, casting dancing shadows on the wooden walls. The scent of cedar and burning logs fills the air, wrapping around us like an old blanket, familiar yet distant. I take a moment to breathe it all in, a pang of nostalgia washing over me. This was the kind of place I had imagined for so long—where stories of adventure could unfold, where hearts could mend, where perhaps, I could find some semblance of peace.

But peace feels elusive tonight. Reed is still standing near the door, dripping and tense, the weight of unspoken words pressing heavily upon us. I shake off the rain and move to stoke the fire, feeding it with dry kindling and watching as the flames leap higher, illuminating the cabin with a warm glow.

"Why are you really here, Reed?" I finally ask, the words slipping out before I can rein them in. He looks up, surprise flickering in his stormy eyes.

"You know why," he replies, his voice steady but low, as if afraid that any louder would shatter the fragile calm.

"I thought I did," I retort, my hands on my hips. "But all I see is a man who is haunted by his past. I want to understand, but you keep pushing me away."

Reed's gaze hardens for a moment, the vulnerability I glimpsed before retreating behind walls that felt like they had been built over lifetimes. He crosses his arms, his muscles tensing, the flickering firelight casting shadows that deepen the lines of his jaw. "Some things are better left unsaid, Ember."

"But this isn't just about you anymore!" I counter, stepping closer, feeling the heat radiate from the fire and from him. "We're in this together now, whether you like it or not."

The air between us crackles, charged with something electric and undeniably real. "Is that so?" he challenges, a glimmer of the old fire in his eyes resurfacing. "And what do you think we're fighting for, exactly?"

I take a breath, my heart pounding in my chest. "For a future, Reed. For a chance at redemption, for both of us. You can't keep running from your past—"

"Maybe I don't want to change," he interrupts, his voice rising, fueled by frustration. "Maybe I'm content to stay in the shadows where I belong."

The truth of his words stings, but something deep inside me refuses to let go. "You don't have to be. You can be more than the choices you've made. We can fight this together," I insist, my voice trembling with the weight of my conviction.

Silence falls, thick and heavy. Reed's gaze softens, and I see the flicker of uncertainty within him. "You don't know what I've done," he whispers, almost pleading. "The lives I've taken—"

"And the lives you could save," I finish for him, feeling the truth of my words resonate in the space between us. The moment stretches, taut with possibility, as he steps closer, drawn to me like a moth to flame.

With a sudden motion, he reaches out, pulling me into his warmth, his lips brushing mine with a gentleness that belies the tempest around us. I can taste the rain on his skin, feel the heat of his breath mingling with the smoky scent of the fire. It's a moment suspended in time, fraught with danger and desire, each heartbeat echoing the uncharted territory we tread together.

In the tangled mess of feelings and secrets, I find a glimmer of hope—a shared breath in the storm, a connection forged not just in conflict but in the promise of something more. In this cabin, with the rain pouring down and the world outside forgotten, I surrender to the pull of a man who, against all odds, has ignited a spark deep within me.

The warmth of the fire wraps around us like a snug quilt, but my heart races with a mix of fear and anticipation. Reed's presence looms large, his silhouette framed by the flickering flames, casting long shadows that dance across the cabin walls. We stand there, suspended in a moment thick with unspoken words, the crackle of the fire punctuating the silence. My mind races with questions, but as I look into his eyes, the weight of our shared secrets hangs between us like a fragile thread.

He pulls back slightly, his breath warm against my cheek, a stark contrast to the chill seeping in through the cabin's wooden walls. "This isn't just a game, Ember," he says, his voice low and steady, but the intensity of his gaze betrays the turmoil inside him. "I'm not the man you think I am."

"Then who are you, Reed?" I challenge, my own voice firm despite the tremor in my heart. "You've painted yourself as a villain, but I refuse to believe that's all there is to you. We all have shadows."

He sighs, a sound that seems to echo the weight of his past. "Some shadows are darker than others. You wouldn't want to be anywhere near me if you knew the truth."

"And yet here we are, trapped in this cabin together," I shoot back, a hint of mischief creeping into my tone. "You might as well let it all out. Who knows? I might still like you after the big reveal."

His lips twitch, and for a fleeting second, I see a glimpse of the man I used to admire—the charming rogue with a quick wit and an infectious laugh. "That's a bold claim," he retorts, his brow arched in mock skepticism. "What if I told you I'm actually a villain with a penchant for world domination?"

I can't help but laugh, the tension easing just a fraction. "World domination? So cliché. I was expecting something a bit more original."

His smile falters, and the levity between us shifts back into the heaviness of reality. "I've done terrible things, Ember. People have died because of me. That's not exactly a résumé you want to brag about."

The fire crackles again, filling the silence that follows. I feel the warmth of the flames but also the cool shadow of his words. "We all have our demons," I reply softly, the sincerity in my voice surprising even me. "What matters is how we face them."

He runs a hand through his wet hair, the motion revealing the tension coiled in his shoulders. "And what if I don't know how to face mine?" he admits, vulnerability spilling out in the confession. "What if I'm too far gone?"

I step closer, feeling the heat radiating from him. "You're not too far gone," I insist, the firelight illuminating the determination in my eyes. "You're standing here, aren't you? You've chosen to come this far. That means something."

Our gazes lock, a storm brewing within the depths of his eyes. He opens his mouth as if to protest, but the words fade into silence as he studies me. It feels like we're caught in a battle neither of us knows how to win. I can sense the weight of his past pressing down on him, and yet, there's a flicker of hope, a spark that ignites within me.

Before I can think better of it, I reach out, placing my hand over his heart. "Tell me, Reed. If you could change anything, what would it be?"

He hesitates, the shadows of his past flickering behind his eyes like ghosts. "I wish I could take back the choices I made. The people I hurt. But those wishes are as empty as the promises I made to myself long ago." His voice drops to a whisper, almost breaking. "I'm afraid that no matter how hard I try, I'll only end up hurting you, too."

I squeeze his hand, feeling the pulse of life beneath my fingers, a steady reminder that he's here, with me, in this moment. "You have to give yourself a chance, Reed. Don't close the door before you've even stepped inside."

His breath hitches, and I can see the internal struggle playing out across his features. "It's not that simple," he murmurs, the fight draining from his voice. "You don't know what it's like to carry the weight of those choices."

"No, I don't," I agree, my heart aching for the burden he bears. "But I do know what it's like to feel trapped by fear and regret. And I'm standing here, ready to face whatever comes next, if you'll let me."

The tension shifts again, an undercurrent of possibility threading through our shared silence. He looks down at our joined hands, then back to me, and in that moment, I see a flicker of something—a realization, perhaps, or a dawning acceptance.

"Maybe I've been running for too long," he concedes, a softness in his tone that makes my heart leap. "But the last thing I want is to drag you into my darkness."

"Then let's face it together," I reply, my voice steady, fueled by an unexpected resolve. "I'm not afraid of the dark, Reed. I've danced with it more times than I care to remember."

He studies me, and the tension between us morphs into something warmer, softer. "You really are something else, Ember," he says, his voice a mix of admiration and incredulity.

"Flattery won't get you anywhere," I tease, a playful smile breaking through the seriousness of the moment. "But keep going. It's nice to hear."

The corners of his mouth lift slightly, and for the first time in what feels like ages, I see the flicker of a genuine smile, a glimmer of the man I once knew. The atmosphere between us shifts, lightening just a fraction, and in that flickering firelight, I realize that whatever comes next, we'll face it together.

And as the storm rages outside, I can't help but feel that perhaps we are both on the brink of something new, something raw and beautiful, where the past doesn't have to define us, but can instead lead us into the light.

The fire crackles softly in the background, a comforting lullaby against the backdrop of the raging storm outside. We stand close, the space between us filled with the unspoken promise of second chances. Reed's gaze is steady, searching my face as if trying to decipher the complex code of emotions that flickers behind my eyes. I can feel the warmth of his body against mine, an anchor in this tumultuous sea of uncertainty.

"You're brave, you know that?" he says, his voice breaking the silence, pulling me from my thoughts. "It's easier to turn away from the darkness than to face it head-on."

"Bravery is just fear in a pretty disguise," I retort with a wry smile, trying to lighten the weight of our conversation. "If I've learned anything, it's that the monsters under the bed are rarely scarier than the ones in our heads."

He chuckles, a sound that feels like sunlight breaking through the clouds. "You should charge admission for that wisdom. It's profound."

I lean against the rough-hewn mantle, enjoying the banter, the way it pulls us closer. "I'd offer a discount for you, but only if you promise to stop brooding like a tragic hero."

Reed's lips curl into a genuine smile, and the tension that had coiled around us loosens just a bit. "I'll try, but no promises. Brooding is an art form for some of us."

We lapse into a comfortable silence, the only sounds the crackle of the fire and the rhythmic drumming of rain against the roof. As the flames dance, casting a warm glow over the cabin, I can't shake the feeling that we're at a crossroads. Outside, the storm rages on, but in here, it feels as if we've created a sanctuary, a pocket of safety amidst chaos.

"Tell me about the key," I finally say, breaking the silence that has grown thick between us. "The one that's supposed to unlock the charm's full power."

Reed shifts, the easy atmosphere evaporating as quickly as it had come. "It's not just a key. It's more like a... catalyst," he replies, his tone now serious. "It's a piece of an ancient puzzle, one that has been guarded for centuries."

"Sounds ominous," I say lightly, hoping to keep the conversation from sinking into darkness again. "What happens if we find it? Do we get our very own magical wish?"

"If only it were that simple." He runs a hand through his hair, his expression clouding. "The key is rumored to be hidden in a place where light and darkness collide—a balance of power that has been sought after by those who wish to exploit it."

"Great," I mutter. "So we're not just dealing with a treasure hunt but a potential magical war zone."

"Exactly." Reed's eyes narrow, reflecting the flames like flickering torches. "And it's not just me who's interested in finding it. There are others—much darker forces at play. They'll stop at nothing to get it."

The weight of his words sinks in, and I can't help but shiver. "So we're not just looking for an ancient artifact. We're also racing against time and some unsavory characters?"

"Precisely," he confirms, his voice steady but low, like a warning bell tolling in the night. "And if we're not careful, we could end up caught in a web that neither of us can escape."

"Perfect," I say with a touch of sarcasm, trying to keep my spirits up despite the rising tension. "So what's our next move? Do we put on our adventure hats and venture into the unknown?"

He smirks, the ghost of a grin crossing his face. "If you keep making jokes, I might just start believing we have a chance."

"Good, because I'm not going to stop until we both believe it," I reply, heart racing at the prospect of what lies ahead. "What if we make a pact? Whatever comes our way, we face it together."

Reed's expression shifts, and I can see the weight of his past still clinging to him. "You have no idea what you're asking for," he warns, but there's a flicker of something in his eyes—an ember of hope, perhaps.

"Maybe I do," I challenge, stepping closer, emboldened by the fire that surrounds us and the one igniting between us. "Maybe I've been looking for something worth fighting for."

His gaze locks onto mine, and I feel the air shift, charged with possibility. "Then we'll find the key together. But know this—if it comes down to you or me, I won't hesitate."

"I wouldn't expect anything less," I say, feeling the gravity of his promise settle over us. "We all have something to lose."

But just as the tension reaches its peak, a sudden crash shakes the cabin, the sound of thunder erupting outside. The windows rattle violently, and the light dims momentarily, as if the storm itself has become an unwelcome guest in our refuge. My heart races as I glance toward the door, the sense of foreboding settling like a stone in my stomach.

"Did you hear that?" I ask, my voice barely above a whisper. Reed's demeanor shifts instantly, the playful banter evaporating as the reality of our situation returns.

"It's just the storm," he says, but I can see the flicker of concern in his eyes.

"It didn't sound like just the storm." I move closer to the door, peering through the glass, my pulse quickening as the rain lashes against the cabin, obscuring my view. But then, through the curtain of rain, a shadow looms—a figure moving through the downpour, heading directly toward us.

Reed steps up beside me, tension radiating from his body as he shifts into a defensive stance. "Stay behind me," he orders, voice low and fierce.

"No way," I retort, adrenaline surging. "I'm not hiding while you do all the heavy lifting."

With a swift motion, he turns to face me, urgency etched on his face. "Ember, this isn't a game! If it's who I think it is, they won't hesitate."

Just as the words leave his mouth, the door rattles violently, and I feel a chill seep into the room. The handle jostles, a rhythmic banging echoing through the cabin. My heart races as I exchange a look with Reed, a mixture of fear and determination flickering in the air between us.

"Get ready," he murmurs, and in that moment, I know that whatever happens next will change everything. As the door bursts open, rain and wind crashing inside like a vengeful spirit unleashed, the figure steps into the threshold, drenched and menacing.

And in that instant, I realize that the storm outside is nothing compared to the tempest that has just entered our lives.

Chapter 15: Bound by Fire

The morning light spills over the horizon, painting the world in hues of gold and soft orange, as if the sun itself is trying to brush away the shadows that loom over us. Each step towards the mountain feels like a march toward destiny, the ground beneath our feet whispering secrets of the ancient gate that stands before us, draped in a shroud of ivy and mystery. I can almost hear it breathe, the wood groaning with age, holding tightly to the legends it has guarded for centuries.

The gate is enormous, towering above us with an imposing grandeur that both thrills and terrifies me. Its surface is etched with symbols that twist and turn like serpents, a language long forgotten, and I can't help but trace the intricate designs with my fingertips, feeling the history seep into my skin. Reed stands beside me, his presence steady and warm, a grounding force in this moment that feels precariously balanced between fear and excitement.

"Do you think it'll really grant us immortality?" Reed's voice cuts through the thick silence, low and filled with a mixture of wonder and skepticism. There's a glimmer of something in his eyes—hope, perhaps, or the beginnings of doubt, and I turn to him, searching for the right words to alleviate his unease.

"Immortality isn't a gift. It's a curse," I reply, my tone more serious than I intended, the weight of the truth heavy in the air between us. "What if we end up losing everything we hold dear instead?"

His brow furrows, and for a moment, I can see the flicker of conflict behind his brave façade. "Then we'll have to make our choices carefully." There's a resolve in his voice that ignites something within me, a spark of courage that drives out my lingering fears. Together, we've faced countless challenges, and it seems only fitting that we tackle this one, too.

Taking a deep breath, I grip the charm around my neck, a small token of magic that has guided me thus far. Its warmth spreads through me, filling the cracks of uncertainty with a steady glow. I can feel the pulse of the chamber beyond the gate, an invitation laced with danger, and I nod to Reed, our silent agreement sealing the bond between us.

As we push against the ancient wood, it creaks in protest, resisting our entry as if it senses the weight of our intentions. The moment we step inside, the air shifts dramatically. It's thick with magic, a tangible force that envelops us like a warm embrace and simultaneously pricks at my skin, sending shivers down my spine. The light dims, replaced by a soft, flickering glow emanating from a pool of fire in the center of the room, its flames dancing like ethereal spirits, alive and hungry for attention.

"Welcome," a voice whispers, smooth as silk yet laced with an underlying fierceness that makes the hairs on my arms stand on end. I squint into the flickering light, trying to make out the source of the sound. The fire shifts, revealing a figure cloaked in smoke and flame, an embodiment of the very essence of the Phoenix itself.

"You seek the power of immortality," it states, each word punctuated with an echo that resonates deep within my bones. "But every gift comes at a price. What will you sacrifice for eternity?"

A shiver runs through me at the mention of sacrifice, and I glance at Reed, his expression a mix of awe and fear. "We're not here just for that," I say, my voice steadier than I feel. "We need the truth, the knowledge of the Phoenix to stop what's coming."

The entity seems to consider my words, the flames swirling in an intricate dance, revealing hints of shadows that whisper of battles long fought and lost. "Truth is a double-edged sword. It can illuminate your path or lead you into darkness."

"Then show us," Reed interjects, stepping forward with a conviction that surprises me. "We're ready to face whatever it is." His bravery washes over me, a wave of strength that propels me to join him. Together, we stand united against the uncertainty that looms like a storm cloud above us.

The Phoenix figure tilts its head, a gesture that feels almost amused. "Bravery and naivety are often two sides of the same coin. To wield the truth, you must first confront your deepest fears."

I swallow hard, the weight of those words wrapping around my throat like a vice. My deepest fears? I had buried them beneath layers of hope and determination, but now they rise like specters, clawing at the edges of my mind. I can't ignore them any longer, and the thought sends a rush of adrenaline coursing through me.

"Show us," I say again, my voice rising above the crackling flames, tinged with defiance. "We'll face them together."

A slow smile unfurls on the Phoenix's face, and the flames flare brighter, illuminating the chamber with a fierce glow. "So be it," it intones, and the world around us begins to shift. The fire swirls, and suddenly, I'm standing in a scene from my past—a memory I had long since buried.

The air is heavy with the scent of rain-soaked earth, and I can see my younger self, a girl filled with hope and dreams, standing at the edge of a vast, empty field. Laughter echoes in the distance, the sounds of friends playing, carefree and unburdened. But as I take a step closer, the laughter fades, replaced by the haunting whispers of loss and regret.

"No..." I whisper, the realization washing over me like ice water. "Not this." I can feel Reed's presence beside me, a reminder that I am not alone, and yet the sight of my past stretches before me like a vast chasm, dark and uninviting.

"You must confront it," the Phoenix's voice murmurs, echoing from the flames, urging me to look deeper. "What do you fear most? What have you left behind?"

The words strike me hard, and I close my eyes, letting the memory wash over me. I see faces, familiar and beloved, but marred by the shadows of what could have been. The truth is painful, a raw ache that claws at my heart. But beneath that pain is a flicker of light, a warmth that calls to me. I can almost hear the voices again, soft and reassuring, reminding me that I am more than my past. I am forged from it, strengthened by it.

Reed's hand finds mine, a simple gesture that ignites a flame of hope within me. "We can do this," he whispers, his words wrapping around my heart like a shield. "Together."

With that, I take a deep breath, the air tinged with the promise of new beginnings, and step forward into the abyss of my fears, ready to confront the darkness and embrace the truth that awaits.

The sensation of stepping through the gate is like plunging into water—surprising and exhilarating, the world morphing around us. We emerge into the heart of the chamber, where the flickering firelight dances against the stone walls, creating shadows that twist and morph into shapes that flicker at the edge of my vision. The air hums with the energy of ages, and I feel it tugging at the strands of magic woven into my very being. Reed stands beside me, his expression shifting from awe to determination as the fiery figure before us pulsates with life.

"Do you always show up in flames?" I quip, trying to lighten the weight of the moment. My voice echoes slightly, swallowed by the vastness of the chamber. The Phoenix figure leans closer, its flames crackling with interest, as if appreciating my attempt at humor.

"Only when I'm feeling particularly fiery," it replies, the words rolling off its tongue like molten honey. I can't help but grin at the wry twist of its response. Reed chuckles softly, a sound that eases some of the tension coiling within me.

The flames shift, casting a vivid orange glow that washes over our faces. "You've come seeking the truth, but be warned, the path is riddled with trials. Each trial will peel back layers of your soul, revealing the very core of who you are." The Phoenix's tone deepens, resonating with an intensity that reverberates through the chamber.

"Great, just what I wanted—a therapy session with a fireball," I mutter under my breath, feeling Reed's elbow nudge me gently in mock admonishment. But beneath my jest lies a quiver of dread. What truths would I face, and what would I sacrifice?

With a flick of its fiery wrist, the Phoenix conjures a swirling vortex of flames, and in the heart of that chaos, visions begin to emerge. My childhood home materializes, familiar yet faded, the edges blurred like a dream I had almost forgotten. I can hear laughter ringing through the air, bright and untainted by the weight of time, the sound of my mother calling me for dinner. I see myself as a small girl, wild-haired and barefoot, dancing in the garden, unaware of the darkness looming in the distance.

"This is where it begins," the Phoenix says, its voice echoing softly, urging me to step closer. The garden is lush and overgrown, a riot of colors that seem to pulse with life. But as I approach, the beauty fades, revealing the sharp thorns of neglect and sorrow that have grown unchecked. I reach out to touch a flower, its petals soft and inviting, yet I recoil as the thorns prick my fingers, a painful reminder of all that was lost.

"Your fear of abandonment runs deeper than you realize," the Phoenix continues, its voice now imbued with a somber gravity. "You were left behind, and the scars still ache."

A lump rises in my throat as memories flood back, ones I thought I had locked away. "It wasn't just abandonment," I whisper, my voice barely a breath. "It was betrayal." The pain of my childhood echoes through me, filling the space around us with an uncomfortable tension. I remember the day my parents packed their bags, leaving me behind to chase after dreams that had no place for me.

Reed steps closer, and I can feel his warmth wrapping around me like a protective cloak. "You're stronger than this," he murmurs, his eyes fixed on the scene playing out before us. "You survived it."

The garden begins to shift, the colors fading into shades of gray as the memory morphs into another—this one cloaked in shadows. I stand outside a high school gym, the sounds of laughter and celebration ringing in the air, but inside, I feel isolated, a ghost among the living. I can see the faces of my classmates, their smiles bright and carefree, but all I feel is the sharp sting of loneliness.

"Why couldn't I just fit in?" I ask aloud, a sense of desperation creeping into my voice. "Why did it always feel like I was on the outside looking in?"

The Phoenix swirls, and the laughter transforms into whispers, sharp and cruel, cutting through the air like shards of glass. "Because you dared to be different. You carried the weight of the world while they reveled in their ignorance."

"But I wanted to belong," I admit, my heart racing as the memories swirl around me like autumn leaves caught in a tempest. "I tried so hard."

"Fitting in comes with a price, my dear," the Phoenix replies, its tone a mix of sympathy and strength. "Sometimes, those who dare to be themselves must walk a lonely path."

Reed's presence beside me is a balm against the rising tide of emotion. "But you didn't let it break you," he says, his voice steady and unwavering. "You forged your own path, even when it was hard."

The shadows waver, and the vision shifts again, bringing me to a moment I thought I had forgotten. I stand before a mirror, a young woman staring back at me with uncertain eyes, her reflection clouded by doubt. The world outside the glass is vibrant, bustling with life, yet here I am, trapped in a moment of despair. "What's wrong with me?" I ask the reflection, the words heavy with longing and fear.

"Everything," the reflection whispers back, a voice filled with venom and self-loathing. "You're not enough. You'll never be enough."

But this time, instead of crumbling beneath the weight of those words, I feel Reed's hand squeeze mine tighter, a lifeline pulling me back from the edge. "You are enough," he states, his voice cutting through the darkness like a beacon. "You've fought battles they can't even fathom. You've risen from the ashes time and time again."

With his words wrapping around me like armor, I face the reflection with newfound resolve. "No more," I say, my voice stronger than before, echoing in the cavernous chamber. "I refuse to let this define me. I choose to embrace every part of who I am."

The Phoenix watches, its flames flickering with a vibrancy that mirrors my awakening. "So, you choose authenticity over acceptance?" it asks, intrigue dancing in its fiery gaze.

"Yes," I declare, the weight of the past lifting from my shoulders. "I choose to be true to myself, no matter what."

With that proclamation, the world around me begins to dissolve, the garden, the gym, the mirror—all fading into a brilliant light that envelops us. The flames of the Phoenix swirl around me, igniting a spark of power that thrums in the air, vibrant and alive.

Reed's presence beside me feels like an anchor in the tempest, a reminder that I am not alone. "What's next?" he asks, his eyes shining with determination.

"Next," I reply, the firelight reflecting the resolve in my heart, "we reclaim our truth and face whatever comes."

The Phoenix nods, approval flickering in its gaze, and the flames spiral higher, beckoning us toward the next trial. Together, we stand on the threshold of transformation, ready to embrace the challenges that await, united in our journey to uncover the secrets that will shape our destiny.

The light flares around us, igniting the chamber in a blaze of color and warmth as the swirling flames of the Phoenix coalesce into a stunning display. The vibrant fire illuminates our surroundings, revealing ancient carvings along the walls—depictions of the Phoenix in all its fiery glory, reborn from its own ashes in a dance of resilience and renewal. The atmosphere crackles with an electric charge, as if the very air is waiting for us to take the next step.

"Are we ready for whatever this is?" I ask Reed, casting a sidelong glance at him. His expression is a blend of excitement and resolve, a reflection of my own thoughts.

"Honestly? No, but since when has that ever stopped us?" His grin is disarming, a flash of confidence that makes my heart race.

With a shared glance of understanding, we step deeper into the chamber, the air thickening around us like a fog infused with energy. As we walk, I feel a tremor beneath my feet—a heartbeat of the mountain itself, urging us onward. The light from the flames dances across our faces, and I can almost hear the whispers of the past echoing in the corners of the room, cautioning us, guiding us, beckoning us closer to the truth that awaits.

The floor shifts beneath us, revealing a new path spiraling downward into darkness. The descent feels both exhilarating and terrifying. My heart pounds in rhythm with the ground, and I can hear the distant echoes of voices, indistinct yet resonant. "What is this place?" I ask, my voice steady despite the underlying current of anxiety.

"An abyss, perhaps," Reed speculates, his brow furrowing slightly. "Or a trial—something that tests us further."

"Isn't that what we came for?" I counter, my own fear dissipating with the rush of adrenaline coursing through my veins. "If we're going to find the Phoenix, we need to see it through."

"Right. Let's go meet our fiery friend," he replies, the wry humor in his voice managing to lift the weight in the air just a little.

We descend cautiously, the light from above fading until only a dim glow from the fire remains, illuminating a vast underground chamber that opens up like a hidden treasure. The space is enormous, its ceiling arching high above, and the walls are studded with glistening stones that reflect the dim light like stars in a night sky. In the center of the chamber lies an obsidian altar, smooth and dark, shimmering ominously.

As we approach, the air grows heavier, filled with an intoxicating blend of anticipation and dread. "This must be it," I breathe, feeling the energy thrumming through the stones beneath my feet. "The heart of the Phoenix."

"Or the heart of darkness," Reed mutters, glancing around as if expecting something to leap from the shadows. "Are you ready for this?"

"Ready as I'll ever be," I reply, trying to project confidence, even as my heart races with uncertainty. Together, we step forward, and the moment our hands touch the altar, a surge of heat courses through us. It's not just warmth; it's a power that races up my arm, sparking a fire in my core that feels as though it could consume me whole.

The flames erupt around us, swirling in a magnificent display that almost feels alive, and the Phoenix appears once more, emerging from the blaze with an intensity that steals my breath. Its eyes, like molten gold, pierce through the darkness, and for a moment, I am rooted to the spot, awash in the fire's glow.

"Welcome, seekers of truth," it intones, its voice a harmonious blend of warmth and authority. "You have faced your fears, and now you stand at the threshold of choice. What do you desire?"

"Knowledge," I answer, finding my voice amidst the swirling heat. "We need to understand how to stop what's coming."

The Phoenix regards us, its flames flickering with intrigue. "Knowledge demands sacrifice. What are you willing to give?"

"Everything," Reed replies, his tone unwavering, his gaze locked on the Phoenix with fierce determination.

"Let's not get hasty," I interject, glancing at Reed. "What if it takes something we can't bear to lose?"

"It's a risk we have to take," he insists, his voice strong but laced with an undercurrent of worry. "We've come too far to turn back now."

The Phoenix tilts its head, the fire illuminating the contours of its majestic form. "Very well. Choose wisely."

Before I can respond, the altar shifts, the dark stone revealing a swirling void—an entrance into the depths of our own desires, fears, and truths. The air grows thick with tension, a palpable sense of impending choice weighing heavily on my shoulders.

"Are you ready?" I ask Reed, my heart racing as I peer into the dark abyss.

"I've never been more ready for anything in my life," he replies, the light of his determination shining through.

We take a collective breath, then step into the void, the sensation of falling enveloping us as we plunge into a whirlwind of emotions and memories. I feel the rush of wind whipping past me, and suddenly, we're thrust into a vibrant tapestry of scenes—moments from my life flashing before my eyes like a film reel on fast-forward.

Each scene reveals a choice made, a path taken, and then, a moment that shatters me. I see my childhood home ablaze, flames licking at the walls, consuming everything in their path. I hear my mother's voice calling out in desperation, a haunting echo that cuts through the chaos, and I can feel the heat radiating toward me. "No!" I scream, reaching out, but the vision fades just as quickly as it appeared.

I am jerked back to the present, panting as the chamber solidifies around us once more. The Phoenix stands before us, its gaze piercing.

"You've seen a glimpse of what you fear. But will that fear bind you, or will it fuel your resolve?"

Reed's expression is one of determination. "We can't let the past control us. We have to move forward."

But before I can agree, the ground trembles violently beneath us, sending ripples through the chamber. The altar shifts again, the void growing wider, threatening to swallow us whole. "What's happening?" I shout, panic surging within me.

"Your choice is upon you!" the Phoenix roars, its flames flaring as the ground shakes. "Embrace the fire, or be consumed by it!"

I grasp Reed's hand, our fingers intertwining as the ground beneath us threatens to split. "What do we do?"

"Together," he shouts above the roar of the chaos, his voice cutting through the confusion. "We stand together!"

With a surge of determination, we take a step forward, ready to confront whatever trials lie ahead. But just as the energy peaks, a shadow darts from the darkness, striking the Phoenix with a force that sends shockwaves through the chamber.

"What was that?" I gasp, my heart racing as I turn to Reed, the ground shifting underfoot.

"I don't know, but we're not alone!" he yells, and the chamber is suddenly filled with ominous laughter, echoing from the depths of the darkness.

In an instant, the room is engulfed in shadow, the fire flickering as if afraid of the encroaching darkness. My heart pounds in my chest, the danger pressing in around us, and I feel the weight of uncertainty settle heavily on my shoulders.

As the laughter grows louder, I realize we've awakened something ancient, something that won't let us leave without a fight. The shadows close in, swirling with malevolence, and I grip Reed's hand tighter, the promise of the fight ahead igniting a flame of determination within me.

"Whatever comes, we face it together," I declare, the words ringing with resolve, just as the darkness lunges forward, swallowing us whole.

Chapter 16: The Phoenix's Flame

The chamber glowed with an ethereal light, an otherworldly shimmer that flickered like a heartbeat, illuminating the intricate carvings on the stone walls—winding vines, celestial bodies, and distant realms all entwined in a tale older than time. Shadows twisted and twirled, painting ghostly images that leaped and danced, making me wonder if the stories hidden within the stones were awakening to life. I felt a pulse in the air, a vibration that thrummed against my skin and quickened my heartbeat, as if the room itself was alive, eager for our presence.

Reed stood beside me, his silhouette sharp against the glow, and I caught the fleeting glimmer of fear in his eyes. It was a rare sight; Reed was usually so steady, so sure of himself. But here, in this ancient sanctum where history and magic entwined like lovers, the weight of our choices hung heavy between us. I clutched the charm in my hand—a simple trinket, yet imbued with the power of countless sacrifices and dreams. The warmth radiating from it sent tendrils of energy spiraling up my arm, filling me with a resolve that mingled with uncertainty. What lay ahead would not just alter the fabric of our lives; it would define who we were.

As I stepped toward the pedestal at the center of the chamber, the glow intensified, wrapping around me like a cloak of promise. I could feel the charm pulsing in my palm, urging me onward. With a deep breath that steadied my quivering resolve, I placed it on the stone surface. The moment it made contact, the air crackled with energy, and the room responded as if awakening from a long slumber. A deep rumble reverberated through the ground, and suddenly, the charm erupted in a flash of blinding light, igniting the space with flames that danced like living beings. They coalesced into the magnificent form of a Phoenix, its wings unfurling in a blaze of color that illuminated the chamber with fiery reds, oranges, and golds.

The Phoenix hovered in the air, surveying us with eyes that shimmered like molten metal, piercing yet tender. It seemed to understand the weight of our decision, the gravity of the choice laid before us. I could feel its essence, a swirling mix of wisdom and power that beckoned me to reach for it. Yet, it was not just power that the Phoenix offered; it held within it the promise of destruction, a duality that made my heart race with fear and excitement.

"Are we really going to do this?" Reed's voice broke the spell, trembling slightly as he stepped closer, uncertainty etched across his face. His gaze flickered between me and the fiery creature, and I could see the struggle within him, a tempest of doubt and hope.

"We have to decide together," I replied, the words emerging steadier than I felt. "This isn't just about power; it's about us—what we stand for, what we're willing to sacrifice. If we harness this, we'll change everything. But we can't lose ourselves in the process."

The Phoenix flapped its wings, sending a wave of warmth over us, as if acknowledging my words. It hovered closer, its fiery feathers brushing against my skin, igniting my senses. The heat was intoxicating, both terrifying and exhilarating. I felt my heart hammering in my chest as I met Reed's gaze, searching for the flicker of trust I so desperately needed.

"I want to protect you, but what if we can't control it?" His voice was a whisper, almost drowned out by the crackling flames. "What if this is too much?"

"We won't know unless we try," I replied, my voice rising above the chaos. "Trust me. We've faced the darkness together before; this is just another shadow we need to illuminate."

The Phoenix tilted its head, its fiery eyes reflecting a thousand possibilities. A soft breeze danced through the chamber, carrying the scent of smoke and something floral, intoxicating and wild. I could see the weight of my words settling over Reed, the conflict etched in his brow slowly beginning to fade.

"You're right," he finally conceded, a spark igniting within him as he stepped closer. "We've come this far; it's not just our lives we're fighting for. We're changing the world."

The fire surged around us, wrapping us in its embrace, as if encouraging our resolve. The Phoenix spread its wings wider, casting an ethereal glow that bathed the room in warmth, filling the space with a vibrant energy. We could choose to harness its power, to wield it as our own, but at what cost? The air crackled with the weight of our decision, a pivotal moment suspended in time, and I felt the urge to reach out toward the Phoenix, to grasp the flame that could either light our path or consume us whole.

"Together?" I asked, my voice steady, a mantra that bound us.

"Together," Reed affirmed, and in that moment, it felt as if the universe held its breath, waiting for us to take that leap of faith. I could feel the threads of fate weaving tighter around us, a tapestry of hope, fear, and love, and I knew that whatever choice we made, it would shape not just our destinies, but the world itself.

The Phoenix gazed at us with an intensity that made me shiver, a creature of myth and fire, waiting for the spark of our intentions. And in that moment of clarity, as the flames licked the air and the scent of ash enveloped us, I understood that our journey was only just beginning. The choice before us was not merely about power; it was about who we would become when faced with the very essence of life itself.

The air around us vibrated with the echoes of our decision, thickening as the Phoenix hovered before us, its fiery form flickering with an intensity that could melt stone. The glow cast long shadows, and I felt as though I stood at the precipice of a cliff, the world beneath swirling with uncertainty. Reed's gaze was locked on the creature, a mix of wonder and trepidation etched across his handsome features. I could see the gears turning in his mind, the way he weighed the implications of our choice. It was a look I'd grown accustomed to over our many escapades, where he balanced the thrill of the unknown against the weight of responsibility.

"What if we choose wrong?" Reed finally asked, his voice low, almost a whisper swallowed by the crackling flames. "What if this…power changes us in ways we can't predict?"

"Or what if it doesn't?" I countered, stepping closer to the pedestal, my heart racing in sync with the warmth radiating from the Phoenix. "What if this is our chance to do something extraordinary? We can't shy away from the possibility just because it terrifies us."

The creature flapped its wings, a surge of warmth cascading over us like a wave, and for a brief moment, I was lost in its beauty—the way its feathers shimmered like molten gold, the way its eyes held the fire of a thousand suns. It was a siren's call, both alluring and dangerous, urging me to reach out, to grasp the power that could elevate us beyond the ordinary. The atmosphere shifted, thickening with anticipation, and I could feel the energy of the chamber wrapping around us, binding our fates tighter than ever.

"Together," I repeated, grounding myself in that promise, the word hanging between us like a lifeline.

Reed took a deep breath, his resolve solidifying as he stepped closer, intertwining his fingers with mine. "Together," he echoed, and the moment felt monumental, charged with an unspoken vow that neither of us would face this alone.

The Phoenix's gaze softened, as if it understood the bond we shared, the trust that had grown through every trial and triumph we had faced. I could feel the mechanism beneath our feet humming, the ancient magic that pulsed through the chamber resonating with our united intention.

Then, in a sudden burst of energy, the Phoenix erupted into a whirlwind of flame and feathers, swirling around us in a dance of light and heat. I gasped as the flames enveloped us, not burning but rather igniting something deep within—an awakening of our innermost desires, fears, and hopes. It was exhilarating, a heady rush that made my skin prickle with anticipation.

As the fire subsided, we stood in a cocoon of shimmering light, and in that space, I felt the boundaries of my being expand. I closed my eyes, allowing the warmth to seep into my bones, to whisper promises of strength and courage. When I opened them again, Reed was gazing at me with an intensity that made my heart flutter. "What do we do now?" he asked, his voice steady yet laced with excitement.

"We choose," I replied, my voice clearer than I expected. I turned back to the pedestal, feeling the charm resonate with my energy, the Phoenix's essence intertwining with mine. "We harness this power, but we do it our way. We won't lose ourselves in the process."

The Phoenix flared its wings, sending another pulse of warmth through the chamber, and I felt a rush of possibilities bloom around us—visions of futures intertwined, of adventures yet to come, of a world that could be shaped by our hands. It was intoxicating, and yet, beneath the thrill lay a whisper of caution, a reminder that the flame was both creator and destroyer.

"Let's make it official," Reed said, a glimmer of mischief lighting his eyes. "I mean, who doesn't want to make a fiery pact with a legendary bird?" He flashed me a grin, and I couldn't help but laugh, the tension of the moment easing slightly.

"Are you suggesting we need to throw a party?" I teased, the warmth in my chest spreading into a full-bodied laugh. "I can just imagine the invitations: 'Join us for an evening of sparks, both literal and metaphorical!'"

"Only if I get to wear the cape," he shot back, mimicking a superhero stance, and I laughed even harder. The laughter broke the weight of the moment, reminding me that no matter the magnitude of our decision, we were still us—two adventurers in a world full of wonders and dangers alike.

ARCANE RISE

As the laughter subsided, a solemnity returned to the chamber. The Phoenix glided closer, its wings brushing against us like a soft caress. It emanated a deep, resonant hum that filled the space, and suddenly, images danced before my eyes—glimpses of futures woven with threads of possibility, battles fought and won, lives transformed. But with every spark of brilliance came shadows, doubts that loomed like dark clouds, whispering the risks we faced.

"What if this goes wrong?" I asked, my voice dropping, the weight of the moment pressing down again. "What if we harness this power and it changes us for the worse?"

"We'll find our way back," Reed replied, his hand tightening around mine. "If there's one thing I've learned, it's that we're stronger together. No matter what happens, we'll face it side by side."

I nodded, feeling a renewed sense of resolve. The Phoenix seemed to sense our hesitation, its fiery feathers flickering in response. It drew back slightly, and as it did, the flames dimmed, revealing a path that glowed faintly beneath our feet, a path leading deeper into the unknown. It was an invitation, a challenge wrapped in the guise of opportunity.

"Shall we?" I said, glancing at Reed, who nodded firmly.

"After you, my fearless leader," he replied, a playful grin breaking the tension. I took a deep breath, feeling the energy of the Phoenix still swirling around us, invigorating and alive, and stepped forward onto the path that would change everything. The air hummed with promise, and as we ventured deeper into the chamber, I felt an electric thrill of excitement. Whatever awaited us, we would meet it with open hearts and unwavering courage, ready to embrace the unknown.

We stepped deeper into the chamber, the air thick with anticipation, and I could feel the energy swirling around us, as if the very walls were alive with possibilities. The faint glow beneath our feet illuminated a winding path leading toward an archway formed by ancient stone, intricately carved with symbols that pulsed softly in time with my heartbeat. Each step we took felt heavier, the weight of the Phoenix's power heavy on our shoulders, yet exhilarating. I glanced sideways at Reed, his eyes sparkling with determination, and the corners of my mouth lifted involuntarily. Whatever awaited us, we would face it together.

"Do you think there's a hidden treasure at the end of this path?" Reed mused, his voice teasingly light, though I could sense the underlying tension. "Or perhaps a grumpy old troll with a fondness for riddles?"

"Considering our luck so far, I'd bet on the troll," I replied, laughter bubbling up. "At least then we could negotiate our way out. I have a decent collection of bad jokes to trade."

Reed chuckled, the sound grounding me amid the overwhelming power crackling in the air. "As long as it's not just a cheesy pickup line about how I fell for you."

"I'd consider it a fair trade if the troll finds it funny," I shot back, the banter providing a momentary distraction from the serious weight of our quest.

We pressed on, the corridor narrowing as the glow intensified, wrapping around us like a warm embrace. The Phoenix's flames had settled into a subtle warmth, a comforting reminder of the choice we'd made, but with each step, I couldn't shake the feeling that the atmosphere was shifting. The walls closed in slightly, and the symbols carved into the stone began to shift and change, like a living puzzle revealing its secrets.

"Uh, are those... moving?" Reed pointed, his voice laced with a mixture of excitement and apprehension. I squinted, watching as the glyphs undulated and twisted, forming shapes that seemed to dance just beyond comprehension.

"They might be," I replied, my heart racing. "It feels like they're responding to us. But why?"

Before Reed could answer, the ground beneath us shuddered, a deep rumble that made the stones tremble. I instinctively grabbed his arm, and we exchanged a look of alarm. The glow shifted from warm amber to a blinding white, and a sudden gust of wind swept through the corridor, sending my hair whipping around my face.

"Okay, this is definitely not a friendly welcome," Reed shouted over the howling wind, pulling me closer as we braced ourselves against the surge.

"Maybe it's the Phoenix testing us!" I shouted back, my voice a mix of exhilaration and dread. "Or—"

The archway loomed closer, and without warning, the wind stopped, leaving us in a suffocating silence. I could feel the heaviness of the air, thick with unspoken words, as if the very fabric of the chamber was holding its breath. The archway pulsed with light, and I took a cautious step forward, my instincts screaming that we had reached a pivotal moment.

As I stepped through the arch, the world shifted again. The chamber expanded into a vast hall, its ceiling lost in shadow, and the walls lined with what looked like thousands of flickering lights—like stars captured within stone. At the center stood a massive altar, intricately detailed, etched with the same symbols we had seen before but now glimmering with a power that set my nerves alight.

"What is this place?" Reed breathed, awe and fear mingling in his voice as he surveyed the scene.

"It feels... sacred," I murmured, stepping closer to the altar, my heart racing as I noticed the shimmering lights were not just random; they formed intricate patterns that danced in response to our presence.

Suddenly, the lights flared brighter, and a figure emerged from the shadows, cloaked in a robe of deep indigo, its face obscured by a hood. My breath caught in my throat as the figure raised a hand, silencing the room with an otherworldly calm that washed over us.

"Seekers of the Phoenix," the figure intoned, their voice echoing around us, resonating with power. "You have come seeking strength and wisdom, yet your hearts are laden with doubt. To wield the Phoenix's flame is a path fraught with peril. Are you prepared to face the consequences of your choice?"

Reed and I exchanged glances, the weight of the figure's words sinking in. This was no ordinary guardian; this was a sentinel of the ancient power we sought. "We are," I declared, my voice steadier than I felt. "We accept whatever comes, together."

The figure lowered their hand, and the lights dimmed slightly, as if gauging our resolve. "Then you must answer a question that will test the very core of your bond. Choose wisely, for the Phoenix will reveal not only your strength but also your vulnerabilities."

"Bring it on," Reed said with a wry smile, his confidence returning, but I could sense the tension creeping back into his posture.

"Very well," the figure replied, their voice smooth as silk. "What is it you value most: the power to change the world or the love that binds you together?"

The question hung in the air, charged with meaning, and I felt the walls of the chamber constrict around us again. My heart raced as the implications unfolded in my mind. This was not just a question about choice; it was a revelation of our deepest selves, of what truly mattered to us.

"I—" I started, my mind racing.

But before I could finish, the lights flared back to life, swirling around us in a frenzy, and the figure vanished in a burst of starlight. The room trembled, and the altar began to glow, a beacon of power drawing me closer, beckoning me to make my choice.

"Wait!" I shouted, panic rising as the energy surged around us, and Reed's expression mirrored my own fear. "What do we do?"

And then, as if the universe was pulling the strings of fate, the chamber trembled violently, and the ground beneath us began to crack, revealing a chasm of darkness.

"Reed!" I screamed, reaching for him as the floor gave way.

He grasped my hand, but the chasm widened, threatening to swallow us whole.

"Hold on!" he shouted, determination etched on his face.

With one last surge of strength, I clung to him, feeling the warmth of the Phoenix's flame flickering in the distance, a promise of what could be—or a warning of what might come.

And then, as we hung in the balance, the walls around us exploded into a whirlwind of light and shadow, the very essence of our choice poised to unleash a force that would forever change our fates.

Chapter 17: Scorched Bonds

The chamber reverberates with the heat of the Phoenix's flames, the brilliant orange and red tongues of fire illuminating the faces of the intruders. Shadows flicker across the stone walls like memories best forgotten, and the air is thick with the smell of sulfur and something sharp, electric. My heart races as Carrick's men pour in, eyes gleaming with ambition and desperation, their swords glinting in the fiery light like stars fallen to earth, ready to wreak havoc.

Reed stands at my side, his silhouette framed by the flames, looking every bit the warrior he is. The space between us crackles with unspoken words and shared glances, our fates intertwined like the threads of a finely woven tapestry. We've weathered storms together, traversed dark corridors of doubt and treachery, yet this moment feels different, charged with an urgency that hums through my veins.

"Are you ready?" I whisper, the heat of the Phoenix at my back, its power coursing through me, igniting my determination.

He nods, but I catch a flicker of hesitation in his eyes as they dart to Carrick, who stands at the edge of the chaos, a dark figure watching the storm unfold with a predator's gaze. Carrick is a ghost of Reed's past, a shadow that looms larger with each passing second. I can feel the pull of that connection, the way loyalty can become a chain, binding someone to a past that threatens to crush them under its weight.

With a fierce roar, the Phoenix rises, casting an iridescent glow across the room, momentarily blinding our enemies. I seize the opportunity, launching myself into the fray with an exhilaration that almost drowns out my fear. My sword slices through the air, meeting steel with a satisfying clang, adrenaline flooding my senses. The first man falls, his surprise at my speed a delicious thrill.

"Nice move!" Reed shouts, his voice cutting through the din like a beacon. We make a formidable pair, and for a heartbeat, it feels as if we can conquer the world together. But the flicker of doubt still lurks in the corners of my mind, and I sense Reed's internal struggle as he grapples with the bonds of allegiance.

Another attacker charges at me, his face a mask of rage and desperation. I sidestep, pivoting on my heel, and the world blurs around me as I counter his attack. The clash of our blades sings a duet of defiance, and I relish the thrill of the fight, even as I know it could be my last. There's something intoxicating about this dance, each movement a testament to our shared survival, but I can't shake the feeling that Reed is still grappling with ghosts that I can't fight for him.

"Focus!" I shout, ducking beneath a wild swing aimed at my head. The sound of clattering metal and the grunts of exertion surround us, creating a chaotic symphony. Yet in the midst of battle, my eyes are drawn to Reed, his form fluid and graceful as he dispatches yet another foe. But there it is again—a fleeting moment of hesitation as his gaze shifts to Carrick, who stands by, arms crossed and a mocking smile playing on his lips.

"Why are you hesitating?" I scream over the clash of steel, frustration clawing at my insides. "We can't afford to lose focus!"

His brow furrows, and I see the struggle etched in his features. "It's complicated," he shouts back, a hint of despair lacing his voice. The way he glances back at Carrick sends a jolt through me, a reminder of the tangled loyalties that threaten to unravel everything we've fought for. I realize, in that moment, that the bond we share is not as unbreakable as I wished.

Just as I prepare to press him further, the ground shakes beneath our feet, a tremor that sends a wave of dust swirling into the air. The Phoenix roars, its flames flickering, casting a golden glow that bathes the room in a surreal light. My instincts scream at me to keep fighting, but the fire dims, and in that brief moment, I see something change in Reed. The flicker of a decision ignites behind his eyes, but it's as if he's trapped in a web of his own making, caught between the flames of our battle and the icy tendrils of his past.

"Reed, fight with me!" I call, desperation lacing my words. The bond we've forged is meant to be a shield against the darkness, a sanctuary where nothing could touch us. Yet here I am, grappling with the reality that loyalty can be as much a weapon as a blessing.

"I'm trying!" he shouts, his voice rising over the chaos, a raw edge of vulnerability cracking through. My heart aches for him; he's a warrior caught in a tempest of memories, and I can't reach him through the din of battle. I can't allow Carrick to take him from me—not now, when we are so close to victory.

In that moment of distraction, another assailant lunges toward me, but I'm ready. My sword meets his with a fierce clang, and the impact resonates through my bones. Yet, even as I fend him off, my mind races, tangled in thoughts of Reed and the fragile ties that bind us. I cannot let fear dictate my actions, nor can I let the past dictate his future.

I turn back to him, my breath coming in quick, fiery bursts. "You have to choose, Reed! Us or him!"

Our eyes lock, and the world falls away, leaving just the two of us suspended in this moment, the flames of the Phoenix flickering behind us like a heartbeat. His expression shifts, something in him igniting—a spark that tells me he understands, even if he doesn't fully know what that choice means yet.

The air thickens with tension, each breath a reminder of the stakes we face. As the clash of steel echoes around us, I catch sight of Carrick, his smile a serpent's hiss in the chaos. He watches with a keen delight, his dark eyes glinting with the anticipation of watching his former ally unravel. "Reed!" I shout, my voice barely cutting through the din. "Don't let him get to you!"

The heat of battle swirls around us, my sword a bright arc of determination as I fend off yet another attacker. I can feel Reed's presence beside me like a steady flame, but his attention keeps drifting back to Carrick, that lingering gaze like a thread pulling at the fabric of our alliance. My heart pounds as I launch myself at the nearest foe, striking him down with a swift, practiced motion. Victory is sweet, but the taste of uncertainty hangs bitter on my tongue.

"Stay with me!" I urge as I evade a swing aimed at my head, the movement graceful yet charged with urgency. I could swear I can feel the very essence of the Phoenix behind me, its energy thrumming through the air, waiting for us to channel it into something greater.

"Don't you think I'd rather be anywhere else?" Reed shoots back, breathless and frustrated, as he dispatches another opponent with a calculated thrust. I can't help but admire his precision, even as my heart sinks at the thought that he might still be torn between the man he once called friend and the path we are forging together.

Carrick's voice rises above the chaos, smooth and taunting. "You think you can save him, don't you? The naïveté is almost charming." There's something in his tone that twists in my gut, a reminder that he's not just a foe; he's a specter of Reed's past, an embodiment of old promises and shattered loyalties.

"Shut up, Carrick!" I shout, my frustration boiling over. "This isn't about you!" My sword clinks against his men's blades as I push forward, the fight igniting a fierce protectiveness in me. I can't afford to lose Reed—not now, not ever.

He steps back, deflecting an attack with a quick flick of his wrist. "I know, I know! I just..." His voice trails off, and I can almost see the wheels turning in his mind, weighing the past against the future. The fight continues to swirl around us, yet we seem to occupy a bubble of uncertainty.

Suddenly, a shout pierces the air, cutting through the clash of swords. One of Carrick's men has snuck behind me, and my instincts kick in just as the man lunges. I turn, my heart pounding in my ears, and with a swift sidestep, I knock him off balance, sending him crashing to the ground. But my moment of triumph is short-lived; I turn back to find Reed entangled in a fierce struggle with another opponent.

"Reed!" I shout, my voice a blend of anger and concern as I push through the chaos to reach him. The fight is a blur, a whirlwind of movement, but my focus is singular. I can see the flash of steel and the grim determination etched on Reed's face as he wrestles with a man who seems to embody all the darkness of their shared history.

"Get out of my head!" Reed snarls, grappling with the man, his muscles taut with effort. The two of them are locked in a deadly embrace, each vying for control, and I can see the toll it's taking on him. I rush to assist, my heart racing with the urgency of the moment.

With a swift kick, I send the assailant sprawling, and in that instant, Reed's eyes meet mine—grateful yet uncertain, the weight of his past still clouding his judgment. "Thanks," he breathes, but I can see the conflict still raging within him.

"Focus on us, Reed! We need each other!" I plead, but even as I say the words, I can feel the weight of their truth. We're more than allies; we're bound by something deeper, something that feels fragile and yet unyielding.

With renewed determination, we push forward, fighting side by side in a rhythm that feels both foreign and intimate. The Phoenix roars in the background, its flames a dance of power that seems to mirror our own struggle. Every clash of swords is a testament to our resolve, a reminder that we have a choice, even in the face of our darkest fears.

As we fend off the remaining foes, I catch sight of Carrick again, his expression shifting from smug satisfaction to something darker, more desperate. "This isn't over!" he bellows, retreating into the shadows, his followers scattering in disarray. But I can feel it—the tides are turning, and as the last of his men falls, a fierce hope ignites within me.

"What now?" Reed asks, panting as we finally take a moment to breathe, our surroundings shifting from chaos to an uneasy silence. The air still buzzes with the remnants of our battle, and I can feel the adrenaline coursing through my veins, but beneath it all lies the weight of our unresolved tension.

"We regroup. We find a way to confront him once and for all." My voice is steady, but inside, I'm a tempest of emotions, torn between my desire to protect him and the knowledge that I can't fight his battles for him. The past looms large, a shadow that threatens to consume us both if we let it.

"Do you really think we can?" Reed's voice is barely a whisper, uncertainty creeping in like a chill wind. I reach out, placing a hand on his arm, grounding him in this moment.

"We have the Phoenix. We have each other. If we face him together, we can break the cycle. You don't have to be tied to him anymore." My words hang in the air, heavy with possibility, and I watch as the flicker of hope begins to kindle in Reed's eyes.

He draws a deep breath, a moment of clarity piercing through the haze of doubt. "You're right. I can't let him dictate my life any longer." The conviction in his voice sends a surge of warmth through me, and in that moment, it feels as if the very air around us shimmers with promise.

We turn toward the remnants of the battle, our path ahead illuminated not just by the flickering flames of the Phoenix, but by the bond we've forged amidst the chaos. The air hums with potential, and though the road ahead is fraught with peril, I know we're no longer bound by the shadows of our past. Together, we can rise, unscathed and resolute, ready to face whatever darkness Carrick tries to unleash.

The echoes of our battle fade into an uneasy silence, the aftermath of our confrontation settling like dust in the air. Reed stands beside me, breathing heavily, his chest rising and falling in a rhythm that matches the pulsing flames of the Phoenix. The remnants of our fight lay strewn around us—defeated foes, scattered weapons, and a lingering tension that feels palpable enough to touch. I can sense Reed's struggle to shake off the weight of his past, the scars of loyalty that cling to him like an unwanted cloak.

"Are you sure you're ready for this?" I ask, my voice low, laced with concern. It feels as if we're standing on the precipice of something vast and unknown, and the gravity of the moment hangs heavily between us.

Reed runs a hand through his hair, the action both familiar and oddly vulnerable. "I've been ready for too long. It's time to stop looking back." His resolve is like a spark in the night, igniting a flicker of hope within me. I take a breath, allowing his determination to seep into my own veins, a shared conviction that fuels our next steps.

"Good," I say, forcing a smile to bridge the gap between our thoughts. "Because I'm not letting Carrick get away with this. Not anymore." As I say it, I can feel the fire of the Phoenix radiating warmth behind me, a reminder that we are not alone in this fight.

We move deeper into the chamber, the walls alive with the flickering shadows of the flames. Each step reverberates with the history of those who have come before us, their spirits lingering like echoes in the stone. There's a tension in the air that prickles my skin, a sense that we are being watched. My instincts scream at me to be wary, to expect the unexpected, and as we venture further, the oppressive silence weighs heavily, as if the very stones are holding their breath.

"What do you think he's planning?" Reed asks, his tone sharp with apprehension. The flicker of doubt I see in his eyes makes my heart ache. I wish I could banish the shadows for him, show him that we can forge a new path, one untainted by the scars of betrayal.

"Carrick thrives on chaos," I reply, scanning the shadows for any sign of movement. "He'll want to regroup, perhaps even come at us from another angle. He'll be planning something."

"Then we need to beat him to it," Reed declares, his voice growing stronger, more assured. I can feel the shift in him, a resolve taking root as he steps closer to me. There's an intensity in his gaze that promises he's with me, ready to face whatever darkness looms ahead.

Suddenly, a low rumble reverberates through the chamber, the ground vibrating beneath our feet. My heart lurches, and I look to Reed, the question unspoken but clear in my eyes. "What was that?"

"Not sure, but it can't be good," he responds, tension coiling in his shoulders. We exchange a glance that speaks volumes—a shared understanding that we are far from finished, that the battle is far from over.

Before I can voice my concerns, the walls seem to shudder as a fissure opens in the stone, a jagged crack that runs like a wound through the very heart of the chamber. Dust and debris tumble from above, and I instinctively reach for Reed, our hands finding each other in a tight grip, grounding us in the chaos.

"Is it supposed to do that?" he jokes, though his voice betrays the tension lurking beneath his bravado.

"Not usually," I mutter, my eyes wide as I scan the opening. The fissure glows with an eerie light, a pulsating energy that seems to draw us in, beckoning us closer. "We should move."

As we retreat, the ground shifts again, and the air crackles with raw energy, almost electric. My instincts scream at me to run, but curiosity pulls me toward the glowing fissure. There's something captivating about it, a promise of secrets waiting to be uncovered.

"Wait, look!" I gasp, pointing to the light spilling from the crack. It swirls and dances, casting shadows that twist and writhe along the walls, almost alive.

"Is it calling to you?" Reed asks, a smirk creeping onto his lips despite the perilous situation. I can't help but smile at his attempt to lighten the mood, but the smile fades as I realize this is more than just a spectacle.

"It feels... familiar," I whisper, stepping closer to the light. It pulls at my core, resonating with the very essence of the Phoenix, a connection that sings within me.

"Maybe it's a trap," Reed warns, his hand tightening around mine. "Carrick could have set this up to lure us in."

"Or it could be our only chance to find the truth," I counter, my heart racing with the thrill of discovery. "If we're going to confront him, we need all the power we can get."

Before Reed can respond, the ground shakes violently, and the fissure widens, spilling forth tendrils of light that weave through the air like ribbons of fire. They spiral around us, teasing and tantalizing, and I gasp as I feel the energy surging through me, awakening something deep within.

"Get back!" Reed yells, pulling me away just as a wave of energy surges forward, threatening to engulf us both. I stumble, but he steadies me, his eyes fierce with determination.

"This is insane!" he exclaims, his voice rising above the chaos. "We need to decide now. Are we going in, or are we running?"

The light flickers, and for a heartbeat, it feels as if the very essence of the Phoenix is urging me forward, whispering promises of strength and knowledge. I can almost hear the echoes of ancient warriors, calling to us from the depths of the light.

But then, from behind us, a sinister laugh breaks through the tension, chilling me to my core. "You think you can escape me that easily?" Carrick's voice slices through the air like a blade, thick with malice.

My heart races as I turn to face him, his figure emerging from the shadows, eyes glinting with a predatory gleam. "I'm afraid you've only just stepped into my web, and now the fun really begins."

Reed's grip on my hand tightens, and I can feel the tension in his body as he squares his shoulders, preparing for the inevitable confrontation. But the fissure behind us pulses with raw energy, and I can't shake the feeling that we are on the cusp of something monumental—an unraveling that could change everything.

"Together," I murmur to Reed, the words a silent vow as we stand united, facing Carrick and the unknown. The energy from the fissure thrums in response, and as the darkness encroaches, I know we have to make a choice that could alter our fates forever.

Just as Carrick lunges forward, a blinding light erupts from the fissure, enveloping us in its radiance, and I can only hope that we are ready for whatever lies beyond.

Chapter 18: Flames of Forgiveness

The air crackled with a palpable tension, thick as the smoke rising from the remnants of what had been. I stood beside Reed, my heart pounding in rhythm with the flickering flames of the Phoenix. The battlefield lay behind us, a chaotic tableau of crumpled bodies and scattered memories. It felt surreal, like stepping out of a fever dream, where the echoes of Carrick's final words ricocheted through my mind, twisting like a vine around my thoughts. "You'll never escape the darkness," he had said, his voice a haunting whisper in the aftermath of chaos.

Reed knelt beside Carrick, whose lifeless form was a stark reminder of the price we had all paid. Sorrow etched deep lines across Reed's handsome face, contrasting sharply with the fiery backdrop of the Phoenix. His fingers trembled slightly as he reached out, brushing against Carrick's shoulder, and for a moment, I saw the boy he once was—a boy who had forged bonds stronger than iron but had also learned that love could cut deeper than any blade.

"Why did it have to be this way?" Reed's voice was a low rasp, weighted by grief. I could see the struggle in his eyes, the battle between the man he had become and the boy he had left behind. I wanted to reach out, to anchor him in this moment, but the air between us felt charged, electric, as if the very essence of our surroundings was urging us to move forward, to release the past.

"It didn't have to be," I murmured, my heart aching with empathy. "But you chose differently, Reed. You chose us." The warmth of his hand around mine was a soothing balm against the uncertainty that still clawed at my insides. I wanted to believe that we could walk away from this, that we could emerge from the shadows that loomed over us.

Reed stood, still holding my hand, his gaze locked on the Phoenix. Its fiery plumage swirled with an otherworldly grace, beckoning us to embrace the power it offered. "We can end this," he said, a newfound determination igniting within him. "We can destroy the charm. We can free ourselves from all of it."

The thought sent a thrill through me, a flicker of hope lighting the way. "Together?" I asked, my voice barely above a whisper.

"Always together." His response was immediate, as if the very fabric of our bond had woven itself tighter in that moment. I felt the weight of our shared history settle around us, heavy but not suffocating.

We stepped toward the Phoenix, the flames licking at our feet, warm and inviting. Each step was a declaration, a promise that we would not shy away from the flames that had once threatened to consume us. As we reached the heart of the fire, the air shimmered with heat, wrapping around us like a second skin. The Phoenix flared brightly, its brilliance illuminating the darkest corners of my heart, revealing the pain and fear I had long hidden away.

With a deep breath, I pulled the charm from beneath my shirt, the smooth surface cool against my skin. It pulsed with a faint energy, a reminder of the power it had bestowed upon us and the darkness it had also unleashed. Reed squeezed my hand tighter, his strength a steady presence beside me.

"On the count of three?" he asked, his voice steady yet laced with an undercurrent of anticipation.

"Let's do it." I nodded, the weight of our decision heavy in the air. "One... two..."

As we both uttered the word "three," I tossed the charm into the flames. Time slowed as it soared through the air, spinning like a falling star, before disappearing into the fiery depths of the Phoenix. The moment it touched the flames, an explosion of light erupted, engulfing us in a dazzling spectacle.

The heat intensified, wrapping around us in a cocoon of warmth that surged through my veins. I felt the charm's power dissipate, swirling away like smoke on the wind. The Phoenix roared, a sound that resonated deep within my soul, as if the very essence of life itself had awakened.

"Is it over?" I gasped, the intensity of the flames making it hard to breathe. My eyes sought Reed's, searching for reassurance, for a sign that we had truly broken free.

He looked back at me, his expression a mixture of relief and disbelief. "I think it is."

But just as the words left his lips, the ground beneath us trembled, and the air crackled with a new energy—one that sent a shiver racing up my spine. The Phoenix's flames flickered, momentarily dimming, and I felt an icy tendril of fear slither through the warmth surrounding us.

"Reed…" My voice quivered as I took a step back, instinctively seeking to distance myself from the brewing storm.

"I know," he replied, his brow furrowing with concern. "Stay close."

The Phoenix surged back to life, its flames flickering wildly as a dark shadow loomed over us. The realization hit me like a bolt of lightning: the darkness we had sought to escape was not just a figment of our past. It was here, alive and hungry, and it would not relinquish its hold without a fight.

Reed pulled me closer, the heat of his body grounding me against the chaos unfolding around us. "We can face this together," he said, his voice steady, unwavering against the rising tide of uncertainty.

With determination burning in our hearts, we braced ourselves for whatever would come next, ready to fight not just for our future, but for the very essence of who we had become. As the darkness approached, I felt a fierce sense of hope ignite within me. Together, we would rise from the ashes, ready to forge a new path in a world that was waiting for us to reclaim our destiny.

The swirling flames cast flickering shadows around us, morphing the landscape into a dance of light and darkness. I could almost hear the whispers of the past in the crackling embers, secrets weaving through the air like strands of smoke. As Reed's grip tightened around my hand, the warmth radiating from him seeped into my skin, igniting a spark of courage that momentarily shielded us from the encroaching shadows. Yet, even amidst the chaos, an unsettling sensation twisted in my gut, the kind that warned of an impending storm.

"Did you feel that?" I asked, my voice a cautious whisper, though every instinct screamed to turn and flee. The heat from the Phoenix felt alive, a beast awakening after a long slumber, its power thrumming in the air around us.

Reed's eyes were sharp, scanning the horizon where the light met the dark. "I did. It's not over yet." His voice was calm, but I could see the tension coiling in the set of his jaw. "We need to be ready."

"Ready for what? A shadow puppet show?" I forced a smile, but the jest felt hollow, overshadowed by the gravity of the moment. "Because I didn't sign up for that."

With a wry grin that flashed like the embers around us, he replied, "Trust me, if it were a puppet show, I'd definitely be the one in charge of the strings."

Laughter bubbled up despite the seriousness of our situation, and in that brief moment, the oppressive weight of dread was lightened. The sound hung in the air, an offering to the fire, a tribute to the hope that still flickered within us. But as the laughter faded, the atmosphere shifted, the air thickening with tension.

A shape emerged from the smoky haze, dark and indistinct at first, before it coalesced into a figure, stepping out of the shadows like a specter from a nightmare. My heart dropped as the silhouette sharpened, revealing the unmistakable features of someone I had once trusted.

"Carrick," I breathed, the name slipping past my lips as though it were a forbidden incantation. His eyes glowed with a malevolent light, and the smile that danced across his lips was anything but warm.

"Did you think you could simply walk away?" His voice was smooth, laced with a mockery that sent a chill racing down my spine. "You've only delayed the inevitable."

Reed stepped forward, a protective barrier between Carrick and me, his posture radiating defiance. "This ends now, Carrick. You can't manipulate us anymore."

Carrick laughed, a sound devoid of warmth, echoing off the stone walls like a jarring symphony. "Manipulate? Oh, darling, you misunderstand. I merely offered you a taste of power. You both had the chance to embrace it, to rise above the mundane. Instead, you choose this pathetic little charade of righteousness."

"Righteousness?" I scoffed, the heat of anger igniting my words. "What you call power is just another chain. We're breaking free, and we won't let you drag us down."

"Brave words from someone who has always played the role of the underdog." He stepped closer, his presence suffocating. "But let's be honest, dear. You are far more like me than you care to admit. You relish the thrill of control, the rush of having power at your fingertips."

I could feel my heart racing, uncertainty battling the bravado that rose to my lips. "I'm nothing like you. I've seen the darkness you embrace, and I refuse to become it."

"Oh, but that's where you're wrong." Carrick's voice dripped with an unsettling confidence. "You see, the darkness doesn't need your permission to exist. It festers, waiting for a moment of weakness. It's a flickering candle in a room full of shadows, and it always finds a way to dance back into the light."

Before I could retort, the ground trembled beneath us, the Phoenix roaring in response to Carrick's words. The flames surged higher, vibrant and defiant, as if in answer to the encroaching darkness. Reed's grip on my hand tightened, his gaze locked onto Carrick with an intensity that set my heart racing.

"Let's show him just how much we've grown," Reed declared, the fierce determination in his voice echoing like a battle cry.

In that moment, I felt a surge of adrenaline coursing through my veins, a visceral reminder of everything we had fought for. "Together, right?" I glanced at Reed, needing the assurance that this wasn't a fight we would face alone.

"Always together," he affirmed, his eyes steady and filled with resolve.

The Phoenix's flames danced around us, creating a protective barrier that pulsed with energy. I took a deep breath, allowing the heat to wash over me, feeling the strength of our bond invigorate my spirit. We were no longer just pawns in a game; we were players, ready to take our stand.

"Your little flames will not save you," Carrick sneered, but there was a flicker of uncertainty in his eyes, a crack in his bravado.

Reed stepped forward, a fierce determination etched on his face. "We're not afraid of you. We've faced the darkness and come out stronger. You may have thought you could control us, but you were wrong."

The Phoenix erupted in a dazzling display of light, igniting the air with a brilliance that momentarily blinded us. I shielded my eyes, and when the glow faded, I found myself standing shoulder to shoulder with Reed, a surge of energy buzzing between us. The darkness that Carrick had once commanded felt less intimidating, a mere shadow against the incandescent light of our newfound strength.

"Let's finish this," I said, my voice steadier than I felt. The moment felt like a leap off the edge of a cliff—terrifying, exhilarating, and filled with the promise of flight.

With a shared nod, we moved as one, weaving through the flames and toward the dark figure that threatened to consume us. Reed and I had forged a bond strong enough to withstand the fiercest storms, and together, we would face whatever lay ahead, ready to embrace the power of the light that flickered within us.

The moment hung in the air, crackling with energy, as Reed and I faced Carrick, the weight of his presence pressing down like a storm cloud on the horizon. The Phoenix's flames surged around us, their warmth a stark contrast to the chill that enveloped Carrick, who stood unfazed by the glow, his shadow stretching menacingly as if seeking to snuff out the light.

"What's the matter, darling?" he taunted, his voice smooth yet cutting. "Afraid the fire won't be enough to keep the darkness at bay? You both seem to forget that power comes at a price. And you've already paid dearly."

"Paid dearly?" I scoffed, drawing strength from Reed's unwavering stance beside me. "You're the one who thinks power is about control and fear. We choose to rise above that."

Reed's eyes blazed with determination as he stepped forward, a barrier between me and the creeping shadows. "We won't let you manipulate us any longer, Carrick. This ends tonight."

With a flick of his wrist, Reed summoned a wave of fiery energy from the Phoenix, sending it cascading toward Carrick. The flames spiraled like living creatures, dancing and swirling, and for a brief moment, I felt invincible. But Carrick simply raised his hand, and a wall of darkness surged to meet the fire, swallowing the flames whole.

"Is that all you have?" Carrick smirked, his confidence oozing with every syllable. "You think your little flames can extinguish the night?"

In that instant, the air thickened, heavy with the weight of his words. My heart raced as I glanced at Reed, who was visibly shaken but determined. "We've come too far to back down now," I whispered, a plea more than a statement.

"Right," he replied, his voice low and fierce, a flame rekindled. "We just need to channel our strength together. You and me. No more hesitations."

"Easy for you to say when you're not the one facing the dark version of your best friend," I quipped, feigning bravado to mask my fear. But the truth was that Carrick's dark magic had always seemed a mirror reflecting the parts of Reed that he tried to hide.

"I think he's only dark because he's scared." Reed's brow furrowed, eyes narrowing as he kept his focus on Carrick. "Fear is a powerful motivator. Look at how he tries to wield it like a weapon."

Carrick laughed, a chilling sound that echoed in the shadows. "Fear? You think this is about fear? No, my dear, it's about strength and control. And you've both been playing a very dangerous game."

Suddenly, the ground trembled beneath our feet, and the air swirled with a tempest of energy. The Phoenix roared, flames licking toward the heavens as if responding to the tension. It was as if the very world was holding its breath, waiting for our next move.

"Together," Reed said, his voice steady, and I felt a rush of hope surge through me. "We can do this."

"Fine," I replied, taking a deep breath to steady my racing heart. "What do we do?"

"We channel everything we've learned, all our emotions, and use it against him." Reed's eyes shone with determination, and I nodded, absorbing his courage.

With our hands still intertwined, we focused on the Phoenix, the heat enveloping us like an embrace. I summoned every ounce of power I had, drawing from the flames and the strength of our bond.

The flames roared louder, intertwining around us, illuminating the darkness that surrounded Carrick.

"Are you ready?" I asked, my voice tinged with urgency.

"Ready as I'll ever be," Reed replied with a small smile that steadied my nerves.

As we concentrated, the fire began to swirl in brilliant shades of gold and orange, a tempest of light and energy that spun toward Carrick. "We are not afraid of you!" we shouted in unison, sending the torrent of flames toward him.

Carrick's face morphed from smug confidence to surprise as the flames surged forward, momentarily illuminating his shadowy form. The fire enveloped him, crackling and hissing, and for a split second, I thought we had done it.

But with a wave of his hand, Carrick transformed, the darkness coiling around him like a shroud, absorbing the flames as if they were nothing. "You've only fueled my power," he hissed, his voice echoing in the recesses of the night. "And now, you will pay the price."

Before I could react, the ground beneath us shattered, and tendrils of darkness shot upward, wrapping around my legs like serpents. I gasped, struggling against the encroaching shadows that sought to pull me down into the abyss. Reed lunged to grab my hand, but the darkness twisted, tearing us apart.

"Reed!" I screamed, reaching for him as the shadows tugged me backward, further away from him.

"I won't let you go!" He fought against the encroaching shadows, desperation etched in his features, but the darkness was relentless.

"Trust the flames!" he shouted, his voice a beacon amid the chaos. "You are stronger than this!"

The shadows tightened around me, squeezing the breath from my lungs, and just when I thought despair would consume me, a surge of warmth flooded through my veins. The Phoenix's flame ignited within me, roaring to life with a force that sent shockwaves through the darkness.

"Together!" I cried, focusing on the bond we shared, the light we had forged through our struggles. With a surge of will, I pulled on that inner fire, letting it blaze against the shadows.

Suddenly, the darkness recoiled, as if stung, and I felt the grip loosen. I glanced back at Reed, his eyes wide with determination, and I knew in that moment we could shatter the chains of fear that bound us.

"Now!" we shouted in unison, and together we unleashed the flames, sending a shockwave of light toward Carrick, igniting the very essence of the darkness he commanded.

But as the flames rushed forward, Carrick's laughter echoed through the air, mingling with the fire, a chilling reminder that this battle was far from over. "You think this is the end? I have just begun!"

The darkness surged back, a tempest of shadows that clawed at the edges of the light, threatening to envelop us once more. I felt the heat of the Phoenix flicker and dim, and my heart raced with the realization that we were on the brink of something monumental—a crossroads where fate would decide our destinies.

As the shadows lunged for us, I braced myself, ready to fight, but a sudden jolt of energy pulsed through the air, and in that moment of uncertainty, a blinding light erupted from the heart of the Phoenix. I squinted against the brightness, and when I opened my eyes, everything had changed.

A figure appeared in the radiant glow, silhouetted against the flames, and as the darkness drew closer, I felt a shiver run down my spine. Was it friend or foe? The light flickered dangerously, and just as I opened my mouth to speak, everything went black.

Chapter 19: Ashes of Rebirth

The air feels different now, charged with a quiet kind of hope that seems to ripple through the very fabric of the world around us. I take a deep breath, letting the crisp morning air fill my lungs, awakening every part of me that has felt dulled by the weight of despair. As the sun rises, casting its golden rays over the jagged peaks, I can't help but marvel at how life blooms anew in the aftermath of devastation. Reed's hand in mine is warm, a solid reassurance against the cool breeze that brushes past us.

"Did you ever think we'd make it out of there?" he asks, a soft smile playing at the corners of his mouth, the tension in his shoulders finally easing. I can see the remnants of the battle etched in his features, the bruises and scrapes telling stories of their own, but they no longer feel like scars; they're badges of honor, reminders of our survival.

"Honestly? I was betting on us being too stubborn to die," I reply with a playful lilt, nudging him gently. There's a lightness to my voice, a bounce that echoes the energy around us. "I mean, we practically defied fate itself, didn't we?"

He laughs, a sound that bubbles up like a spring thawing after a long winter. "True, but there were moments when I thought we might just end up as dust in the wind, or worse, a cautionary tale."

"Cautionary tales are overrated," I counter, my gaze drifting to the horizon, where the sun has now climbed higher, illuminating the landscape with a brilliance that feels almost surreal. "What matters is we're here. Together. After everything."

A comfortable silence envelops us as we walk, the only sounds being the rustle of leaves and the distant call of a bird taking flight. The forest around us feels alive, the trees swaying gently as if in celebration of our victory. I let the warmth of the moment wash over me, a stark contrast to the chill that once gripped my heart.

Then, as if the universe has a penchant for drama, a sharp sound pierces the tranquility—a crack like a branch snapping underfoot, but heavier, more foreboding. Reed and I exchange glances, the comfortable warmth of our earlier banter now replaced with a cautious alertness.

"What was that?" I whisper, instinctively gripping Reed's hand tighter.

"Stay close," he murmurs, his voice low and steady as he scans the surroundings.

I can feel the tension in the air, thick and electric. Every instinct in me screams that something isn't right. The forest that once felt like a sanctuary now looms ominously, shadows stretching unnaturally as if the light is being swallowed whole.

"Should we investigate?" I ask, though the quiver in my voice betrays my hesitation.

Reed considers for a moment, his brow furrowing as he weighs our options. "Let's not rush in blindly," he finally says, and I nod in agreement. "We've already faced enough danger for a lifetime. Let's approach this one step at a time."

As we tread lightly forward, the underbrush crunches beneath our feet, each sound amplifying the anticipation swirling in my chest. The trees part to reveal a clearing, and what I see takes my breath away. At the center lies a small, makeshift camp, but it's the flicker of flames and the unmistakable shapes of figures that send a chill down my spine.

There, gathered around the fire, are silhouettes clad in dark cloaks, their faces obscured by shadows. I recognize the sigils embroidered on their garments, remnants of the very forces we thought we had vanquished.

"Reed," I hiss, my heart racing as the reality sinks in. "It's the Shadow Council. They're back."

His expression hardens, a flicker of resolve igniting in his eyes. "We need to get closer, gather information."

"What if it's a trap?" I protest, the fear clawing at my insides. "We can't just waltz into the lion's den."

Reed squeezes my hand, grounding me amidst the whirlwind of my thoughts. "We won't, but we need to know what they're planning. This might be our chance to finally end them."

Against every instinct telling me to turn and run, I nod. I can't deny the fire of determination burning in my chest, urging me forward. Together, we creep closer, using the natural camouflage of the foliage, hearts pounding in tandem as we inch into the clearing.

As we draw nearer, the murmurs from the cloaked figures become distinct, sharp words slicing through the air like blades. They speak of resurrection and revenge, of gathering strength and plotting against the very fabric of our world. My stomach twists at the mention of ancient rituals, the kind that could twist life and death into a grotesque dance.

"We can't let them summon the Phoenix again," I whisper, a sense of urgency flooding through me. "If they manage that, everything we've fought for will be for nothing."

Reed nods, his expression fierce. "We'll stop them, but we need a plan."

Just as we turn to retreat, the ground beneath us shifts. A low growl emanates from the shadows—a creature, half-formed and glistening with malice, emerges from the underbrush. Its eyes are fiery, glowing with a hatred that makes my blood run cold.

"Looks like we've been discovered," I say, the irony of the situation not lost on me. "Great. Just when I thought today couldn't get any worse."

Reed's grip tightens around my hand as the creature lunges, its teeth bared in a snarl that sends a shiver down my spine. I'm not ready for this, but the flicker of determination ignites in me once more.

"Together," I say, and I can feel the strength of our bond surging through me, propelling us forward into the fray.

With our backs against the wall, it's now or never. This is our moment to rise, to harness the power of the ashes that surround us and become more than we ever thought possible.

The creature lunges, teeth gleaming like sharpened knives in the slanting sunlight, and instinct kicks in as I barely dodge to the side. The adrenaline rush is both exhilarating and terrifying, my heart pounding like a war drum in my chest. Reed is at my side, moving fluidly, his presence a reassuring anchor in the chaos. Together, we form a solid front, a duo forged in the fires of countless battles and bound by something deeper than mere survival.

"Not exactly the reunion I envisioned," I mutter, breathless, as I sidestep the creature's snapping jaws. Its growl reverberates through the clearing, a sound that seems to draw the shadows closer, as if they're alive and watching our every move.

"Maybe we should've brought party favors," Reed quips, darting to my right, his eyes alight with a mix of mischief and determination. "You know, to lighten the mood."

"Perhaps a bottle of wine would've been better than our battle scars," I retort, deflecting the creature's claws with a well-timed kick, my foot colliding with its side. It stumbles, letting out a furious snarl that sends a shiver racing down my spine.

We're no longer just fighting for survival; we're fighting for our future, for the fragile thread of hope woven between us like a tapestry. With every strike, every moment spent battling this twisted creature, I feel that connection growing stronger, fueling my resolve.

"Focus!" Reed shouts, and I snap back into the fray, adrenaline sharpening my senses. The creature shifts, its glowing eyes locking onto me with an intensity that feels almost personal.

"Does it look at you like that, too?" I yell, my voice tinged with mock horror, hoping to distract both Reed and the beast. The corner of his mouth quirks up, and for a brief moment, the tension eases.

"Maybe it has a thing for fierce redheads," he shoots back, and I can't help but laugh, even as I duck and roll to avoid another swipe from the creature. It's a strange comfort, our banter, a reminder of why we've fought so hard to get here.

The creature recovers, lunging again, but this time I'm ready. I sidestep its charge, feeling the rush of air as it narrowly misses me. Reed takes advantage of its momentary distraction, launching himself at it with a grace that leaves me momentarily breathless. He strikes with precision, a series of blows that send the creature reeling.

"Now's your chance!" he calls, and I leap forward, feeling the ground firm beneath my feet. Channeling every ounce of my energy, I focus on the small charm still clutched in my hand—a remnant of our victory over the Phoenix. It glows faintly, pulsing with an energy that resonates with the very core of my being.

I throw the charm at the creature, and it hits with a soft thud, the air shimmering around it as if reality itself is bending. The charm reacts violently, releasing a blinding light that engulfs us all.

"Reed!" I scream, but my voice is swallowed by the brilliance. I shield my eyes as the light pulses, wrapping around the creature like a noose, binding it in place. It writhes and howls, its dark form becoming more insubstantial, more ethereal, until it dissolves into a shower of shimmering particles.

As the light fades, the clearing stands silent and still, a serene calm washing over the chaos that moments before had consumed us. Reed stands beside me, his breath coming in heavy gasps, a wide grin breaking across his face.

"Did we just—?" he begins, but the words die on his lips as he looks around, taking in the clearing's peacefulness.

"I think we did," I say, disbelief mixing with a sense of triumph that threatens to burst from my chest. "We actually did it."

The remnants of the battle linger in the air, a palpable energy that vibrates with the promise of new beginnings. I can feel the weight of the world lifting, the shadows that once loomed over us retreating into the corners of the forest.

As we stand in the aftermath, I can't help but notice the stillness of the camp in the distance. The cloaked figures who had once filled the space now lie dormant, their shadows retreating like the tide.

"Should we check on them?" Reed asks, a flicker of concern crossing his features.

"Maybe they'll wake up with a newfound appreciation for morning sunlight," I suggest, a teasing lilt to my voice. "But in all seriousness, we should keep our guard up. I wouldn't be surprised if they're planning a welcome-back party just for us."

"Or a revenge plot," he adds, the playful tone slipping from his voice.

"Right. Let's not give them any ideas," I agree, a steely resolve hardening my stance. "We need to figure out what they were planning and put a stop to it before they gather strength again."

As we cautiously approach the camp, the air shifts, a sudden chill creeping in that prickles my skin. Shadows seem to cling to the figures huddled around the smoldering fire, flickers of darkness whispering secrets too dangerous to overhear.

"Do you hear that?" Reed murmurs, his eyes narrowing as he focuses on the group.

"It's like they're... chanting," I reply, straining to make out the words, which flutter like leaves in the wind, tantalizingly close yet just out of reach.

"What if they're summoning something?" Reed's voice is grave, the playfulness gone as he steps closer, positioning himself protectively in front of me.

"Then we'd better interrupt their little soirée," I say, a rush of adrenaline surging through me. "Are you ready?"

"Always," he replies, and with a nod, we spring into action.

With swift movements, we charge into the camp, startling the cloaked figures who whirl around, their expressions a mix of shock and fury.

"Surprise!" I shout, my voice ringing with a mix of bravado and disbelief at our own audacity.

The figures recoil, confusion momentarily freezing them in place. Reed and I share a glance, an unspoken agreement sparking between us.

"Let's show them what happens when you mess with the Phoenix's champions," he growls, and I can feel the electric charge of determination surging through him.

With a deep breath, I prepare to unleash the strength we've forged through every trial and tribulation. This is it—the moment we turn the tides, not just for ourselves but for everyone who has suffered at the hands of the darkness.

"Together," I whisper, as we charge forward, ready to face whatever awaits us in this battle against the encroaching shadows.

The cloaked figures are still reeling from our sudden intrusion, their initial shock morphing into fury as they scramble to regain their composure. The air hums with tension, the thick energy of their dark intent lingering like smoke in the aftermath of a fire.

"Who dares to interrupt our gathering?" a voice booms, deep and resonant, emerging from the throng like a serpent slithering through the grass. It belongs to a figure larger than the rest, draped in layers of tattered black fabric that seem to absorb the light around it.

"Just two people with a knack for terrible timing and a taste for adventure," I call out, trying to sound braver than I feel. Reed stands beside me, a reassuring presence as I feel the weight of their collective gaze settle upon us.

"You should have stayed away," the figure sneers, his words dripping with contempt. "You think you can thwart our plans? You are nothing but ashes in the wind."

"Sounds poetic," Reed replies, crossing his arms and leaning casually against a nearby tree. "But if you wanted to impress us with your vocabulary, you might want to rethink your delivery."

The cloaked figures murmur among themselves, their unease evident. I take a moment to scan our surroundings, searching for anything that might give us an advantage. The fire crackles ominously, casting flickering shadows that dance on the forest floor like spirits caught between realms.

"Let's see how clever you are when we unleash the power of the Phoenix!" the leader roars, raising his hands toward the heavens. I feel the air shift, a palpable energy beginning to swirl around him, tendrils of darkness coiling like smoke, forming a vortex that threatens to consume everything in its path.

"Guess we really hit a nerve," I say, my voice low as I lean closer to Reed, adrenaline pumping through my veins. "We can't let him finish whatever ritual he's starting."

"I'm on it," Reed replies, determination flashing in his eyes. "Distract him while I look for a way to break this up."

"Easier said than done," I mutter, but the spark of adrenaline urges me forward.

"Hey! Over here!" I shout, waving my arms theatrically. The leader turns, his eyes narrowing as he focuses on me, the swirling darkness hesitating momentarily.

"Foolish girl!" he snarls, but there's an edge of uncertainty in his voice, a crack in the armor of his bravado. "You'll regret this!"

"Regret? Nah, that's reserved for the people who thought they could take down a Phoenix," I shoot back, my voice gaining confidence as I inch closer, my heart pounding like a drum.

Reed takes advantage of my distraction, moving stealthily behind the leader. I can see him inching closer, his face a mask of concentration. Just as I think we might have a chance, the leader suddenly turns, his dark powers surging forth like a tidal wave.

"Enough of your games!" he bellows, and the darkness erupts around him, shooting outwards in jagged spikes that seem to pierce the very fabric of reality.

I dive to the side, narrowly avoiding a shard that whizzes past me, embedding itself in the tree with a sickening crunch. "You know, this is starting to feel like one of those terrible horror movies," I yell, scrambling to my feet.

"I'd take a slasher flick over this any day!" Reed calls back, ducking and weaving as he dodges another volley of dark energy.

"Let's just make sure we're the ones with the happy ending," I reply, a surge of defiance swelling within me.

"Hold on!" Reed shouts as he lunges for the leader, but the moment he makes contact, the figure twists, and with a flick of his wrist, Reed is thrown backward, crashing into a pile of crates with a dull thud.

"Reed!" I scream, fear gripping me as I rush toward him.

The leader laughs, a cruel, chilling sound that sends shivers racing down my spine. "You think you can defeat me? I have harnessed the power of the Phoenix! Your bravery is nothing more than a dying ember."

In that moment, I can feel the weight of the world pressing down on me, but amidst the fear, a fire ignites within. "You may have the power of darkness," I shout, "but we have something you can never understand—hope, love, and the will to fight for what's right!"

With that declaration, I dig deep into my core, pulling from the remnants of the Phoenix's light still lingering within me. The charm I had thrown earlier flares brightly, igniting with a warmth that spreads through my fingers.

"Let's see how you handle this!" I call out, thrusting my hand forward as the light bursts forth, illuminating the clearing in a radiant glow. The darkness recoils, the shadows retreating in the face of such brilliance, shrieking as they fade away.

The leader falters, his confidence shattered as he shields his eyes from the blinding light. "No! This can't be happening!" he cries, his voice trembling with disbelief.

I press forward, feeling the power surge through me, igniting a fierce determination I never knew I possessed. "You don't get to take away our future! This ends now!"

Suddenly, from behind me, I hear Reed's voice, low but steady. "Together."

With a fierce nod, I channel the light toward him, and as our energies intertwine, a radiant beam shoots forth, engulfing the leader in a torrent of warmth and brilliance. The shadows scream, writhing against the onslaught, but it's clear they're losing ground.

"Hold on!" Reed shouts as the dark figure attempts to fight back, summoning the last remnants of his strength. But the more he struggles, the more the light envelops him, banishing the shadows that have clung to him for so long.

Then, just as victory seems within our grasp, a piercing cry echoes from the forest, a sound unlike anything I've ever heard. It reverberates through the trees, shaking the very ground beneath us.

"What was that?" I gasp, the light faltering as I turn to face the sound, dread pooling in my stomach.

"It can't be—" Reed begins, but before he can finish, the trees themselves seem to twist and warp, and from the depths of the forest, a new figure emerges, cloaked in an aura darker than night, with eyes like burning coals.

"Your battle is far from over," the figure hisses, and with a flick of its wrist, the world around us begins to crumble, the very ground splitting apart like the fabric of reality itself.

I barely have time to react as the ground beneath my feet shifts and breaks, and I reach for Reed, but the chasm widens, separating us in a flash.

"Julia!" he screams, desperation etched across his face as I feel the pull of the darkness dragging me into the abyss.

"Reed, no!" I cry, my voice swallowed by the chaos.

As I'm yanked away, I grasp for the light, for him, for anything solid, but the shadows wrap around me, pulling me deeper into the unknown.

In those last moments, as the world fades into darkness and despair, I hear his voice one last time—a promise, a vow that we will find each other again.

And then, silence.

Chapter 20: Sparks of Freedom

The air is electric with the scent of damp earth and blooming wildflowers, the remnants of the mountain still clinging to us like a second skin. Each step feels like shedding the weight of a past too heavy to bear, a burden shared between us. Reed walks beside me, his presence steady and grounding, a reassuring anchor amidst the uncertainty that stretches out ahead. I can hear the rustle of leaves in the gentle breeze, a soft melody accompanying our descent, whispering secrets that only the mountains understand.

"You know," Reed says, breaking the comfortable silence that has enveloped us, "if we survive this, I might actually have to start believing in miracles."

I chuckle, a sound that feels foreign but welcome. "And what makes you think this is a miracle? We still have to find a way to pay rent, and I don't see any job offers flying our way."

He raises an eyebrow, a playful grin tugging at the corners of his mouth. "Oh, come on. You can't tell me you don't feel it. The world is literally at our feet. You've got to admit it's a little miraculous."

I roll my eyes, but the smile on my face betrays me. "If by miraculous, you mean terrifyingly unpredictable, then yes. Let's add that to the list." We share a moment of laughter, a brief escape from the reality that looms over us like a shadow, heavy and omnipresent.

As we reach the bottom of the mountain, the landscape shifts. The wildflowers give way to the more structured chaos of the city, where streets pulse with life, people rushing past like currents in a river. The juxtaposition is striking. Here, life moves at an alarming pace, contrasting sharply with the tranquil isolation we've just left behind. I'm struck by how different it all feels; once vibrant and full of possibilities, the city now feels like a cage, with bars forged from the memories of what we've escaped.

"Are you ready for this?" Reed asks, his voice low, eyes scanning the crowd as if searching for the ghosts of our pasts lurking among the throngs of people.

"Not even close," I admit, the weight of truth settling heavily on my chest. "But it's not like we have a choice. We keep moving, right?"

He nods, resolute. "Right." We step onto the sidewalk, the pulse of the city thrumming beneath our feet. The cacophony of sounds swirls around us—honking cars, distant laughter, the rhythmic clatter of shoes on pavement, each sound a reminder that life goes on, regardless of the storms that rage within us.

As we navigate the crowded streets, I can't help but notice the subtle changes in Reed. The way he holds himself a little straighter, his jaw set with determination, as if he's pulling strength from the very ground we walk on. I wish I could claim the same confidence, but my mind is a maelstrom of worry and regret, each thought vying for attention. I'm not sure how to silence them, or if I even want to. There's a certain comfort in the chaos, a familiar ache that reminds me of everything we've survived.

We pass by a café, its inviting aroma of freshly brewed coffee wafting through the air. My stomach grumbles, a rebellious reminder that even amidst the turmoil, some needs remain constant. "Coffee?" I suggest, unable to suppress the hopeful lilt in my voice.

"Only if they have pastries," Reed replies, and I can't help but laugh, the sound ringing clear and bright against the backdrop of the bustling street. "I need fuel for whatever comes next."

Inside the café, the atmosphere shifts. The hum of conversation is warm and welcoming, the clinking of cups a soft percussion to our entrance. I glance around, taking in the mismatched furniture and the eclectic décor that feels like a comforting embrace. Reed heads to the counter, his broad shoulders blocking my view as he orders. I take a moment to breathe, to absorb this fleeting sense of normalcy, an oasis amidst the chaos of our lives.

When Reed returns, he's carrying two steaming mugs and a bag that crinkles with promise. "I got you a blueberry scone. Just trust me on this," he says, presenting it to me like a prize.

I raise an eyebrow, feigning skepticism. "What's wrong with the chocolate croissant? You know I'm a chocolate girl at heart."

He shrugs, a mischievous glint in his eye. "You can have your chocolate, but this blueberry scone? It's life-changing. I promise."

With a dramatic sigh, I take the scone, and a small part of me is willing to forgive him for abandoning my beloved croissant. The first bite is a revelation—sweet, tart, and buttery, a reminder that even in the midst of uncertainty, joy can be found in the simplest of pleasures.

"Okay, I'll admit it," I say, savoring another bite. "This is pretty spectacular."

Reed beams, triumphant. "Told you. Now, let's take a moment to plan our next move before we dive headfirst into the madness of our new life."

As we find a corner table, the tension of our reality settles back in like a heavy fog, but the warmth of the café, the sweetness of the scone, and Reed's steady presence offer a brief reprieve. I glance out the window, watching the world move around us, a swirling tapestry of lives intersecting, all oblivious to the battles we've fought.

"I guess we need to figure out where we go from here," I say, my voice softening, uncertainty creeping back in. "It's not like we can just pretend everything's fine."

Reed leans back in his chair, a contemplative look crossing his face. "No, we can't. But we can make a choice about how we face it. Together."

The weight of his words hangs between us, a lifeline thrown in the midst of our turbulent sea. I nod, feeling the warmth of hope flickering to life within me, a small flame against the darkness that lingers at the edges of my heart.

As we settle into a small corner table at the café, the hum of conversation washes over us, enveloping us in a comforting cocoon. The aroma of freshly brewed coffee mingles with the sweet scent of pastries, grounding me in this moment. Reed takes a sip from his mug, his brow furrowing slightly in concentration as he contemplates our next steps. I can see the gears turning in his mind, a hint of the determination that has driven him through every obstacle we've faced.

"What do you think our first move should be?" I ask, my voice laced with curiosity and a hint of apprehension. The truth is, the uncertainty of what lies ahead fills me with a mix of dread and exhilaration. "Should we look for jobs, or maybe a place to stay?"

"Both," he replies without hesitation, leaning forward as if the very act of planning could change our fate. "But we need to prioritize. A place to crash first. If we're going to tackle this city, we need a base camp. A fortress against the chaos."

I laugh at his dramatic flair. "Fortress, huh? You make it sound like we're preparing for battle rather than just finding a roof over our heads."

"Same difference," he says with a wink, raising his mug in mock toast. "Let's just hope our fortress doesn't come with a moat full of alligators."

"Or an overly friendly landlord who thinks 'No pets allowed' means he can keep a dozen ferrets," I counter, taking a sip of my coffee and feeling the warmth spread through me.

With each passing moment, the laughter lightens the air between us, dissolving some of the tension. The café is filled with a colorful array of patrons—students hunched over laptops, couples lost in whispered conversations, and families sharing stories over plates piled high with pancakes. I can't help but feel a pang of nostalgia for the simpler days when my biggest worry was whether I'd have time to grab a coffee before class.

We finish our drinks, and I can feel the shift in the atmosphere. The outside world calls to us with its vibrant pulse, and with it comes a swell of anxiety, a reminder that our newfound freedom is both exhilarating and terrifying. Reed stands first, motioning for me to follow him.

"Let's hit the pavement," he declares, determination etched on his features. "We'll find our new fortress and plot our next course. Adventure awaits!"

"Adventure, or chaos?" I tease, but I can't help the smile that breaks through. There's something undeniably infectious about his enthusiasm, a spark that ignites a flicker of hope within me.

Outside, the city unfolds like a sprawling tapestry of opportunity and uncertainty. Each street is a vein pulsing with life, the sounds and sights merging into a chaotic symphony that feels both thrilling and overwhelming. I pull my coat tighter around me, the cool air nipping at my skin, and I fall into step beside Reed, who strides forward with a confidence that both reassures and surprises me.

As we navigate the bustling sidewalks, Reed spots a "For Rent" sign plastered on a charming brick building. The words jump out at us, an unexpected beacon amid the chaos. "What do you think?" he asks, his eyes lighting up with possibility. "It looks promising."

"It's adorable," I admit, taking in the ivy that crawls up the façade, the way the sun casts a warm glow on the red bricks. "But we need to be practical. What's the rent? And are we ready to jump in?"

Reed shrugs, a playful smirk dancing on his lips. "Why not? What's life without a little risk? Besides, we can always negotiate. Just think of it as a daring adventure!"

I can't help but chuckle at his enthusiasm. "You do realize this isn't a treasure hunt, right? We can't just barter for rent like we're at a flea market."

"Who says? We can give it a shot," he insists, a twinkle of mischief in his eyes. "Worst case, they laugh us out of there. Best case, we find a place that's ours."

"Okay, I'm in," I say, caught up in his enthusiasm. "Let's see if our daring adventurers can convince the landlord to take a chance on two vagabonds."

The door swings open with a creak, and we step inside to find a small, cozy space filled with an eclectic mix of mismatched furniture and a faint scent of cinnamon. An older woman stands behind the counter, her silver hair neatly pinned up, and she looks up from her newspaper with an air of practiced curiosity.

"Welcome! What can I do for you?" she asks, her voice warm and inviting, but her gaze sharp, as if sizing us up.

Reed clears his throat, stepping forward with his trademark charm. "We're interested in the apartment for rent. We might have a few questions."

She raises an eyebrow, intrigued. "Questions, you say? Let's hear them, then."

As we converse, I can't help but admire Reed's ability to weave magic with his words. He paints a picture of us as responsible, motivated tenants, eager to find our place in this bustling city. I chime in occasionally, adding my own anecdotes, and soon the atmosphere shifts from businesslike to almost familial, as if we're old friends rather than strangers looking for a home.

"I like your energy," the woman says, leaning back in her chair, her eyes sparkling with approval. "It's refreshing. Most people just want to know about the rent and the utilities. What about the spirit of the place?"

Reed and I exchange glances, and I can see the gears turning in his mind. "Well, the spirit is everything, isn't it? We want a home that feels like a safe harbor, where we can recharge and plot our next great adventure."

She nods slowly, clearly amused by our banter. "I appreciate that. But let me warn you—this place isn't without its quirks. The plumbing's a bit... unpredictable."

"Unpredictable can be fun!" Reed quips, nudging me playfully. "Adds character, right?"

With each laugh and shared story, I feel a thread of connection weaving between us and the woman, her initial skepticism melting away like ice in the sun. The prospect of finding our new fortress begins to feel tangible, as if it's within reach, waiting for us to take the leap of faith.

As we leave the café, the weight of what lies ahead still looms, but for the first time in a while, the future feels less daunting and more like an open road, lined with possibilities and unexpected delights. I glance at Reed, whose eyes shine with determination and a hint of mischief. In this moment, amidst the swirling chaos of the city, I can almost believe that we have a chance to carve out our own little slice of happiness, together.

The sun hangs low in the sky, casting long shadows that dance along the sidewalk as we venture deeper into the city's vibrant chaos. Reed's laughter lingers in the air, a buoyant reminder that joy can still seep through the cracks of uncertainty. We weave through throngs of pedestrians, each lost in their own stories, a tapestry of lives intersecting briefly, only to drift apart again. I feel the pulse of the city thrum beneath my feet, an electric rhythm that syncs with the beat of my heart.

"Okay, fortress of our dreams," Reed announces, gesturing dramatically toward a narrow street lined with charming brownstones. "This is where we find our next adventure. A slice of heaven in this concrete jungle!"

"Or a pigeon-infested nightmare," I quip, eyeing the droppings dotting the sidewalk. "Let's not get ahead of ourselves."

He feigns offense. "Pigeons are just urban chickens, and they're misunderstood! Besides, think of the ambiance."

"Right. Because nothing screams 'cozy living' like dodging airborne feces," I retort, but the playful banter brings a smile to my face. It's in these lighthearted moments that I can almost forget the weight of our past, the shadows that cling to our thoughts like a stubborn fog.

As we approach a particularly quaint brownstone, my heart quickens. The building stands proud, its dark wood façade gleaming in the soft light, an inviting front stoop adorned with flowering pots that sway gently in the breeze. "This one looks promising," I say, my voice filled with a mixture of hope and apprehension.

"Let's make our move," Reed replies, his eyes twinkling with mischief. He bounds up the steps two at a time, the very embodiment of youthful enthusiasm. I follow, my heart racing as if we're about to embark on an expedition into the unknown.

The door creaks open, revealing a cheerful woman with curly hair and a welcoming smile. "Welcome! You must be the new tenants I've heard whispers about."

"Whispers, huh?" Reed replies, a grin plastered across his face. "We're not that mysterious, I promise."

"Well, I suppose everyone has a little mystery in them," she replies, gesturing for us to enter. "Come in! I'm Angela, the landlord. You're just in time; I was about to brew some coffee. Would you like some?"

"Is that even a question?" Reed shoots back, his excitement palpable. "We'd be fools to turn down coffee."

I chuckle at his eagerness and step inside, immediately struck by the warmth of the space. The walls are painted a soft yellow, and the sunlight spills through large windows, illuminating the cozy living area filled with eclectic furniture. A worn but inviting sofa beckons, and the faint scent of vanilla and cinnamon drifts from the kitchen, wrapping around us like a comforting embrace.

"Make yourselves at home!" Angela calls from the kitchen as she prepares the coffee. "I've just finished decorating for spring, so don't mind the chaos. It's a work in progress."

"I'm already in love," Reed murmurs, surveying the room with wide eyes. "This is perfect."

I nod in agreement, feeling a sense of belonging wash over me. It's a far cry from our past, a sanctuary where the weight of the world feels just a little lighter. We settle onto the sofa, and I can't help but smile at the way Reed's eyes dance around the room, absorbing every detail with childlike wonder.

"Tell me, what's your story?" Angela asks as she pours steaming cups of coffee, her gaze soft and inviting.

I glance at Reed, and he gestures for me to take the lead. "Oh, just the classic tale of two people trying to escape their pasts," I reply, a hint of sarcasm lacing my words. "And possibly pigeons."

Reed snorts, and Angela laughs, her eyes sparkling with intrigue. "Aren't we all running from something? But what matters is where you land."

Her words settle over me like a warm blanket, and for the first time in what feels like forever, I begin to feel like we might actually find our place in this world. As we sip our coffee, we share snippets of our lives, the highlights and the lowlights, weaving a tapestry of experiences that bind us in this fleeting moment.

After what feels like hours of laughter and stories, Angela leans back, her expression shifting to something more serious. "Listen, I want you both to know that this building has a history. Some say it's haunted."

"Great. Just what we need," I joke, but there's a small shiver running down my spine.

Reed shoots me a look. "Haunted? That could add some flair to our adventure."

Angela chuckles softly. "No, really. A lovely young woman lived here years ago, and she vanished without a trace. The neighbors still talk about the strange occurrences—the flickering lights, the music playing late at night. You know how rumors go."

"Music, you say?" Reed raises an eyebrow, clearly intrigued. "Sounds like a party."

"Or a ghost in desperate need of attention," I retort, a nervous laugh escaping my lips. But as Angela shares more stories, I feel a chill creeping into the air, a reminder that our past isn't the only thing we might have to contend with.

As we leave the cozy haven, the afternoon sun dips lower in the sky, casting a golden hue across the city. I glance at Reed, who seems lost in thought. "What do you think?" I ask, breaking the comfortable silence that has settled between us.

"I think we need to explore more places like this," he replies, his voice thoughtful. "But I also think we need to decide quickly. The city waits for no one, and if we're going to make a life here, we need to act fast."

I nod, the weight of his words sinking in. Time is not on our side, but neither is the weight of our past. We step back onto the busy street, and as we walk, a shadow flickers in the corner of my eye. I turn, scanning the crowd behind us, but nothing seems out of place.

"Did you see that?" I ask, my pulse quickening.

"See what?" Reed replies, glancing back.

"Just... something. I don't know." I shake my head, trying to shake off the unease that has settled over me. "Maybe it's just my imagination."

"Or the ghosts," he teases, but there's a hint of concern in his eyes.

We continue walking, but the feeling lingers, a gnawing sensation that something is watching us, lurking just beyond the veil of the ordinary. As we round a corner, I hear a faint melody drift through the air, hauntingly familiar yet just out of reach.

"Is that—?" Reed starts, but I don't have time to answer. The music rises, enveloping us, and suddenly the world feels more intense, more vivid.

And then, just like that, everything changes. The street we were walking on shifts, the buildings around us warping and twisting as if the very fabric of reality is fraying at the edges. I grasp Reed's hand tighter, my heart racing as I look at him, confusion mirrored in his eyes.

"Do you feel that?" I whisper, fear threading through my voice.

Before he can respond, the ground beneath us trembles, a low rumble that seems to resonate deep within my bones. Panic rises in my chest as I realize we're no longer standing on the familiar street but in a place that feels both otherworldly and eerily reminiscent of our past. The shadows deepen, and the music crescendos, enveloping us in a cocoon of sound.

"What's happening?" Reed's voice is taut with concern, and I can see the storm brewing in his eyes.

But just as I open my mouth to respond, everything goes dark, a whirlpool of uncertainty pulling us under, leaving only the echo of the music lingering in the air. The world shifts around us, and with it, our fate hangs in the balance, suspended on the brink of a new and terrifying adventure.

Chapter 21: Whispered Shadows

The night air clung to our skin like a damp cloak, heavy with the scent of rain-soaked asphalt and the distant echo of laughter spilling from the nearby taverns. Each step we took seemed to reverberate in my bones, a rhythmic reminder of the danger that loomed just beyond the flickering streetlights. Reed walked beside me, his silhouette cutting a determined figure against the urban backdrop, but there was an unmistakable tension in his posture—a coiled spring ready to snap. The hustle and bustle of the city felt like an elaborate dance, yet we were two weary performers on the fringes, ever vigilant, ever haunted.

"Are you sure this is the right way?" I asked, my voice low, as if the shadows themselves might overhear our doubts. I trusted Reed, but with the stakes higher than ever, a whisper of uncertainty crept into my mind.

He turned to me, his expression a mixture of resolve and concern. "If there's any hope of finding allies, it's here. The old district is still a hub for those who dare to stand against Carrick. We just have to keep our heads down." His hand brushed against mine for a moment, a fleeting touch that sent warmth coursing through me, a brief reminder of the bond we shared amidst the chaos.

The old district was a labyrinth of narrow streets and crumbling buildings, where the past lingered like a stubborn ghost. Each corner we turned revealed remnants of a city that once thrived, now overgrown with weeds and forgotten dreams. I spotted a faded mural on the wall, vibrant colors struggling to break through layers of grime, a phoenix rising from ashes—a silent testament to resilience. It resonated with me, a flicker of hope against the encroaching darkness.

"Look at that," I murmured, tilting my head towards the artwork. "Maybe we're not as lost as we think."

Reed's gaze softened as he followed my line of sight. "Sometimes, you have to create your own light in a world that's determined to snuff it out." There was a gravity to his words, a promise that flickered in the depths of his dark eyes.

As we pressed on, the sounds of the city began to shift, fading into a low hum that mirrored my racing thoughts. I caught snippets of conversations, laughter, and the distant strum of a guitar. The tension in the air was palpable, charged with the electric pulse of a city that never truly slept. But beneath the surface, I could feel the whispers—an undercurrent of fear threading through the vibrant life, echoing the danger we were trying to escape.

Reed suddenly halted, drawing me close, his breath hot against my ear. "Stay behind me," he whispered, his voice a low growl that sent a shiver down my spine. I strained to see what had caught his attention, but the shadows obscured my view. A figure loomed at the far end of the alley, partially hidden beneath the eaves of a dilapidated storefront.

"Who is it?" I asked, my heart pounding as I instinctively reached for the small blade tucked in my waistband.

"Not sure. Could be one of Carrick's scouts. Let's find out." Reed's tone was calm, but I could sense the storm brewing beneath his exterior. He took a cautious step forward, and I followed, adrenaline sharpening my senses.

The figure shifted, revealing a face half-hidden by the brim of a weathered hat, a flash of recognition hitting me like a bolt of lightning. "Milo?" I exclaimed, the name slipping from my lips before I could stop it.

The figure straightened, eyes narrowing as they fell on us. "What are you doing here?" The voice was gravelly, rough around the edges, but the concern was unmistakable.

"Milo, we need your help," Reed said, stepping closer, the urgency in his voice slicing through the tension.

"Carrick's men are everywhere," Milo replied, glancing around as if the very shadows might betray us. "You should have stayed hidden. It's too dangerous."

"Too late for that," I said, frustration bubbling to the surface. "We can't run forever. We need allies, and you're the only one we could trust."

Milo sighed, running a hand through his unkempt hair, his expression a mix of annoyance and concern. "Fine, but you need to understand something—trust is hard to come by these days. We can meet at the old diner, but we have to move fast."

Before I could respond, Reed had already nodded, determination etched across his features. "Lead the way, Milo."

As we slipped into the shadows, I couldn't shake the feeling that we were teetering on the edge of a precipice, every step drawing us closer to a confrontation we could neither predict nor avoid. The streets seemed to constrict around us, narrowing with each passing moment, as if the city itself were conspiring against us.

In the old diner, the air was thick with the scent of stale coffee and greasy fries, a ghost of warmth lingering in the faded booths. The neon sign flickered erratically outside, casting jagged shadows on the walls, and the worn floorboards creaked beneath our weight, a nostalgic symphony of secrets and stories. I could almost hear the laughter of strangers from another time, echoing in the corners as we took our seats, the weight of the world pressing heavily on my shoulders.

"This better be worth it," Milo said, a glimmer of defiance lighting up his weary eyes. "I've got a bad feeling about this."

"I do too," I admitted, glancing at Reed, whose intense gaze was fixed on the door. "But we have to try."

And in that moment, as the door swung open to reveal a gust of cool night air and a flicker of uncertainty, I realized that we were more than just survivors. We were warriors in a game far larger than ourselves, and as the shadows whispered around us, I knew we were about to step into a storm that would change everything.

The diner buzzed with a low, rhythmic hum, a chorus of murmured conversations and the clinking of silverware against chipped ceramic plates. I could feel the tension pooling between us, thick enough to slice through with a knife, as Reed and Milo exchanged guarded glances. The flickering neon sign cast a kaleidoscope of colors across our faces, painting us in shades of uncertainty and resolve.

"Do you really think they'll come?" I asked, my voice barely above a whisper, as if raising it would summon the ghosts of our past failures.

Milo leaned back in his seat, his brow furrowed. "They might, but it's a gamble. Carrick's men are always watching. Trust is a luxury we can't afford." He reached for his coffee, fingers trembling slightly as he lifted the cup to his lips.

"Trust may be scarce, but it's what we need right now," Reed interjected, his tone firm yet weary. "We can't face this alone."

As if to punctuate his point, the bell above the door jingled, drawing our attention to the entrance. A figure stepped inside, silhouetted against the glow of the streetlights, their features obscured by the shadows of their hoodie. The air shifted, thickening with the weight of impending confrontation.

"Who's that?" I murmured, my instincts on high alert.

"Only one way to find out," Reed said, his voice low and steady.

The figure approached our booth with a confident stride, the kind that commands attention, yet I felt an uneasy flutter in my stomach. They stopped short, tilting their head slightly to reveal a glimpse of a familiar face framed by unruly curls.

"Fancy meeting you here," said a voice that wrapped around my senses like a warm blanket, both reassuring and alarming. It was a mixture of familiarity and danger, like a melody I couldn't quite place but knew by heart.

"Lena?" I breathed, disbelief flooding my senses. I hadn't seen her since everything fell apart, since the day we thought we'd lost each other for good.

"Who else?" she grinned, her eyes sparkling with mischief. "I heard you two were in town, stirring up trouble."

Milo leaned forward, suspicion etched on his face. "You're a long way from home, Lena. What do you want?"

"Easy there, hotshot," she replied, holding up her hands in mock surrender. "I'm here to help. Or at least to keep an eye on you two idiots."

Reed's expression remained guarded as he appraised her. "Help isn't something we can take lightly right now. We need to know you can be trusted."

"Trust is overrated," Lena replied, her tone playful, but the weight of her words settled heavily on my chest. "But if you're looking for someone who can walk between shadows and make enemies disappear, I'm your girl."

"Last I checked, you were on Carrick's radar," I pointed out, folding my arms across my chest. "What's changed?"

Lena's smile faltered for just a moment, a flicker of vulnerability beneath her bravado. "Let's just say the last time I saw Carrick, I made it clear I wasn't going to be his pawn anymore. I've got my own agenda now."

Reed leaned closer, eyes narrowing with interest. "What's your agenda, exactly?"

Lena glanced around, ensuring no one was eavesdropping. "I have information. Carrick's men are more disorganized than you think. There's a fracture in his ranks, and I might be able to exploit that. But I need your help to set it in motion."

My heart raced at the prospect. "What kind of help?"

"Let's just say it requires a little bit of misdirection and a whole lot of guts. You in?"

Reed's jaw tightened as he exchanged glances with me, and I could sense the internal debate raging within him. "This isn't a game, Lena," he warned, the weight of his protectiveness evident.

"Neither is our situation," she shot back, her voice sharp yet earnest. "I'm offering you a chance to turn the tide. Think about it: we can either sit here waiting to be picked off, or we can make a move. I know how Carrick operates. I can get us in."

A charged silence enveloped the booth as we weighed our options, the lingering taste of uncertainty mingling with the bitterness of the coffee. It was a precarious balance—trusting Lena, a friend turned rogue, versus the risks that came with aligning ourselves with someone walking such a thin line.

"We're in," I said suddenly, surprising even myself with my conviction. "But if we're going to do this, we need a solid plan. We can't afford any missteps."

Reed's gaze met mine, and in that moment, I saw a flicker of approval, a silent acknowledgment of my decision. "Fine. But if this goes sideways, I'm holding you responsible, Lena."

Her laughter rang out, light and defiant, as if she thrived on the chaos we were about to unleash. "You have no idea how much I missed you two. This is going to be fun."

"Fun?" I echoed, arching an eyebrow. "Is that what we're calling it now?"

"Oh, come on. You're not a little nervous?" she teased, leaning back in her seat with a casual ease that belied the tension bubbling beneath the surface.

"Terrified," I replied, unable to suppress a smile. "But if we're going to do this, let's do it right."

"Right," Reed agreed, the spark of determination returning to his eyes. "First, we need to gather intel and identify our targets. No half-measures."

Lena leaned forward, her expression shifting from playful to serious. "I've got contacts who can help us. We need to move quickly before Carrick's men can regroup."

And just like that, a plan began to take shape, woven from the threads of uncertainty and desperation. We were three misfits standing on the precipice of something reckless yet exhilarating, and I could feel the energy crackling in the air around us. It was a dangerous game, but for the first time in a long while, I felt alive—caught in the whirlwind of whispered shadows, ready to face whatever storm awaited us.

The diner began to feel like a war room, the clatter of dishes and the low hum of conversation fading into the background as we huddled together, eyes fixed on Lena. She laid out her plan with an infectious energy, her hands gesturing animatedly as she spoke. The weight of our circumstances pressed against my chest, but there was something exhilarating about plotting our next move, like drawing a line in the sand and daring the tide to come in.

"First, we'll need to make contact with the Black Market," Lena explained, her voice steady as she outlined the path ahead. "They know the ins and outs of Carrick's operations. If anyone knows how to get to him, it's them."

Milo scoffed, his skepticism evident. "And you trust these people? They're just as likely to sell us out."

"True, but they're also desperate," Lena shot back, her eyes gleaming with mischief. "And desperate people can be surprisingly useful. Besides, they owe me a favor. It's time to collect."

Reed leaned back in his seat, arms crossed, a storm brewing in his expression. "We can't afford to take unnecessary risks. If this goes wrong, we'll be on Carrick's radar faster than you can say 'betrayal.'"

I placed a reassuring hand on Reed's arm, feeling the tension in his muscles beneath my fingers. "We need to trust Lena, at least for now. She's right; we're out of options."

Lena grinned, the familiar spark in her eyes. "See? A little faith goes a long way. I'll arrange a meeting tonight. It won't be easy, but we'll have a chance to gather intel and potentially turn the tide."

As the plan took shape, I felt a shift within me, a flicker of hope igniting in the depths of uncertainty. There was still danger lurking around every corner, but with every word exchanged, I felt more emboldened, as if we were forging our own destiny instead of running from it.

"Let's move then," Reed said, his voice steady, resolve returning to his demeanor. "We need to get to the meeting before Carrick's men figure out what we're up to."

Lena slid from the booth with a confident flair, and I followed suit, slipping on my jacket and tightening the laces of my worn boots. As we stepped outside into the brisk night air, the city felt alive around us—cars honked, street vendors shouted, and music pulsed from the bars lining the streets. It was a world teetering on the brink of chaos, and we were at its center.

We navigated the winding streets with urgency, the glow of streetlights casting long shadows that danced at our feet. My heart raced, not just from the thrill of what lay ahead but also from the weight of the risks we were taking. Every passing figure was a potential threat, every alley a possible ambush. Yet, I held on to the glimmer of hope that this night might just change everything.

The Black Market was hidden away beneath the city, a place known only to those who danced on the fringes of legality. As we descended the narrow staircase leading to the underground lair, a sense of foreboding settled over me. The air grew thick with the scent of sweat and desperation, a stark contrast to the clean, polished world above.

"Stay close," Reed instructed, his voice a low murmur as we stepped into the flickering dimness. The space was a cacophony of voices and laughter, punctuated by the clinking of glasses and the occasional shout. It felt alive, but also perilously unpredictable.

We wove through the crowd, a sea of faces blending into one another, each hiding their own secrets. I caught snippets of conversations about deals struck and betrayals made, the murmur of ambition thick in the air. The atmosphere buzzed with adrenaline, and I couldn't shake the feeling that we were stepping into a spider's web, with every thread leading to danger.

Finally, we reached a bar at the far end of the room, where a heavyset man with a bushy beard and an eye patch presided over a collection of mismatched bottles. He looked like someone who had seen it all and then some, and his gaze was as sharp as the knives gleaming on the wall behind him.

"Rico," Lena called out, flashing a smile that felt more like a mask than genuine warmth. "Long time, no see."

"Lena," he replied, his tone neutral but his eyes narrowed. "What brings you to my humble abode?"

"I need a favor," she said, leaning closer, her voice low and conspiratorial. "We're looking for intel on Carrick's operation."

Rico's brow arched, the tension in the air thickening. "You know that information comes at a price. What do you have to offer?"

Before Lena could respond, a commotion erupted on the other side of the bar. A scuffle broke out, two men grappling over a stack of cash that glimmered like a beacon in the dim light. The ruckus sent a ripple through the crowd, and I instinctively stepped closer to Reed, feeling the surge of adrenaline heighten my senses.

"This is not what we need," Reed muttered, scanning the room for any signs of trouble.

"Hold on," Lena urged, her eyes glued to the unfolding chaos. "Let's see how this plays out."

The fight escalated, shouts echoing as others jumped in, fueled by the thrill of conflict. In the midst of the fray, a figure caught my eye—tall, imposing, and all too familiar. My stomach dropped as I recognized him, a man I'd hoped to avoid at all costs. Carrick's right-hand man, Hunter, prowled through the crowd with a predatory grace, his gaze sweeping over the chaos with interest.

"Damn it," I whispered, panic surging within me. "He's here."

Reed stiffened beside me, his jaw clenching as he scanned the room. "We need to move. Now."

Just as we turned to slip away, a cold voice sliced through the din. "Where do you think you're going?"

I froze, heart pounding in my chest. Hunter's icy stare locked onto us, and in that moment, I realized we were trapped—caught in the web of whispered shadows, with no clear way out. The laughter and shouts faded into a low hum as dread washed over me, and I could feel the walls closing in, the reality of our choices crashing down like a relentless tide.

Chapter 22: Bonds Tested by Flame

The air in the bunker was thick with a mix of damp earth and the metallic scent of old machinery, the kind that lingered in the back of the throat and sparked an unsettling feeling in the pit of my stomach. As I stepped further inside, the low, flickering light cast shadows on the stone walls, twisting their forms into eerie shapes that seemed to dance in time with the unease swirling around us. I could feel the weight of the fighters' gazes on my back, their mistrust palpable as I walked beside Reed, his presence both a comfort and a source of simmering tension.

"Just keep your mouth shut, okay?" he whispered, the faintest edge of urgency in his tone. I turned to him, my brow furrowing.

"I'm not the one they're worried about," I replied, my voice a murmur. The fighters, all weathered by hardship and resolve, had their eyes narrowed in scrutiny. Each wore the marks of battles fought—nicks in their skin, scars like stories etched into flesh. It wasn't just their lives at stake; it was their fight, their hopes. And here we were, two outsiders with a history that hung between us like a noose.

"Look," Reed said, his expression softening. "I know this isn't ideal, but we need their trust if we want to figure out how to take down Carrick."

"Trust? Is that what you call it?" I shot back, glancing over my shoulder at the rebel who stood watch like a sentinel. His face was a mask of skepticism, arms crossed tightly against his chest as if he could physically shield his doubts from us. "This isn't about trust for them, Reed. They want answers. They want to know if you're still one of Carrick's loyal lapdogs."

His jaw tightened, and for a fleeting moment, I wondered if he would reveal the truth of his past—those murky shadows that clung to him like ghosts. But we were interrupted by a voice that cut through the tension like a knife.

"Enough of this." A woman stepped forward, her eyes sharp and calculating, the flicker of the light catching the glint of steel in her grip. "If you want our help, you'll need to prove your worth. We can't afford to have anyone in our midst who isn't on our side."

"What do you want me to do?" Reed asked, his tone steady despite the storm brewing around us.

"Tell us about the weapon Carrick has been developing," she demanded, her stance unwavering. "And don't even think of lying. We know you were involved in the early stages."

I watched as Reed's features hardened, his eyes momentarily clouding over with something I couldn't quite decipher. The shadows danced across his face, a tempest of emotion flickering in the depths. "I'm not going to spill secrets like some sniveling traitor," he replied, a note of defiance lacing his words. "I might have worked on his projects, but that doesn't mean I agree with them."

The woman scoffed, her skepticism unfurling into a full-blown glare. "You expect us to believe you've had a change of heart? After everything?"

"People can change!" I interjected, the heat of passion rising in my chest. I stepped forward, meeting the eyes of each fighter, feeling their judgment like a thousand tiny arrows piercing my resolve. "Reed isn't the same man he was before. We've all been caught in this mess. We're here because we want to help. That has to count for something."

A tense silence followed, heavy with doubt and the lingering scent of sweat and earth. The others exchanged glances, the unspoken battle of wills crackling in the air like static electricity. I could feel the resistance melting into something almost tangible, the burden of our shared fears pulling at the seams of our tenuous alliance.

"Fine," the woman relented, her voice colder than the walls that surrounded us. "We'll give you a chance to prove it. But understand this: one wrong move, one slip of loyalty, and you'll find yourself on the wrong side of a gun."

Reed nodded, his expression inscrutable, and I wished I could read the thoughts that twisted within him, like tendrils of smoke rising into the darkness. "I'll share what I know," he said, his voice firm, yet the uncertainty lingered like a specter.

As he began to explain the intricacies of Carrick's weapon, I felt the weight of the moment settle over me. The bunker around us transformed from a shadowy space into a war room, filled with tension and resolve. Every word Reed spoke felt like a bridge spanning a chasm of mistrust, a tentative step toward rebuilding what had frayed between us.

"Do you even understand the consequences of what you're asking?" I challenged, my heart racing as I turned back to the fighters. "You're putting your lives in his hands—he might have a history, but he's here now. Isn't that what matters?"

"History is all we have to judge you by," the woman replied sharply, her expression unwavering. "And we've seen too many who say they want to help, only to betray us when the time comes."

"Then ask your questions," Reed said, his voice steady despite the tension vibrating between us. "I'll answer everything, and if you think I'm lying, then... well, I guess you'll have to make your own choices."

I felt a chill run through me, the gravity of our situation settling heavily. The fire of defiance flickered within me, battling against the tide of doubt swirling around us. We were standing on the edge of something monumental, the choices we made echoing in the depths of our souls. In that moment, as the fighters began to scrutinize Reed with renewed intensity, I realized that we weren't just fighting for survival. We were fighting for our very selves, battling against the flames of our past to forge a new path forward, one that could bind us together in ways we hadn't yet begun to understand.

The rebels leaned in, their bodies a wall of tension, as Reed laid bare the details of Carrick's weapon. I watched his face, the way his brow furrowed as he navigated the memories like a treacherous path, each step a potential misstep. "It's a project called the Scourge," he said, the name slipping from his lips like a secret too dangerous to hold. "Carrick's aiming to create something that can not only control the population but eliminate any dissent with... a flick of a switch."

A low murmur swept through the group, disbelief mingling with outrage. The woman who had first confronted him, Mara, leaned forward, her dark eyes glinting like sharpened blades. "Control? You expect us to believe that you're spilling this because you're suddenly filled with remorse?"

I could see Reed's fists clench at his sides, the fight in him bubbling just beneath the surface. "I'm telling you because you need to know what you're up against. If we're going to bring him down, we have to understand his plans."

Mara scoffed, crossing her arms defiantly. "And why would we trust you? You've been playing both sides for too long."

The tension escalated, thickening the air around us until it felt electric, charged with the potential for conflict. "I'm not playing any sides," Reed snapped, his voice rising slightly. "I was trying to survive. Just like you all."

"Survive?" Mara echoed, her laugh bitter. "You call working for the enemy surviving? You were complicit in all of this!"

"Enough!" I interjected, my voice slicing through the room. The fighters turned to me, surprise etched on their faces. "We're not here to point fingers. We're here because we all want the same thing—freedom from Carrick's reign. If Reed is willing to help, we need to give him that chance."

The silence that followed was pregnant with tension. It was as if I had tossed a stone into a still pond, the ripples spreading wide, forcing everyone to confront the truth hidden beneath the surface. Mara's expression softened slightly, but I could see the remnants of her doubt lingering like a shadow.

Reed took a step toward her, his voice calmer now. "I can prove my loyalty. Just give me a chance to help you—us. You have my knowledge; I can share everything I know about Carrick's operations. Together, we can dismantle his plans piece by piece."

"Dismantle? That's cute," one of the fighters scoffed from the back, a burly man with a scruffy beard that looked like it had weathered many storms. "And what do we do when Carrick sends his army after us? You think some pretty words will save us?"

"No," I said, my heart pounding in my chest as I felt the weight of their skepticism pressing down on me. "But knowledge is power. We can prepare. We can outsmart him."

"Outsmarting Carrick is a death wish," Mara replied flatly, her tone like ice. "He doesn't play games."

"Maybe it's time we stop playing by his rules," Reed shot back, his confidence building. The energy in the room shifted slightly, the tension morphing into something more productive—an alliance born out of shared desperation.

"Let's say we entertain your proposal," Mara said slowly, her gaze piercing through the dim light. "What's your plan?"

Reed glanced at me, and I could see the spark of hope flickering in his eyes, almost as if he was waiting for me to jump in and bolster his claim. "We gather intel on his operations," he explained, drawing the others in with his words. "We need to know the locations of his supply routes, the numbers of his soldiers, anything that can give us an edge."

"And what makes you think you can just waltz back into Carrick's camp?" the bearded fighter asked, skepticism coating his voice.

"Because I know how he thinks," Reed replied, his voice low and steady. "I was in the inner circle. I can get close, and once I'm in, I can gather information, sabotage his efforts from within."

The room buzzed with murmurs, doubt still lingering in the air, but there was an unmistakable shift—the hint of curiosity piqued by the possibility of a plan. I could feel my heart racing as I realized that this was a fragile moment, the balance hanging by a thread.

"And what about you?" Mara turned to me, her gaze sharp as a dagger. "What role do you play in all this?"

"I'm with him," I stated firmly. "If Reed goes in, I go in. I've learned a thing or two about surviving under pressure. I won't be left behind."

"That's your choice," Mara replied, a hint of reluctant respect in her tone. "But understand, once you step into that world, there's no turning back."

As the fighters deliberated, I could sense the bonds of trust beginning to form, fragile and tentative, yet undeniably present. I shared a look with Reed, and in that moment, I knew we were in this together. Whatever awaited us beyond these walls, we would face it as allies, and perhaps something more.

Suddenly, a loud crash echoed from the entrance of the bunker, a deafening interruption that sent everyone into a defensive stance. The heavy door swung open, revealing a silhouette cloaked in shadows, breathless and wild-eyed.

"Carrick's men are coming!" the newcomer shouted, panic threading through the air like a live wire. "We have to move! Now!"

Instinct kicked in as the fighters sprang into action, their movements fluid and practiced. Reed grabbed my arm, pulling me close. "Stay close to me," he urged, urgency lacing his tone. "We can't get separated."

"Right," I replied, adrenaline surging through my veins. The stakes had just been raised, and the reality of our situation struck like a hammer. We were no longer just dealing with mistrust; we were in the thick of a battle that would test our limits, both individually and as a unit.

As the rebels rallied, I caught a glimpse of Reed, determination etched on his features, the weight of the world seemingly resting on his shoulders. We were bound now, not just by choice but by necessity, our fates intertwining like the roots of a great oak, searching for stability in the chaos that threatened to engulf us. And as we prepared to face whatever horrors lay ahead, I couldn't shake the feeling that this moment—this rush of adrenaline and fear—would forever alter the course of our lives.

The moment the heavy door burst open, a rush of chaos flooded the bunker. The newcomer—a wiry man with wild hair and frantic eyes—skidded to a halt, panting as if he'd sprinted miles instead of just a few feet. "They're closing in fast!" he gasped, urgency seeping into his words like a crack in a dam.

I felt the blood drain from my face as panic surged through the room, a wave of disbelief mingling with dread. The rebels began to move with purpose, adrenaline igniting a fire in their movements. "Where's the main exit?" I asked, forcing my voice to remain steady despite the anxiety coiling in my gut.

"Follow me!" the man shouted, darting toward a narrow corridor shrouded in shadow. I exchanged a frantic glance with Reed, who nodded, determination hardening his features. He grasped my hand, and together we plunged into the darkness behind the newcomer, my heart pounding in sync with the pounding of footsteps echoing against the stone walls.

As we sprinted through the winding passage, the air grew thick with dust and the faint scent of dampness, a reminder of how far beneath the earth we were. I could hear voices in the distance—angry shouts and the clanking of weapons—drawing closer. We had little time. "Who are they?" I called out, breathless.

"The militia," the newcomer replied, glancing over his shoulder, his eyes wide. "Carrick's goons are hunting us down. They caught wind of our operations and want to wipe us out."

"Great," Reed muttered, his grip tightening around my hand as we veered around a corner, the passageway narrowing dangerously. "Just what we needed—an ambush."

"Not if we're smart about it," I replied, my mind racing with possibilities. We were outnumbered, but if we could get to the main exit, we might have a chance to escape into the city streets where we could blend in with the shadows.

We burst into a dimly lit chamber, where the walls were lined with makeshift maps and charts, evidence of countless plans forged in secrecy. A group of fighters huddled around a table, their expressions tense as they strategized their next move. "What are you doing here?" one of them snapped, eyes narrowing at our intrusion.

"Carrick's men are coming!" the wiry man shouted, urgency spilling from his lips. "We need to move, now!"

"Right. Let's split up," the fighter at the table ordered, his voice low and controlled. "If they want to hunt us down, let's give them a chase. Some of us can draw them away while the rest escape through the back exit."

"I'm not leaving anyone behind," I declared, a surge of conviction rushing through me. "We stick together, or we don't go at all."

Mara, who had remained silent in the background, stepped forward. "You have guts, I'll give you that. But it's not about bravery; it's about survival. If we want to make it out of this, we need to be smart."

Reed's eyes met mine, and in that moment, we shared an unspoken agreement. We had survived too much together to walk away now. "Then let's create a diversion that gives us all a chance," he suggested, the fire of determination igniting within him.

Mara considered it, her brow furrowing as she calculated the risks. "Fine. But it's going to be dangerous. We'll need a solid plan."

"Who's going to be the bait?" one of the fighters piped up, looking around the group as if weighing the options.

"I'll go," the wiry man said without hesitation, a fierce resolve flashing in his eyes. "I know the terrain. I can draw them away long enough for the rest of you to escape."

"No way," I protested, feeling a cold wave of dread wash over me. "We're not sacrificing anyone."

He shrugged, the determination in his stance unwavering. "This is my fight too. We all have to do our part, or none of us get out alive."

Mara nodded, recognizing the resolve in his eyes. "You won't be alone. A few of us will go with you to cover your escape."

"Fine. But I'm sticking with the group heading to the back exit," I insisted, glancing at Reed, who nodded in agreement. We had each other's backs; there was no way I was letting him out of my sight now.

As the rebels organized, the tension in the air shifted, anticipation mingling with fear. It was a delicate balance, one that could tip in an instant. I could hear the distant echoes of footsteps, growing louder, a reminder that time was slipping away.

The fighters moved with urgency, preparing weapons and gathering supplies as I felt Reed's presence beside me, a steady anchor in the midst of chaos. "Are you ready for this?" he asked quietly, the weight of his question hanging in the air like a leaden cloud.

I nodded, forcing a smile that didn't quite reach my eyes. "As ready as I'll ever be."

"Let's make it count, then," he replied, the flicker of determination returning to his gaze. "Together."

As we gathered by the back exit, adrenaline coursed through my veins, heightening every sense. The air was electric, crackling with the promise of confrontation. "On my signal," Mara whispered, her voice steady despite the tension surrounding us. "We'll burst out and create as much chaos as we can."

We took our positions, the adrenaline thrumming in my ears, drowning out the shouts growing louder outside. I could feel the heat of Reed's body next to mine, grounding me as we prepared for the chaos to come.

"Three... two... one... go!" Mara shouted, and we sprang into action.

The door burst open, and we spilled into the alley, the cool night air rushing over us like a wave. The moonlight cast an eerie glow on the narrow street, illuminating the chaos unfolding in front of us. Shadows moved quickly, darting through the darkness, and I could see Carrick's men advancing, their figures looming like ominous specters against the backdrop of the night.

I glanced back at Reed, my heart racing as the sounds of shouting and clashing metal filled the air. "We need to split up!" I yelled over the chaos, my voice barely rising above the din. "Head for the rooftops if you can!"

Before he could respond, a deafening crash echoed through the street, and I turned to see one of Carrick's men barreling toward us, his weapon raised. My instincts kicked in, and I pushed Reed behind me, ready to face the threat.

Just as I prepared to fight, a flash of movement caught my eye—one of the fighters had leaped into action, taking down the attacker in a swift motion. Relief surged through me, but before I could breathe, a sharp pain erupted in my shoulder, and I stumbled back, feeling the world tilt dangerously.

The last thing I saw was Reed's expression morphing into horror as I collapsed to the ground, the cold cobblestones biting into my skin. My vision blurred, the sounds of chaos fading into a dull roar, and all I could feel was the overwhelming sense of dread as I slipped into darkness.

Chapter 23: The Rising Storm

The moon hung low over the city, a luminous pearl casting its soft glow on the twisted alleyways and crumbling facades that seemed to sigh beneath the weight of the world. I could hear the distant murmur of the marketplace, the clamor of merchants hawking their wares, oblivious to the storm brewing just beyond their sight. Reed stood beside me, his silhouette stark against the flickering streetlamps, the tension in his frame palpable.

"Are you ready for this?" he asked, his voice barely above a whisper, yet it cut through the night like a knife. I had known him long enough to read the lines of worry etched on his brow, a stark contrast to the bravado he often donned like armor.

I nodded, though uncertainty coiled in my gut like a serpent. "Ready as I'll ever be." But inside, I felt like a fragile ember, dancing precariously on the edge of extinction.

We had rallied our meager forces, a motley crew of rebels and weary souls who had learned to survive on scraps of hope. Each face held a story—some etched with scars of loss, others shining with the fierce light of determination. We were bound by a singular goal: to dismantle Carrick's empire before his shadow stretched further, choking the life from our city. The resistance had offered us sanctuary, but tonight, it felt more like a noose tightening around our necks.

The plan was audacious, an echo of desperation and defiance. We were to infiltrate Carrick's stronghold, a dilapidated warehouse on the edge of the docks, where the salty air mingled with the acrid stench of industry. As we moved through the labyrinth of alleys, my heart thundered in my chest, the pulse of adrenaline spurring me forward even as my mind flashed with images of what could go wrong.

Reed and I fell into step beside one another, our hands brushing occasionally—a fleeting contact that sent sparks dancing up my arm. The intimacy was dangerous, a tether that could either strengthen our resolve or unravel us in the face of chaos. He glanced at me, his blue eyes glinting in the dim light, and for a moment, the weight of the world melted away.

"I know this is just a job," he said, breaking the silence, "but what if we survive? What if we actually win this?"

His words hung between us, thick with possibility. I dared to imagine a future where we could leave the horrors of our past behind, where laughter replaced the sounds of gunfire and bloodshed. But the thought felt too fragile, too delicate to hold. "And if we don't?" I countered, trying to reign in the wild surge of hope.

Reed's expression hardened, resolve flooding his features. "Then we fight like hell."

The alley opened into a wide square, the moonlight spilling over the cobblestones, illuminating the shadows where we stood. I caught sight of the others—our comrades, each preparing in their own way, some whispering quiet prayers while others sharpened blades, steeling themselves for the night ahead. It was a strange mix of fear and bravery, woven into the very fabric of our alliance.

We approached the warehouse, a hulking behemoth of steel and stone, where the faintest hum of machinery pulsed within. As we drew closer, I caught the faint whiff of something metallic, the tang of impending violence. My heart raced as we slipped through a gap in the rotting boards, the darkness enveloping us like an old friend.

Inside, the air was thick with anticipation, a palpable energy that prickled my skin. Reed and I exchanged glances, an unspoken understanding passing between us. We were no longer just soldiers; we were the tip of the spear, charged with piercing the heart of Carrick's regime.

The layout of the warehouse was a maze of crates and shadows, each corner concealing secrets and threats. I led the way, my instincts honed by countless skirmishes, every step a careful dance between courage and trepidation. My senses were on high alert, each creak of wood beneath our feet echoing like a siren's call.

"Do you hear that?" Reed's voice cut through the silence, a sharp edge of urgency.

Before I could respond, the unmistakable sound of footsteps echoed in the distance, reverberating off the cold walls. My blood ran cold. We weren't alone.

"Back," I hissed, retreating into the shadows. Reed pressed close, his breath warm against my ear, and I could feel the heat radiating from his body, a stark contrast to the chill in the air.

We melted into the darkness, hearts pounding in sync as the footsteps grew louder, a regiment of shadows marching toward us. I could barely breathe, the tension coiling tighter in my chest. My mind raced with the implications of being discovered. Would it be a swift end, or a prolonged nightmare?

As the figures came into view, my heart sank. They were heavily armed, their faces obscured by masks, eyes gleaming with a predatory hunger. I recognized them immediately—Carrick's enforcers, a brutal force trained to snuff out any flicker of resistance.

In that moment, everything shifted. The future Reed had whispered about felt further away than ever. We were on the precipice of war, and I realized that our fragile alliance, our hopes, and dreams hung in the balance. With a shared glance, we prepared to fight, but in my gut, I sensed that the battle for our city was only just beginning.

In the suffocating shadows of the warehouse, the atmosphere crackled with tension. The enforcers moved like a pack of wolves, their instincts honed and lethal, as they patrolled the labyrinthine aisles between the crates. My heart thudded in my chest, a relentless drumbeat urging me to flee, yet I was rooted in place, compelled by the magnetic pull of Reed's presence beside me.

"Is this the part where we become a tragic story?" I whispered, attempting to inject a thread of humor into the dire situation. My attempt at levity fell flat, drowned by the oppressive air, but Reed smirked nonetheless, his eyes glinting in the dark.

"Only if we don't do something," he replied, his tone light but laced with urgency. "You have a plan, right?"

"Me? A plan?" I feigned indignation, though my mind was racing. The enforcers drew nearer, their voices low and conspiratorial, the sound a reminder of the stakes. It wasn't just our lives at risk but the very essence of the rebellion we had fought to protect.

As the figures turned a corner, I seized the moment. "We need to split them up," I said, my voice barely a whisper. "If we can lure one away from the group..."

Reed nodded, his expression serious, the playful banter replaced by the steely determination I had come to rely on. "You think we can draw them into a trap?"

"Only one way to find out," I replied, steeling myself. With a quick glance at our surroundings, I spotted a stack of crates teetering precariously at the far end of the warehouse. "If I create a distraction, you can take out the others while they're busy."

"Brilliant. Just don't get yourself killed while being brilliant." His voice held a trace of concern, a reminder of the fine line we walked between hope and despair.

"Only if you promise to stay alive long enough to see my brilliance," I shot back, a smirk teasing my lips as I melted into the shadows. My heart raced as I darted toward the crates, the cool air sharp against my skin. I could feel the adrenaline coursing through me, sharp and exhilarating, propelling me forward.

As I reached the precarious stack, I hesitated, weighing the risk. But a deep breath steeled my resolve. If we didn't act now, we might lose everything. I knocked against the crates, creating a cascade of sound that echoed through the vast emptiness of the warehouse. They tumbled to the ground with a thunderous crash, splintering against the concrete floor.

The enforcers stopped, their heads snapping in my direction, eyes narrowing in suspicion. "What was that?" one barked, his voice gruff and commanding.

I turned to run, knowing that the moment of truth had arrived. My feet pounded against the ground as I led them deeper into the maze of crates, the sound of their footsteps reverberating behind me. I glanced back, and for an instant, our gazes locked. Their eyes burned with an intensity that sent a chill down my spine, but I couldn't stop.

"Come on, slowpokes!" I called over my shoulder, my voice dripping with bravado. "You can do better than that!"

The bait had been taken, and I felt a surge of exhilaration mingled with terror. Reed, I hoped, was ready. I rounded a corner, my heart in my throat as I spotted a side door. The exit loomed before me, a sliver of salvation in a world painted with shadows.

I slipped through the door just as the enforcers rounded the corner, their expressions morphing from irritation to surprise. "After her!" one shouted, and I could hear them barreling into the space behind me.

The night air hit me like a wave as I stumbled outside, gasping for breath. I whirled around to catch a glimpse of Reed, who had emerged from the shadows like a vengeful ghost.

"Now!" I shouted, pointing back into the darkness of the warehouse.

He took off, his movements fluid and swift, darting into the chaos. The enforcers had fanned out, confusion written across their faces as they tried to locate the source of the disturbance. It was a moment suspended in time—one that felt both exhilarating and terrifying.

With swift precision, Reed struck, taking down the first enforcer before the others had a chance to react. I watched, a mixture of pride and fear swirling within me, as he moved with purpose and determination. But I couldn't linger; there were still others to confront.

I picked up a stray piece of metal lying on the ground, a makeshift weapon in my trembling hands, and joined the fray. The adrenaline fueled my every movement, the thrill of battle igniting something primal within me. With each strike, I felt a surge of power, a reminder that I was not merely a pawn in this game of survival.

But then, in the midst of the scuffle, I heard a voice that sliced through the noise. "Stop! Stand down!"

It was Carrick's voice, smooth and commanding, resonating with a chilling authority that made the hairs on the back of my neck stand on end. My stomach twisted, the familiar fear settling in like a heavy fog. I turned, my heart racing as I faced him, framed in the doorway of the warehouse, an ominous specter against the night.

He surveyed the scene, amusement dancing in his eyes as he took in the chaos. "You think this little rebellion of yours is going to change anything?" he taunted, his tone laced with condescension. "You're all just pawns in a game far beyond your understanding."

A surge of anger ignited within me, pushing me to take a step forward. "You underestimate us," I said, my voice stronger than I felt. "We're fighting for our lives, for our city. You may have power, but you will never have our will."

Carrick's laughter echoed through the night, a dark sound that twisted the air around us. "Will? Such a quaint notion. Will doesn't save you when you're outnumbered. You're in way over your heads."

But before I could respond, Reed appeared at my side, bloodied but unbroken, a fierce glint in his eyes. "We're not outnumbered," he said, his voice low and steady. "We have something you don't."

"Please," Carrick sneered, brushing off the threat with a flick of his wrist. "What do you think you have? A few misguided souls? You're nothing."

At that moment, I felt it—a shift in the air, a ripple of energy that promised change. The enforcers hesitated, caught between their loyalty to Carrick and the audacity of our defiance. The tide of the battle was turning, and I could almost taste the victory that hung tantalizingly close.

With a shared glance, Reed and I braced ourselves, ready to fight against the odds. Whatever came next, we would face it together, defiant against the storm that loomed over us, prepared to carve our own fate in the chaos that followed.

The tension in the air was electric, palpable enough to reach out and snag at the edges of my mind as Carrick stood before us, a malevolent puppet master savoring the chaos he had orchestrated. I felt a pulse of anger and desperation surge through me, igniting my resolve. "You think we're nothing?" I shot back, my voice steady despite the pounding of my heart. "We're the people you've underestimated for too long. This ends now."

Carrick's smirk faded slightly, his eyes narrowing as he assessed the determination in my stance. "You talk a good game, but words alone won't save you," he retorted, a flicker of annoyance flashing across his face.

Behind him, the enforcers shifted, their loyalties wavering like a candle's flame in the wind. I could sense the shift in the atmosphere—their hesitance hung between us like an invisible thread, fragile yet promising. Reed and I shared a quick glance, a silent exchange of courage and strategy, and I could see in his eyes the same fire I felt roaring within me.

With a calculated leap, I surged forward, driven by a surge of adrenaline and purpose. "What's wrong, Carrick? Afraid of a little challenge?"

His gaze darkened, and in that moment, I understood that I had crossed a line. "Foolish girl," he hissed, and with a flick of his wrist, he signaled the enforcers to advance.

"Now, now," I said, feigning nonchalance even as panic clawed at my throat. "You don't want to make this too easy for us, do you? Where's the fun in that?"

Reed stepped in beside me, his stance unwavering, ready to face whatever madness Carrick unleashed. "We're not backing down," he declared, voice firm and resolute. "Not now, not ever."

A battle cry erupted from the enforcers, a discordant chorus of fury and determination as they charged toward us. Time slowed, every heartbeat stretching into eternity as the world around me narrowed to the immediate threat before us. The clash of metal rang out, echoing in the cavernous space, and I lunged into the fray.

I swung the makeshift weapon with all my strength, adrenaline coursing through my veins like wildfire. The enforcer before me dodged with an agile grace, his eyes glinting with the thrill of the fight. My instincts kicked in, honed by countless hours spent training with Reed and the resistance. I ducked and weaved, the dance of combat fueling me with a heady sense of purpose.

But just as I found my rhythm, the warehouse door burst open, and a new wave of figures flooded in, cloaked in darkness and armed to the teeth. "We've got company!" someone shouted, the urgency in their voice cutting through the chaos.

My heart sank as I recognized the insignia on their uniforms—Carrick's reinforcements, his elite guard, and they were not here for a chat over tea. The tide had turned, and the battle was morphing into something far more dangerous.

"Reed!" I yelled, but the words barely escaped my lips as I felt a heavy hand grasp my arm, yanking me away from the fray. I swung around, ready to strike, only to find one of Carrick's men staring back at me, a twisted smile stretching across his face.

"Got you," he sneered, tightening his grip. I fought against his hold, but he was too strong, and the weight of the chaos around me threatened to swallow me whole.

"Let her go!" Reed roared, his voice a beacon of defiance amid the turmoil. He lunged forward, but two enforcers quickly blocked his path, shoving him back into the throng of combatants.

I kicked and struggled, desperation flooding my limbs. "Reed!" I called, my voice laced with panic, but the din of battle swallowed my words.

"Focus on getting out of here!" he shouted back, and though his voice was strained, it held an unwavering strength that anchored me.

With a sudden burst of adrenaline, I twisted my body, leveraging my weight to break free from my captor's grip. I stumbled back, heart racing as I regained my footing. The scene before me was a cacophony of shouts and clashes, a whirlwind of bodies and blurred faces, but I spotted Reed fighting valiantly, his fierce determination shining through the chaos.

Before I could take another step, I felt a presence behind me—a shadow that loomed larger than life. I turned, and a figure emerged from the darkness, tall and imposing. My breath hitched in my throat as I recognized the unmistakable features of Carrick himself, anger radiating from him like heat from a flame.

"You've meddled in my affairs long enough," he said, his voice a silky menace. "It's time to teach you a lesson."

Just as I prepared to confront him, a surge of movement erupted in the corner of my eye. A flash of silver gleamed under the dim lights—a knife aimed straight at me, hurled from the chaos. Time slowed as I instinctively ducked, the blade whistling past my ear. My heart raced as I spun around, adrenaline coursing through my veins.

"Duck!" Reed shouted, but it was too late. The enforcer behind me, now seemingly empowered by Carrick's presence, surged forward, the desperation of the moment overwhelming him.

In one fluid motion, I sidestepped, pivoting just enough to allow the enforcer to stumble past me. Reed took advantage of the opening, launching himself at the man and taking him down with a well-placed strike.

"Stay close!" he ordered, his voice firm, but I could see the strain on his face, the fatigue from the relentless battle.

But the reinforcements poured in like a dark tide, a relentless wave crashing against our fragile defenses. I fought to stay at Reed's side, but the chaos swirled around us like a tempest, separating us amidst the clamor of clashing steel and desperate shouts.

"Reed!" I called, desperation creeping into my voice. I glanced around, searching for a glimpse of him, the shadows swallowing his figure. A knot of fear tightened in my chest, and for a moment, I felt completely and utterly lost.

Then, just as hope began to slip through my fingers, I spotted him—locked in combat with Carrick himself, their struggle a dance of skill and fury. Carrick's face was a mask of rage, while Reed fought with everything he had, the intensity of their clash sending shockwaves through the air.

"Reed!" I screamed, adrenaline sharpening my senses as I charged toward them. But just as I reached out, a sharp pain lanced through my side. I gasped, stumbling to the ground, the world blurring around the edges.

The laughter of Carrick echoed in my ears, a cruel sound that reverberated through my bones as darkness threatened to overtake me. My vision dimmed, and I struggled to stay conscious, fighting against the encroaching shadows.

But just as my world began to fade, I felt a hand grasp mine—a warmth in the frigid air. I turned my head, finding Reed's face, determination etched into his features even as he fought against the tide of chaos around us.

"Don't you dare close your eyes!" he shouted, his voice a lifeline in the storm. "We're getting out of this!"

With a sudden surge of energy, I gripped his hand tighter, refusing to let the darkness claim me. I could hear the fight raging on, feel the world spinning out of control, but I wasn't ready to give in—not now, not when everything we had fought for hung in the balance.

Yet just as I drew in a breath, a flash of movement caught my eye. A figure cloaked in shadows stood at the edge of the chaos, a sinister smile playing on their lips as they raised a weapon—pointed directly at Reed.

Time froze as my heart sank, fear clawing at my throat. "Reed, look out!" I screamed, but my voice was lost amid the cacophony.

As the weapon fired, the world tilted, and everything I had fought for teetered on the brink of oblivion.

Chapter 24: Flames of War

The air in the industrial district was thick with the scent of oil and burnt metal, a bitter reminder of the war that had taken root in every corner of our once-thriving city. As we maneuvered through the maze of factories, I could hear the distant clang of machinery mingling with the sharp retorts of gunfire, each shot echoing like a warning bell through the grim landscape. Shadows danced around us, cast by the flickering flames of our resistance's assault. It was a desperate gamble, one that felt like a twisted game of chance, and I had never been one to trust luck.

Reed moved beside me, a silent sentinel with an intensity that drew my gaze like a moth to a flame. His dark hair was tousled, sweat glistening on his brow as he scanned the area with an unwavering gaze. I had seen him handle a weapon with the grace of a dancer, each movement precise and calculated, but today there was something different in his demeanor—a palpable tension that wrapped around us like a shroud. My heart raced, not just from the adrenaline coursing through my veins but from the unspoken connection we shared, a bond forged in the heat of battle and tempered by our shared struggles.

"We need to head for the old mill," Reed whispered, his voice low but steady, cutting through the chaos like a blade. "It's the only way we'll regroup with the others."

I nodded, though the knot in my stomach tightened. The mill was a relic of a bygone era, its walls scarred by time and neglect. It would be a risky move, one that could either secure our position or expose us to Carrick's forces. "What if they're waiting for us?" I asked, my voice barely above a whisper, the fear creeping in despite my attempts to suppress it.

"Then we'll give them a fight they won't forget," he replied, the flicker of a smile playing on his lips, even as the shadows loomed larger around us. There was a wildness to him, a spark of determination that ignited something deep within me. I had always admired that about Reed; he faced danger head-on, an indomitable spirit that somehow made me feel invincible alongside him.

As we approached the mill, the sounds of battle grew louder, the cries of our comrades mingling with the thud of heavy boots on concrete. I felt the weight of the world on my shoulders, the burden of hope and fear intertwining until they became indistinguishable. Each step I took felt like a decision etched in stone, a commitment to a cause that was as much about survival as it was about liberation.

The mill loomed ahead, its silhouette stark against the backdrop of an orange sky, the remnants of the day slipping away. As we rounded a corner, I spotted a familiar figure—a soldier with a fierce look in his eyes and a rifle slung over his shoulder. It was Marcus, a loyal friend and ally, his expression a mix of relief and determination.

"Over here!" he called, waving us toward a side entrance where shadows huddled close, blending with the darkness. As we ducked inside, the cacophony of the outside world dulled to a distant roar, the sanctuary of the mill offering a momentary reprieve from the chaos.

"Have you seen the others?" Reed asked, urgency lacing his tone as he stepped closer to Marcus, scanning the dimly lit space for any signs of life.

"Not yet, but we need to move fast," Marcus replied, his voice tight with concern. "Carrick's men are closing in, and they're not taking prisoners."

The gravity of his words hit me like a punch to the gut. We were running out of time, and every heartbeat felt like a countdown. Just then, the sound of boots thudding against the floor above us sent a chill down my spine. The lieutenant's men had followed us, and the game was about to change.

"Take the back exit," Reed instructed, his tone firm but quiet. "I'll hold them off."

"No way. We stick together," I insisted, defiance igniting in my chest. The thought of losing him in the chaos was unbearable, and I could feel the tension thickening in the air, the unspoken connection between us growing heavier with each passing moment.

"Do you trust me?" Reed asked, his gaze piercing into mine, searching for something beneath the fear.

"More than anything," I breathed, the truth hanging between us, as palpable as the danger lurking just outside.

"Then go," he urged, his expression fierce, a mask of determination. "I can't let you get caught in this."

A sudden crash above us shattered the moment, dust raining down as footsteps pounded closer. "Now!" Reed barked, and with a nod that felt like a promise, I turned to follow Marcus, my heart pounding in my chest like a war drum.

We slipped through the back exit into the cool night air, the chaos of the city swirling around us, but my thoughts were consumed by Reed's words, by the intensity of his gaze as he prepared to face the enemy alone. We had fought side by side for so long, and the thought of him standing against Carrick's lieutenant without me felt like a betrayal of everything we had endured.

As we darted into the shadows, I couldn't shake the fear gnawing at my insides, the realization that this battle was not just about our survival, but about everything we had fought for. We were not just fighting for freedom; we were fighting for each other, and I could only hope that Reed would be waiting for me when this was all over.

The chill of the night air wrapped around me like a shroud as Marcus and I darted away from the mill, the faint flicker of flames casting eerie shadows across the asphalt. I could feel my heart racing, a relentless rhythm that seemed to echo in the silence that followed the chaos of battle. The distant sounds of conflict faded, replaced by the rustling of leaves and the soft whisper of the wind, yet every nerve in my body remained taut, alert to the lurking danger. It was a game of cat and mouse, and we were the prey.

"Do you think he'll be okay?" I asked, the words tumbling from my lips before I could stop them. Panic seeped into my voice, the unease creeping into my chest like a shadow stretching across the fading light.

Marcus glanced back at me, his expression a mixture of concern and resolve. "Reed knows what he's doing. He's a fighter," he replied, though the tightness around his eyes suggested he was trying to convince himself as much as me. "We can't dwell on that now. We need to keep moving."

I nodded, forcing myself to focus on the path ahead. We veered into an alley, the narrow passageway flanked by crumbling brick walls that seemed to close in around us, suffocating yet oddly protective. My mind raced with thoughts of Reed, of the way his eyes had burned with intensity and determination just moments ago. I could still see him standing there, poised to face the enemy, and the image filled me with both admiration and dread.

"Are you sure we should take this route?" I asked, squinting into the darkness. Shadows pooled around us, and I felt a prickling sense of foreboding that made my skin crawl. "I've heard stories about these back alleys. They're not exactly safe havens."

Marcus chuckled softly, a sound that somehow eased the tension hanging in the air. "Safe? This is a war zone, remember? I think we've officially abandoned any notion of safety. But I promise you, I've scouted this area before. It's our best shot at getting to the rendezvous point without running into Carrick's patrols."

His confidence was infectious, and I found myself drawing strength from it. With every step, I reminded myself of what we were fighting for—the chance to reclaim our lives, to break free from the shackles of oppression. It was a battle larger than ourselves, yet it felt intensely personal, fueled by the sacrifices of those we had lost and the hope that still flickered like a candle in the dark.

As we turned a corner, the alley opened up into a small courtyard, overgrown with weeds and littered with debris. My heart sank at the sight; it felt abandoned, desolate, yet a flicker of movement caught my eye. "Did you see that?" I whispered, gripping Marcus's arm.

"See what?" he asked, peering into the shadows, his posture instinctively tense.

"Over there!" I pointed toward the far side of the courtyard, where a figure emerged from the darkness. My breath caught in my throat as the shape materialized—a woman, cloaked in shadows, with a hood that obscured her features.

"Who are you?" I called, my voice steadying despite the apprehension knotting my stomach.

"Friends," she replied, her voice low and confident. "At least for now. I've been watching you two."

Marcus took a step closer, eyeing her warily. "Watching us? What do you mean?"

"Word travels fast in these parts," she said, lifting her hood slightly to reveal striking blue eyes that glinted like shards of ice. "Your little group has been causing quite the stir, and Carrick isn't pleased. I've got information that could help you."

Intrigued yet cautious, I exchanged a glance with Marcus. "And why would you want to help us?" I asked, my suspicion thickening the air between us.

"Let's just say I have my reasons for wanting Carrick out of power," she said, a flicker of something dark passing over her expression. "But if you want my help, you need to move fast. Carrick's men are already scouring the area, and you're not safe here."

Marcus straightened, a sense of urgency blooming in his eyes. "What do you know?"

She gestured for us to follow her deeper into the shadows, the night swallowing us whole. "The lieutenant is on his way to find you. He's not just a ruthless soldier; he's smart. He knows how to play this game, and he won't hesitate to use you against Reed."

A chill slithered down my spine at the thought. "What do you mean?"

"The lieutenant's been watching Reed, studying his patterns. He knows the bond you two share, and he'll exploit that," she replied, her voice grave. "If you want to save him, we need to move."

With each step we took, the urgency of our situation settled deeper into my bones. I was torn between the desire to rush back to Reed and the harsh reality of the situation. I knew the risks, yet the thought of facing the lieutenant without Reed by my side felt like stepping into a lion's den with a blindfold on.

"Where are we headed?" I asked, my voice barely more than a whisper as the woman led us through a labyrinth of alleys, the darkness enveloping us like a cloak.

"To a safe house," she replied, glancing back at me. "But we need to be quick. The lieutenant is relentless, and if he catches wind of your movements, he won't hesitate to strike."

As we continued to weave through the shadows, the tension between us tightened, an invisible thread binding us together in this moment of peril. I couldn't shake the feeling that the woman knew more than she was letting on, but I didn't have time to question her motives. My mind was racing, each thought spiraling into the next as I wondered how we would turn the tide in this battle and what sacrifices we would have to make.

"Do you really think we can win?" I asked, the question tumbling out before I could filter it through the haze of fear.

The woman paused, her eyes reflecting the dim light like embers. "Victory isn't about numbers. It's about will. If you believe in your cause, if you fight for what matters, you can defy the odds. But you must be willing to pay the price."

Her words hung heavy in the air, a reminder that every victory came at a cost. I clenched my fists, determination igniting within me as I thought of Reed and the battle that lay ahead. This was not just about survival; it was about fighting for the future we envisioned, a future worth every sacrifice.

We moved swiftly through the labyrinth of alleys, the woman leading us with an agility that belied her apparent frailty. I couldn't shake the feeling that she was more than she appeared, a specter of the city's underbelly, familiar with every hidden corner and darkened path. With each turn, the atmosphere thickened, a mix of adrenaline and apprehension swirling in the air around us like the smoke from the distant fires.

"Why did you choose to help us?" I pressed, trying to gauge her intentions. "You could easily walk away."

She glanced back, her blue eyes sharp, and for a fleeting moment, I thought I detected a hint of vulnerability. "Because I've lost too many people to Carrick's regime. I'm tired of running," she said, her voice steady but laced with an undercurrent of pain. "If I can help end this, then it's worth the risk."

Her words resonated with me, stirring a flicker of shared anguish. We were all fighting our own battles, and the thought of uniting for a common cause filled me with renewed determination. "What's your name?" I asked, feeling the need to know the woman who might hold our fate in her hands.

"Celia," she replied, as we navigated another narrow passage. "And you're the one they're talking about—the girl who stands against Carrick."

I hesitated, the weight of her gaze igniting a blend of pride and pressure within me. "I'm just trying to survive like everyone else," I countered, my voice firm despite the tremor beneath it.

"Survival is a noble pursuit, but you're more than that," Celia said, stopping at a battered door that looked as if it had seen centuries of struggle. "You've inspired others to fight back. You've become a symbol of hope."

As she pushed the door open, the creak of the hinges echoed through the dimly lit space, and I stepped inside, inhaling the musty air mixed with something more invigorating—determination. The safe house was sparse but functional, filled with makeshift furniture and maps plastered across the walls, each marked with the locations of Carrick's strongholds. It was a command center in the heart of chaos, a place where plans were forged and destinies altered.

Marcus was already poring over the maps, his brow furrowed in concentration. "We need to regroup with the others before we make our next move," he said, tracing a line on the map with his finger. "If we can strike at Carrick's supply lines, we might level the playing field."

Celia nodded, her expression serious. "Exactly. But we need to be swift and strategic. Every moment we waste gives him time to retaliate."

"Then we'll have to make our move before he knows we're here," I chimed in, feeling the fire of defiance stoke within me. "We can't allow him to dictate our fate any longer."

As we plotted our next steps, I couldn't shake the weight of Reed's absence. Every plan felt incomplete without him by my side, and the gnawing worry about his safety threatened to overwhelm me. "We can't leave him behind," I insisted, the urgency thrumming in my veins. "He'll be looking for us."

Celia placed a steadying hand on my shoulder. "I promise, if we act quickly, we can find him. He's resourceful, and he knows the risks. We can't let fear dictate our choices."

Just then, the sound of hurried footsteps echoed outside the door, and the atmosphere shifted instantly, tension electrifying the air. My heart raced as I exchanged a glance with Marcus. "Get ready," he whispered, his voice low but urgent.

The door burst open, and I spun around, bracing for a confrontation. Instead, it was one of our scouts, a young man with disheveled hair and wild eyes, panting as if he had run a marathon. "We have a situation!" he gasped, his face pale. "Carrick's lieutenant has called for reinforcements. They're coming this way, and fast!"

Celia's expression hardened. "We don't have much time. We need to move now."

Before I could react, she turned to me, urgency radiating from her. "You need to trust us, but I can't promise you safety. If we're going to find Reed and fight back, we have to be prepared to face whatever comes next."

A thousand thoughts swirled in my mind as I nodded, knowing deep down that the time for hesitation had passed. "Then let's go," I said, steeling myself for whatever lay ahead. We had fought so hard to reach this moment, and I wouldn't let it slip away.

We dashed through the door and into the chaotic night, the city alive with the sounds of conflict. I could feel the pulse of the battle surrounding us, each heartbeat resonating with the promise of freedom and the peril of defeat. As we maneuvered through the narrow streets, the faint glow of fires painted the scene in hues of orange and red, the flickering flames a reminder of the fight we had ignited.

As we reached the edge of a larger street, a plan began to form in my mind. "If we can create a diversion, we might be able to draw the lieutenant's forces away from Reed," I suggested, glancing at Marcus. "We could use the old warehouse as a decoy. It's close enough that they'll think we're there."

"Brilliant," Marcus said, his eyes lighting up with the spark of action. "We'll need to set it ablaze to draw their attention, but it'll give us a chance to slip in and find him."

Celia looked at me, her expression serious. "Are you ready for this? It could get dangerous."

I took a deep breath, allowing the adrenaline to wash over me like a cleansing tide. "I've never been more ready for anything in my life," I replied, my voice unwavering.

Together, we made our way to the warehouse, weaving through the shadows as the tension thickened around us. As we approached, I could see the silhouette of Carrick's men gathering at the far end of the street, their figures tense and alert. The fire in my gut ignited, and I knew that we were on the precipice of something monumental.

"Let's make this quick," Marcus urged, his voice steady as he prepared to ignite the flare we had brought.

I nodded, my heart pounding with a mix of fear and exhilaration. Just as he struck the match, a loud explosion rocked the street, sending debris flying into the air, and the ground trembled beneath our feet.

"What was that?" I shouted over the din, eyes wide in shock.

The moment hung suspended in time, a heartbeat stretched too thin. Then I caught sight of the unmistakable figure of Reed, sprinting toward us, his expression fierce and resolute, a storm of emotions swirling in his eyes.

"Get down!" he shouted just as a bullet whizzed past my ear.

I dove to the ground, heart racing as the world erupted into chaos once more. The lieutenant's men poured into the street, and as I looked up, I saw Reed charging forward, determination etched on his face. I reached out for him, but before I could close the distance, everything around us ignited into a whirlwind of fire and chaos, and in that moment, I realized that this battle would determine our fate, whether we were ready for it or not.

And then, in the midst of the fray, I felt the ground shift beneath me, a sense of foreboding rising like the tide. A blinding flash erupted around us, and in the chaos of the moment, everything went dark.

Chapter 25: Fractured Hearts

The house stands at the edge of the city like a weary sentinel, its windows boarded and its paint peeling, reminiscent of a forgotten dream. Shadows stretch across the floorboards, where dust motes dance in the slivers of moonlight that seep through the cracks. Outside, the wind whistles through the trees, an eerie lullaby that sets my nerves on edge. I can still hear the echoes of what happened, the chaos that tore through us like a storm, and the haunting cries of those we couldn't save. Each breath I take feels like a betrayal to their memory.

Reed stands near the broken window, silhouetted against the pale light. His shoulders are hunched, as if the weight of the world rests on them alone. I want to reach out, to bridge the chasm that has opened between us, but the space feels insurmountable. "You should have left me," he mutters, his voice a gravelly whisper, barely breaking the silence. The guilt that hangs in the air is almost palpable, a thick fog that clouds everything.

"What good would that have done?" I counter, my tone firmer than I feel. "You know that. We're a team, Reed. We have to face this together." My words hang in the air, an offering wrapped in desperation, but I can see his resolve harden.

"It's my fault," he insists, turning away, his fists clenching at his sides. "All of it. If I hadn't dragged you into this—"

"Stop it!" I interrupt, unable to hide the tremor in my voice. "You think I didn't choose to be here? You think I'm some innocent bystander in this nightmare?" The tension in the room snaps like a taut string, and for a moment, we are both just two souls caught in the crossfire of our own making. I step closer, my heart pounding, each beat a reminder of how fragile life has become. "We need each other now more than ever. I won't let you push me away."

He finally meets my gaze, and for the first time, I see the flicker of vulnerability beneath the hard exterior he's crafted to shield himself. "I never wanted to put you in danger," he says, the words laced with remorse. "Every day I wake up knowing I might lose you. It's unbearable."

In that moment, the air shifts, and the wall he's built begins to crumble. "I'm not going anywhere," I assure him, my voice softer now, wrapped in the warmth of truth. "You don't get to decide that for me. Not when we've come this far."

Silence stretches between us, heavy and electric, as if the universe is holding its breath, waiting for us to make a choice. Reed takes a step forward, his resolve wavering like a candle flickering in a draft. "You don't know what I've done," he says, and the pain in his voice twists something deep within me. "What I'm capable of. I'm not the man you think I am."

"Who are you, then?" I challenge, my heart racing. "Show me. I want to know the real you, not the shadows you hide behind."

His breath hitches, and for a heartbeat, I think he might pull me into his world, but then the moment passes, slipping through our fingers like sand. He turns away, and the moment I dread most unfolds—a slow retreat into darkness.

"Reed, please," I plead, my voice catching in my throat. "Don't do this. We've fought too hard to let fear dictate our lives."

The night presses in around us, a heavy cloak of uncertainty. Reed runs a hand through his hair, and I can see the muscles in his jaw tightening. "What if I hurt you?" he says, almost to himself. "What if I drag you down with me?"

I can feel the pulse of my heartbeat in my ears, the urgency rising like a tide. "What if you don't?" I counter, stepping closer until I can feel the heat radiating from his body. "What if together, we find a way through this?"

His eyes dart to mine, searching for something—hope, perhaps, or a glimmer of faith in what we could become. "I can't promise that," he admits, a crack forming in his stoic facade.

"Then don't," I whisper, daring to close the gap between us. "Just be with me now. That's all I'm asking."

Time seems to freeze as the weight of our shared pain settles around us, and I reach up, brushing my fingers against his cheek. The contact is electric, a reminder of the life we've fought for. "We're stronger together," I say, and in that moment, the air shifts once more, thick with unspoken words and a tentative understanding.

He captures my hand in his, a spark igniting between us as our fingers entwine. "You're too good for me," he murmurs, his voice a low rumble, thick with emotion.

"Maybe. But I'm not letting go."

The tension that had built between us begins to dissolve, replaced by a shared determination. There's a flicker of something deeper in his gaze now, a promise that perhaps we can heal, that the fracture in our hearts can be mended, stitch by careful stitch.

The darkness outside seems less daunting, and as I lean into him, feeling the warmth radiate from his body, I know that this moment, however fleeting, is a step toward reclaiming the parts of us that have been shattered. In the silence, we hold each other, two broken pieces finding solace in the cracks of our fractured hearts.

As the darkness outside deepens, the abandoned house seems to cradle our secrets, each creak of the floorboards resonating with the weight of our unspoken fears. I nestle closer to Reed, determined to bridge the emotional distance that stretches between us. The warmth of his body is a balm against the chill of our shared trauma, yet I can still feel the invisible barrier he's erected. The silence that envelops us is oppressive, punctuated only by the occasional rustle of leaves outside, a reminder that the world continues to turn even as we are caught in this moment of uncertainty.

"Do you think they're okay?" I ask, breaking the stillness, the question lingering in the air like a ghost. The memories of our fallen comrades tug at my heart, their faces flickering through my mind like a cruel slideshow. "The others, I mean. Did we do enough?"

Reed's brow furrows, and he shakes his head slightly, as if shaking off a bad dream. "I don't know," he admits, his voice thick with remorse. "I keep replaying it in my head. If I'd only..." His words trail off, and the guilt in his eyes deepens.

"We did what we could," I say firmly, willing the conviction into my tone. "You can't carry that burden alone. We made choices, and sometimes those choices come with consequences we can't predict. But we're still here. That counts for something."

He nods, but I can see the battle raging within him, a war of self-reproach that threatens to consume him whole. "But did it have to come at such a cost?" he whispers, his voice barely audible, each word weighted with grief.

"Life doesn't come with a manual," I reply, striving to inject a touch of levity into the heaviness between us. "It's more like a particularly tricky crossword puzzle—filled with dead ends and cryptic clues. Just when you think you've got it figured out, you realize you've spelled 'cat' instead of 'dog.' And look where we are now." I gesture around the decrepit room, a half-hearted attempt at humor.

For the briefest moment, a flicker of amusement dances in his eyes, the corners of his mouth twitching upward. "So you're saying we've solved a lot of puzzles that lead us here? To a derelict house on the edge of town?"

"Exactly! A real estate agent's worst nightmare." My playful banter hangs in the air, a thin thread of connection woven through our pain. Reed chuckles, and the sound is like a healing balm, soothing the raw edges of my heart.

But then the laughter fades, replaced by a heavy silence. I glance at the boarded windows, the shadows lurking just outside, and I realize that our laughter feels like a fragile truce. "We have to make a plan," I say, the gravity of the situation sinking in once more. "We can't stay here forever, pretending the world isn't crumbling around us."

He nods, the humor dissipating like morning fog. "I agree. But what can we do? We're running on empty."

"We regroup," I declare, determination flaring within me. "We find a safe place, gather what we can, and figure out our next move. Together."

"Together," he echoes, but I sense a lingering hesitation in his voice. I can't blame him. The path ahead is littered with uncertainty, the future a twisted maze that may lead us further into danger. But the alternative, allowing fear to paralyze us, feels even more daunting.

Just then, a sound outside catches my attention, a rustling in the underbrush. My heart quickens, and I instinctively grab Reed's arm, my grip tightening. "Did you hear that?"

He nods, his body tense as he moves closer, his instincts on high alert. "Stay low," he whispers, slipping into a crouch as we inch toward the window.

I peer through a crack between the boards, my breath hitching as I scan the shadows. A figure moves through the trees, stumbling slightly as they emerge into the moonlight. "Who is that?" I murmur, my pulse racing.

Reed shifts closer, straining to see. "I can't tell. But if it's who I think it is..." His voice trails off, and I can feel the weight of his worry, the unspoken fear that shadows every syllable.

As the figure steps into the light, I squint, recognition washing over me like a tide. "It's Lila!" I exclaim, the joy bursting from me in a gasp. Relief floods through me, warming the cold edges of dread that had settled in my chest. "Thank goodness she's alive!"

Before Reed can respond, I dart toward the door, flinging it open to call out to her. "Lila! Over here!"

She looks up, her eyes wide with surprise and relief. "I thought you two were—" She stumbles over her words, catching herself. "I thought you'd left me."

"Never," I assure her, rushing to her side and enveloping her in a tight embrace. She feels fragile in my arms, but there's a spark of resilience in her that I've always admired.

"What happened?" Reed asks, emerging from the shadows, his voice a mixture of concern and urgency. "We thought we lost you."

"I got separated during the chaos," she explains, her breath coming in quick bursts. "I've been hiding, trying to find my way back to you. It was a nightmare."

As she speaks, I can see the weight of her fear in her eyes, but beneath it all lies a fierce determination that mirrors my own. "You're safe now," I promise, stepping back to look her in the eye. "We'll figure this out together."

Just then, a distant rumble echoes through the air, sending a shiver down my spine. Reed's gaze snaps to the horizon, where dark clouds gather ominously. "We need to move. Now."

With Lila beside us, our small group feels whole again, but the urgency of the moment propels us forward. Together, we turn our backs on the dilapidated house, stepping into the unknown, determined to carve our path amid the chaos that threatens to engulf us.

The air outside crackles with tension as we push away from the house that had sheltered our secrets, now just a shadow behind us. Lila keeps close, her expression a blend of fear and determination, mirroring the unsteady rhythm of my heart. We weave through the narrow alleys, our footsteps muffled by the overgrown weeds and crumbling concrete beneath us. The moon hangs high, casting an eerie glow that feels more like a spotlight on our plight than a comforting presence.

"Where are we even going?" Lila asks, glancing around as if expecting a savior to emerge from the shadows. "Do we have a plan, or are we just hoping for the best?"

Reed's gaze is fixed ahead, a mask of focus etched on his features. "We need to get to the warehouse district," he replies, his voice steady but laced with urgency. "There's a chance we can find supplies there, maybe even others who made it through."

"A treasure hunt for survival," I quip, trying to lighten the mood despite the heavy weight pressing down on us. "Is there a prize for that, or is it just bragging rights?"

Lila shoots me a look, half amused, half exasperated. "I'd settle for food and water right about now. Bragging rights sound a bit... hollow."

"Fair point," I concede, my own stomach rumbling in agreement. "But let's not underestimate the power of a well-crafted story. They could serve us well as we recount our heroic escape over a feast of canned beans."

Lila snorts softly, and I catch a glimpse of the old spark in her eyes, the one that used to light up our banter before everything turned upside down. It fuels me, reminding me that amidst the chaos, laughter is still a weapon we can wield against despair.

Reed leads the way, his footsteps sure and steady, but I can feel the current of anxiety swirling beneath the surface. Each shadow seems to pulse with hidden dangers, and I can't shake the feeling that we're not as alone as we hope. The streets are eerily quiet, the usual sounds of city life silenced, replaced by the occasional rustle of the wind and the distant sound of sirens that wail like mourning doves.

As we navigate the maze of abandoned buildings, I can't help but wonder what horrors await us in the warehouse district. "What if we're too late?" I ask, my voice barely above a whisper. "What if there's no one left?"

"Don't think like that," Reed says, his voice firm. "We have to believe there are others out there. If we lose hope, we lose everything."

His words hang in the air, a thread of strength woven into our frail tapestry of survival. Just then, a flicker of movement catches my eye, and I instinctively halt. "Did you see that?"

"What?" Reed asks, his eyes scanning the dimly lit surroundings.

"There!" I point towards a flicker in an alleyway across the street. "Something moved. I swear."

Reed squints into the shadows, tension coiling in his posture. "Let's check it out," he says, and I can hear the pulse of adrenaline in his voice, matching my own racing heartbeat.

We creep toward the alley, each step a careful negotiation with the silence that hangs in the air. Lila hangs back slightly, her eyes darting nervously. "Maybe we should just keep moving..."

"No," Reed replies, his tone resolute. "We need to know if it's a threat or an ally. We can't afford to leave anything unchecked."

I nod, adrenaline surging as I push forward. As we approach the mouth of the alley, the darkness feels thick, almost suffocating, and I can sense the danger lurking within. "On three," Reed whispers, and I can almost feel the electric charge of anticipation building between us.

"One, two..."

Before he can finish, I lunge into the alley, heart racing, and there, illuminated by the moonlight, stands a figure—a man, disheveled and dirty, but unmistakably alive.

"Hey!" I call out, relief flooding through me. "Are you okay?"

He jumps at the sound of my voice, eyes wide with fear, and stumbles back against the wall. "Stay back!" he warns, raising his hands in a defensive gesture. "I'm not looking for trouble!"

"We're not here to hurt you," I assure him, glancing at Reed, who stands at the ready, tension radiating from him. "We're just trying to survive."

The man hesitates, his gaze flicking between us. "You're not with them?"

"Who?" Reed asks, stepping forward cautiously.

"The ones who've been hunting us down," he replies, his voice trembling. "They've been sweeping through the city, looking for anyone who survived. You have to hide—"

But before he can finish, the ground beneath us trembles, and a low rumble rolls through the air. My heart sinks as I realize it's not just a minor quake; it's something much worse. A thunderous explosion erupts from a nearby building, sending a shockwave that knocks us off our feet.

"Get down!" Reed shouts, pulling me close as debris rains down around us. The world blurs into chaos, the air thick with dust and confusion. My heart races as I struggle to regain my footing, the panic of the moment sharpening my senses.

We scramble to find cover as more explosions echo in the distance, a chain reaction of destruction that sends plumes of smoke spiraling into the night sky. "We have to move!" Lila cries, her voice barely audible over the cacophony.

The man from the alley is still on the ground, fear paralyzing him. "They'll come! We need to go!"

"Come on!" Reed yells, reaching down to pull the man to his feet. "There's no time!"

But just as we manage to regroup, a figure emerges from the smoke—a silhouette against the inferno, larger than life and dripping with malice. "Well, well, what do we have here?" the voice booms, dripping with mockery, sending chills racing down my spine.

Reed tenses beside me, and I can feel the weight of the moment crashing over us like a tidal wave. We're not safe. Not yet.

"Run!" Reed orders, and we break into a sprint, adrenaline surging through my veins. But as we dart into the maze of alleys, I can't shake the feeling that the hunt has only just begun, and with every step we take, the darkness closes in, ready to swallow us whole.

Chapter 26: The Burning Choice

The air crackled with tension, the horizon painted in hues of orange and crimson as the sun dipped below the crumbling skyline of our city. Shadows danced across the debris-strewn streets, the remnants of homes and lives we once knew. I could feel the weight of the world pressing against my chest, each breath a struggle as the echoes of distant shouts and the clatter of boots on pavement reached my ears. I stood on the rooftop, my heart pounding in rhythm with the war drums of the approaching storm, my fingers intertwined with Reed's, a lifeline amidst the chaos.

"Do you hear that?" I asked, my voice barely a whisper, though the air felt thick with the impending clash. It was a sound that reverberated in my bones—a chorus of hope mingled with despair, a symphony of defiance from those who had chosen to stand their ground against Carrick's advancing forces.

Reed nodded, his jaw set tight, the stubble on his chin catching the fading light. "They're gathering. It's now or never, Kyra." His gaze drifted toward the distant horizon where the enemy's banners flapped like crows' wings against the setting sun. I could see the resolve in his eyes, but I also sensed the fear, the nagging doubt that lingered just beneath the surface.

What lay before us was not merely a choice between safety and danger; it was a collision of dreams, of futures imagined and then shattered by the relentless march of war. To stay meant embracing the possibility of a final, glorious stand—a chance to fight for the soul of our city, for the people who had become our family in the shadow of the collapsing walls. To flee was to surrender, to abandon those who depended on us, but it also held the promise of a life unshackled from the chains of conflict, the tantalizing thought of freedom echoing like a sweet song in my heart.

"I can't just walk away," I said, my voice rising as frustration boiled over. "Not now, not when everything we've fought for is within reach. We can't let Carrick win, Reed. Not after all this." The memories flashed before me—faces of friends who had stood by my side, laughter shared in stolen moments, the warmth of unity against the coldness of oppression.

He squeezed my hand, grounding me, but I could see the internal battle raging behind his eyes. "And what about our future? What about the life we dreamed of?" His voice cracked, and I felt the pull of his unspoken fears tugging at my heart. "Is it worth the risk? What if we don't make it? What if—"

"Stop." I cut him off, the weight of his words pressing down like a leaden shroud. "What if we do?" The question hung between us, heavy with possibilities. "What if we fight, and we win? What if we actually change things?"

Silence enveloped us, a cocoon spun from the tension of our unresolved hopes and fears. Reed's gaze softened, a mixture of admiration and frustration. "I want to believe that, Kyra, I really do. But what if—"

"What ifs can't dictate our choices anymore," I interrupted, my tone sharp yet pleading. "We've spent too long living in the shadow of fear, letting it control us. What if we choose to believe in something bigger than ourselves? What if we stand together and make a difference?"

As if to punctuate my words, the ground beneath us trembled, a distant rumble signaling the arrival of Carrick's forces. My heart raced in response, and the urgency of our moment crystallized. I could feel the flicker of resolve igniting within me, a fire kindled by the passion of those around us, the cries of the resistance echoing in the back of my mind.

"Fine," Reed finally relented, his expression a mix of resignation and determination. "But we do this together. No more secrets, no more hiding our fears. If we're going to fight, we fight as one."

I nodded, relief washing over me. In that moment, I could almost envision the possibilities blooming like flowers after a long winter. "Together," I echoed, the word a promise—a bond unbroken by the threats that loomed outside our fragile sanctuary.

As the shadows deepened, I glanced out over the cityscape, my heart swelling with a blend of hope and dread. The streets that had once felt suffocating were now alive with the fervor of rebellion. Men and women were gathering, their faces set in grim determination, each one a thread in the tapestry of our cause. A banner unfurled in the wind, its colors vivid against the encroaching darkness, a beacon of our shared defiance.

Reed tightened his grip, drawing my attention back to him. "Are you ready?"

A thrill shot through me, an electrifying mix of fear and excitement. "As ready as I'll ever be," I replied, my voice steady, though my heart raced like a wild stallion.

With a deep breath, we descended from the rooftop, the world below pulsating with anticipation. The air tasted of smoke and adrenaline, the promise of battle thickening the atmosphere. I could hear the voices of the resistance rising, a symphony of determination, each note ringing with the fervor of hope.

"Let's give them a fight worth remembering," I said, my spirit alight with the fire of a thousand dreams.

Reed's gaze held mine, the warmth of his presence a steadfast anchor amidst the storm. "For us," he replied, and I saw the shadows of his fears begin to lift, replaced by a flickering flame of hope.

We stepped into the fray, ready to carve our names into the annals of history, to embrace our destinies entwined in the fire of rebellion. The battle awaited, and with it, the chance to claim our future.

The streets surged with a pulse of energy, each step resonating with the fervor of defiance. Together, Reed and I plunged into the thrumming heart of the resistance, a sea of determined faces blending into one collective spirit. The air was thick with a mixture of hope and trepidation, each breath a reminder of the stakes we faced. Flickering torches cast ghostly shadows on crumbling walls, illuminating a world caught between despair and the possibility of something greater.

"Kyra!" a voice cut through the murmur of the crowd, sharp and urgent. It was Elara, her fiery hair dancing like a beacon as she approached us. Her expression was fierce, eyes blazing with a mix of fear and resolve. "We need you at the front. The scouts just returned with news—Carrick's army is closer than we thought. We have to act now."

I exchanged a glance with Reed, a silent understanding passing between us. The time for hesitation had slipped away like sand through our fingers. "Lead the way," I replied, my heart racing with a blend of exhilaration and dread.

As we followed Elara through the throng, the sounds of the resistance grew louder—clashes of metal, the rhythmic thud of drums urging us onward, a symphony of voices rising in solidarity. Each face we passed told a story, every furrowed brow and set jaw a testament to the sacrifices made in this fight. My heart swelled with pride, an undeniable sense of belonging wrapping around me like a warm blanket. We were more than just individuals; we were a force to be reckoned with, a community forged in the fires of hardship.

"Do you think we stand a chance?" Reed asked, his voice low as we navigated the tight spaces between barricades and makeshift stalls. The doubt lingered in his tone, a shadow that threatened to eclipse the light of our resolve.

"More than a chance," I replied, feeling the weight of my words settle into my chest. "We've fought too hard to turn back now. This is our moment." I could see the doubt flickering in his eyes, but determination began to blossom within him, a flicker of hope igniting.

We reached the central command area, where the leaders of the resistance gathered around a makeshift table covered with maps and blueprints, each marking a point of interest, a potential battleground. The air was thick with tension, the kind that crackled like static before a storm. The leaders were deep in discussion, their voices a low hum that drew me closer.

"Elara, Kyra, good to see you both," one of the leaders, a grizzled man named Magnus, greeted us with a nod. His face was lined with age and worry, but his eyes held a fierce determination. "We're preparing our strategy for the assault. Time is of the essence. Carrick won't give us a moment's rest."

"What's the plan?" I asked, stepping forward, adrenaline coursing through my veins. The stakes had never felt higher, the air buzzing with the thrill of the impending clash.

Magnus pointed to a cluster of dots on the map. "We'll divide our forces—some will engage directly with Carrick's main body, drawing their attention, while others will flank from the east. We need to create chaos among their ranks. It's our best chance to gain the upper hand."

Elara's eyes sparkled with intensity. "And we'll need to ensure the civilians are evacuated. They shouldn't be caught in this crossfire."

My heart twisted at the thought of the innocents, those who had already suffered too much in this relentless conflict. "I can help with that," I volunteered. "I know the streets well; I can guide them to safety."

Reed's brow furrowed as he considered my proposal. "It's dangerous, Kyra. What if—"

"No." I cut him off, a sudden surge of fierce determination igniting within me. "This is what we signed up for. I won't sit idly by while others fight."

His expression softened, the worry still etched across his features, but he nodded, an unspoken agreement hanging between us. "Just promise you'll be careful."

"Always," I replied, forcing a smile, but the truth gnawed at me like a persistent itch. Care was a luxury I could hardly afford in these times.

As the plan solidified, we broke into groups, the atmosphere charged with the electric energy of impending conflict. The air was thick with the smell of smoke and the sounds of hurried footsteps, all mingling into a chaotic symphony. I felt a palpable sense of purpose thrumming in my veins, each heartbeat echoing the urgency of our mission.

"Kyra!" A familiar voice called out, and I turned to see Finn, a young boy who had been among the first to join our cause. His innocent enthusiasm was a stark contrast to the harsh realities we faced, a reminder of everything we fought for. "I'm ready to help!"

I knelt to his level, smiling despite the heaviness in my chest. "I'm glad you're here, Finn. We need all the help we can get."

"What do you want me to do?" His eagerness was infectious, a spark in this dark time.

"Stay close to the back of the group. We'll be evacuating the civilians. I need you to help keep them calm, alright?"

He nodded vigorously, determination shining in his eyes, and I felt a swell of pride for this brave child.

The crowd began to mobilize, energy building as we prepared to enact our plan. I could see Reed across the way, his own group gearing up for their role in the assault. Our eyes met briefly, and in that fleeting moment, I saw the weight of our choices reflected back at me.

"Be safe," I mouthed, hoping my message would bridge the distance between us.

"Always," he replied, a determined nod punctuating his words.

With one last look at him, I turned and joined my group, the weight of my resolve settling firmly on my shoulders. Together, we moved out into the labyrinth of the city, the familiar streets now cloaked in an uneasy tension. Each corner we turned felt like a step into the unknown, every shadow potentially hiding the enemy or, worse yet, a trap.

The first few civilians we encountered were hesitant, fear etched on their faces as they clutched children close, eyes darting toward the horizon where the echoes of chaos loomed. "Please, we're here to help," I urged, my voice steady, trying to inject a sense of calm into the whirlwind of anxiety swirling around us.

As we led them through the winding alleys, I caught glimpses of the preparations unfolding on the main streets. The resistance had mobilized into action, a determined army united by a common cause, their hearts ignited with the hope of liberation. I could hear the shouts of leaders rallying their troops, the clash of metal against metal as they braced for the confrontation that would determine our fates.

The rhythm of my heart matched the beat of the city, a fragile pulse amidst the encroaching storm. Each step forward felt heavy with consequence, but within that weight lay an undeniable sense of purpose. As we neared the designated safe zone, I couldn't shake the feeling that this was just the beginning—a spark that could ignite a flame, or perhaps, it would be the last flicker of light before everything was swallowed by darkness.

We reached the evacuation point, and my heart raced at the sight of families huddled together, each one a reminder of what we stood to lose. The thought of a life stripped away, of dreams extinguished before they had a chance to take flight, was a bitter taste in my mouth. I steeled myself, ready to lead them to safety, determined to protect these lives against the encroaching shadows of war.

But as the first family stepped forward, a low rumble echoed through the streets, a sinister omen that sent chills down my spine. The ground shook, and with it, the world around me began to unravel.

The earth trembled beneath us, a primal warning that surged through the air like an electric current, snapping me back to the immediate danger. The first family, a mother clutching her child, hesitated at the entrance to the makeshift safe zone, their faces a mix of hope and fear. My heart raced as I met the mother's gaze, her eyes wide with uncertainty.

"Come on," I urged, my voice steady despite the chaos swirling around us. "You're safe here. We need to move quickly." I reached out, hoping to convey a sense of urgency as well as reassurance, but the ground shook again, this time more violently, a reminder that time was slipping through our fingers like grains of sand.

As we pressed forward, leading the families toward safety, the air was punctuated by shouts and the sound of footsteps pounding against the cobblestones. The vivid colors of the banners flown by the resistance rippled in the wind, a stark contrast to the gray dust settling over the streets. I turned to glance back, and what I saw sent a jolt of panic through me.

Carrick's forces were in motion, a wave of soldiers advancing through the streets, their armor glinting ominously in the fading light. They moved like a dark tide, a relentless force intent on crushing everything in their path. My stomach knotted at the sight, and I felt the world around me dim, the reality of our precarious situation flooding my senses.

"Kyra!" Elara's voice sliced through the air, pulling me from the clutches of my dread. She stood a few yards away, her hand raised in a desperate signal. "We need to create a diversion! Now!"

"What do you mean?" I called back, glancing over my shoulder as the first of Carrick's soldiers began to round the corner, their faces set in grim determination.

"There's a supply cache nearby. If we can blow it up, we can slow them down!" Her eyes glinted with fierce resolve, and in that moment, I knew she was right. Time was our enemy, and we had to act.

"Let's do it!" I shouted, the adrenaline surging through me. I turned to the civilians. "Stay here! I'll be back!"

"Don't go!" the mother called out, panic lacing her voice. But I could see the fire in Elara's eyes, a spark that ignited my own resolve.

"We don't have a choice," I said firmly, moving toward Elara, who was already racing down the street. "Stay put. Trust us."

We dashed through the alleys, every footfall echoing with the weight of our mission. The air thickened with tension, the distant sounds of chaos growing louder as we neared the supply cache. I could feel Elara's presence beside me, a fierce warrior in her own right, and together we forged ahead, our hearts beating in sync with the urgency of the moment.

"There!" Elara pointed as we reached the entrance to the cache, a nondescript building cloaked in shadows. "The explosives should be inside. We'll need to move quickly."

I pushed the door open, the creaking hinges protesting as if reluctant to reveal what lay beyond. Inside, the space was dimly lit, boxes stacked haphazardly against the walls, the smell of gunpowder permeating the air. My heart raced as we rummaged through the supplies, our fingers brushing against the cold metal of weapons and the reassuring heft of explosives.

"Elara, over here!" I called, spotting a crate labeled with warnings in faded red ink. Together, we pried it open, the contents revealing several sticks of dynamite wrapped in oilcloth.

"Perfect," Elara grinned, her expression a mix of excitement and resolve. "This should do the trick."

We quickly set to work, our hands deftly assembling the explosives, the urgency of our task lending us an almost unnatural focus. Outside, I could hear the sounds of the resistance clashing with Carrick's forces, the shouts and the sounds of steel on steel mingling into a cacophony that mirrored the pounding in my chest.

"Do you think we'll make it back in time?" I asked, my voice barely above a whisper as we worked.

"Of course we will," Elara replied, her confidence a balm against my nerves. "We have to."

We finished packing the explosives, my hands shaking slightly as I lit the fuse. "On three," I said, nodding toward the door. "One, two—"

Before I could finish, a resounding crash echoed from outside, and the ground shook once more, a reminder that our time was slipping away. "Now!" I yelled, and we burst from the building, the world outside a blur of chaos.

The sight was jarring—soldiers clashing, shouts filling the air like the cracking of thunder. I glanced back at the supply cache, the fuse trailing smoke as it flickered ominously. "Let's get to safety!"

We sprinted through the alley, adrenaline propelling us forward, and as we turned a corner, the explosive went off behind us with a thunderous roar. The ground quaked, and the shockwave hit us like a tidal wave, nearly knocking me off my feet. I dared a glance back to see a plume of fire erupting into the sky, smoke billowing upward in a dark column that twisted into the air.

"Did we do it?" I shouted over the din, a mix of fear and exhilaration coursing through me.

"Looks like we bought them some time!" Elara's laughter was a wild, infectious sound, and I couldn't help but grin despite the chaos.

We ducked and weaved through the narrow streets, pushing ourselves toward the safe zone. But as we reached the corner, a sharp cry split the air. "Kyra!" A familiar voice, laden with urgency, drew my attention.

I turned, my heart dropping at the sight of Reed, fighting through the chaos, his face a mask of concern. "You shouldn't have left!" he yelled, desperation etched into his features. "I was worried sick!"

"I had to!" I shot back, a mix of frustration and relief flooding through me. "We had to create a diversion!"

His expression softened for a split second, but then his eyes darkened as he glanced over my shoulder. "We need to move. Now!"

In an instant, the reality of the situation crashed down around us. A squadron of Carrick's soldiers had flanked us, closing in with a ruthless efficiency that sent chills down my spine. The air thickened with tension, each heartbeat echoing the urgency of our predicament.

"We need to run!" Reed shouted, his grip tightening around my arm as he pulled me away from the oncoming threat. But before we could react, a figure emerged from the shadows, blocking our path.

It was a soldier, his eyes cold and calculating, a smirk playing at the corners of his lips. "Going somewhere?" he taunted, the sneer on his face igniting a flicker of anger within me.

"Back off!" I growled, stepping forward instinctively. But before I could react further, a sharp noise cut through the chaos—the unmistakable sound of gunfire.

The world slowed, my heart hammering in my chest as I turned to see Reed pushing me behind him, his protective instinct kicking in. "Run, Kyra! Now!"

But the soldier lunged forward, a glint of metal flashing in the dim light. I reached for Reed, my breath catching in my throat as I struggled against the tide of panic surging through me.

"Kyra!" Reed's voice was a desperate cry, echoing in my mind as the world narrowed to a single, horrifying moment—the clash of our fates hanging by a fragile thread, poised on the brink of chaos.

And then, just as the chaos reached its peak, everything shattered, spiraling into darkness.

Chapter 27: Battle of the Phoenix

The sun hung low in the sky, casting an eerie orange glow that mingled with the billowing smoke, transforming the city into a grotesque painting of chaos. Shadows danced around us, shifting in the flickering light of distant flames. I felt the heat of the inferno wrap around me, a living thing that threatened to swallow us whole. The battlefield was a cacophony of clanging steel and anguished cries, and amidst it all, my heart raced not from fear, but from an electric anticipation that crackled in the air.

Reed was a force beside me, his presence a constant reassurance against the pandemonium swirling around us. He moved with a grace that belied the violence of the moment, each swing of his weapon a testament to his strength and determination. I mirrored him, our bodies synchronized in this deadly ballet, dodging blows and returning strikes with precision. The adrenaline coursing through my veins was intoxicating, urging me onward, even as the weight of what lay ahead pressed down upon my shoulders.

"Watch your left!" he shouted, his voice cutting through the din like a beacon. I spun, feeling the rush of air as an enemy soldier lunged at me, only to find my dagger buried deep in his chest. I breathed hard, the sound echoing in my ears as I stepped back to catch my breath. The tang of blood filled the air, mingling with the acrid scent of smoke and charred earth.

But the moment of reprieve was short-lived. From the corner of my eye, I caught a glimmer—metal reflecting the dying light. I turned, my heart dropping into my stomach as Carrick stepped onto the battlefield. He was a dark figure, formidable and menacing, and in his hand, he held a weapon that crackled with energy, remnants of the charm's power pulsating along its length. It was a sight that froze me in place, terror coiling around my heart like a serpent ready to strike.

"Reed!" I cried out, panic spilling into my voice. He had seen it too, his eyes narrowing as he faced the man who had once been his ally, now turned enemy. The battlefield faded into the background, time itself bending as the two men squared off. Their past loomed between them, a tapestry woven with betrayal, loyalty, and a history that would not easily be forgotten.

"Carrick," Reed growled, his voice low but steady, the tension vibrating in the air like a plucked string. "You don't have to do this."

A sardonic smile stretched across Carrick's face, a grimace that seemed to revel in the chaos around him. "But I do, Reed. It's time to settle our differences once and for all." He raised his weapon, and the energy thrummed like a heartbeat, vibrating through the ground beneath our feet.

I felt the chill seep into my bones, but I couldn't falter now. I needed to fight, not just for Reed but for the city we loved, for everyone who had been caught in the crossfire of this relentless war. My feet moved of their own accord, adrenaline flooding my system, pulling me toward the confrontation unfolding before me.

"Stay back!" Reed barked, his eyes fierce as he prepared to engage Carrick. I could see the muscles in his jaw clench, the determination radiating off him in waves. But there was an underlying fear that gnawed at me—fear for him, fear for us.

"No!" I shouted, pushing through the chaos, my own weapon raised, ready to join the fray. I couldn't let him face this alone. This was our battle, and together, we were stronger than we could ever be apart.

As I closed the distance, Carrick's eyes flicked to me, a glimmer of surprise flickering across his features. "You've chosen the wrong side, dear friend," he taunted, his voice smooth like silk but laced with malice. "You think you can win against me?"

"I don't think," I shot back, my tone sharp, fueled by desperation. "I know we can win, together!"

The energy around Carrick surged as he charged forward, and Reed intercepted him with a swift movement, their weapons clashing with a metallic ring that resonated in the chaos. I could almost feel the impact reverberate through the ground beneath my feet, a jolt of energy that made my heart race.

"Reed!" I called, my voice a thread in the whirlwind of battle. He glanced at me, a brief flicker of reassurance before he turned back to face Carrick, their eyes locked in a deadly stare. I took a breath, steeling myself for what was to come. This wasn't just a fight for survival; it was a fight for everything we had built together, for our hopes and dreams forged in the fires of this relentless war.

I rushed forward, determined to flank Carrick, my movements fueled by the love I felt for Reed, by the memories of laughter shared and dreams whispered under starlit skies. In this moment, the battlefield faded away, leaving only Reed and me against the darkness threatening to consume us.

"Let's end this," Reed growled, his voice a low growl as he pushed Carrick back, each thrust of his weapon more powerful than the last. I stepped in, the rhythm of our movements syncing effortlessly, an unspoken bond carrying us through the chaos.

But as we fought, I couldn't shake the feeling that this was just the beginning. Carrick's eyes glinted with something darker, a desperation that made the air around us thick with tension. The past was catching up with all of us, and I could feel the shadows closing in, ready to unleash their wrath upon us.

The battlefield stretches out before us, a grim tapestry woven with the threads of chaos and courage. Each clash of metal sends vibrations through the ground, echoing the tension in the air. I can hardly breathe, each inhale laden with the acrid scent of smoke and the metallic tang of blood. Reed and I move in a practiced rhythm, our bodies anticipating each other's every turn, each swing, each parry. It feels as if we've trained for this moment our entire lives, and yet nothing could have prepared us for the ferocity of the fight.

"Remember that time you tried to teach me how to throw a dagger?" Reed shouts over the cacophony, his eyes sparking with determination even amidst the chaos. I can't help but chuckle, despite the gravity of the situation.

"I think I was just trying to keep you from accidentally slicing your own foot off!" I shout back, my voice laced with affection and adrenaline.

"Good thing I've learned to keep my toes intact," he retorts, a grin breaking through the grim facade as he deflects an incoming strike. For a moment, we lose ourselves in the banter, the darkness of our reality fading as laughter bubbles up, a bright beacon in the thick haze of despair.

But then, a shadow falls over us, heavy and suffocating. Carrick steps forward, his presence a palpable chill that freezes the very air around us. The weapon he wields pulses with an eerie glow, its energy crackling like the tension between us. The memories of our past collide in that instant—Carrick's relentless ambition, his desire for power that burned like a wildfire, consuming everything in its path.

"Reed," I breathe, the weight of fear settling in my stomach. I reach for him, but the space between us feels insurmountable. Carrick raises his weapon, and for a moment, the world hangs in balance.

"Did you really think you could hide from me forever?" Carrick sneers, his voice a chilling whisper that slices through the din of battle. "You've always been weak, Reed. Always relying on others to fight your battles."

"Strength isn't measured by how many fights you've won, Carrick," Reed counters, his voice steady, unyielding. "It's about who you choose to fight for."

With that, they charge at each other, a collision of wills that sends shockwaves through the air. I watch, my heart racing, feeling as if the very ground beneath us might swallow me whole. Reed ducks under a swing and counters with a strike of his own, but Carrick is relentless, his movements fueled by a desperate rage.

"Is this what you've become?" Carrick taunts as they circle each other, the flames licking at the edges of the battlefield. "A mere pawn in someone else's game? Do you really think you can protect her?"

I swallow hard, the implication of his words sinking into my bones. I can't let fear consume me; I won't. I grip my own weapon tighter, ready to support Reed even if my heart trembles at the thought of facing Carrick myself.

"Enough!" I scream, stepping into the fray. "You don't get to decide who we are or what we become!"

Carrick's eyes flash with surprise, a flicker of uncertainty that ignites a spark of hope within me. For just a moment, the tension between them falters.

"Step aside, love," Reed urges, his voice low, a mix of concern and fierce protectiveness.

"No!" I protest, shaking my head. "You're not doing this alone. We fight together."

The energy in the air shifts, crackling with the weight of our combined resolve. Carrick sneers, an expression of disdain twisted across his face. "How quaint. But your little alliance won't save you."

With a swift motion, he lunges toward us, and instinct kicks in. I sidestep and thrust my weapon forward, adrenaline surging through my veins. The blade finds its mark, but Carrick brushes it off like an annoying gnat, his focus still locked on Reed.

In that split second, I see Reed's face, a mixture of surprise and admiration. "You've grown," he says, a flicker of pride illuminating his expression even as he dodges another of Carrick's vicious strikes.

"And I'm not done yet," I retort, my voice steadier than I feel. I move to flank Carrick, weaving through the chaos, determined to reclaim our ground. The battle rages around us, a chaotic symphony of clashing steel and anguished cries, but our focus narrows to the three of us—Reed, Carrick, and me.

Carrick's eyes narrow as he realizes our strategy. "You think you can defeat me together?" he snarls, a cruel smile creeping onto his face. "You'll both fall before this day is done."

"Not today," I declare, my heart pounding, fueled by the urgency of the moment. I feign left, drawing Carrick's attention, then pivot sharply to the right as Reed strikes from the opposite side.

The clash of our weapons reverberates through the air, and for a heartbeat, I think we might actually have a chance.

But Carrick is not easily subdued. He retaliates with a flurry of strikes, each one more desperate than the last, fueled by a venomous anger that permeates the air. "You'll pay for this," he snarls, fury twisting his features as he focuses on Reed, his old rival.

"Reed!" I shout, trying to break through the fog of Carrick's wrath. I need to help, to do something—anything—but I feel so small amidst the whirlwind of power and emotion.

But Reed stands firm, his expression set with determination. "You don't get to take anything from us," he growls, his voice cutting through the chaos. With a fierce drive, he launches himself at Carrick, and I follow suit, our movements becoming a synchrony of will and defiance.

In that moment, the world narrows to the three of us, the battlefield around us fading into a distant murmur. This is not just a fight for survival; it's a battle for our future, our choices, our very selves. And together, we will rise, unyielding in our fight against the darkness that seeks to consume us.

The din of battle swells around us, an orchestra of chaos with Carrick as the conductor, pulling the strings of destruction with a twisted glee. My heart races as I watch Reed confront his past, his face set in grim determination, a mask of defiance against the overwhelming tide of Carrick's wrath. Each blow exchanged between them sends shockwaves through the air, reverberating deep within me. I can feel the tension curling in my stomach, a mix of fear and fierce loyalty that propels me forward.

"Nice moves, Reed! Did you take a few lessons from my 'How to Not Get Yourself Killed' manual?" I call out, attempting to lighten the weight of the moment.

Reed shoots me a glance, his lips twitching as he dodges a particularly vicious swing. "I didn't realize you were an expert in self-preservation!" he retorts, his voice laced with that familiar teasing warmth.

The banter is a brief respite in the whirlwind of violence, but as Carrick presses forward, rage fueling his every action, I know we have little time to spare. I shift into position, ready to flank Carrick again, determined to find a way to give Reed the upper hand.

"You think this is just about you?" Carrick snarls, his eyes glinting with a manic intensity. "This is bigger than your pathetic little bond. This is a reckoning."

"Reckoning?" I echo, incredulous. "Is that what you call throwing a tantrum with a fancy sword?"

The momentary surprise on Carrick's face is worth it. It gives Reed the opening he needs to strike, landing a blow that momentarily pushes Carrick back. But Carrick recovers quickly, his anger coiling around him like a venomous serpent. "You'll regret those words," he growls, lunging forward with renewed ferocity.

"Is that a promise or a threat? Because I'm getting mixed signals," I shoot back, adrenaline coursing through me.

The ferocity of our struggle intensifies, the battlefield becoming a blur of faces, weapons, and the crackle of energy. I catch glimpses of others fighting, comrades and enemies alike, their fates entwined in this moment of chaos. But all my focus is on Reed and the storm brewing before us.

Carrick's weapon glows brighter, drawing power from the very chaos he has wrought. "You think you can defeat me? I have become something greater than either of you can comprehend!"

"Greatness? That's rich coming from someone who needs a magic sword to feel powerful," Reed shoots back, his confidence unwavering despite the gravity of our situation.

With each exchange, I feel the fabric of our reality stretching thin, a taut wire ready to snap. I slip into the fray, my instincts guiding me as I move to support Reed, but Carrick, like a predator, seems to anticipate my every move. With a flick of his wrist, he sends a blast of energy toward me, and I barely dodge it in time, feeling the heat singe my hair.

"Watch out!" Reed shouts, his voice slicing through the cacophony as he dives in front of me, absorbing the brunt of Carrick's attack.

I scream, reaching for him, but the force of the blast throws Reed back, and he crashes to the ground, pain etched on his face. "Reed!" My heart skips a beat, terror clawing at my throat.

"I'm fine," he grunts, struggling to rise, but I can see the effort it takes him, the shadows of exhaustion clinging to him. "Just a little—ouch."

I rush to his side, determination igniting within me. "You're not fine! We need to finish this together."

Carrick cackles, a sound that makes my skin crawl. "Together? You're both so delightfully naïve. This is not a game. You're fighting against forces you cannot possibly understand!"

"Then enlighten us, oh wise one," I challenge, forcing a steadiness into my voice. "What is your endgame? A throne made of ash?"

"Isn't it obvious?" Carrick's voice drips with condescension. "Power is not just about ruling; it's about instilling fear, about breaking those who stand in your way."

"Your idea of power is twisted," Reed says, pushing himself to his feet. "You're just a child with a toy, and you've forgotten that strength comes from unity."

With a fierce shout, I surge forward, determination fueling my every movement. Carrick's laughter echoes around us, and I can see the darkness surrounding him, a vortex of raw, unbridled energy. My heart pounds in my chest as I take a deep breath and call upon everything I've learned, everything I am.

"Reed, we need to synchronize," I say, my mind racing with strategies and possibilities. "We can outsmart him. Let's use his arrogance against him."

Reed nods, and for a moment, the world narrows to just the two of us, our breaths synchronizing as we prepare for our next move.

As we charge, I feel the power between us crackling, a shared energy that flows through our movements. But just as we close in on Carrick, a blinding flash erupts from his weapon, engulfing us in a blizzard of light.

"Together, then!" Carrick's voice booms, a chilling declaration that echoes in my ears as the brightness swallows us whole.

In that blinding moment, reality twists and warps, and I reach out for Reed, feeling his hand brush against mine, warmth amidst the cold. But just as quickly as the light appears, it vanishes, leaving only darkness, an oppressive void that wraps around us like a shroud.

"Reed?" I call out, panic rising in my chest as I struggle to adjust to the sudden absence of sound and light. "Where are you?"

Silence answers, thick and suffocating. My heart races, fear clawing at my insides. I spin in place, desperate for any sign of him. "Reed!"

And then, from the depths of that silence, a sinister chuckle pierces through, sending chills down my spine. "You really thought you could defeat me?"

I freeze, recognition flooding my senses as I realize the voice belongs to Carrick. "What have you done?"

"Welcome to my domain," he taunts, the darkness pulsing around us as if it were alive. "Here, your bonds are meaningless. Here, I hold all the power."

The realization crashes over me like a wave—this was not just a battle for our lives; it was a battle for our very souls. And I am left standing alone, surrounded by shadows, with only the echo of Reed's last words ringing in my ears, a chilling reminder that the fight was far from over.

Chapter 28: Ashes of Sacrifice

The scent of charred earth hung in the air, mingling with the acrid smoke that coiled upward in dark tendrils, twisting into the unforgiving sky above. My heart pounded in a frantic rhythm, the beat echoing in my ears like the war drums of a battleground, relentless and insistent. I had always imagined that the world would end in fire and fury, yet I had never envisioned it would feel so intimate, so cruelly personal. The chaos around us blurred into insignificance as I locked my gaze on Reed, the man whose very existence had turned my life into something vibrant, something worth fighting for.

Time seemed to stretch and twist as Carrick advanced, his weapon glinting ominously in the dim light, a cruel mockery of the promise of safety Reed had given me countless times. I felt the world shift beneath my feet, and for a heartbeat, I wished we could be anywhere but here—anywhere that didn't involve the grim specter of death lurking just behind the promise of victory. I had fought my way through so much to reach this moment, only to find it teetering on the brink of annihilation.

"Get back!" Reed's voice rang out, fierce and protective, slicing through the haze of despair. It was a command that ignited something primal within me, something that urged me to act, to scream, to do anything but stand frozen in horror. But before I could move, before I could comprehend the full weight of his sacrifice, Reed lunged forward, positioning himself between me and certain doom.

The blade met flesh with a sickening finality. A gasp tore from my lips, raw and ragged, as Reed's body crumpled like a marionette with its strings cut. The world around us faded, a distant echo overshadowed by the thundering of my own heart as I caught him, cradling him against me as if I could somehow shield him from the pain that was already seeping into the ground beneath us.

"Reed!" I cried, my voice shattering like glass against the concrete reality of his injury. The warmth of his blood soaked into my clothes, mingling with my tears as I pressed my hands against his wound, futilely willing the life to return to his body. His eyes fluttered open, and in that moment, a million emotions played across his face—fear, pain, love, and a deep, abiding regret.

"Why did you do that?" I choked out, desperation clawing at my throat. "You should have run! You shouldn't have—"

"Because I'd do it again," he interrupted, his voice a strained whisper that cracked with the effort of speaking. "You are everything. I couldn't let him take you." His fingers found mine, the warmth of his touch a stark contrast to the chill creeping in around us.

My heart twisted, a dark knot of anguish tightening with every shallow breath he took. The world felt unsteady, like a ship tossed in a storm, and yet, in the eye of that tempest, there was a stillness that anchored me to him. "You can't leave me," I pleaded, clutching his hand as if it were a lifeline. "Not now. Not when we finally found our way back to each other."

"Listen to me." His voice was softer now, laced with an urgency that demanded my full attention. "Promise me you'll keep fighting. Not just for us, but for everyone. There's so much more at stake..." His eyes drifted, losing focus for a fleeting moment as he struggled against the encroaching darkness. "You're stronger than you know. Don't let this be the end."

In that instant, the weight of his words wrapped around my heart, squeezing tighter than the grip of his hand. I nodded, knowing my promise was more than just a vow; it was a pact forged in the fire of our shared history, of our dreams and our love that had weathered storms far greater than this.

"I promise," I whispered, my voice trembling as the first echoes of grief bubbled up from the depths of my soul. I felt the ground beneath me tremble, the earth shaking with the remnants of our battle, but all I could focus on was Reed, the man who had sacrificed everything for my sake.

His gaze held mine, a silent conversation passing between us, filled with love and regret, a lifetime condensed into the mere moments we had left. I could see the flicker of hope dimming in his eyes, and with a sudden surge of ferocity, I pulled him closer, determined to infuse him with every ounce of my strength.

"Stay with me," I implored, a wild desperation creeping into my voice. "Please, just stay."

As if sensing the tide of despair rising, Reed forced a smile, though it was fragile and tremulous, a shard of sunlight breaking through the clouds. "I'll always be with you," he said, his breath a shuddering sigh that escaped his lips. "In every choice you make, in every fight you fight. You're not alone."

The flicker of life in his eyes dimmed, and my world tilted dangerously as I felt the warmth of his body slip away, a candle extinguished far too soon.

I could hear Carrick's laughter ringing in my ears, a cruel reminder that the battle was not yet over, but I felt a fire ignite within me, fueled by grief and love, promising retribution for what had been taken from us. With a final, deep breath, I closed my eyes against the sting of tears, letting them spill unchecked as I prepared to rise, armed with the memories of a man who had shown me that love was not just a word but a weapon capable of carving out a new destiny, even in the face of despair.

I was perched on the precipice of despair, the weight of Reed's sacrifice pressing down on my chest like a boulder. The battlefield faded around me, transforming into a surreal landscape of shadows and echoes. The last remnants of our fight danced in the corners of my vision, but all I could focus on was the warmth slipping away from his body, the gentle ebb of life that I couldn't halt, no matter how fiercely I clung to him.

"Just hold on," I murmured, as if my words were a lifeline, something tangible to keep him tethered to this world. "You can't leave me. Not like this."

The ground beneath us was still slick with the remnants of chaos, a grim reminder of what we had faced, yet now it felt like a sepulcher—both sacred and suffocating. Carrick had retreated, but his laughter echoed in my mind, a haunting reminder of our unfinished business. I could feel him lurking just out of sight, biding his time like a snake in the grass, waiting for the moment I would let my guard down.

"Isn't it a bit cliché to hold someone while they bleed out?" Reed's voice, though weak, held a spark of that wry humor I had come to love. I glanced down at him, a bittersweet smile cracking through the veneer of my grief.

"If you think I'm going to let you go that easily, you must be delusional." I fought against the tears, feeling a surge of indignation. "I need you to stay alive long enough to mock me for my melodrama. Come on, Reed, you're not done with me yet."

His eyes glimmered with a hint of mischief, a flicker that reminded me of summer days spent laughing over ice cream cones, the sun warm on our skin. "Melodrama? Please, you're practically the queen of it. It's part of your charm," he teased, even as his breath grew shallower.

The juxtaposition of our circumstances—a life hanging by a thread, laced with moments of dark humor—felt surreal. I wanted to laugh, to hold on to those fleeting memories, but the urgency of our reality clawed at me, demanding action. I couldn't let this moment be our last. Not when we had fought so hard, not when I could still feel the fire of our connection burning bright amidst the shadows.

"Reed," I said, firm and resolute, "I'm going to get you out of here. I'm not losing you, not now, not ever." I cradled him against me, my heart pounding with the realization that I had never truly understood the depths of my own determination until this moment.

His gaze softened, a hint of something deeper lurking behind the pain. "You're going to need a plan for that," he murmured, a teasing lilt in his voice that made my heart swell, even as dread gnawed at my insides.

"Trust me, I thrive under pressure," I replied, forcing a confidence I didn't fully feel. I had faced down the darkness before, and I wasn't about to let it swallow me whole now. "I just need to buy us some time."

With every ounce of strength I possessed, I pushed myself up, feeling the cold earth shift beneath my feet. The air was thick with tension, and I could sense the unease creeping back in, the remnants of battle hanging in the air like a ghost. I had always been a fighter, and now it was time to unleash that spirit.

"Stay here," I instructed Reed, knowing he wouldn't take it lightly. "Just for a moment. I'll be right back."

"Not a chance," he protested weakly, attempting to rise, but I pressed my hands on his shoulders, urging him to remain still. "You need to be safe."

"And you need a doctor," I countered, my tone sharp. "So let me handle this. Just…don't move." The uncharacteristic stubbornness that swelled within me felt like a familiar armor, protecting me against the fear of losing him entirely.

As I moved away from him, the ground beneath my feet felt like an unstable bridge, ready to collapse at any moment. Every instinct screamed for me to run, to retreat to the safety of Reed's side, but I had to be brave—no, brave wasn't the right word; I had to be strategic. I would not let Carrick dictate the terms of our story any longer.

I scanned the battlefield, the remnants of the clash still raw and vivid. Bodies lay strewn across the ground, the remnants of my friends and foes alike, their sacrifices a haunting reminder of the stakes we faced. Yet amidst the chaos, I saw the glimmer of an opportunity—a broken piece of metal from one of Carrick's discarded weapons. It caught the dying light and shimmered like a beacon of hope.

I lunged toward it, heart pounding in my chest as I grabbed the weapon, the weight of it surprisingly comforting in my hands. It felt solid, a promise of protection and retaliation. As I turned back, my gaze swept over Reed, who remained slumped against the earth, his breath coming in shallow gasps.

I hurried back to him, the metal gleaming like a shard of destiny. "This should keep us safe for a bit," I said, determination tightening my grip on the makeshift weapon. "We'll figure this out together."

"Together," he echoed, his voice barely a whisper, but it carried the weight of a shared promise, a lifeline amid the storm.

Just as I was about to suggest a retreat to the nearest cover, a noise interrupted—the telltale crunch of footsteps approaching, deliberate and menacing. My heart leaped into my throat as I turned, the world narrowing down to a singular focus, ready to confront whatever darkness was closing in on us.

There, emerging from the shadows, stood Carrick, a predatory smile stretching across his lips. "Well, well, what do we have here?" he drawled, his voice dripping with mockery. "A brave little fighter and her wounded knight. How quaint."

I could feel Reed's presence behind me, a steady reminder of what I was fighting for. The room spun with possibilities, the tension thick enough to cut with a knife. But I refused to show fear. If Carrick thought he could intimidate me, he had underestimated the strength forged in love and desperation.

"Get away from us," I snapped, my voice steadier than I felt. "You don't have to do this."

"Oh, but I do," Carrick replied, stepping closer, eyes gleaming with malice. "It's far too late for mercy now. You've made this personal."

I gripped the weapon tighter, steeling myself against the tide of fear threatening to drown me. This was it—the moment I would either break or rise from the ashes. I had no intention of going down without a fight, and as I met Carrick's gaze, I felt the embers of determination flare to life within me. The battlefield was set, and I wouldn't let this be the end of our story.

The battlefield, once vibrant with the promise of hope, lay cloaked in shadows, the air thick with the acrid scent of smoke and despair. I felt as though time had suspended itself, wrapping around me like a thick fog, making every heartbeat feel like an eternity. Reed's body, cradled in my arms, was a testament to the fragility of life, and I couldn't shake the overwhelming dread that enveloped me. His eyes, once sparkling with the fire of determination, now flickered like the last embers of a dying flame, fighting against the encroaching darkness.

"Stay with me," I whispered, my voice barely a breath against the cacophony of the battlefield. "Please, Reed, don't leave me."

He smiled faintly, a ghost of his former self. "I'm right here," he murmured, though I could hear the tremor of uncertainty threading through his words. It was a desperate promise, one that felt both comforting and cruel. I wanted to believe him, wanted to cling to that last thread of hope, but the reality was stark and unyielding. Blood pooled around us, a dark halo that marked our moment of reckoning, and I felt the world around us tilt precariously on the edge of a knife.

Carrick lay defeated in the distance, a shadow of his former menace, yet victory felt like a hollow consolation. The cheers of our allies rang out, distant and disconnected, as if they were celebrating a triumph that belonged to someone else entirely. My heart was heavy with loss, a weight that threatened to crush me under its enormity. Reed's fingers, once so strong, twitched weakly against my palm, and I squeezed them tighter, willing warmth back into his body.

"Remember the sunsets?" he asked, his voice a threadbare whisper. "We used to watch them from the cliff. You said they looked like fire."

A smile quirked at the corners of my lips despite the gravity of the moment. "And you insisted they were more beautiful because of the ashes left behind. You always had a way with words, didn't you?"

His eyes shimmered with something that felt like pride mingled with pain. "That's the trick, you know. Beauty lives in the aftermath. It's the scars that tell the real story."

His words resonated deep within me, igniting a flicker of resolve amidst the chaos. The world around us, painted in hues of destruction, had a strange beauty of its own—an echo of sacrifice and love intertwined. I could feel the weight of his sacrifice pressing down on me, urging me to rise above the ashes. It was a call to action, one that demanded I honor his legacy by living, by fighting for all that we had dreamed of together.

Just as I began to summon the strength to stand, to turn this moment of despair into something that would propel me forward, a sudden movement caught my eye. Emerging from the shadows, a figure clad in dark robes materialized, their presence looming like a storm cloud on the horizon. I felt a chill race down my spine, an instinctive warning that sent adrenaline coursing through my veins.

"Ah, the phoenix rises from the ashes," the figure drawled, voice smooth and laced with malice. "How poetic."

"Who are you?" I spat, instinctively tightening my grip around Reed, as if my body could shield him from any further harm.

"Just a humble spectator, my dear," the figure replied, stepping into the dim light. A flicker of recognition twisted my stomach into knots. It was Maren, Carrick's closest confidante, her gaze as sharp as the dagger glinting at her waist. "You've made quite the mess, haven't you?"

"What do you want?" I demanded, my heart racing, the looming specter of fear clashing against the raw determination that had taken root in my chest.

"Oh, it's not what I want—it's what I'm owed," she said, the corners of her lips curving into a sly smile. "You see, every sacrifice has a price. Reed's death has opened a door for me. You can't possibly believe you're done here, can you?"

I could feel the blood drain from my face, my mind racing with possibilities, none of them good. "You're a monster," I spat, fury and fear blending in a toxic mix. "What are you planning?"

"Simple, really. I'm here to collect what's mine." She gestured with a languid flick of her wrist, and I felt a surge of energy crackle in the air around us. "Reed may have shielded you, but that doesn't mean I won't take what I deserve."

Desperation clawed at my throat. "You won't touch him! You can't!"

Her laughter was cold and cutting, slicing through the tension like a blade. "Oh, my dear, I already have. He sacrificed himself to protect you. Isn't that just tragic? And yet, so wonderfully convenient for me."

As she stepped closer, the air around her shimmered with dark energy, and I felt an invisible force pushing against me, trying to pry me away from Reed. My heart raced with panic, and I shook my head violently, unwilling to let go. "You won't win! I won't let you take him!"

"Oh, but you already have," she hissed, the darkness swirling at her fingertips, ready to snatch away everything I held dear. The battlefield fell silent, the very air crackling with the tension of our confrontation. I was out of options, out of time, and I could feel the world closing in around me, suffocating in its urgency.

"Let go of him!" I screamed, the words tearing from my throat as I summoned every ounce of strength I possessed.

But as Maren's laughter echoed in my ears, sharp and taunting, I knew I was standing at the precipice of a choice that would alter everything. In that moment of desperation, as the darkness threatened to consume us both, I felt the weight of Reed's hand in mine—a tether to the world I fought to protect, a reminder that love could rise even from the ashes of sacrifice. And yet, the cliffhanger of our fate hung in the balance, a tenuous thread ready to snap.

Chapter 29: The Phoenix Rises

The world around me pulses with a vibrant energy, a kaleidoscope of colors shimmering in the sunlight as I stroll through the streets of a city that has been forged anew. Every corner I turn whispers tales of resilience, the remnants of destruction woven into the very fabric of our surroundings. The air is thick with the scent of fresh paint and blooming flowers, an intoxicating blend that sharpens my senses. I can almost hear the laughter of children echoing through the alleyways, their joyous shouts rising like music, mingling with the clang of hammers and the soft murmur of hope.

Beside me, Reed walks with a renewed vigor that defies the shadows of his recent struggle. His fingers entwine with mine, a simple gesture that sends warmth racing through my veins. I catch glimpses of the man he once was, his spirit flickering like the flames of a phoenix, each step we take together reigniting the spark within. I am in awe of him, not just for the physical battle he has fought, but for the emotional turmoil he has weathered. His resilience becomes a part of me, like an electric charge weaving through the very marrow of my bones, urging me to believe in brighter tomorrows.

As we pass a group of volunteers repainting the faded murals that tell the story of our city's history, I pause, drawn to the vibrant strokes of color that breathe life into the brick walls. Each brushstroke seems to encapsulate a moment in time, and I am transported back to when the city held its breath, waiting for the dawn after the darkness. "Look at this," I say, pulling Reed to a halt. "They're bringing the heart of the city back to life."

He studies the mural, a depiction of a fierce lioness guarding her cubs, her eyes fierce and unyielding. "It's beautiful," he replies, a hint of admiration in his voice. "It reminds me of you."

My cheeks warm at his words, and I can't help but smile. "A lioness? Strong and fierce?" I raise an eyebrow, teasingly.

"Absolutely," he grins, his blue eyes sparkling with mischief. "But also soft and nurturing."

"Alright, I'll take that compliment," I laugh, my heart soaring. The air feels lighter around us, the tension of the past days lifting like morning fog.

With each passing hour, we explore the city, a tapestry of laughter and tears, joy and pain interwoven in our shared journey. The sounds of construction fill the air, a symphony of determination as new life emerges from the ruins. Everywhere I look, people are working together, hands joining across divides that once seemed insurmountable. I see neighbors offering smiles, strangers lending a hand, a community rising together, echoing the very spirit that drives Reed and me forward.

As the sun sinks low in the sky, casting long shadows that dance across the pavement, we find ourselves drawn to the heart of the city. The central square, once a battlefield, is now a vibrant marketplace bustling with life. Vendors shout their wares, the scent of freshly baked bread mingling with spices from distant lands, creating an aroma that wraps around me like a comforting embrace. I take a deep breath, filling my lungs with the scents of resilience, the flavors of renewal.

"Do you want to grab something to eat?" Reed asks, his gaze scanning the colorful stalls, his appetite awakened by the tantalizing offerings.

"Absolutely!" I respond, my stomach growling in agreement. "How about that stall over there?" I point to a vendor frying up golden pastries, their steam curling into the air like an invitation.

As we approach, a woman with kind eyes and flour-dusted hands greets us. "Freshly made! They're stuffed with cheese and herbs. You won't regret it!"

"Two, please!" I reply enthusiastically, my excitement bubbling over as she fills our hands with the warm, flaky pastries. We step aside to sample our treats, the crunch of the outer shell giving way to a gooey center that bursts with flavor.

"Delicious!" Reed exclaims, his eyes widening with delight. "This might be the best thing I've ever eaten."

"Don't get too carried away," I tease, taking another bite. "You've just woken up from a coma. Your taste buds might be exaggerating."

He chuckles, shaking his head. "I can assure you, these are amazing even in the most lucid states."

In that moment, surrounded by laughter and the hum of life, I realize how deeply I've missed these simple pleasures. The world feels less burdensome, more alive, as though each bite we take is a celebration of everything we've endured and everything we're becoming.

As dusk settles, the square transforms, strings of twinkling lights hanging from the trees casting a golden glow over the gathering crowd. Music fills the air, lively notes that invite even the most reluctant to sway to the rhythm. Reed pulls me closer, our bodies moving instinctively to the beat, the music wrapping around us like an embrace.

With the stars emerging above, I can't help but feel a spark of hope igniting within me. Perhaps this is the new beginning we've been searching for—a chance to forge ahead, to rebuild not just the city around us, but the life we want to create together.

"What do you think?" Reed asks, his voice a gentle whisper against the backdrop of laughter and music. "Do you believe in second chances?"

"I do," I reply, meeting his gaze with unwavering certainty. "But I think they're a lot like these pastries—full of unexpected flavors that take time to appreciate."

He nods, a thoughtful smile gracing his lips. "Then let's savor every moment, shall we?"

And as we sway beneath the shimmering lights, I know in my heart that together we'll discover the sweetness hidden within each new day, finding joy in the flavors of life, love, and the promise of tomorrow.

The night envelops us, a blanket of velvet darkness sprinkled with a million stars, their distant glimmers punctuating the vast sky. Reed and I find ourselves drawn deeper into the heart of the celebration, the music beckoning us like a siren's call. We weave through the crowd, laughter and chatter swirling around us, an intoxicating blend of freedom and joy that wraps us in its embrace. Each smile we share feels like a promise—a vow that we will not only survive but thrive in the wake of the chaos that has threatened to consume us.

As we pass a makeshift stage, a local band strikes up a lively tune, the infectious beat sending shivers of delight through my limbs. "Let's dance!" I exclaim, my heart pounding with anticipation. Reed raises an eyebrow, a teasing grin spreading across his face, as though he's weighing the pros and cons of such an outrageous proposition.

"Dance? You must be mistaken," he replies, his voice a mock-serious whisper. "I'm known for my unparalleled grace, or lack thereof."

"Please," I laugh, pulling him toward the stage, "you're not that bad. Besides, we could both use a little practice. Just think of it as a spontaneous, and perhaps slightly embarrassing, date night."

With a reluctant chuckle, he relents, allowing me to guide him to the edge of the crowd, where a few brave souls have already begun to sway to the music. As the first notes envelop us, my body instinctively moves, and I can't help but twirl, the skirt of my dress flaring out like a burst of confetti.

Reed watches for a moment, a look of awe mixed with amusement etched across his face. "You've really lost your mind, haven't you?"

"Absolutely," I declare, spinning again, this time landing in front of him, my hands reaching for his. "Now come on, unleash your inner dancer!"

Reluctantly, he steps forward, his strong hands finding my waist as he pulls me closer. We move awkwardly at first, laughter spilling from our lips as we try to find our rhythm. But soon, we slip into an easy flow, the music guiding us like a gentle tide.

I lean in, my forehead brushing against his. "See? Not so bad, right?"

"Maybe you're the one with the unparalleled grace," he replies, his breath warm against my skin. The chemistry between us crackles with an intensity that sends my heart racing.

The crowd around us seems to fade, the world narrowing to just the two of us, cocooned in our bubble of laughter and warmth. With every twirl, every shared glance, I can feel the threads of our connection strengthening, weaving us tighter together. The past may have brought us darkness, but in this moment, we are light—illuminated by each other's presence, by the promise of what lies ahead.

Just as the song shifts to a slow ballad, a murmur of excitement ripples through the crowd. I glance over my shoulder and see a familiar face emerging from the throng—a face that sends a chill creeping down my spine. It's Mark, Reed's old acquaintance, and a man I never quite trusted.

My heart stutters as he approaches, his presence casting a shadow over the joyous atmosphere. "Reed," he calls out, his voice dripping with a mixture of familiarity and something more insidious. "I see you've decided to join the living again."

"Mark," Reed acknowledges, a note of caution in his tone. I can feel the tension rising, a storm brewing on the horizon of our blissful evening.

"Quite the gathering," Mark continues, his gaze sweeping over the crowd before landing on me, his expression unreadable. "You've picked quite the partner, haven't you?"

The way he looks at me sends a wave of unease coursing through me. "What do you want?" I ask, my voice steadier than I feel.

"Just checking in," he replies, his smile too wide, too sharp. "You know, seeing how things are now that the city is... changing."

"Things are looking up," Reed interjects, his tone firm. "And if you're here to stir trouble, you can leave."

Mark chuckles, a sound devoid of warmth. "Oh, trouble? Me? You've got me all wrong. I'm just a concerned friend."

The tension in the air thickens, an unspoken challenge sparking between the two men. "We don't need your concern," I say, stepping slightly in front of Reed, feeling a surge of protectiveness. "Why don't you go find someone else to bother?"

Mark raises an eyebrow, his amusement palpable. "Feisty. I like that."

"Back off, Mark," Reed warns, his voice low and steady.

For a moment, the air crackles with unresolved conflict, the music around us fading into a distant hum. I can see the storm brewing in Reed's eyes, the struggle between wanting to keep the peace and the fierce protectiveness that rises within him.

Then, as suddenly as it began, Mark throws up his hands in mock surrender. "Fine, fine. I'll leave you to your little fairy tale." He smirks, glancing at me once more, and then he turns, blending back into the crowd, leaving a lingering unease in his wake.

"Let's get out of here," I say, my heart racing.

"Are you okay?" Reed asks, concern etching his features.

"I will be, but that was... unsettling."

He nods, pulling me into the shadows of a nearby alley where the sounds of the celebration fade, allowing me to breathe again. "I'm sorry you had to deal with him. He's not someone you can trust."

"I figured that out on my own," I reply, trying to shake off the lingering chill. "Why does he have to show up now?"

"Some people just don't know when to quit." His voice is laced with frustration.

"Or how to respect boundaries," I add, feeling the adrenaline still coursing through me.

"Let's focus on what we can control," Reed suggests, his hand finding mine once more, grounding me in the moment. "What do you want to do now?"

I look up at him, and suddenly, the shadows of uncertainty lift, replaced by the warmth of his presence. "I want to dance," I declare, a mischievous glint in my eyes.

"Then dance we shall," he replies with a smile, pulling me back toward the music, ready to face whatever may come next—together.

The music beckons us back to the square, vibrant and alive with laughter and the sweet, melodic notes of a song that promises adventure. Reed's grip on my hand tightens as we step into the thrumming heart of the celebration, the atmosphere electric with hope. We slip back into the crowd, lost among a sea of smiling faces and swaying bodies. The earlier tension fades like the last vestiges of twilight, replaced by a buoyant energy that seems to pulse through the very ground beneath us.

"See? Nothing to worry about," I tease, nudging Reed with my elbow as we join a small group dancing near the front. "Just a friendly reminder that not everyone appreciates a happy ending."

He smirks, his eyes bright with mirth. "I'll remember that next time I'm faced with a man who has the charm of a snake in a suit."

"Oh please, I think he's more of a garden-variety toad, if we're being honest."

We both laugh, the tension of Mark's visit dissipating like mist in the morning sun. As the tempo shifts to something upbeat, I throw myself into the dance, letting the rhythm take over, my body moving with abandon. Reed watches, an amused expression on his face, and I can't help but perform a little spin, my dress flaring around me like petals in the wind.

"Do you ever get tired of being this happy?" he calls out over the music, a hint of disbelief lacing his words.

"Not a chance!" I shout back, twirling again. "If anything, I've been waiting for this moment for far too long!"

He shakes his head, stepping forward and pulling me close again, our bodies aligning in a way that feels both familiar and electric. "You're going to exhaust me with your enthusiasm," he says, laughing softly, and I can feel my cheeks flush at the intimacy of the moment.

"Good. It means I'm doing my job right," I counter, a playful glint in my eye.

We lose ourselves in the music, moving as one, the world around us fading away until it's just the two of us dancing in our own universe. The moments stretch into a delightful haze, filled with laughter and warmth. As the stars twinkle above us, each one feels like a shared secret between Reed and me, a reminder that we've emerged from the darkness and into the light, ready to embrace whatever life throws our way.

Yet, just as I begin to let myself fully revel in our new reality, the sound of chaos disrupts the harmony. A sudden commotion erupts at the far end of the square, a loud crash echoing through the night, drawing our attention. I glance toward the noise, my heart sinking as I see a group of men pushing through the crowd, their faces hardened and determined.

"Reed," I whisper, the weight of dread settling heavily in my stomach.

He turns, tension rippling through him. "Stay close," he orders, his voice a low rumble.

As the men draw closer, I see the glint of metal in their hands, and my breath catches. The festive atmosphere shifts abruptly;

laughter turns to screams as people begin to scatter, the joy of the evening evaporating in an instant.

"Everyone out!" one of the men shouts, his voice sharp and commanding. "This is your only warning!"

Panic erupts like a wildfire, the crowd pushing back in a frenzy, desperate to escape the impending danger. Reed grabs my hand, pulling me toward the nearest alley, his grip a lifeline against the chaos swirling around us.

"Where do we go?" I gasp, my heart racing as we dash away from the fray.

"I don't know!" he replies, glancing over his shoulder, his expression a mix of fear and determination. "We just need to get somewhere safe!"

We weave through the narrow streets, the sounds of chaos fading behind us as we dart down an alley. My mind races, trying to comprehend what's happening. Who are these men? What do they want? And why now, when everything seemed to be turning around for us?

As we reach the end of the alley, I pull Reed to a halt, my chest heaving. "What's going on? Why would they—"

"Shh!" he interrupts, his finger pressed to his lips. His eyes scan the area, searching for signs of danger. "We need to figure out what they want."

I nod, forcing myself to focus. "There must be a reason they're here. Could they be connected to Mark?"

Reed shakes his head, frustration knitting his brow. "No, this feels different. Mark's a snake, but he's not violent. He just enjoys watching the chaos unfold."

Just as I'm about to respond, a loud crash echoes from the direction we came, followed by shouts that send fresh chills through me. My instincts kick in, a sense of urgency flooding my veins. "We can't stay here. They'll find us."

"Okay, let's move," Reed says, determination hardening his features. He pulls me further down the alley, urgency driving us forward. The sounds of the celebration fade into the background, replaced by the echo of our footsteps against the pavement, our breath coming in quick bursts as we navigate the unfamiliar streets.

Suddenly, Reed stops abruptly, pulling me behind a dumpster. "Wait."

"What?" I whisper, trying to peer around the edge.

"Listen."

The sounds of chaos grow closer, muffled voices and footsteps echoing in the distance. My heart races as the reality of our situation sinks in. I can't shake the feeling that we've stumbled into something much larger than ourselves, something that could threaten the fragile peace we've only just begun to savor.

"Do you think they're looking for us?" I ask, my voice trembling slightly.

Reed's jaw tightens, his expression resolute. "I think they're looking for something," he says quietly, his eyes narrowing as he listens intently. "And we might have just found ourselves in the middle of it."

A sudden crash reverberates through the alley, and I freeze, my heart in my throat. The men are closer than I anticipated, their voices growing louder, more frantic.

"We need to move!" Reed urges, pulling me along as we dart deeper into the shadows. My pulse quickens, a mix of fear and adrenaline propelling us forward.

Then, without warning, the sound of a gunshot rings out, echoing through the night like a death knell. My blood runs cold as I realize the danger has come to life, and in that moment, the world around us fractures, shattering the fragile illusion of safety we had just begun to build.

As the chaos closes in around us, I glance back at Reed, the resolve in his eyes mirroring my own. We have to escape this, to find a way out of the darkness that threatens to swallow us whole. But the question lingers in the air: how do you outrun a storm that's already upon you?